FOR BETTER OR CURSED

BOOKS BY KATE WILLIAMS

The Babysitters Coven
For Better or Cursed

FOR BETTER OR CURSED

KATE WILLIAMS

DELACORTE PRESS

Text copyright © 2020 by Katharine Williams
Jacket art copyright © 2020 by Rik Lee

All rights reserved. Published in the United States by Delacorte Press, an imprint of Random House Children's Books, a division of Penguin Random House LLC, New York.

Delacorte Press is a registered trademark and the colophon is a trademark of Penguin Random House LLC.

Visit us on the Web! GetUnderlined.com

Educators and librarians, for a variety of teaching tools, visit us at RHTeachersLibrarians.com

Library of Congress Cataloging-in-Publication Data
Names: Williams, Kate, author.
Title: For better or cursed / Kate Williams.
Description: First edition. | New York : Delacorte Press, [2020] | Series: The babysitters coven ; vol 2 | Audience: Ages 12+. | Audience: Grades 10–12. | Summary: When the Synod, the Sitterhood's governing circle, calls a once-in-a-generation Summit, Esme should be excited to get the answers she wants, but she is struck, instead, by a building sense of panic.
Identifiers: LCCN 2020008913 | ISBN 978-0-525-70741-7 (hardcover) | ISBN 978-0-525-70742-4 (library binding) | ISBN 978-0-525-70743-1 (epub)
Subjects: CYAC: Babysitters—Fiction. | Clubs—Fiction. | Witchcraft—Fiction.
Classification: LCC PZ7.1.W5465 For 2020 | DDC [Fic]—dc23

The text of this book is set in 12-point Baskerville MT.
Interior design by Ken Crossland

Printed in the United States of America
10 9 8 7 6 5 4 3 2 1
First Edition

To my archangel ninja turtle—

you are very cowabunga!

CHAPTER 1

The sun was setting, and up and down the street, I could see Christmas lights flicker on and blow-up snowmen fill with air. It was supposed to be festive, but I found it ominous, the snowmen especially. I'd seen demons that looked almost exactly like them, and now anything white and puffy automatically put me on guard. My breath billowed in front of me, and I pulled up the collar of my shearling-lined jacket, accidentally tugging it too close to my nose. I stifled a gag and immediately folded it back down.

The jacket was killer. It was pale-peach suede, had a '70s *Foxy Brown* cut, and was about the warmest thing I owned. I'd found it at a thrift store the night before, and it was a serious score except it was dry-clean only. I thought I could get away with wearing it without spending more to have it cleaned than it actually cost, but nope. Breathe too deeply and I definitely got a whiff of weed, BO, and a third note I couldn't identify. Maybe canned corn? I tried breathing through my mouth.

Cassandra wasn't wearing a coat. Of course. Even in December. She sat next to me on the wooden bench, in just one of her brother's hoodies over a flannel, her hair pulled back into a ponytail and anchored with a plain old rubber band. Cassandra doesn't worry about split ends. She was gnawing on her thumbnail, making really gross sounds that were at odds with her I-sell-detox-tea-on-my-Instagram kind of beauty. Her right leg bounced at 180 bpm, and she spit a piece of nail onto the ground.

There were only three kids left on the playground, all bundled up like little marshmallows. Their shouts echoed off the school's brick walls, and the swings made a metallic creak in the wind. The kids were taking turns throwing a red rubber ball at a basketball hoop, and one of the boys hurled the ball at the girl. She caught it and immediately turned and drop-kicked the ball away from him, sending it flying out into the playground. I stifled an urge to cheer her on.

"What do you think?" I asked.

"I swear it's here," Cassandra said. "It's just weird that it's waiting so long."

Cassandra was right. It was here. I could tell by the sadness that tickled the edges of my mind, and the way I shivered more from disgust than the cold every time the air moved around me. It was the reason Cassandra was so nervous, even though we were about to do something that, in the past month, had become as routine to us as going to school or not doing homework. We'd been in its presence for a while now, and exposure to a Negative demon always brings nerves and despair. Even to Sitters.

On the basketball court, one of the little boys was on the ground crying, while the little girl stood over him doing some sort of dance and kicking at his shins, her dangling mittens giving her the appearance of having four hands. I was trying to decide whether I was still on her side when Cassandra jumped up and started running across the playground. I was right behind her, my eyes straining in the crepuscular light, to make out what she saw.

There. By the monkey bars. A Shimmer. Barely visible, but I saw it nonetheless, like a glitch in reality. I detoured to the basketball court and held up my hands, palms facing the kids. "Mnemokinesis!" I shouted at them. They stopped fighting and turned to look at me with blank stares, arms hanging limply at their sides. Cass and I now had five minutes to do what we needed to do before the spell wore off and the kids would remember everything they saw.

Except Cassandra had stopped, and she was bent over, staring at the ground. I caught up to her, my heart pounding. "Cass! Are you okay? What's wrong?"

She looked up at me and smiled. Her pupils were huge, which made her dark eyes look like deep black holes. Her expression was peaceful. More than peaceful—euphoric. "Esme," she said, her voice an excited hush. "Have you ever noticed there's glitter in the concrete? Look at how it sparkles." She reached down and ran a hand over the dirty ground. "We are literally walking on rainbows. A million tiny rainbows."

What the?

"Are you serious?" I looked away from her as something

flickered in the corner of my eye. Now that we were stationary, the Shimmer thought it was stalking us, and not the other way around. I looked back at Cassandra, and her expression shifted in a split second, like she'd just been snapped by a rubber band. She gave her head a quick shake and broke into a run again, jumping a merry-go-round in two strides. She collided with something midair and went pixelated as she crashed to the ground. Shoot. The Shimmer was on top of Cassandra, and her limbs were going in and out of focus as she thrashed. My breath caught in my throat as the Shimmer surrounded her head, lifting it like it was about to smash her skull against the teeter-totter.

I held out my palm and wedged my powers between Cassandra and the ground so the Shimmer was just pounding her into the air. The sensation disoriented the Shimmer enough that it loosened its grip for a second, and a second was all Cassandra needed to wrench free. She rolled away and pushed herself up to her knees, her palms held out in front of her. Instantly, the Shimmer erupted in a blaze. With it outlined in flames, I could see that it was as big as at least two jungle gyms. It let out a piercing hiss, and I clamped my hands over my ears.

Her fire bathed Cassandra in flickering orange light for an instant. Just as quickly as the flames appeared, they were out again. She'd put them out. She had one palm extended and was gripping something tightly in her other fist. She raised it, but in a split second the Shimmer swung and connected with her, knocking her through the air. I winced as she smacked against the monkey bars and she fell to the ground in a heap.

"Cassandra!" I yelled. "What are you doing?"

She was back up in no time, her fist raised again, and now I could see what she was holding: a rope I didn't know she'd had. She unfurled a length of it behind her and started to swing it over her head. I was so confused that I stopped for a second. Was she trying to lasso this thing?

"Pin it!" she yelled back at me. "Don't let it go!"

I glanced up. The Portal was here, swirling over the playground like a curdled latte, which meant we only had a few seconds to flush the Shimmer before the Portal closed again. Pinning the Shimmer and not letting it go was not part of the plan. "What?" I screamed back, but before I could do anything, Cassandra had swung the lasso. Only, instead of being pinned, the Shimmer caught the rope and gave it a hard yank, pulling Cass off her feet and toward it.

"What are you waiting for?" I screamed. "Torch it!" That was how we usually did this: she set something on fire, which disabled it just long enough for me to grab it and flush it into oblivion. But she was over there playing tug-of-war like we were at a barbecue, and the Shimmer seemed to be having a grand old time.

I glanced up. The Portal was already starting to shrink, and Cassandra was still cowgirling. I had to act. I held up a hand and took hold of the demon, then focused my energy and gave it the biggest, hardest yank I've ever given anything. And, *crap*, it weighed as much as a baby elephant. Who'd been snacking on Kälteen bars. I held out my other palm, as this was a two-powered-hands job. Cassandra was yelling something at me, but I couldn't make it out. I sucked a breath in through my nose, and yanked.

I felt the Shimmer's energy course through me. It was hot and angry and still writhing in pain, and I didn't care one bit. I started to swing it around in a circle, gathering speed. With each swing, I grew more powerful and it got lighter. I looked back at the Portal, still burbling above us, and took aim. With a final swing, I let go of the Shimmer. It hurtled toward the swirl and sailed right through the middle. As it always did, the Portal flushed, a sound that never failed to send a rush through my body, from my eyebrows down to the tips of my toes.

Then I turned to Cassandra. "What the crap was that? Did you want it to stick around and hang out?" She wouldn't meet my eyes as she stood there, dirty from the scuffle and trying to catch her breath. "And that whole walking-on-rainbows thing? When did you become a flower child?"

Her eyes locked on mine. "What are you talking about?" she said. She seemed genuinely confused, but I was not going to let her put me on the defensive.

"You were wasting all sorts of time out there!" I snapped. "And you got distracted by the concrete! Of all things."

She was coiling the rope back up. "I just wanted to do it a bit differently this time."

"And you didn't think that this was something you should tell me?"

"It's no big deal," she said.

"Yes, it is, Cassandra," I said. "It could have gotten loose. What were you trying to do, anyway? Tie it up?"

She turned and started to walk away from me. "I wanted to interrogate it," she said. Which made such little sense that I needed her to repeat it.

"You wanted to do what to it?"

"Interrogate it," she said. "You know, ask it some questions."

I still didn't get it. "I know what interrogate means, Cassandra," I said. "But it's a Shimmer. It doesn't even have a mouth." We passed a trash can and she tossed the rope in it. It landed on a bag of dog poop and a Wendy's box. A bigger question hit me, and I stopped. "Wait, you wanted to *talk* to it?"

I stared at the back of her head as she kept walking. She reached up to redo her ponytail as she nodded, and I winced when she ripped the rubber band out of her hair, taking several strands with it. "What did you think it would say?" I asked, catching up to her. But she picked up her pace and I could tell she was starting to get annoyed with me.

"I don't know," she said. "I thought maybe we could learn something. Let's drop it, okay? I won't do it again." Then she said something that really blew my mind. "I'm sorry."

Wow. I had to play my cards right with this one. What she had just done was weird, there was no doubt about it, but it was also clear that she didn't want to discuss it. She so seriously didn't want to talk about it that she'd even apologized, which she never did. I wasn't going to get anything more out of her, so sure, I'd drop it. For now, at least. It was hard to tell when Cassandra was being weird and when she was just being Cassandra. I did know that she kept her word, though, so if she said she wouldn't do something again, she wouldn't. But interrogate a demon? Maybe she'd been watching too many cop shows? "What about the sidewalk rainbows, though?" I asked, figuring that was at least a different subject.

"Huh?" she asked, looking over at me like I was the one not making any sense.

"Do you not remember that? Your pupils were huge. It looked like you were on a different planet." Something flickered across her face, too fast for me to decipher it.

"I don't know what you're talking about," she said, looking away from me and down the street. "I got really light-headed there for a minute. I didn't really eat anything today."

"Oh," I said. "You should eat lunch. And breakfast." She nodded. "Something with protein, like yogurt, or an egg . . ." Cassandra smirked.

"What'd you have for breakfast today?" she asked. I knew exactly what I'd had for breakfast: six Reese's Peanut Butter Cups and a venti iced coffee.

"Irrelevant," I said, "as I'm not the one who had a . . ." I wasn't sure what to call what had just happened to Cassandra. "Tripping balls" seemed most apt. "Episode," I said finally. "In the middle of a Return. It did not seem like you were okay."

"Thank you for your concern, Nutritionist Esme," she said, reaching out to squeeze my shoulder. "I will make sure it doesn't happen again." Before either of us could say anything else about the subject, my phone started ringing. An incoming call from Jim Halpert, which is how I had Brian Davis—Cassandra's and my Counsel, and also my dad's best friend, hence the code name—saved in my phone. Brian always called me because he knew that Cassandra's phone was usually broken, missing, or dead, and sometimes all three.

I answered and put him on speaker so Cassandra could hear too. "Hey," I said. "What's up?"

"Where are you?" he asked, his voice sounding more clipped and businesslike than usual.

"At the playground by Woodland Elementary," I answered. "We just Returned a Shimmer."

"Stay there," he said. "I'm coming to get you."

"It went well!" Cassandra called out. "Thanks for asking." But Brian had already hung up.

"What do you think this is gonna be about?" I asked her.

She shrugged. "Something to do with his balls, probably."

I nodded. She was probably right. Brian's true passion was interior design, and he had a flair for mixing boho patterns and textiles with mid-century silhouettes. Overall, his style was very sophisticated and clean, yet it still felt cozy. But I digress, because Brian's day job was as the football coach at our high school, and "his balls," as Cassandra fittingly called them, stressed him out to no end. So much so that he neglected our training, which resulted in serious disaster. In the month or so since then, even though the Spring River Bog Lemmings (yep, the lemming is our school mascot) managed to close out the season and take home a trophy that they all spit in, or whatever it was you did with a trophy, Brian had been working overtime to get us up to speed. Which meant that Cassandra and I were working overtime too. We hadn't planned to meet up to train tonight, so Brian's urgent call was kind of a bummer. I was looking forward to a night off. I had plans. I mean, I was going to put a blackhead mask on my nose and watch the Versace *American Crime Story* for the fourth time. Those were plans, right?

Wherever Brian had been calling from must have been close, because his Ford Explorer was already rounding the corner. I wiped my palms on my smelly coat and realized I was still in the thralls of a post-Return comedown, shaky and sweaty and starving. Cassandra recovered from Returns much faster than I did, almost as if it was something she'd been doing her whole life. As Brian stopped the car across the street, Cassandra turned to me. "Don't say anything," she said. She didn't say about what, but I knew: the rope, and the rainbows. I stepped off the curb into the street to follow her, and I heard the kids start yelling and playing again. The spell had worn off, and for Cassandra and me, that was another Return sorta well done.

Then it hit me. A realization that brought with it a pit-drying chill. Up to this point, I'd been pretty sure Cassandra wasn't afraid of anything. The look that I'd seen flicker across her face earlier? That was fear.

CHAPTER 2

My life has changed a lot in the past couple of months, since I met Cassandra and found out I was a Sitter—aka, a superpowered female tasked with protecting the innocent and keeping evil at bay. Most Sitters spend a lifetime preparing for their seventeenth year, when they'll assume their role, but Cassandra and I were thrown in. The Spring River Portal, which is the interdimensional doorway between our regular old world and the demon-infected Negative dimension, was supposed to be sealed, so our Counsel, Brian (who also happens to be an interior designer turned high school football coach and my dad's best friend), was tardy with our training. Sure, he showed us a fancy PowerPoint, but demons? Dimensions? Magic spells? Kinetic powers? It's going to take a while for all that to sink in, much less make sense.

Maybe this wouldn't have been such a big deal, but things hit code red on Halloween, when Cassandra's brother, Dion kidnapped my babysitting charge MacKenzie to use her in a powerful ritual to blast through the sealed Portal. MacKenzie got sucked into the Negative, Cassandra dove in after her, and I had to form a coven with my dog, my mom, and my best friend to get them back.

It turned out that Dion had been acting under the influence of their dad, Erebus, who had acquired illegal powers through the use of Red Magic, which is a kind of perverted Sitter magic that can be used for all sorts of evil.

About fifteen years ago, the Synod caught Erebus using Red Magic and banished him to the Negative. He's still pissed about it and wants out. He even cursed my mom to try and tried to ransom her for his release, but the Synod has never bit.

Mom has been cursed for as long as I can remember, and she can barely interact, much less take care of herself. Underneath the curse, she's loving, funny, and the best mom anyone could hope for. I know, because I met the real her on Halloween.

Dion's ritual worked, Erebus escaped and her curse lifted for a few, brief, glorious hours before the Synod showed up and put Erebus back where he belonged, which brought the curse clanging down again. Before that, I'd always just thought my mom was mentally ill, and I'd pretty much accepted it. I was still getting used to the fact that Mom didn't have to be the way she was, and that was harder. Actually, I was still getting used to a lot of things, and they were all hard.

Brian's car smelled different. Normally, it smelled like a new car, because he had an air freshener on the dash that was literally called New Car Smell. In my opinion that's weirder than having your old car smell like old car.

But now the car smelled fresh. Crisp. Green, and seasonal AF. I leaned forward from the backseat and sure enough, New Car had been replaced with Balsam Fir. "I like this one better," I said. "It's less headache and more nature."

"Good," Brian said. "It's my seasonal scent. I find it very festive." "Jingle Bell Rock" was playing softly on the radio, a countrified version that I had already heard seventeen billion times this year, even though Christmas was still three weeks away. Cassandra reached out to change the station, and Brian swatted her hand from the knob like she was trying to steal his last mozzarella stick. "I like this song," he said. Of course he did.

"Okay," she said. "What's up? Why are you so snappy? That is not the holiday spirit."

Brian sighed, then flipped down his visor, and a piece of thick white paper fell into his lap. He picked it up and handed it to Cassandra. "This," he said.

She looked at the paper for a second, then handed it to me. The paper was so thick and soft it felt like it was made from bedsheets. It was blank, so I flipped it over and saw six words in ornate purple script printed right in the middle of the page.

The Summit
Spring River, Kansas
Friday evening

"What is this?" I said, passing it back to Cassandra, who held it out to Brian. He rolled through a stop sign, and that's when I knew beyond a doubt he was upset.

"The Sitters are coming," he said.

His pronouncement sounded both innocuous and ominous at the same time. "Okaaay," I said. "Which ones?"

"All of them," he answered.

The traffic light in the distance turned red, and Brian kept driving as if he was going to run it. Then, at the last second, he slammed on the brakes, sending Cassandra pitching forward into the dash.

"Maybe you should pull over so we can talk about this?" she said, and I nodded vigorously in agreement.

The light changed and Brian gunned it, cutting across two lanes of traffic to the side of the road and pulling to a stop. I'd known Brian for a long time, and I'd never seen him this flustered. He took a deep breath.

"The Synod has called a Summit, to be held here in Spring River."

"Brian," I said, "you're doing it again." Brian had this thing where he talked about Sitter stuff like Cassandra and I had been doing it our whole lives and knew exactly what he was talking about, like he forgot that we were brand-new and basically clueless.

"A Summit is a gathering of all the Sitters from our region," he explained. "Which is the entire country. They rarely happen. But one is happening now. And it is happening here."

There was a sound of grinding metal, and then the car filled with light. Cassandra leaned forward and looked in the side mirror. "Coach," she said, "it appears you have parked at a bus stop." The words were barely out of her mouth before the bus driver laid on the horn, a blaring that caused Brian to throw the Explorer into drive and move forward half a block before pulling to a stop in front of a pawnshop.

"So that piece of paper," I said, "that's the invite." Brian nodded. "There's no more information?" I asked, and he shook his head. "Which Friday?"

"This Friday," he said, and swallowed. "Keeping things last-minute makes it safer."

"So, all the Sitters are going to come here?" I asked, and Brian nodded again. "Doesn't that leave all the other Portals unprotected?"

"They'll be sealed," he said, drumming his fingers on the steering wheel. "Including this one. That's why Summits happen so rarely. Sealing all the Portals is a huge drain on powers. And such seals are not without consequences—for individual Sitters too."

"Like what?" I asked.

"Sitters are intuitively connected to the Portal that they are charged to protect. That's why it opens automatically when you are set to do a Return. When the Portal is sealed, that connection is blocked. All of your senses will be off. It's like being psychically constipated."

"Wow," I said. "Thanks for that, B." I had definitely hoped to go my entire life without hearing the football coach refer to me as being any kind of constipated, but what Brian had said did have a ring of truth to it. My mind was clearer now. I felt more in sync with everything around me. And even though life was about ten million times more stressful, I had fewer moments of wanting to climb inside my locker and never come back out. Don't get me wrong, it wasn't like I liked school now. It was more like I could see where school ended and the world began. There was just something about chasing monsters that helped put a chem quiz in perspective.

The sound of Cassandra playing with the lock on the passenger-side door pulled me back. "So, if seals make everyone constipated," she said, and I cringed again at that word, "they must have really not wanted my dad to get out after they put him down there. Otherwise, they wouldn't have gone to all that trouble of draining their powers and plugging up everyone's pipes."

"Cassandra!" I hissed. "Can you stop with the poop metaphor?"

"You're the first one to mention poop here, Esme," she said.

Brian ignored us both. "I guess not," he said. "To be quite frank, it was a controversial decision. Many in the Sitterhood thought it was an overreaction, but Wanda insisted it was necessary and pushed it through. I think she wanted to make an example of your father and send a message that Red Magic would not be tolerated. Wanda was the Synod's HBIC, and definitely someone not to be messed with."

"Some seal if my idiot brother could break it with a Magic 8 Ball," Cassandra muttered. "Like he did on Halloween. . . ."

"Dion didn't break it," Brian answered, ignoring her tone. "He was a vessel, like an empty bottle; Red Magic is what opened it. But right now, we need to talk about the Summit. Fortunately, I already had a few things prepared in case such a thing was to ever happen." He cleared his throat. "Esme, there are a few binders in the box back there, with just a few of my ideas for the Summit."

There was a cardboard box on the seat next to me that I had just assumed was full of jockstraps and mouth guards, or whatever it was that Brian drove around with in the backseat of his car. I flipped open the top, and just as he'd said, there were binders. But more than just a few—the box was filled to the brim with them. I pulled out a navy-blue one and read the label: TABLE DECOR. It had to be an old binder, reused without Brian's changing the label, so I flipped it open.

No. Inside were pages and pages of pictures of . . . table decorations. Eucalyptus sprigs, quartz crystals, pillar candles, holly branches, air plants, river rocks, vases. I pulled out another binder. This one was labeled MAIN STAGE, and it was full of pictures of podiums. A clear acrylic podium, a wood podium, one that looked like it was made from brushed steel . . .

I looked up at Brian. "What is this?" I asked.

"I know." He sighed. "The metal one is my favorite too, and I keep asking myself, 'Is it really a good idea to use that much of the budget on a podium?' But I think it's very chic, and it sends the right message about who we are here in Spring River."

"'Chic' isn't the word . . . ," I started, but then stopped myself. That wasn't the point. The point was I had no idea what Brian was talking about. "You haven't even really told us what a Summit is, much less what it has to do with podiums and table decor."

"Ah yes," he said, nodding, "I do get carried away with the fun stuff. A Summit is when the Synod summons all of the Sitters to one location for further training, education, and connection. They happen approximately once a decade, but the exact timing is up to the Synod's discretion, as is the location."

I pulled out two more binders, one labeled LIGHTING and another CANAPÉS. I didn't even know what canapés were. "Where was the last Summit?" I asked Brian.

"San Francisco," he said. "The one before that was in Dallas."

"Well, I can see why they chose Spring River for this one, then," Cassandra said. "Top-tier destinations only."

Brian stiffened in the driver's seat. "The locations are not chosen haphazardly," he said. "Sitters have always been on the forefront of technology, and it was very important for us to understand what was going on in Silicon Valley, as it was a hotbed of some of our greatest hopes and threats in 1999."

"And Dallas?" I asked.

"There had been an unfortunate incident at Six Flags," he said. "I'm not at liberty to say more."

"Okay," I said, nodding slowly. "And Spring River is a hotbed of what? Aside from oral herpes, of course."

"Don't be daft, Esme," he snapped. "If the Summit is coming to Spring River, then it means the events that transpired on Halloween are more serious than we thought."

"Oh," I said, and swallowed. "Does this mean we're in trouble?"

"Not necessarily," he answered. "But it does mean all eyes are on us."

I passed one of the binders up to Cassandra, and she flipped through it quickly. "So, what do centerpieces have to do with it?" she asked.

"If the Summit is to be held at our Portal, then we are the hosts," Brian answered. "And there are a lot of responsibilities that come with that."

"Such as?" Cassandra said, holding the binder up to reveal a page of colored sprinkles pictured alongside corresponding Pantone colors.

"Such as decorating," Brian said. "As well as welcoming everyone and making sure they are comfortable, and, most important . . ." He took a big breath and paused dramatically before continuing. "Planning and executing the closing event."

"And by closing event, you mean like making sure everyone gets to the airport on time?" I asked, hoping I was right about that.

Brian cleared his throat. "No, I mean a party," he said.

And that was when it hit me: Yes, Brian was terrified of all the Sitters coming to town and what that might mean for us, but he was also excited. Excited as hell.

"A party?" I repeated, as I was significantly less excited. Mass socializing? I preferred demons.

"Esme, if you could, in that box, there's a yellow binder," Brian said. "It details past closing ceremonies, so you can get an idea."

I looked in the box and pulled a yellow binder out from the bottom of the stack. I started to flip through it, and within two pages, my jaw dropped. The pictures looked like they had been taken at the Olympics. Or the CFDA Awards, or the VMAs. These were ragers, where everyone looked glam and cool. One party looked like it took place in a museum, another in an airport hangar, one in a stadium. Oh my FG. I looked up at Brian.

"These are all past parties?" I said. "They look epic."

Cassandra reached around and took the binder out of my hands. She flipped a page, then held it up so she could get a closer look.

"Is that Angelina Jolie?" she asked, pointing to a young, pouty-lipped woman in one of the photos.

"Yes," Brian said. "She studied with several Sitters to prepare for her role in *Tomb Raider* and was given special dispensation to attend the closing event. From all accounts, she had a wonderful time."

"Brian," I said, beginning to lose my cool, "I don't want to be the one to burst anyone's bubble, but this is Spring River. Angelina Jolie does not want to come here."

"That was twenty years ago, Esme," he said. "She's a mom now. I'm sure she has other things to do."

"No, I'm not talking about Angelina Jolie," I said, not quite able to keep the exasperation out of my voice. "I'm speaking metaphorically. I mean cool people. There's nothing to do in Spring River. The closest we have to a music venue is the karaoke machine at the Ford dealership."

"Can you rent the dealership out?" Cassandra asked. I shot wads of chewed-up gum into the back of her head with my eyes. Cassandra should be helping me out, but instead this was one of those times when she seemed to be opting for the deliberately dense route.

"No one wants to sing 'Single Ladies' to a bunch of four-door Fiestas," I said. "We can't do a party like this. I would say we can't do a party at all, but somehow I know that is not an option."

"You are correct," Brian agreed. "You have no choice. You don't have to like it, but you are required to throw a party."

"So, we have to lower expectations," I said, grabbing the yellow binder back from Cassandra. "A lot."

Brian gestured to the box. "I think there are a lot of good ideas in there."

He was right. There were a lot of good ideas in the binders, if we were planning a wedding for a couple of forty-something divorcées. But it was going to take a lot more than a hot-chocolate bar to have a good party in Spring River. For one thing, Brian was talking about a budget—so who exactly was going to pay for all of these podiums?

"What if we got a ton of those sub sandwiches that are big enough to feed a whole party?" Cassandra said. "What are those called again?"

Oh my God. "Party subs, Cassandra," I answered. "They're called party subs."

"Yeah, those," she said. "I really like the meatball ones." Brian pulled out a notebook and, with a shock, I realized he was actually writing that down.

"People your age like those?" he asked.

"Well, *I* love them," Cassandra said. "Especially when they have melted provolone. . . ."

I slumped back in the seat. I was outnumbered. It was two against one. I cringed at the thought of trying to make small talk while attempting the delicate operation of cramming a meatball into my mouth without getting sauce up my nose. Meatballs weren't finger food, even when you shoved them between bread. I massaged my temples. Brian was right. Like so many things in my life, this party was happening whether I wanted it to or not. "Okay," I said. "So, the invite says Friday." Brian nodded.

"And today is?" I asked.

"Tuesday," Brian said.

I nodded. "That's what I thought," I said. "So that means we have"—I counted the days off on my fingers—"three days to plan this party."

"Exactly," Brian answered. "Which is why it is so fortunate that I've been preparing for this. Of course, as the host Sitters, you two have to make the final party decisions. And I can only guide you. . . ." His voice drifted off, a little wistfully.

"Right," Cassandra said, "party subs. What's left to plan?" Brian looked like he might have a coronary.

"Place cards, for example," he said. "And floral arrangements." He cleared his throat. "I was thinking we should go with dried. Something seasonal—it's what I'm seeing right now."

"Why would anyone want dead flowers?" Cassandra asked.

"Not dead," Brian said. "Dried."

"What's the difference?"

"There's a big difference," Brian scoffed. "For one . . ."

My brain whirred and tuned them out. To say I'd never planned a party before was a lie. I'd arranged many a soiree for my dolls, and after our dog, Pig, moved in with us, I even had a living, breathing guest, though she didn't bring much to the table conversation-wise. But planning a party for a whole bunch of Sitters in three days? Barf me out the door—I'd rather do extra-credit homework.

The front seat was still arguing about dead versus dried flowers, and it sounded like Cassandra was winning. "I hate to interrupt this debate," I said, sticking my head in between their seats, "but how are we supposed to do this in three days?" My question united them, and they both looked at me like I was five cans short of a six-pack.

"I figured that would be obvious," Brian said.

"Yeah," Cass echoed.

"We use magic?" I guessed.

Brian nodded.

"Duh," Cassandra said.

"And this," Brian said, holding something up. In the dark, I couldn't quite see what it was.

"A credit card?" I asked as Cassandra snatched it out of his hand. She looked at it and guffawed.

"Nope," she said, "try again. Gift card. To someplace called Party Town."

"There's five hundred dollars on it," Brian said haughtily. "And we get an employee discount."

"Have you been to Party Town?" I asked him. "They

sell blow-up—" I stopped myself before the word "penises" came out of my mouth. "Body parts," I said, finally.

"I have not," Brian said, as he grabbed the card back from Cassandra and handed it to me. "But this gift card was sent to us directly from the Synod, so I assume they have done their research and Party Town is awash in seasonal decor." I tucked the card into the front pocket of my backpack. "Do not waste it," he continued. "And please shop economically."

I sat back again as Brian put the car in drive and pulled away from the curb. "So, you had no idea this was happening?" I asked him, and he nodded.

"Then what's with all the binders?" I asked. "You certainly did a lot of research for something that surprised you."

"I, uh, well, I thought this might happen someday," he said. "I just didn't think that someday would be so soon." We passed under a streetlight, and I got a good look at Brian's face in the rearview mirror. He was biting his lip. Oh, of course. He wasn't *expecting* this to happen—he was *hoping* it would. Brian had been waiting for this. The next thing I knew, we were in front of Cassandra's house. She had climbed out of the car and turned around and was looking at me expectantly.

"Oh," I said. "Am I getting out here too?" She nodded.

"I have to run," Brian said, by way of explanation, so I just mentally shrugged and started to climb out. I was now farther from my own house than I had been when he picked us up. "Don't forget the binders!" he added as I started to shut the door. With some effort, I managed to tug the box out of the back and around the passenger seat, and then dropped it with a thud at my feet. "We'll meet at my house tomorrow night. And I expect you two to have some solid ideas for the event," he added.

"We should have one of those things they have at the fair," Cassandra said, excited. "Where you swing a hammer and it says how strong you are? And also one of those people who guesses how much you weigh!" Sometimes I swore that Cassandra was just a frat dude trapped in the body of a teenage Jessica Alba. I was glad she couldn't see me shake my head in the dark.

Brian drove away, and as I was bending down to pick the box of binders up, I looked over at Cass. "Can you help me with this?" I asked. "This much inspiration can really weigh you down."

"Leave it," she said. "I'll make Dion come out and get it." Dion's van was in the driveway, and through the house's front window, I could see him sitting on the couch, watching TV.

"How's that going, by the way?" I asked.

Cassandra gave a little laugh. "Well, the house is super clean, and once I get home from school, I barely have to get off the couch if I don't want to. He made me chocolate chip cookie dough yesterday."

"Did you bake any?"

"No, chocolate chip cookie dough ice cream," she clarified.

"Oh, wow." That was impressive. "How did he even know how to do that?"

"He didn't. He stayed up until three a.m. to learn."

"Doesn't he have to get up for work at like five?"

"Yep."

I would be lying if I said I knew how to respond to that. "Well," I said finally, "was it any good?"

CHAPTER 3

At one point, it seemed like Cassandra's older brother, Dion, and I were maybe someday going to have something. That was before, of course, he let his father take over his mind, kidnapped my babysitting charge, and performed a Red Magic ritual that got Cassandra and the eleven-year-old girl sucked up into the Negative. It was as complicated as it sounds, and Dion didn't remember any of it.

There were a lot of things Cassandra could have done to punish him, and maybe she still would, but for now she seemed content to use him as her slave by way of a custom-tweaked memory spell that I was pretty sure wasn't legal by Sitter standards. In some ways, it seemed like she was letting him off easy—after all, staying up late to make your sister ice cream hardly seemed like a fitting punishment for kidnapping—but then Dion hadn't totally been acting on his own free will, and besides, he was the only family Cassandra had. I could see why she didn't want to lose him, even if she also didn't want to let him off the hook.

As we walked into the living room, Dion was, I swear to goddess, watching *Love Actually*. He looked up and smiled at me. "Hey, Esme!" he said, way chirpily. "Have you seen this movie? It's pretty good!" He was wearing a sweatshirt, and when he pushed one of the sleeves up, I could see his horrible tattoo, a botched homage to his mother's Mexican heritage and love of Greek myths. I'd used a spell to fix it for him, but it had reverted to the original version when the Synod had reversed all our powers while cleaning up the mess from Halloween.

"I prefer movies where people get stabbed," I said, then turned away to signal the end of the conversation.

"There's a box of stuff on the curb," Cass told him. "Go bring it in." Dion jumped up off the couch and was out the door in a flash. I followed Cass to her room, then picked my way over to her bed and sat down in the one clear spot I could find.

Her room looked like she was auditioning for *Hoarders*. It was hard to walk on the floor because it was covered with so much stuff. Old dolls' heads, spools of thread, dead plants (Brian might have called them "dried"), Popsicle sticks, bags of expired bubble gum, spray deodorant, silly string, old bathing suits, a plastic kiddie pool, a bicycle wheel, press-on nails, anything and everything. Her desk was covered with jars and bags of spices—cardamom, anise, rosemary, cloves—and herbs, and dried flowers (Cassandra might have called them "dead"), like crispy crushed rose petals and lavender buds.

Rocks and crystals, tigereye, garnet, onyx, and what looked like parking lot gravel. Being a Sitter inspired pack-rat tendencies. Our spells required all kinds of ingredients, and the spells updated themselves all the time, so you never knew what you were going to need. Cassandra, I guess, had decided it was good to keep stuff on hand. It didn't look like she had thrown anything away, ever.

There was something new too: a mini freezer that was plugged in, whirring away in one corner like Cassandra was worried she'd have a Fla-Vor-Ice craving in the middle of the night and not have time to get to the kitchen.

"What's up with the freezer?" I asked.

Wordlessly, she opened the door. Cold air rushed out and I bent down to look at the contents. It was empty, save for a large block of ice with something black and round frozen right in the middle of it. It took me a second to realize what it was: a Magic 8 Ball.

"Is that the one from Halloween?" I said, knowing even as the words came out of my mouth that it was a stupid question. Cassandra wouldn't buy (or acquire, since I wasn't sure she actually bought the things she needed) a freezer just to hold a random toy. Through some combination of Red Magic and sheer a-holery, Erebus had managed to turn a Magic 8 Ball into a multidimensional communication device, and that was how he'd sent Dion the directives for his dirty deeds. If anyone else had done it, I would have found it quite clever.

It turns out that Erebus, Cassandra and Dion's dad, was a pretty powerful Red Magician, and years ago, he'd been banished to the Negative for doing a bunch of awful stuff.

Like, oh, cursing my mom. But his extreme d-baggery didn't stop there: the whole reason he'd enchanted the 8-Ball was so he could manipulate Dion into doing a Red Magic ritual that would break him out of the Negative, and it involved sacrificing a child. In short: Erebus was human garbage. There was only one reason I didn't want him to stay exactly where he was: If Erebus got out, Mom's curse came off. Just thinking about all this made me feel like my heart was going to implode. I turned my attention back to Cassandra.

"I was keeping it in the kitchen," she said, "but I started to get nervous that Dion would find it again, so I spelled this room to keep him out."

"Do you think the 8 Ball still works?" I asked.

"I have no idea," she said. "But I'm not trying to find out." She shut the freezer door and turned and started to rummage through the stuff on her desk. "At least not right now." This last part made me give her a strange look, one she didn't catch.

"You think you might want to find out if it still works later?" I asked.

"Maybe," she said. "I just think it's a good idea to keep our options open, don't you?" She had found what she was looking for: a piece of wintergreen gum. She popped a piece into her mouth, and then smoothed out the wrapper and tucked it in an envelope.

"No, actually, I don't," I answered. "I don't think we should be keeping any of our options open. I think we should unfreeze that thing, take it outside, and run over it with the van. I don't want anything to do with Red Magic."

"You don't have to do anything," she said. "He's my dad, and I'll keep him in my freezer if I want to. Besides, we don't really know that much about Red Magic." That last statement made my stomach cartwheel. Red Magic terrified me, but it intrigued Cassandra. Her dad had obviously been very powerful, and I wondered whether there was something in her blood that drew her to it.

"I don't think you need to take a class on it to know it's bad," I said, trying as I always did to steer us into more benign territory. "I mean, the Synod basically nuked the Spring River Portal because your dad did some dabbling." But a part of me understood, because Cassandra and I had the same weakness: family. That was the reason our villain was in her freezer, and why his imbecile sidekick was down the hall acting like his sister's house elf. I knew what it was like to grab the shards of a connection and hold on until it cut your fingers.

"Do you miss Dion?" I asked her, and as if on cue, we could hear him laugh at the TV.

"He's just in the other room," she said.

"Cass, you know what I mean," I said. "He has no idea what's going on. He's more like a Roomba than a person these days. You can't have a real conversation with him."

She shrugged and attempted to blow a bubble, which popped on her lip. "We didn't have a ton of conversations before."

"Then who do you talk to?"

"I talk to you," she said. "I'm talking to you right now." She kicked some stuff out of the way, and then dropped to the floor and started to do push-ups. Cassandra liked doing push-ups.

I sighed. "Yeah, but you won't talk to me about Halloween. What was it like down there?"

She stopped doing push-ups and looked up at me. "Esme, did you ever think that maybe I don't talk about it because I don't want to talk about it? You want to know what it was like? It sucked. That's why it's called the Negative."

I got to my point. "Does being in the Negative have anything to do with why you wanted to talk to the Shimmer?"

Cassandra answered me by getting up and walking out of the room. After a bit, I heard a toilet flush and then she reappeared, acting like she hadn't heard my question. Who knew, maybe she hadn't, but I did know Cassandra well enough to know that when she didn't want to talk about something, me pushing her was going to accomplish jack squat. "Come on," she said, "Dion will give you a ride home." I followed her back through the house. "Dion, take Esme home," she said once we got to the living room.

"Not a problem," he said, getting up off the couch and grabbing a jacket from a nearby chair. As he pulled it on, his T-shirt rose a little, just enough to reveal a strip of skin above his jeans. I swiveled my head, looking away, and ended up looking at my own reflection in the picture window.

Cassandra and Dion had mythological names, and they also both looked like Greek gods. There was no doubt they were physical perfection; I had to admit that, even though I hated Dion's guts. I had no idea whether Cassandra understood how she looked, and that it wasn't normal. She treated her beauty like it was an unsquanderable resource. The only time I'd ever seen her wash her face, she'd used dish soap. But Dion knew, and he understood the power it gave him; that week before Halloween, he knew I'd swoon and play right into his hands. Or did he? That was what I didn't know—how much of me and Dion getting to know each other had been his father, Erebus, and how much of it was Dion? It was one of those things that I was starting to realize I might never know.

His jacket on, Dion stood to the side of the door to let me go first. I walked out onto the porch and then turned around. "You know, I think I'm just going to walk," I said to Cassandra.

"Okay," she answered with a shrug. I was starting to learn that the parts of Cassandra I found the most disconcerting were also the parts that were the most comforting. She wouldn't ever ask how you were doing, but that also meant she wouldn't ever pry. I turned and started my walk.

Instead of going home I started to walk to my mom's, a place with locked wards where she wasn't allowed to have anything sharper than a spork. Which happened on Halloween but—thankfully—just for a hot minute. Now he's back down there, doing whatever it is he does. The dark side of that is that mom is still here.

It was getting late, but I still had time for a quick visit. I signed the visitors' log at the front desk, and Marie, who'd worked there as long as I'd been coming, smiled at me.

"Hi, Marie," I said. "It looks nice in here. Did you do this?" There was a tiny Christmas tree covered in white twinkle lights, cotton-ball snowmen on the wall, and a flickering menorah (no real candles, of course). A small radio was turned to the same station Brian had been listening to, and it was playing "Jingle Bell Rock." Again. Marie's fingernails were candy-cane-striped and she drummed them on the desk in time to the music.

She nodded in answer to my question. "Make sure you come next week," she said, smiling. "I'm making my rum balls!"

"Yum," I said, though I was pretty sure rum balls were not something I would like. I'm not a Scrooge, it's just that the holidays have never been that big of a deal in my house. Mom is in here, and Dad is the kind of person who thinks toasting waffles counts as home cooking. He's not all that great at gifts either. Two years ago, it was a Target gift card. Last year, it was a Starbucks gift card. This year, I have my fingers crossed for a gift card to the Starbucks in Target.

Thank God for my best friend, Janis. Janis may have Rihanna's cool and Claudia Kishi's closet, but when it comes to Christmas, she turns into a Hallmark-watching, gift-wrapping, tree-decorating elf in vintage Burberry. And her presents are epic. Last year, she gave me an Edward Scissorhands diorama that she made herself. I gave her some socks. But Janis's and my friendship is so strong that she persists, in spite of my anti-Christmas attitude.

Marie walked me down the hall and used her key card to swipe me into Mom's ward.

"Thanks," I said, as she turned to leave. "I'm not going to be long."

I'd been here every day since Halloween, when Mom's curse was briefly lifted. Which also had meant Mom's curse was lifted, also for a hot minute. She was herself, and she was whole, and then, just like that, she was gone again. Since then I couldn't help it; I needed to see her every day to search for some shred, some sign that the Mom I met on October 31 was still in there somewhere. Also, I didn't want her to be bored, or to hate what she was wearing, because now I knew that Mom was aware of everything, even though she couldn't do anything to let me know. I tried to comfort myself with this small fact, because I used to think that Mom couldn't tell the difference between me and an Elvis impersonator.

I made my way down the hall and found Mom's room. The door was open a few inches, and I knocked, then let myself in. Mom was lying on her stomach across her bed, her feet hanging off one side and her head hanging off the other, the ends of her black hair touching the floor.

"Hey, Mama," I said. She rolled over so that she was facing the ceiling, but she still didn't look at me. She was wearing teal leggings that were stretched out at the knees and a too-large purple sweatshirt with a glittery iron-on decal of Christmas ornaments. I had no idea where those clothes came from, because they were nothing I'd ever bought her.

I dropped my backpack at my feet and pulled out the clothes I'd thrifted for her when I got my suede jacket. "Look at this," I said, holding up a bright-blue peasant blouse embroidered with red, yellow, and white flowers and trimmed with lace. "It's definitely not a fall-winter look, but it was too good to pass up. I figure we can save it for vacations or something." I hung it up in her closet and then pulled out my next find: an '80s-esque wrap dress, black run through with gold threads. "You look so good in black," I said. "And the wrap style means it's easy to put on and take off." That was super important, since sometimes Mom couldn't dress herself. The final find was an oversized, probably hand-knit sweater coat of marled red wool. "This is for walks outside," I said. "I figured you needed something warm, but something a little less . . . athletic." I'd seen the coat they'd been putting her in, and again, it was one of those things I didn't know where it came from—an orange and blue leather jacket with a giant Denver Broncos logo on the back. I imagined that every time Mom wore it, the little tiny shred of herself still locked inside was screaming in protest.

I took a Post-it and a Sharpie out of my backpack and wrote "Please have Theresa wear this coat for excursions." I stuck it to the plastic hanger. "So, what do you want to wear tomorrow?" I asked Mom. She was watching me now but still didn't say anything.

I went back into her closet and pulled out a gray turtle-neck sweater, a pair of navy-blue high-waisted pants, and a herringbone tweed blazer. "Lady lawyer who lunches," I told her, and then hung them on the door. I glanced behind me into the hall to make sure no one happened to be walking by, then held out my palms and kinetically lifted the bed about six feet in the air and spun it around a couple of times. I set it back down and checked Mom's face for a hint of a reaction, but still nothing.

When she came back on Halloween, Mom said things that let me know she loved me and had my back. She was a guiding star, a bright light I could follow through the darkness. Then, the same night, the same babysitting gig, I'd lost her again. My universe had been turned completely upside down in the past month. It turned out nothing was what I thought it was. I wasn't who I thought I was. I could move things with my mind. I fought monsters. I was the kind of person movies were made about. I was fulfilling my destiny. But . . . meh. I'd give it all up if I could bring Mom back for good.

Mom brought one foot up to her mouth and tried to bite her big toenail. I sighed and flopped down in a chair across from her. "Mom, don't do that. It's gross," I said, and then I really started talking. I told her about my day at school, and the Shimmer, and how I was worried about Cassandra. The only thing I didn't tell her was that I was worried about her too. And about Cassandra's freezer. I wasn't sure she'd like those thoughts, and I didn't want to stress her out because she couldn't do anything about it.

I kept rambling, and rambling, until there was a knock on the door. I looked up to see the kind face of a nurse smiling at me. "I hope I'm not interrupting," she said, "but it's time for her nighttime meds." She was holding a tiny white cup filled to the brim with pills, probably hundreds of dollars of medication that Mom would swallow in one gulp, a waste of time and money. Powerful Sitter spells couldn't even remove

Mom's curse, so a pharmaceutical cocktail wasn't going to do a damn thing. The only thing that would work was Red Magic, but I certainly couldn't tell her doctors that. I took the nurse's presence as my cue to go. I stood up, walked over, kissed Mom on the forehead, then slipped out of the room.

"Have a good night," the nurse called after me, but I just waved, afraid that if I tried to speak, my voice would crack, and the tears would flow. I'd been missing Mom every day for almost my entire life. I thought that wound had scabbed over, but Halloween had ripped it open again, and now it wouldn't stop bleeding.

I caught the city bus home, the last one of the night, and the same line that had honked at Brian just a few hours earlier. The house was dark when I let myself in, so I figured Dad must have gone to bed early, but I heard grunts and jingles coming from the kitchen. Scritch-scratching on the hardwood floor, and she was swarming me before I'd even taken off my shoes: Pig, my girl. Head like a wrecking ball, heart like pink Starburst. I bent to give her a kiss and gagged.

"Your face smells like sardines," I said. "I don't even want to know who or what you've been sniffing." Pig was unoffended by such insults and followed me into my room.

As soon as I saw my bed, exhaustion hit me like a beanbag. My body still wasn't used to the physical demands of being a Sitter, and I was tired. I dropped down onto my bed and used my powers to close the bedroom door and open the one to my closet.

I pulled out different items of clothing and sent them spinning through the air as I decided what to wear to school the next day. Pig let out a low growl as skirts and shoes swirled over her head. She'd seen my powers in action enough that she'd stopped barking when I used them, but apparently it was still unsettling.

I finally settled on a black, white, and gray patchwork blazer—thrifted, of course—with the shoulder pads still in, a pleated gray knee-length skirt, and blue tights. It was inspired by *Heathers*, of course, and I dubbed it "Brain Tumor Breakfast" and sent Janis a text.

I was about to fall asleep when I remembered Brian's binders, still sitting on the floor at Cassandra's. I'd completely forgotten about them, and I was sure Cassandra hadn't cracked them either. Our party planning was off to a banger of a start. Maybe we could cash in all our irony points and just go with "tHiS PaRty sUx" as the theme. I drifted off as I was mentally adding songs to the perfect rap-rock playlist.

CHAPTER 4

When my alarm went off, I hauled myself out of bed, put on Brain Tumor Breakfast, dragged myself to the kitchen, and helped myself to what was left of the coffee. Since I hadn't eaten dinner the night before, the coffee hit my stomach like gasoline on hot asphalt, but at least it woke me up.

Dad had been going to work early and coming home late the last couple of weeks, and he was already gone. I let Pig out, and she drifted around the front yard, looking for the exact right spot to pee, before finally settling on the cement deer in our next-door neighbor's flower bed. This was the exact wrong spot to pee, of course, because Mrs. Burgelman hated dogs. Oh well.

When Pig came back in, I fed her breakfast, which I couldn't do for myself, since the contents of our fridge were limited to leftover lo mein and a lone pickle floating in its jar. I was sure it was fine, but there was something sad and creepy about eating the last pickle. Dad must have felt the same way, because that pickle had been there for as long as I could remember.

Janis normally picked me up when Dad couldn't give me a ride, but she was getting her tires rotated—whatever that meant—before school, so I caught the bus. My stomach was growling by the time I stepped off, and I had just enough time before my first class to grab a weird granola bar (Apple Rain, whatever the heck kind of flavor that is) and some gummy sharks from the vending machine.

Today was going to go by fast, because I actually had something to look forward to at school, thanks to Mrs. Winchester. Mrs. Winchester was our Earth Sciences teacher, and I was pretty sure she taught that subject because she had actually been around when there were dinosaurs. Usually she was responsible for a good number of things I dreaded about school (inanity, stupidity, stab-my-eyes-out boredom), but today the fact that she thought Tumblr was something you used for rocks was working in our benefit. She was letting us leave campus to go to the city library because she had assigned us research papers that were supposed to be researched with books, something called a microfiche (which sounded like a minnow to me), and basically anything that was not the internet. I bet she'd award extra credit to anyone who scratched their essay onto a piece of stone. But, bonus: Earth Sciences was the one class Janis and I had together, so getting to go to the library was pretty much like hanging out, just an hour earlier than usual.

I suffered through gym, which actually wasn't too bad since we were doing yoga and I could basically just lie on the floor for an hour, then I changed quickly and booked it to the parking lot to meet Janis. She was already in her car, sitting behind the wheel and tapping away at her phone. I tossed a Taco Bell cup and a pair of leggings into the backseat, and climbed in.

Janis, as always, was dressed like a queen. Last week, she'd gotten a new hairstyle, rope-thick braids dusted with various shades of green and silver ("I thought straight-up red and green would be too on the nose," she'd explained of her holiday lewk), a voluminous forest-green hoodie, which she'd cropped so that the front was way shorter than the back, black leather leggings, vintage Nike Cortezes with a silver swoosh, and a puffer jacket so puffy that I was surprised she fit in the driver's seat.

"What's this look?" I asked.

"Off day," Janis said. "I stayed up late last night making ornaments, so I was super tired this morning." She pulled up a photo on her phone and held it so I could see. "Look! Aren't they cute?" She had crocheted tiny ugly sweaters, and they were indeed cute. "If I don't use them for the tree, I might use them for present toppers."

"What are present toppers?"

"They're like little presents that you put on presents," Janis explained, putting her phone down.

"Of course," I said. She punched a button on the stereo, and the radio came on—"Jingle Bell Rock," of freaking course. Just a few seconds, though, before she put a playlist on. The soothing sounds of non-holiday music were like a poem whispered in my ear. The first song was Aaliyah's

"Rock the Boat," one of Janis's favorites. "What's this playlist called?" I asked, since Janis got very specific when naming her playlists.

"'Leaving school early to go to Chick-fil-A,'" she said as we pulled out of the parking lot.

"I thought we were going to the library?"

"We are," she said. "After we go to Chick-fil-A."

"You know they're homophobes, right?" I asked.

Janis grimaced and nodded. "I know, I know," she said, "but . . ."

We finished the sentence together: "Waffle fries."

By the time we got to the library, my fingers were greasy, and I felt like a hypocrite, but my belly was full. Janis's car smelled like chicken, but instead of throwing the stained paper bags away, we crumpled them up and shoved them into the cupholder and door pockets.

"This is the dumbest assignment we've ever had," Janis said, looking around the parking lot. "The whole class is supposed to be here, but it's just us. And we're here a half hour later than we were supposed to be. But nothing says Spring River High School like research conducted on out-of-date technology."

I nodded. "This is almost as bad as freshman year, when Mr. Riley made the whole class write raps about Anne Frank," I said.

Janis grimaced. "I will never forget Todd Spano rhyming 'boss' and 'Holocaust.'" She shuddered so hard her

braids shook. "I wish I could erase it from my memory."
I shuddered too, but also at her reference to erasing her
memory. On Halloween, Janis had helped me get Cassandra and MacKenzie back, and she'd even beaned Dion
with a chair. She doesn't remember any of it, though, because the Synod used a powerful memory-altering spell to
make sure the entire town of Spring River thought that
Halloween passed with nothing more mischievous than a
few smashed pumpkins and stolen Snickers. Janis didn't
know that she'd had her memory erased, which was one of
the trillion secrets I was keeping from her and it's kind of
breaking my heart.

"Come on," Janis said, opening her door. "Let's go get
our technological time warp on." I followed Janis's lead and
got out of the car. She locked the car behind us, and the beep
of the alarm echoed through the parking lot as we started
up the library's concrete steps. I didn't realize how slowly
Janis was walking until I bumped into her, which she barely
noticed. Her attention was fixed over her shoulder.

"What are you looking at?" I whispered, because Janis
acting suspicious made me think I should probably be acting
suspicious too.

"That guy," she whispered back.

"Ugh," I said, pulling my coat over my chest. As far as
I was concerned we should report all creepos to the library
security guard. Unless, of course, the security guard was the
creepo, which was a distinct possibility.

"No," Janis said. "He's hot, which means he is definitely
not from around here." I relaxed and stood up straighter and

followed Janis's gaze. As soon as I saw him, I sucked in my breath. How did I not notice him as we were walking up? He was sitting on a concrete ledge next to the stairs. He had on black high-top Chucks, skinny black jeans, and a padded black Dickies jacket zipped all the way up. His skin was dark, but his hair was bleached blond, and just a little bit peeked out from underneath a red knit beanie. He wasn't playing with his phone, vaping, reading, or doing anything but looking like he was in a designer denim ad.

And, he was also staring right at me.

Something about him made my mouth go dry and my stomach feel like it was about to belly flop off the high dive. I spun on my heel and started walking, smashing right into an old lady in a purple knit hat. "Oh dear," I said, "I am so sorry! Are you okay?" She didn't answer, just gave me a look and muttered something under her breath that definitely sounded a lot like the *c*-word. By the time I got myself together and looked again, the guy was gone.

It took us a little while, but Janis and I found the microfiche machine. It looked like a disappointing television set and we'd barely figured out how to use it when Janis got a text reminding her that she had to pick her brother up. "Eff it," she said, handing her phone to me. "Take a picture of me. I'll just look everything up when I get home and turn this in as proof we were here." She draped herself across the front of the machine and I climbed onto a chair so I could get the best angle. I kept snapping because the pictures were as awesome as they were hilarious. We switched places so she could take some of me.

I had my tongue out, pretending like I was about to lick the microfiche, when someone cleared their throat behind me. I jumped up and turned around to see a librarian who did not look pleased at how the youth of today were using this hallowed institution of learning. Janis and I gathered up our stuff and headed out. Janis flicked through the photos as we walked back to her car. "I'm calling this shoot 'Research, but make it fashion,'" she announced. "And I'm going to frame one so that Winchester can keep it on her desk." She stopped. "Huh, that's weird."

"What?"

"I thought I locked my car."

"You did lock it," I said. "I remember the noise."

"Well, it's not locked now." She opened the driver's-side door and tossed her bag into the backseat, which was met with a frantic screech. A black shape flapped out of the car, hitting Janis in the face with a wing. Janis let out a blood-curdling scream as the shape took off into the sky.

I was next to her in a second, yanking the door fully open and peering into the car. "What the hell was that?" Janis asked, sounding like she was about to scream again any second. My own heart was pounding, and I started to realize what it was. Not a tiny flying demon, but . . .

"A crow," I said. "There was a crow in your car."

"What was it doing in there?"

The panic in her voice inspired me to instill mine with extra calm. I took in the interior of the car again. The passenger seat was covered with shreds of white paper. "Eating trash and looking for fries, I think."

"How did a crow get into my car?"

I shook my head. "I have no idea," I said. And honestly, I didn't, but there was a little something inside of me, about the size of a micro fish, that disagreed and was telling me that that crow had something to do with me.

As Janis drove me home, I could tell she was still pretty shook, and I dug deep to come up with something that would explain the crow away. At least to her.

"Okay," I said. "So, I bet someone tried to break into your car, and left the door open after they realized there wasn't . . ." I paused, trying to think of a nice way to point out that Janis's car was a mobile dumpster that would intimidate even the messiest petty thief. "Anything they wanted to steal," I continued. "And a crow flew in, and while it was in there, someone else came along and decided to be a Good Samaritan and shut your door, not realizing there was a bird inside. Eating Chick-fil-A . . ." I realized it sounded ridiculous, but it was as good as I could do in the moment.

"Okay," Janis said, sounding unconvinced.

When we pulled up outside my house, Janis was still quiet, but she perked up a bit when I reminded her to text me some of the photos. As she drove away, something in me relaxed. I never thought I'd be so nervous around my best friend, but then these days, I was doing a lot of things I never thought I'd do.

CHAPTER 5

At home, I had the house to myself—except for Pig, who was sleeping in a position best described as "melted"—so I made myself some dinner and watched *Wheel of Fortune*. When the puzzle was revealed to say "Piece of My Heart Attack," I called a car.

When my ride pulled up to Brian's, the clock on the dash said 6:55. "Jingle Bell Rock" came on as I was closing the door. Cassandra was already sitting on the front porch.

"There was a crow in Janis's car," I said as I sat down next to her. "Is that an omen?"

Cassandra thought for a second, then shook her head. "I wouldn't think so," she said. "They're everywhere, so if it was, it'd be like, 'Oh, look, there's an omen freaking out over a hamburger wrapper, and another omen over here, trying to eat a shoe.'" She bit at her nail. "Crows are really smart, though. I read once that they remember faces."

"Oh yeah?" I said, not sure whether I found that cool or just really freaky.

Cassandra clasped her hands between her knees, and then leaned forward a little.

"Can I ask you something?"

This kind of prepping was not Cassandra's typical MO. "Sure," I said, my interest piqued.

"So, yesterday on the playground, when I did something weird . . ."

"You mean when you tried to hog-tie the Shimmer instead of Return it?" I asked.

She shook her head, still hunched over. "No, not that," she said. "The other thing, where I kind of went someplace else for a minute."

"Oh yes," I said. "When you were one with the concrete."

"How long did that last?"

I thought about it. "I don't know," I said. "Not very long. Less than a minute, probably. It just felt longer because it was a crucial minute." Cassandra nodded but didn't say anything. "Why do you ask?" I pressed.

She looked around, like she was worried someone might hear her. "I think it happened again."

My eyebrows shot halfway up my forehead in alarm. "When?" I asked quickly.

"Today," she said. "I was in my bedroom, and then the next thing I knew, I was standing in the bathroom. I don't remember walking from one room to the other."

"Do you know whether you did anything weird?"

She nodded and pulled out her phone. "Yeah," she said, swallowing with a gulp, "this." She tapped her phone a couple of times and then showed me what she'd pulled up. It was a picture of her bathroom, and it would have been a selfie, except her reflection in the mirror was totally obscured by a word written in thick, soapy lines: "Goodbye." As I looked at the photo, the skin on the back of my neck pricked up and a chill ran down my spine.

Cassandra clicked her phone off and slid it back in her pocket. "I had to have done it," she said. "Dion wasn't home, and I was the only one in the house."

Brian's car turned in to the driveway, and Cassandra jumped up. I followed. "What do you think it means?" I asked.

"I don't know," she said. "But don't tell anyone."

"Cass," I started, "this is getting weird. That," I said, pointing at her phone, "is scary." She didn't answer. "Doesn't it scare you that you're doing things you don't remember?"

"Of course!" she hissed, her lips barely moving. "You think I like being out of control? But whatever this is, I don't want to become even more out of control by handing this—whatever it is—over to someone else. It's my problem, and I will solve it."

"You went to the Negative," I protested. "You had a serious shock. This could be totally normal. It could be something Brian knows how to fix. He could help you find help."

She shook her head sharply. "I don't want help," she snapped. Brian was halfway down the walkway. Our meeting hadn't even started yet, and he already looked ticked off.

"Where are the binders?" he asked, as he brushed past us to open the door.

"Oh, those," I said, revving up for an excuse that would at least make it seem like we hadn't totally forgotten about them.

"We totally forgot about them," Cassandra said, and followed him into the house. Brian's house was basic witch heaven. I pulled the door shut behind me and inhaled deeply: fresh-cut evergreen and cloved cider. Sure enough, Brian's mantel was draped with juniper boughs, and a diffuser in one corner was pumping out clouds of spicy "seasonal" scent. Janis would have clapped her hands and squealed with glee over the very tasteful terra-cotta nativity scene set up on a side table. I wove around a leather pouf and a potted fiddle-leaf fig in the living room, walked past the white tiled kitchen, and into Brian's bedroom, where, I happened to notice, he had added a salt lamp next to his bed. That gave me the opportunity to deploy one of my favorite bad pickup lines.

"Hey, girl," I said, "are you a Himalayan salt lamp? Because when I stand next to you, I feel nothing." I made myself laugh, but Cassandra just rolled her eyes and Brian just looked at me and raised his eyebrows.

"Are you finished?" he asked, pulling a gold necklace out from under his shirt. I nodded as he opened his closet door, pushed about twenty tracksuits out of the way, and then held the gold charm from his necklace up to a special spot on the wall. There was a click, and then a whir, and then the wall slid open to reveal the Bat Cave.

Unlike the rest of Brian's house, which looked like an

Anthropologie photo shoot, the Bat Cave was straight out of *American Psycho*. It was sleek and modern and there wasn't a speck of shabby chic in sight. One whole wall was lined with Tools, which were weapons so elaborate that even fourth-grade boys would have a hard time dreaming them up; the wall opposite it was covered with photographs of well-known Sitters. My mom's photo was up there, as was Cassandra's. Save for a large screen, the wall behind Brian's desk was stacked floor to ceiling with books, and not the kind you could check out from the Spring River library. Sitter books. Grimoires and weapons guides and demon encyclopedias, plus biographies and Sitter history dating back centuries. The books updated themselves periodically, which was part of why being a Sitter required constant studying, and I'd come to think of the books as living creatures. Sometimes, when things got very quiet, I could swear I heard them breathing.

Brian walked behind his desk, and as Cassandra and I took our usual spots in the chairs opposite him, something hit me, a question I'd never asked. "Brian," I said, "how'd you become a Counsel, anyway?"

He sat down in his chair and leaned back, a faraway look crossing his face. "I was living in Denver," he said, "where I had my interiors business, and I made the news when I saved a dog from a burning building." I saw Cassandra rock a little in her chair—she'd clearly never heard this story either.

"You saved a dog?" she asked, and Brian nodded.

"Technically, eight," he said. "A mother and her pups. It made the news, and the Synod found me shortly after that. They made their case, and it was an easy decision."

"So you gave it all up?" I asked.

"Of course," he said. "And I'd do it again. Protecting the innocent is a noble mission."

"The powers are pretty cool too, huh?" Cassandra said.

The quickest smile flicked across his face, and Brian nodded curtly.

"The Synod has been very generous with me," he said. "And I would be lying if I said I did not enjoy the powers at my dispensation." Then he leaned forward and did that thing where he made a triangle with his fingers. Unlike Sitters, Counsels could be men or women, and though they weren't born with kinetic powers, they could use spells to manipulate magic and from what I'd seen, Brian was pretty powerful.

"Now back to business," he said. "Since you completely forgot about the binders, and the hundreds of hours of research that went into them, I am going to assume that the ideas you are bringing to the table are minimal."

"I, uh . . . ," I started, but I wasn't sure what to say. It wasn't that I'd deliberately avoided thinking about the party we were supposed to be planning. It was more like every time I started to think about it, my mind did that thing it always did when it was trying to protect me from something unpleasant: I locked it away and pretended it was not happening and did not exist.

"I voiced my ideas last night," Cassandra said. "So, I don't know about Esme over here, but I'm tapped out."

"Got it," Brian said. "Submarine sandwiches and feats of strength. This will certainly go down in history as one of the classiest ways the Sitterhood has ever closed a Summit." I had been engrossed in a bit of fuzz on my knee, but I looked up quickly. Brian being sarcastic always caught me off guard. He sighed. Cassandra met his sigh with a sigh of her own, and I couldn't help it, I joined in. We were like three leaky tires. I squirmed in my seat.

"Listen, Coach B," Cassandra said, sitting up straight. "Let's be real here. Most of the parties I've been to have ended with a fight breaking out." She shifted. "Or sometimes it was a fight and then a party broke out, but that's kind of beside the point. I don't have much experience in this area. And Esme's a wallflower." I started to protest, but then realized it wasn't an insult, just the truth. "Her favorite thing to do at a party is sneak out of it. I don't think this is really our thing. You, on the other hand, seem to have a real vision for what this could be."

"I do," Brian said, nodding.

"And it also seems like you have a flair for this kind of thing."

He nodded again. "I have planned a few events in my day," he said. "And they all went quite well. I had quite the Rocky Mountain reputation, if I do say so myself."

"You can say so," Cassandra said. "And I totally believe it." I watched her, wondering where she was going with this flattery. "So out of the three of us here," she went on, "you're probably the best suited to planning a Summit closing event, and it also seems like you would enjoy it the most."

"Oh, I'm sure you two could have fun with it," he said. "Who doesn't love parties?"

"Esme hates them," Cassandra said. "Like we were just saying . . ." They both looked at me and I nodded vigorously.

"Parties," I said. "Puke." I had taken the backseat, and wherever Cassandra was heading, I was along for the ride.

"But you can't plan the party," Cassandra continued, "Esme and I have to do it."

"I can only guide you," Brian said. "And it appears that even with all the guidance in the world, this will still be a disaster."

"Well, what if you did all the work and Esme and I took the credit?" I almost laughed out loud—such a blatant suggestion could only come from Cassandra. But Brian wasn't saying anything. He was still doing that triangle thing with his fingers and looking like he was actually considering her offer. "Everyone would be super impressed with how well you'd guided us, and whenever people would tell us what a great party it was, we could be all like 'Oh, well, Brian practically did everything. . . .'" He leaned back in his chair and rocked a little. Cassandra continued. "I mean, that whole 'Counsels can't help plan parties' rule is a stupid one anyway."

"It is," Brian said. "And I'm sure, when it comes down to it, the Synod would rather have us bend this one rule and throw a good party than be sticklers and end up with a few marinara-stained paper napkins."

I sat up in my chair. "I'm sure they would," I agreed.

Brian moved back and forth slightly, making his chair squeak a little. "It will be tough," he said. "But it's nothing I haven't done before, and sometimes I start to get worried that all my design dreams are going to die and I'll just be stuck on the sidelines for the rest of my life." He stroked his mustache. "Literally speaking, not metaphorically." He was quiet for a few moments, then snapped his fingers. "Okay, let's do it. I have the perfect idea for a theme." He leaned back in his chair again and beamed, then leaned forward again. "Après-ski!" he said, so excited that he smacked his palms on the desk.

"What the heck is that?" Cassandra says.

"Après-ski?" Brian said, looking at her as if she were the one speaking a foreign language. "After-ski?"

"I know that," she said, "I took one semester of French. But how is that a theme?"

"Chalets?" he said. "Chunky sweaters? Lots of candles. Fondue?" He paused. "No meatball subs, of course, but we can have poutine and hot cocoa." He paused again, like he was waiting for us to say something.

"Okay," I said, and Brian smiled.

"Think about it," he said. "It's perfect. It's very cozy, seasonally appropriate, and yet nondenominational. It feels holiday without being about 'the holidays.'"

I looked over at Cassandra, who met my eyes. "Sounds great," she said, and I nodded vigorously.

"Perfect!" Brian said, and made a note on a legal pad. "Now, on to the next order of business. We have to commandeer a place for everyone to stay. I started to put together some lodging ideas. I found a couple that aren't dreadful."

He opened a drawer in his desk, and pulled out—yes, you guessed it—another binder. The man had more three-rings than Office Depot. He flipped it open to the first page, which was a printed-out Yelp page, complete with notable reviews highlighted in yellow. I recognized the building in the picture at the top as the Riverbend Hotel—tall and brick, with a front fountain pavilion that was popular with the few skaters this town had. "This one seems to be lacking in—"

"Ooh," Cassandra said excitedly, leaning forward and tapping the paper with one of her chewed fingernails. "I've stayed there before. The pillows kind of sucked, but other than that, it was really nice."

Brian looked skeptical. "And the food was okay?"

She nodded. "I loved the omelet bar."

He looked at me. "Esme?"

"If it's okay with you two, it's fine with me."

Brian smiled and slapped the binder shut. "That's settled, then," he said, happily. "I'll contact the Synod and we can initiate the reservation tonight."

"How does that work?" I asked. "The Summit is only a few days away. That hotel is probably booked."

"Oh, they don't have a single room available," Brian said. "I checked this morning. The Synod will clear the bookings and reserve the hotel for the Summit."

"Won't that cause a scene? People will be pissed if their reservations are canceled."

"That's where magic comes in," Brian said. "No one who had a reservation will remember. Same with the hotel staff who are working there for the duration of the Summit. Their memories will be modified so that all they are experiencing is another day of work."

Something in what Brian was saying gave me pause. Mind

erasure seemed like a pretty big thing, a potent combo of hypnosis and amnesia, but the Synod was handing it out like candy canes. They'd erased the entire town of Spring River after Halloween to cover up the fact that Brian, in his incognito role as football coach, had been falsely arrested so that he'd be MIA for the night. Janis, Dad, Dion, and MacKenzie had gotten extra muddling—I'd even muddled MacKenzie myself. I also had to assume that Pig's memory had been erased, though I had no idea how to confirm that, her being a dog and all.

Now the Synod was going to zap a whole hotel staff and anyone who had a reservation. And probably more too, since you couldn't ship in a bunch of girls from all over the country without raising a few eyebrows. "Is it safe?" I asked. "I mean, for all these people to get their brains messed with all the time."

"Esme, the Sitterhood exists to keep people safe," Brian said. "So, if the memory altering wasn't safe, then we wouldn't do it." He leaned over and opened a laptop. "Now, if you'll excuse me, I have to get to work. I'll put together a task list for you tomorrow."

"Task list?" Cassandra asked as I stood up.

Brian narrowed his eyes at her. "Errands for you to run. Supplies that need gathering," he said. "I may be the brains behind this operation, but you two are the muscle. Now, I trust that you girls can show yourselves out. I've got some Pinteresting to do." I bit my lip to keep from smiling as I stood up. Cassandra and I started to leave, but I turned back when Brian said my name, right as I was about to walk out the door.

"Actually, Esme, could you stay a minute longer?" I looked at Cassandra, who raised her eyebrows.

"I'll wait for you outside," she said, "and see what Coach has in his fridge."

"Cassandra!" Brian started, but she was already gone. I walked back to the chair and sat down.

"What's up?" I asked.

"I've been looking into your mother's condition," he said. I felt a little tingle run through me. Brian had promised that he would help me find a way to break Mom's curse for good, but he hadn't mentioned it in a while.

"And what did you find out?"

He moved a few things around on his desk, and then leaned back in his chair. It creaked a little.

"Unfortunately, not much. There is not a lot of information on curses in the Sitter books," he said. "Which is disappointing, if not surprising."

"Why isn't it surprising?" I asked.

"Curses are tricky," he said. "Since they're Red Magic, they are technically not under our realm. People have been able to pervert Sitter magic before to do small amounts of harm, of course." As soon as he said that, my mind flashed to Cassandra, and Dion, her brother/personal valet. "But nothing to the scale of what has been done to your mother."

I nodded and swallowed. So basically, what he had for me was nothing. "Thanks," I said, "for trying, at least."

"I will continue to try," Brian said. "And I know you are not looking forward to this Summit, but I ask that you change your attitude. This country's foremost Sitters and magical experts are basically coming to our doorstep. There could potentially be lots of opportunities for you to learn more about your mom and how you might help her."

Oh man. He was right. I hadn't even thought of that. With the Synod here, and whoever else they were bringing with them, I'd be able to go straight to the source and not have Brian be my intermediary.

"Thanks, Brian," I said as I stood back up, and I meant it. I left the room, then walked back through the house to find Cassandra in the kitchen, sitting on a counter and drinking eggnog out of the carton. "Ugh," I said, disgusted. "How can you drink that stuff?"

She hopped down, then closed the carton and stuck it back in the fridge. "I like it," she said. "It tastes like melted ice cream."

"So, when did you stay at the Riverbend?" I asked as we stepped back out onto the porch.

"Never," Cassandra said. "I sensed that he was about to start spiraling out over the difference between a Hilton and a Hyatt. Better to just prevent that entirely."

I nodded. She had a point. Brian was definitely someone who couldn't see the party for the invites, a whole forest-trees situation.

The temp had dropped a lot in the time we were inside, and now the air was cold and tinged with a damp that blew right through my tights. "I don't think there's anything to Return tonight, do you?" Cassandra asked.

I shook my head. What Brian had said earlier was true—as Sitters, we were connected to the Portal. When demons came through, we knew. It wasn't like a flashing light or a siren; it was just a tickle, like throwing a filter on our senses that made everything clearer and brighter, and us more alert. In the short time we'd been doing this, we'd learned we could count on at least a demon a day, with the tickle starting in the morning, then slowly building until it felt like a full-on itch. Demons weren't big on mornings or afternoons, which was good for us, since that meant we were out of school when they came through. Not that Cassandra would have cared—I got the sense she came to school only because she hadn't found anything better to do yet. She would have welcomed a high-noon demon duel, while I was still pretending that school was important. For now, at least.

I looked up and down Brian's street. "I haven't felt anything at all today," I said, and then ran one hand over the back of my neck. That was where my tickle usually started. Cassandra nodded. "When they come, do you feel it?" I asked.

"I hear it," she said. "It's like a buzzing streetlight. Not loud enough to pay attention to, at least not at first, but there when I stop and really listen for it." She rubbed an ear. "But yeah, now I don't hear anything."

Dion's van was parked on the street, so I knew Cassandra had driven. "You want a ride?" she asked.

"Sure," I said, and then stepped back so she could help me wrench the passenger door open. I climbed in and used all my might to pull the door shut again. Cassandra climbed into the driver's seat, and after a few turns of the key, the van sputtered to life. I was sure that right now, at this very moment, every radio station in Spring River was playing "Jingle Bell Rock," but I was saved from the aural assault by the fact that Dion's radio didn't work.

I was always surprised by how carefully Cassandra drove. Arm-out-the-window turn signals and all. But I suspected the reason was that she didn't want to get pulled over because she didn't have a license.

"I don't like it," I said, giving words to a feeling that had been burbling inside me ever since Brian had picked us up and flashed that creamy piece of paper.

"No one likes this van," she said. "Not even Dion."

"No, not that," I said, because truth be told, I was starting to like the heap of rusty metal. It was like an ugly dog that kept growing on you until you thought it was cute. "The Summit," I said. "It just doesn't make any sense. We've known we were Sitters for barely a month, and this town is hardly a destination, so why have the Summit here, of all places? Why make us the hosts?"

"I think I know," Cassandra said.

I turned to look at her, surprised. I had no doubt Cassandra was capable of keeping secrets from me, but if she knew why the Summit was coming to Spring River and she hadn't told me, I was going to be more than a little PO'd. "And you were going to share this with me when?" I asked.

"I can't," she said. "Because I don't remember."

"W-what?" I stammered. "You don't remember?" Then Cassandra slammed on the brakes, and the van squealed to a stop. She threw the van back into park and started fumbling with her seat belt.

"You need to drive, Esme," she said. "Switch places with me, now!" Suddenly she was standing between our two seats, pawing at my seat belt. Then, just as suddenly, she stopped and dove into the back of the van. The driver's seat was empty, and we were sitting at an intersection, the red light in front of us ready to change to green at any second.

"What is going on?" I yelled. I could barely drive a go-kart. "What are you doing?" There was no way I knew what to do with Dion's van. But Cassandra didn't answer. Instead, she was rolling back and forth on the carpet in the back, giggling up a storm. I had no choice, so I jumped over to the passenger seat and got the van back into drive right as the light changed.

I pressed on the gas, and nothing happened. "Cass! I don't know how to drive this thing." She was humming, and then her humming turned into singing: "Ninety-nine bottles of beer on the wall, take one down!" she belted, then laughed again. "Pass it around! *Ninety-nine bottles of beer on the wall!*"

I decided, for the moment, to focus on driving. Instead of just pressing the gas pedal, I stepped on it, mashing it to the floor. It took a second, but the van started to move. I got us through the intersection and used all my might to crank the no-power-steering wheel to the right and pull us to the curb. In back, Cassandra was doing a handstand and kicking the ceiling, still singing, though never changing the number: always ninety-nine bottles of beer, never ninety-eight. She gave the ceiling one last kick, and then crumpled into a ball. The singing stopped. My heart was pounding, and I was still gripping the wheel even though I'd turned almost all the way around in the seat so that I could look at her.

"Esme?" she said, and then coughed a little. "Are you driving?"

I was almost mad and wanted to yell at her that she'd left me no choice, but I wasn't, and I didn't. "Are you okay?" I asked instead. "You didn't, uh, take anything, did you? I won't judge, I just want to know so we can get help."

"I didn't take anything. I don't do drugs." Her voice was small, and I knew she was telling the truth. Cassandra didn't even drink coffee. "It happened, didn't it?" she said. "I was driving, and now I'm in the back of the van, lying on the floor."

I nodded. "But you caught it, whatever it is," I said. "You stopped driving before you, uh, started singing."

"I was singing? What song?"

I shook my head. "'Ninety-Nine Bottles of Beer.'" Cassandra got up off the floor and climbed into the passenger seat.

"I don't even know that song," she said.

"Well, the lyrics are real easy." I swallowed.

She leaned her head against the window. "I think you better drive for a while. I always feel a little woozy after."

I nodded, and bit my lip. I could feel the pedal hit the floor under my foot and we inched away from the curb. The speedometer read seventeen mph.

"Be careful," Cassandra said. "It can pick up speed real fast."

"Oh." I let up on the gas, and we slowed down to eleven.

"I just pump my foot up and down real fast the whole time," she said, "and hope it kind of evens out."

I started to do just that, and thought about how they'd never mentioned anything like this in driver's ed. We drove in silence for several minutes. "Cass, what is going on?" I finally said. "You know why the Summit is coming here, but you don't remember?"

"I just keep blacking out," she said.

We were at a four-way stop and it took my full concentration to balance the delicate pedal ballet with figuring out when it was my turn to cross. I decided to go for it, and no one honked, so I could finally exhale.

"Was the other night the first time it happened?" I asked.

"I don't know," she said. "It might have just been the first time I was with anybody when it happened. I've been feeling weird since Halloween. All of a sudden, I'll feel like I had a glitch. Nothing major, just like I missed a few seconds or something. But today, in the bathroom, and now, they're getting longer. I think it started . . ."

"After you got back from the Negative," I finished for her. "Is that why you wanted to talk to the Shimmer?" I looked over at Cassandra and she nodded.

"It's like the blackouts are so that I won't remember the thing I can't remember. I have no idea what it is, but I know there's a hole where a memory is supposed to be. I want to talk to something that might know what that was." She laughed, a quick snort. "It's stupid, but I figured a Shimmer was as good a source as anything."

By the graces of the traffic goddess, we had reached my house, and I stopped at the curb by using both feet to press on the brake.

"And you think that this thing you can't remember is why the Summit is coming to Spring River?" I asked, turning the van off.

She nodded again. "I have zero proof," she said. "It's just, you know, a feeling."

I didn't press her any further, because I knew exactly what she was talking about. For us, a feeling *was* proof. There was something else that I was thinking, but I didn't want to tell her. Cassandra's episodes were strange and unusual, but they were also familiar. To me, at least: They brought flashbacks of watching my mom try to make a phone call with a banana, or serving powdered Jell-O for dinner. Things that seemed funny . . . until they didn't. Cassandra sounded cursed.

But I wasn't going to tell her that, and I was going to hope, with everything I had to hope with, that that was not the case. "We should talk to Brian," I said finally, to say something.

She shook her head. "No way."

I sighed. "Cass, needing help, being sick, doesn't mean you're weak. It just means you're a human being. Whatever this is, it's nuts, and I don't want you to get hurt."

She was silent, and then she peeled her forehead off the window. "I don't want to make a big deal about it, and I *am* asking for help. Your help, to make sure, for now at least, nobody knows about this but us."

"Okay, fair enough," I said. "How can I help?"

She gestured at her head. "This whole thing. Whatever is going on with me. Just, like, if you see me getting weird, help me get out of there. Wherever it is we are."

"So, I'm supposed to babysit you, basically."

"Ha," she said, instead of actually laughing. "When you put it that way, it sounds less appealing. But basically, yes."

I pulled the keys out of the ignition. "Well, my first order of business as your babysitter is to not let you drive home. Do you want to call Dion?"

She shook her head. "I appreciate it, but I'll be fine for a while. The episodes are happening more frequently, but they're not irregular. I've got at least a couple of hours before I have to worry about it again. Plenty of time to get home."

I was conflicted. There was a part of me that didn't want to let her drive because I was worried about her, but I also knew it was a big deal for Cass to share this with me, and for her to ask me for help, and if I started using her confidence to restrict her autonomy, then she'd never do it again.

"Okay," I said, unbuckling my seat belt and starting to get out of the car. "But if you so much as have to sneeze, pull over. And text me as soon as you get home. Promise."

I held out the keys. Cass took them and nodded. "I promise."

I stood on the sidewalk and watched her drive away, wondering whether I had just made a huge mistake. So far, being a Sitter felt like schlepping secrets with you everywhere you went, and I'd just added another one to my already pretty heavy burden. Also, what if Cass really needed help? What if what was happening to her wasn't magical at all, but medical?

But, still, I could see why she didn't trust Brian. Sure, he was all we had, but even so, I wasn't sure I trusted Brian. He seemed way better at withholding information—about my mom, about Cassandra's family, about this Summit—than he was at sharing it. No matter how much time we spent with him, training or studying, the Sitterhood remained a puzzle, and we were still missing most of the pieces.

But there was one thing about this whole Sitter thing that I was sure of, and that was that I could trust Cassandra. The back of my neck told me so. Everything that was shady about her, the shoplifting and the bad attitude, it was right there on the surface. And I definitely trusted Cassandra to watch out for Cassandra. So if she wanted me to keep her secret, I would, even though I didn't know what that secret was.

CHAPTER 6

By the time I let myself into the house, Dad was already asleep. Lately, he and I were passing each other like cat burglars in the night. Dad didn't know I was a Sitter. He didn't know Mom was a Sitter. He didn't know that his only friendship was a sham, and that Brian, his best friend, was magically implanted into our lives to keep an eye on me. Basically, Dad didn't know his whole life was a lie, and there wasn't a day that went by that I didn't feel guilty about that.

And by the way he'd been acting lately, I was starting to think Dad had some secrets of his own. He was stressed all the time, and the mailbox was always full of bills. I think he thought I didn't know, but sometimes, when I was expecting a package, I got to the mailbox before him. Now I just put everything that's addressed to him back where I found it, ever since I saw the look on his face when I handed him a notice that was clearly from a collection agency.

I assumed that he had fed Pig, because she was only

at about a six on the pathetic scale, and if she hadn't had dinner, she would have quickly turned it up to eleven. She followed me into my room, her tags jingling along the way, and then she curled up on a pile of stuff in the corner before she started snoring with her eyes wide open. I kicked my shoes off and climbed into bed. It was an Olympian feat to keep my eyelids open, but I managed to just finish my Earth Sciences paper before falling asleep with my computer as a pillow.

Dad was already up when I stumbled downstairs in the morning. I could see a little gray sprouting in the stubble on his chin, and there was a coffee stain on his polyester long-sleeved polo shirt. He slurped his coffee like it was a punishment inflicted on him by Satan himself.

"Hi, sweetie," he said, and then yawned.

"Tough week at work?" I asked as I poured some coffee into my Snoopy mug.

"Oh, the worst," he said. "In fact, I should probably get to the office early. You ready to go?"

I was still in my pajamas, which were purple flannel printed with black bats. Dad would be the first to admit that he had zero fashion sense, but he was tripping if he thought that was an outfit.

"I need at least twenty," I said. "But don't worry about it. Janis can give me a ride."

"Sounds good, kid," he said, reaching out to muss my hair like I was five. "Have a good day at school." He patted his pockets for his keys and wallet, then pulled on his jacket and headed out the back.

When the door slammed shut behind him, I sent Janis a quick text. When I looked up from my phone, Pig gave me a heart-melting mournful look. "Oh, girlie," I said, "he didn't feed you breakfast? How rude." I dumped some food into her bowl, and as the kitchen filled with sounds of serious nomming, I drained my coffee and raced to my room. Last night, I'd made the rare decision to spend my remaining drops of energy on doing homework instead of planning my outfit, so now I needed to throw something together fast. I still hadn't had time to wash my suede jacket, which was too bad because I had a really rad pair of go-go boots that were made for it, but high school was not the place where you wanted to take chances with BO twice in one week.

I settled for the go-go boots—made of shiny black pleather—with a pair of cropped red velvet bell-bottoms, a black ribbed knit mock turtleneck, and my purple fake-fur coat. The first time I'd ever worn it to school, Shauna Derks had wrinkled her nose and said, "Oh my God, Esme, is that real fur?" even though it was the color of Dimetapp.

I added my rubber snake earrings and my round Beatles sunglasses. The whole look was "Go-go goes Hot Topic," and it was very warm. I grabbed my backpack and stepped out onto the porch, locking the front door behind me right as Janis rounded the corner, practically on three wheels. She dinged the neighbor's trash can as she pulled up to the curb. I ran down the sidewalk to meet her and opened the passenger door. My jaw dropped. The car was clean. Not even a gum wrapper in sight, and it looked like the floors had been vacuumed.

"Whoa," I said. I climbed in and took a deep breath, catching not even a hint of mildew. "What did you do?"

"I don't want any more vermin in here," Janis said. "So it was either clean it out or set it on fire, and I figure I still need it to get to school, so . . ."

"It looks good," I said.

"Thanks," she said, ramming it into drive. "I feel classy. Oh, and I got new nails!" She waved her fingers at me: black with delicate white snowflakes.

"Nice!" I said, taking in the rest of her outfit. Earlier, she'd texted me "Lenny is a good husband," which was the name of her Lisa Bonet–inspired look for today: gray top hat, patchwork velvet jacket, a mess of necklaces made of several rosaries, including one that looked like it glowed in the dark, and a black maxi dress so long she had to hike it up with one hand when she walked. She also had on thermal long underwear, because Janis got cold easily.

Once we got to school, it went by in a blur, thank goddess. We handed in our Earth Sciences papers with two of the most basic photos of us in the library paper-clipped to them as proof we had done the thing required of us. After school, I was babysitting MacKenzie McAllister, the little girl whom Dion had kidnapped on Halloween. There were times when MacKenzie seemed more like a bank branch manager than an elementary schooler, but no matter how mature a kid was, you never wanted to see her get nabbed, and I had a definite soft spot for MacKenzie. She was braver than me.

I was walking to the bus to go to the McAllisters' house when I heard Cassandra calling my name. I turned around and she was strolling toward me, clutching something to her chest with both arms. When she got closer, I could see what it was: a three-ring binder.

"So, either you decided to step it up in the hole-punch-and-homework department, or—"

"Yep," she answered before I could finish. "Coach HGTV is at it again." She flipped open the binder and held it out to me. "He says we're supposed to get all this stuff today."

"It's an entire binder for a shopping list?" I asked, surprised, but not really.

Cassandra pointed to a page with pictures of paper plates, cups, and utensils, each with a number underneath it. "Yes. The entire binder is a shopping list," she answered. "He told me, and I quote, to 'put it on the gift card.'" She flipped to another page and read off Party Town's address.

"I know where that is," I said.

"Well, come on, then," she said. "I've got the van and you've got the card, so let's go."

"Not so easy," I said. "I have to babysit and it's too late to cancel. It's for MacKenzie." At the name, Cassandra's face softened a bit, no doubt because of their shared experience in the Negative.

"How is she?" Cassandra asked.

"Good, I guess," I said. "I mean, every time I've seen her, she's seemed fine. I'm taking her to her hip-hop dance class today."

Cassandra snorted. "MacKenzie's taking hip-hop?" I

nodded, and I couldn't help but smile. Cass smiled back, and then she got serious again. "You should watch her," she said. "To make sure that what's happening to me isn't happening to her."

"I will," I said, and nodded to the binder. "So, the list?"

"We'll go when you're done," she said. "Text me, and I'll pick you up."

"Are you okay to drive?" I asked.

She grimaced and pulled a piece of paper out of her back pocket, unfolded it, and scrutinized what she'd written.

"I don't know," she said. "I started writing dates and times down, and I don't see much of a pattern. Nothing has happened today, but I'm not taking any chances. Fortunately, Dion has nothing better to do than be our chauffer. So when I said, 'I'll pick you up,' I meant '*We* will pick you up,' but I didn't mention Dion, because Dion's not worth mentioning." She spoke ten miles a minute, and it was conversations like that, that made me wonder what Cassandra would be like if she did drink caffeine.

"Got it," I said. "I'll text you when I'm done."

Janis and I started our babysitting club in seventh grade, after Janis came up with the theory that the Baby-Sitters Club books were really about entrepreneurship and economic autonomy as a way to topple the patriarchy. Janis's parents were college professors, and her bedtime stories were by bell hooks.

My motives for babysitting were less noble than Janis's—I

saw it as a way to have fun and make a few bucks. I didn't really like people my own age, and I was pretty meh about most adults, but I'd always liked kids. They were like the more authentic, more honest version of humans.

Also, I wanted to do it because of Mom. I knew now that, like me, Mom was both a Sitter and a babysitter. I didn't know that at the time, of course. I just knew that, weird as it sounded, when I was chasing a three-year-old around a swing set, I somehow felt closer to my mother.

When Janis and I started the club, we had four members. Cassandra briefly joined when she arrived in Spring River earlier this year, but she was 100 percent Sitter and zero percent babysitter. She'd sooner get chopped into a million pieces by a Hash demon than help wipe one toddler bum. And after the events of Halloween, Janis was too freaked out to babysit anymore, even if she didn't totally remember why. Now, she had a thriving Depop store. Maybe it was thriving *too* much. Janis loved thrifting, styling, taking photos, and posting things to the internet. What she did not love was going to the post office, and it turned out that when people buy things online, they actually want to receive them. She was a seventeen-year-old sorely in need of an assistant. So now the babysitting club was a club of one: me. At least it means meeting minutes are super short.

MacKenzie McAllister's family lived in a super-posh part of town that looked like the inside of a snow globe this time of year. There were white lights on everything, and I would not be surprised if some of the neighbors had snow trucked in so that their kids could be the first on the block to serve up a Frosty. MacKenzie was an only child, and both her parents were lawyers who worked all the time. When her mother asked me whether I would be up for a regular gig taking MacKenzie to dance classes, I said yes right away. Easy money—I'd just sit in the back of the studio. I thought MacKenzie's mom was talking about ballet; I had no idea she meant hip-hop. MacKenzie taking hip-hop classes made me bite my lip to keep from laughing. She had braces, glasses, and freckles, and she was all lanky spaghetti limbs. She was also very, very into her hip-hop classes.

When I rang the doorbell, MacKenzie answered dressed for class and ready to go. Today, she had on high-top sneakers with neon pink laces, baggy purple shorts that came down past her knees, sweatpants underneath them, an oversized T-shirt with Daisy Duck dressed up like Left Eye from TLC (I have no idea where she could have gotten something like that, as it was actually pretty cool), and a flat-brimmed baseball cap that she wore cocked to one side. She liked her outfit so much that she put up serious resistance when I told her she had to put a coat on over it.

"I won't get cold," she said, stubbornly.

"It's a ten-minute walk to the dance studio, M," I said. "Put on a coat, or we're not going." Finally, she sighed, disappeared down the hall, and came back wearing a red-and-black plaid peacoat. I tried to keep my face totally neutral because I could see why she didn't want to wear the coat. Still, backing down would be bad for babysitters everywhere, and MacKenzie may have looked like a hot mess on the way to dance class, but at least she would be a warm hot mess.

At the dance studio, I sat in the back with all the mothers and babysitters, and for an hour and a half, I resisted the urge to cover my ears, as the "hip-hop" that the kids danced to consisted mainly of remixes so bad I wanted to remix them back to normal. Poor MacKenzie had about as much rhythm as you'd expect, but at least she managed to not trip over her own feet. And, I had to give her credit, she wasn't the worst in the class either—that title belonged to a curly-haired kid with a red-and-green cast on his left arm who did manage to trip over his own feet in the middle of a rap version of "Grandma Got Run Over by a Reindeer." He seemed like the kind of kid whose reality show audition would someday go viral.

The class ended with a dance-off, which was basically ten minutes of chaotic flossing to "Christmas in Hollis." It was all I could do to keep from finding something sharp and repeatedly ramming it into my ear canals. Then things got better, because MacKenzie and I went to the ice cream shop down the street. MacKenzie didn't like candy, but she did like ice cream. Not normal-kid flavors, of course, so she got a triple scoop of matcha, lavender, and cardamom, and shot me a look when she saw me raise my eyebrows at her order.

"I can eat it all, Esme," she said, taking off her hat and swiping at her bangs, which were plastered to her forehead with sweat even after a freezing block-and-a-half walk. "I really worked up an appetite today." I said nothing further, because while I may insist on bundling up, I was most definitely not the kind of authority figure who would try to come between a girl and her junk food.

The ice cream shop was surprisingly crowded for such a cold day, but we found a seat by the window and settled in. MacKenzie had already finished the matcha and started in on her scoop of cardamom. "So," she said, her gaze flicking out the window, "you must be quite the heartbreaker, Esme. It's something I also aspire to. When I'm your age, of course."

"MacKenzie, I don't know what you're talking about," I said, taking a lick of my own double scoop of espresso chocolate cookie crumble.

"Your boyfriend," she said. "Or ex, I assume. Considering that he's following you around and you're ignoring him." With that, she pointed behind me, and I turned, my gaze following her small, skinny finger. It was the guy from the library parking lot. He was leaning against a stark, leafless tree. Still in all black with the red beanie. Still looking cool, and hot. My mouth fell open, mid-lick.

"He was outside of hip-hop too." MacKenzie must have misinterpreted my shock as apprehension. "Don't worry," she added. "I won't tell my parents. He doesn't look scary, and he's kind of a dreamboat."

For a split second, I met the guy's eyes and had that same belly-flop feeling, though this time it was like I had landed in ice water. A sharp sound made me look away, but it was just MacKenzie's chair scraping as she pushed away from the table, and by the time I looked out the window again, the guy was gone, no trace of him left, just the white fairy lights looping through the trees. The back of my neck started to buzz.

"You can finish your ice cream on the way home," I said

to MacKenzie as I hurriedly gathered up our stuff. "We should get going."

"My mom said we don't have to be back until dinner," she protested. I didn't answer as I helped her put her coat on, and even though her hand was sticky, I held it as I pulled her out of the shop, and I didn't let go, the whole way back to her house. The guy might be hot, but I didn't know who he was or what he wanted, and when it comes to the kids I'm babysitting, I don't take chances anymore.

When MacKenzie's mom got home, I hung out for a few minutes while MacKenzie showed off her new moves. From what I could tell, the routine they were learning was a mix of viral video routines and country line dancing. By the time Mrs. McAllister paid me, I was super ready to get out of there. I was feeling really anxious, and it wasn't because there were demons to hunt down or because my mom was cursed or because my dad's whole life was a lie or because I lied to my best friend about seventy-two times a day. Something else was making my stomach do a floor routine, and I didn't know what it was.

I texted Cassandra that I was done, and then walked to the corner to wait. Once I got there, I pulled my coat tighter and texted Janis before I really thought about it.

> **I saw him again**
>
> Who?
>
> **The guy from the library**

The cute one

> Did you talk to him? What's his deal?

No

> No what

I didn't talk to him

> So. . . .

I looked up from my phone and sighed. There was no sign of Dion's van, and I felt like I might cry. There was no way I could keep this up. There was no way that Janis's and my friendship was going to survive me being a Sitter. Even when I wasn't lying, there were things that Janis just wouldn't understand, and that I couldn't make her understand.

For her, seeing a cute guy you've never seen before twice in one week was a pleasant coincidence. For me, there was no such thing as coincidence, and I didn't trust anyone. Fortunately, Janis knew that I was a tortoise when it came to guys, so she chalked my reluctance up to my awkward shyness, and started texting me about a pair of leggings she was trying to tie-dye when a gunshot-like backfire let me know that my ride was approaching.

CHAPTER 7

The van stopped and Cassandra jumped out of the passenger side to open the sliding door so that I could climb in the back.

"Hey, Esme!" Dion called from the front seat. "It's good to see you!"

I guess I too would be very cheery if memories of all the bad things I'd done had been erased from my mind.

"Uh, you too," I mumbled, as Cassandra slammed the door closed and I took my place on the floor. Dion's van was basically rust held together with rubber bands, but it was clean as could be, and I was the dirtiest thing on the floor.

"So, you're planning a party for your dad, huh?" he asked. "That's so cool." Cassandra turned around in the passenger seat and caught my eye.

"Sure," I said. "It's his birthday. I mean, anniversary."

"Anniversary of what?" Dion asked.

"His, uh, knee surgery," I said. "Three years since he's been able to walk in a straight line again."

"Good for him!" Dion said as he forced the van away from the curb. "Guess what?" he asked, then answered his own question when neither Cassandra nor I showed any interest in playing along. "I got the radio fixed!" He reached over and turned it on, and the sounds of "Jingle Bell Rock" filled the van. Cassandra reached over and turned it off.

"I hate Christmas," she said.

"Me too," I interjected from the backseat floor.

"Why do you both hate Christmas?" Dion asked, drumming his fingers on the wheel.

"You know why I hate Christmas," Cassandra said. "Because it has always sucked. No matter where we were living, we were last on everyone's gift list."

"Yeah, but that was then," Dion said. "We've got our own place now. We should put up some lights, get a tree, hang some socks. All of it."

Cassandra was looking out the window, and to my surprise, she nodded. "Yeah," she said. "Maybe we should."

We pulled into the Party Town parking lot, and Dion drove us up to the door. "So, text me when you're done, and I'll come back for you," he said.

"No, you'll wait here," Cassandra said, holding her hand out, palm facing him and her fingers toward the sky. "In the car," she added. "No radio, no phone, you just stare out the window and think about algebra."

"Got it," he said. "Will do."

I grabbed my bag and jumped out of the van, following Cassandra toward the store. I looked back right before we were about to walk in. Sure enough, Dion had his hands on the steering wheel at ten and two, and he was staring out the windshield, a slightly confused look on his face. I wanted to laugh, but at the same time, it sent chills down my spine. There was no way this was legal in any universe.

Inside, Party Town looked like someone had just detonated a holiday bomb—it was dripping with fake trees, fake snow, fake mistletoe, fake holly, fake icicles, fake reindeer, and even—for all the nonbelievers out there—fake reindeer poop. "Wow," Cassandra said, taking in a cardboard cutout of Mrs. Claus that looked like it had been modeled on Lizzie Borden. "This place is a circle of hell."

It took almost all the strength I had, and I seriously had to resist breaking out my powers, to dislodge a shopping cart from the train wreck it was part of. I steered the cart out of the way and Cassandra deposited Brian's shopping list binder into the child seat. I pulled the binder out and flipped through it as Cassandra grabbed a cart of her own.

"Wow," I said, skimming the list. "I don't know why I'm surprised, but the man is thorough. So, it looks like we need seventy-five slate-blue plates and seventy-five slate-gray plates." I looked closer at the list. "That's basically the same color. And he wants us to get one hundred and fifty napkins in a color called 'ash,' and then all the cups should be 'puce.'" I looked up. "He is planning a party that is *Fifty Shades of Grey*."

Cassandra pushed past the holiday sputum and turned her cart down a fiesta-themed aisle. "Right," she said. "So, seventy-five gray plates, and seventy-five more gray plates."

"I guess," I said, turning my cart to follow her and continuing to read from the binder. "And fabric holly and greenery, but no plastic flowers. He put that in all caps, twice." Cassandra, though, wasn't listening, and as she walked, she stuck one arm out and started shoveling everything into her cart: cactus pitchers, tiny sombreros, donkey piñatas, serape-striped place mats, everything.

"These," she said, "are amazing." She turned around wearing a pair of avocado-shaped sunglasses. "Too bad they only have about twenty pairs—people will have to fight over them." She threw all of the sunglasses into her cart. I pretended to flip through the binder.

"Ah yes, food-shaped eyewear," I said. "It's right here on page nowhere." I picked up a maraca from Cassandra's cart and shook it at her. "Seriously, Coach is not going to be happy about any of this stuff."

Cassandra yanked the maraca out of my hand and shook it at me. "Come on, Esme," she said. "Of course he's not going to be happy about any of this stuff. But you know who will be? Us!" She reached across the aisle and grabbed an entire rack of unicorn horn headbands and tossed them into my cart. "So let's just get it all!" She gave her cart a big shove and it rolled down the aisle, knocking into a cluster of fake palm trees. Cassandra grabbed an armful of leis, and instead of putting them in the cart, she thrust them over my head.

"If we're planning a party, which is supposed to be *fun*,

we might as well have a little fun," she said. I was about to protest again when I spotted an aisle of wigs. I walked over, grabbed several, and tossed them in my cart. Cassandra had a point.

By the time we were finished, Cassandra and I had five incredibly unorganized carts and one incredibly unhappy cashier staring us down. "You've got to be kidding me," he said as he sized up our purchase.

"Nope," Cassandra said. "Bag it." I had managed to find a few things on Brian's list: white pillar candles and a pack of gray napkins. And by gray, I mean printed with manatees. As a concession to the season, I picked up a lime-green adult onesie with a Grinch hood and STINK STANK STUNK printed on the front in all caps.

I pulled out the gift card and handed it to the cashier. "I think there's five hundred on here," I said.

"With an employee discount," Cassandra added.

"But you don't work here," he said, but Cassandra didn't look up from playing Animal Crossing on her phone. With the sound on so I could tell she was turning her campsite into a gym.

"Just ring up as much as you can," I said, "and we'll take whatever we can afford."

"So, you really think the other Sitters will like this stuff?" I asked as I shoved handfuls of wigs into a plastic bag.

"Well," Cassandra said, not looking up, "I like it. Do you like it?"

I had to admit that I did, especially the tropical bird curtain that I planned to take home after this whole thing was over. "Yes," I said.

She pocketed her phone. "We're Sitters and we like it, so I think the other Sitters will like it too." Cassandra's words made me stop for a minute. I hadn't been thinking about it like that at all. I'd been thinking about how different all the other Sitters were going to be, whereas Cassandra was assuming they were going to be just like us. She held up a blow-up doll of a very hairy policeman in a very skimpy uniform. "We'll just have to keep it all out of Coach's sight until the weekend."

It turned out that five hundred dollars, with an employee discount, will buy a lot of crap at Party Town, and we only had to leave one shopping cart behind. Dion helped us load everything into his van. Or, to be precise, he did most of the loading. Cassandra took shotgun again, so I sat in the back with the plastic palm trees, wedged next to a canister of black gumballs that rattled every time we turned a corner. We hit the drive-through to get burritos, and when we pulled up in front of my house, Cassandra came around to open the door and pull me out from the party supply abyss.

"So, I'll see you at school tomorrow?" I asked Cassandra.

She wrinkled her nose. "Probably not," she said, which wasn't a surprise.

"We should meet up and go to the Summit together," I said. The idea of walking into this thing on my own made my chest grow tight, yet I could imagine Cassandra not even thinking twice about rolling up to the Summit like it was no bigger deal than going to the store for chips. But I didn't need to worry—at that exact minute, both of our phones dinged with a text. It had to be Brian.

I take it you got all the supplies?

I was about to text back, but Cassandra beat me to it.

Yes. Xtra vases 2 in case some get broken

Good thinking. We'll meet at my house tomorrow right after school, and we'll all go together.

Cassandra wrote quickly:

Wut if I hav other plans?

Brian responded:

Unless it's a spelling lesson, you don't.

I swallowed to turn my laugh into a cough before I waved goodbye and headed inside.

When I walked in, Dad was in the kitchen, loading the dishwasher. Neither of us really cooked, but we blew through spoons and coffee mugs like we were trying to tunnel out of here. I felt like Dad and I needed to have a talk, but I didn't know where to begin. "Are we running out of money?" was a definite opener, but one that might not steer the conversation in the right direction.

"How was your day?" I asked instead.

He picked up a coffee mug, looked in it and grimaced, then put it in the top rack.

"Just fine," he said. "How about you?"

"Good," I said. "A few adults tried to educate me, and then I babysat. Same old, same old."

"That's nice," he said, clearly not listening as he tried to shake some detergent out of a nearly empty box.

"What about you?" I asked, casually. "How's everything going with work?"

He pressed a button on the dishwasher. Nothing happened. He pressed it again, then mumbled "Damn it" before pressing all of the buttons, several times, and something finally started up. "It's good," he said. "I mean, it's okay. I'm thinking about looking for a new job." He turned around and gave me a smile, though it was clearly a fake one.

"That'd be cool," I said. "In the new year?"

"Nah," he said. "I figure I might as well start now. No time like the present, right?" Then he yawned and stretched. "I'm bushed," he added before I could say anything. "Figure I'll head to bed early and read for a bit." He came over and gave me a squeeze on the shoulder, and then headed out of the kitchen. "Oh, the school called!" he yelled from down the hall, and I stiffened. "They said they didn't have a permission slip on file, but I told them it was fine."

"Oh, really?" I called back. I had no idea what he was talking about.

He appeared in the doorway again, toothbrush in hand. "I'm surprised you're going," he said. He had a tube of toothpaste that had been rolled all the way up, and he was using both thumbs to try to squeeze out a dab. "A school trip to the capital is not how I would imagine you wanting to spend your weekend, but I'm proud of you for expanding your horizons." He gave up on the toothpaste and tossed the tube into the trash.

It was starting to dawn on me what he was talking about. "I forget when we're leaving," I said, and Dad gave me a funny look.

"Tomorrow, right after school," he said.

"Ah yes," I said. Dad ran his toothbrush under the faucet and walked back to the bathroom, brushing his teeth with water. I couldn't help but feel both relieved and creeped out. I was glad the Synod wasn't planning on taking care of my absence with another mind erasure, but it also made me uneasy to know that while I was ensconced in the Riverbend, less than a mile away, doing goddess knows what at the Summit, Dad would think I was in Topeka, taking selfies in front of the capitol building. What was my life anymore?

I planned out my day-to-Summit outfit, and decided to keep it subtle and comfy, since I had no idea what the Summit would entail. I settled on my floral Doc Martens, my black cropped bootcut jeans, a black ribbed turtleneck sweater, and my *That's So Raven* hot pink corduroy fisherman's vest, the one I thought Janis was going to fight me for when I saw it before she did. I called it "Quoth the Raven . . . Oh snap!" Thinking about ravens made me think about crows, and that made me shudder. I still couldn't believe that the crow in Janis's car was just a run-of-the-mill avis, so maybe that was something I could figure out before the weekend was over.

It was getting late and I was exhausted from my after-school double feature of hip-hop babysitting and party shopping, so I set my alarm for extra early so I could get up and pack everything I needed for the weekend, which would be a fairly difficult task since I had no idea what I needed. Fortunately, the Docs went with everything, and I figured I'd pack one skirt—to get semi-dressed-up for the closing event/disaster—and stick with pants for everything else. I'd been burned too many times before by wearing a miniskirt to something that ended up requiring sitting on the floor.

I followed Dad's lead and brushed my teeth with water, swiped my face with a wet washcloth, plugged in my phone, and then crawled into bed. When Pig started to garumph outside my room, I used my powers to open the door and let her in. I was asleep before she'd even settled into bed with me.

CHAPTER 8

When I woke up the next morning, the house was quiet and bright. Quieter and brighter than it should have been. The sun was coming in my window and hitting me smack in the face. My alarm hadn't gone off yet, so I rolled over and grabbed my phone to see what time it was. I clicked the button, but nothing happened. It was dark because it was dead. Which meant . . . *Crap!*

It was so bright outside because I'd overslept. I threw off the covers and jumped out of bed, startling Pig. Worried, she followed me down the hall and into the kitchen. But the clocks on the stove and microwave weren't even blinking. They were just completely off. I walked to the wall and flipped the light switch. Nothing happened. The power hadn't gone off in the middle of the night. It was still off. That was why it was so quiet. Not even a whir from the fridge or a sputter from the coffee maker. Ugh! No power meant no coffee, among other things, and I still had no idea what time it actually was.

I walked back down the hall and knocked on Dad's door. I heard a grunt, and then a muffled "What?" I pushed the door open to find him sitting up in bed, looking confused.

"Dad, the power's out!" I said, not yet sure whether I was mad, annoyed, confused, or all three. He rubbed his face, then looked over at his bedside alarm clock, which, like everything else, was off.

"Huh," he said, reaching out and giving the alarm clock a slap. "I just bought this thing."

"It's not the clock, Dad," I said. "It's the whole house." I flipped his light switch to illustrate.

A look flashed across Dad's face, but he recovered quickly and hopped out of bed. He went to the window, opened the blinds, and looked out. "I bet it's just a power line out somewhere." I joined him and looked at the houses across the street. The Wilsons' blow-up reindeer was still inflated, and when I squinted, I could see that its LEDs were glowing.

"I don't think so," I said. "I think it's just us. I don't even know what time it is." Dad held up his wrist to look at his Casio watch.

"Eight-fifteen," he said.

"My first class started fifteen minutes ago!" I groaned, and swallowed a lump of panic. I really, really hoped the bad start wasn't a sign of how the rest of the weekend was going to go. "And that means you're late for work!" Dad made a big deal about the fact that he was at his desk by eight every morning.

"It's okay," he said, seemingly unfazed. "I can be late for once. Come on, I'll give you a ride." I knew this was all somehow Dad's fault, and his being oh-so-chill about it was just making me angry, but I didn't have time to argue with him right then. I didn't have time for anything. So much for waking up early to plan my outfits for the weekend.

I raced back to my room and threw some stuff into a weekend bag and got dressed. I met Dad in the kitchen, to find him wearing sweatpants and slippers. "That's what you're wearing to work?" I asked.

He shrugged. "It's casual Friday. No one else will be in the office today anyway." This was weird, but I was too concerned with my own inauspicious start to the day to press him. Pig looked at the keys in Dad's hand, and the bag in mine, and let out a mournful whimper. I crossed to the pantry and pulled out her dog-food Tupperware, but it was still empty.

"We're out of dog food!" I said, slamming the pantry door behind me.

"I'll get some after I drop you off," Dad said, rubbing the back of his head.

"Dad, what is going on?" I asked, exasperation leaking into my voice. "We're out of everything! Even electricity!" Dad just turned and started to walk out to the car.

"I'm surprised you noticed," he said. "Considering you're never here."

"What's that supposed to mean?" I snapped. "I have friends, and I have school, and I have babysitting. I'm doing all of the things I'm supposed to be doing. I'm the kid here, remember?"

He stopped halfway to the car, and I could tell by his shoulders that he was taking a breath. He turned around so that he was facing me again. "I'm sorry, you're right," he said. "I shouldn't have said that. This . . ." He paused and pinched the bridge of his nose, his forehead wrinkled. "The job search has me stressed. It's not your fault. And I know you've got a lot going on, and that you're growing up and that you're not going to tell your old dad everything anymore." He held up his hands and smiled. "And that's okay. That's what's supposed to happen. It'd just be nice if we could hang out more."

Here I was, late for school on the day of the Summit, and my dad was about to make me cry in the driveway. "If it makes you feel any better," I said, smiling to keep the tears from flowing, "I never told you everything."

He smiled back. "Haha, I know," he said. "But how about this—as soon as you're back from this trip, let's get dinner. I need to talk to you about some things, and I want to hear more about what you've been up to lately." Then he held out his arms and motioned me in for a hug. When I pulled away, I looked up at him.

"I'm serious, Dad," I said. "Figure out this electricity stuff. Teenagers need to charge their phones."

"I will," he said. "And teenagers also need to get to school." We walked to the car and got in, Dad blowing on his hands to warm them before he put them on the cold steering wheel, then he turned the key to start the car, and pulled out of the driveway.

At the intersection, I, momentarily forgetting what time of year it was, leaned over to turn on the radio. The sounds of "Jingle Bell Rock" filled the car.

"Jesus Christ!" Dad said, reaching over and turning the radio right back off. "Every time I get in the car, this song is on." He looked at me and smiled. "I'd rather listen to your music than this Christmas crap."

"Same," I said. "I would rather listen to your music. What do you like again? Football anthems?"

"Hey," he said, "those football anthems are classics, and they are way better than your music, which as far as I can tell is the sound of someone howling into a bucket."

"It's called noise rock, Dad," I said as we pulled up to the high school. "I'll make you a playlist." I gave him a hug when I got out of the car, and then, halfway up the sidewalk, I turned around to wave to him again. I half expected him to still be watching me, but instead he was just sitting there, staring straight ahead. Then, after a couple of seconds, he drove off. Sad Dad mode was in full effect, and I couldn't help but feel like the whole thing was my fault since his brain had been hole-punched on the reg for my entire life. But he was right. I was never home, and when I was, I was lying to him. I couldn't help but wonder—had Mom lied to him this much too? I added "Be better daughter" to my mental to-do list as I walked up the stairs and went into the building.

I was late for first period, so I made my way to the first outlet I could find and plugged my phone in. Phones were a serious no-no at school, and blatantly charging one in the hallway was like sacrificing my lunch-hour freedom to the detention gods, but at this point, I didn't really care. It took a few seconds for my phone to turn on. I had a couple of texts from Janis asking me what I was wearing, and then asking if

I was okay. Blergh—Janis! The Synod had covered for me with Dad, but what was I going to tell Janis about why I was going to be MIA all weekend? At least I still had a couple of hours before I had to come up with a plausible excuse, so I quickly texted her back that I was fine, and I'd fill her in at lunch.

Then I texted Dad in the language that he understood: all caps. LOVE YOU BUY DOG FOOD SEE YOU ON MONDAY!

I watched as the message tried to send and then eventually turned to green. Crap. Of course, his phone was dead. I sighed and pulled my charger out of the wall right as the bell rang. So much for first period.

I didn't have to wait for lunch to see Janis. She was waiting for me at my locker. Sure enough, her nostrils flared as soon as she registered my *That's So Raven* vest. Seeing her outfit, my mind flashed to one of her texts from this morning, which I had seen but had not digested: "college dropout." Now that she was standing in front of me, I could clearly see it was a nod to pre-Yeezy Kanye—she had on a knit Polo Bear crewneck and a pale-blue oxford button-down under a tweed blazer with brown leather elbow patches. She had on big tortoiseshell aviators (fake, because Janis had perfect vision) and a chunky gold chain that hung almost to her waist. Skinny jeans, argyle socks, penny loafers, and she'd swapped her backpack for a briefcase.

"How many books can you fit in that thing?" I asked.

"Only one," she said. But cute, right? So, what's the drama with your dad?"

"I think he forgot to pay the electric bill," I said. "So I overslept and woke up to no power."

"Well, you look good," Janis said. "Even if that vest is a little too big." I pretended not to hear her and started to shove my weekend bag into my locker. "Oh, good, you brought your stuff. You want to just come over right after school?"

It took me a second to realize what she was talking about, and then I remembered with a panic. Somehow, with the events of the week, I had completely forgotten that I was supposed to spend the weekend with Janis while her parents were out of town, a hard-won freedom she had spent weeks negotiating. I wasn't going to have to just lie to Janis about being gone all weekend, I was going to have to flake on our plans. Big-time. And she could read it on my face.

"What's up? You're still staying with me this weekend, right? My parents left this morning."

"J, I'm so, so sorry," I said. "I completely forgot. My aunt is sick, on top of everything, and now my dad and I have to go visit her. I just found out this morning. I would never cancel, but this might be the last time I get to see her."

I could tell that Janis was waffling between being mad and being worried, and my heart twisted at yet another abuse of her kindness. "You have an aunt?"

I nodded. "Great-aunt. In Oklahoma. I'm so sorry, J. I should have told you as soon as I found out."

She shifted. "That's okay. I mean, there's nothing you could do about it anyway. I guess I'll just *Home Alone* it." The warning bell cut through the hallway chatter.

"Are you sure?" I said. "You've never stayed by yourself before."

Janis shrugged. "Yeah, I'll be fine. I'll just turn the alarm on, never answer the landline if it rings, and sit up in bed all night holding a knife." My face must have betrayed something. "Kidding," she said. "I'll be fine. Go visit your aunt. It's Spring River. The worst that can happen here is that I die of boredom." Then she turned and headed to class.

Oh, Janis, I thought, I'm glad you don't know how wrong you are.

I sent Dad several texts throughout the day, but never got a response. The only text I did get was from Brian, who said that, due to an unfortunate incident involving two students and a pommel horse, he had been pulled into an athletic department meeting and would see us at the hotel, right before the Summit.

Cassandra, of course, hadn't come to school today, and just before the end of the day, she texted to tell me that she'd pick me up and that all our party supplies were loaded and ready to go. When the final bell rang, I grabbed my overnight bag from my locker and, keeping an eye out for Janis, found a clandestine perch where I could watch for Cassandra and Dion.

When they pulled up, I threw my stuff in and climbed in the back with all the bags. Dion was his usual cheery, oblivious self. "Boy, you two sure do have a lot of stuff for one party," he said.

"We do," I said, wondering what Cass had told him we were doing this weekend. "You know how girls are, we need a lot of outfit options."

The drive to the Riverbend was short, and when Dion pulled into the parking lot, I was a little disappointed that everything looked totally normal. A fountain was spraying mist into the cold air. A classic winter scene had been erected out of lights, complete with pine trees and reindeer. A lone mallard paddled in a circle, and a duck-sized Santa hat would not have looked out of place on its head. The hotel's big double doors were adorned with greenery and wreaths outfitted with shiny gold and silver balls and big red flocked ribbons. It looked cozy and festive, and I felt somewhat disappointed. I didn't know what I had expected—a bubbling cauldron? Demons in cages? Something to hint that this was a gathering of supernatural women, or maybe at least a balloon arch? Dion drove right up to the door, and two hotel employees appeared to help us with our stuff. They unloaded all of the bags from the back of the van onto a wheeled cart without so much as a hello. Then, without even asking us where it was supposed to go, they started to push it away.

That was when I realized maybe things weren't totally normal. I looked over at Cassandra, who was standing on the sidewalk next to me. "Are they, uh . . . ?"

She nodded, and started to walk into the hotel. "They seem to be under some sort of spell or something," she said, her voice low. "Like, they're here, but not really here."

"Have a great weekend!" Dion called from behind us. "Enjoy your staycation! Have fun at the party!"

I turned and waved to him before he drove away, but Cassandra didn't even give him a backward glance. At first I thought this was Cass just being her stone-cold self, but then I noticed her jaw. It was tight and clenched, like she was grinding her teeth. I glanced down at her hands. Sure enough, her nails were chewed to the quick, and it almost hurt to look at them. Cassandra wasn't just being a jerk because she was a jerk. She was being a jerk because she was stressed. Big-time.

I followed her into the lobby, which, aside from smelling like it had been sprayed down with a mix of juniper and chocolate Santas, seemed pretty normal. We made our way to the front desk, but when the woman behind it looked up from her computer, I gasped, and not because of her blinking Christmas-light-bulb dangly earrings. I hadn't made eye contact with either of the two men who had been helping us with our bags, but the woman staring at us had eyes as black as 8 Balls. It was like a negative image of what eyes were supposed to look like: white dots in the center surrounded by liquid pitch black, the opposite vibe from the glitter holly-branch pinned to the front of her jacket, right above her name tag.

"Welcome to the Riverbend and the 2020 Sitter Summit," she said, her voice bright as lemons. Her hair was brassy blonde, and her name tag said SUZANNE. "You're the first to arrive. We can hold your bags for you," she said, and gestured at my duffel.

"Sure," I said, and slid it across the counter. "Cassandra, do you want to leave your stuff?" As I said it, I realized Cassandra hadn't brought a bag with her, but she walked over to the counter, took a toothbrush from her back pocket, and slid it across the counter next to my bag. Suzanne smiled, affixed a tag to my bag and then, amazingly, one to Cassandra's toothbrush, and put them on a luggage dolly behind her.

"We're here to do some setting up," I said when she turned back around. "We had some other bags of stuff, and, uh . . ."

"They've been taken to the conference room for you," she said, gesturing down the hall. Her nails were painted red and green. "The last door on the left."

"Thanks," I said.

"Happy holidays," she responded, her hole-eyes staring someplace just past my shoulder. I turned and started to walk in the direction she had pointed when something scraped the back of my ankle. Specifically, Cassandra's foot from walking too close.

"Sorry," she mumbled as I straightened out my shoe.

"No problem," I said. "But are you okay?"

"Yeah," she said. "I mean, no. These things. Whatever they are, they're stressing me out." She dropped her voice and looked around, making sure we were alone. "This morning, I woke up, poured all the orange juice into a bowl, then carried it into the living room and put my feet in it. Fortunately, Dion's so stupid he just thought I was giving myself a pedicure." She paused and swallowed. "But no one here would think that."

I nodded. "Do you want to talk to Brian? Or someone who might be able to help us figure out what's going on?"

She shook her head. "Stop asking that," she said. "They

could want to help me, or they could make me leave. No offense, Esme, but look at your mom. The Sitterhood isn't exactly lined up to help her."

"No offense taken," I said. Cassandra had a point, and it was something I'd thought about a million times since Halloween. Where was everyone? Why was I the only one who seemed to care about helping Mom? Why didn't Sitters take care of their own? I swallowed. "So, what do you want to do?"

"I'm going to try my hardest to keep it together this weekend, and you're going to try your hardest to help me, and we're also going to try to find out as much as we can. About me, about your mom, about my mom, about my dad. About all of it, basically. I'm tired of being in the dark." She pulled her ponytail out and refastened it. "Deal?"

"Deal," I said, looking at her. Cassandra's face, normally as smooth and tawny as a Krispy Kreme, was splotchy and her eyes looked almost puffy. "Let's get you a drink of water or something," I said, because that seemed like the kind of thing you were supposed to do for someone who was clearly upset. I walked back to the desk. Suzanne was gone, and a new woman had taken her place. She had thick hair that was a blonde that could have easily been gray, and her makeup looked like it had been put on with a spatula—contouring several shades darker than the rest of her skin, glossy raisin lipstick, and blue eye shadow. Her eyes were the same shocking black-and-white configuration, but unlike Suzanne's, they were teary. She dabbed at them and smeared a bit of eyeliner.

"How can I help you?" she asked, smiling at me but looking at Cassandra. I shot Cass a glance to make sure she wasn't doing anything strange, but she was just chewing her nail again and looking around the lobby.

"Hi, Cybill," I said, reading her name tag. "Is there a drinking fountain or vending machine around here?"

"Of course," she said, sticking out her hand to point. "We have water right over there." She kept blinking, and a tear escaped and rolled down her cheek. I almost asked her if she was okay, but then I decided against it. The back of my neck was telling me that I didn't want to know the answer. The Synod had clearly worked their magic on all the hotel employees so that once we were here, we could be totally out in the open and no one would go home and tell their spouse about the strange convention that had come to town. I could just imagine that conversation: "I swear, dear, it was like they were lifeguards but also maybe a little bit dogcatcher? It was the weirdest thing. . . ."

I walked across the lobby to where Cybill had pointed and got Cassandra a little plastic cup of water from a cooler containing lemon and orange slices. "Here," I said, holding the cup out, but Cassandra shook her head.

"I'm not thirsty," she said, so I drank the water myself, then tossed the cup in the trash and started to walk toward the conference room. Cassandra stayed close on my heels, but this time not too close. It was funny to have her walking behind me instead of her usual three feet in front. The carpet was maroon with a forest-green pattern that looked like dead leaves and paint splatters, and at the end of the hallway, there was a set of fake-wood double doors. Inside was a slightly raised stage with a podium—it looked regulation, though, and not like anything in Brian's binders—and a row of chairs behind it. In front of the stage were rows and rows of chairs, and at the back of the room, all of our party supplies. I was just about to dig in and look for a wig that I'd bought for myself when I heard the door open. I spun around to see Laurie Strode striding in.

"Oh dear," she said, gesturing at the Party Town bags. For a moment, I panicked, thinking that she'd seen what was inside them. "These should have gone to the ballroom. Someone will need to move them." She turned back to me and Cassandra, and before my shyness took over, I took a few steps toward her and held out my hand. "I'm Esme," I said. "We met on Halloween, but I didn't get a chance to introduce myself."

Faux Laurie ignored my outstretched hand and went straight in for a hug. "Esme Pearl, of course!" she said. "It's so good to see you again. I'm Wanda." She turned and went over to Cassandra. "And Cassandra Heaven." She wrapped Cass in a hug too. "How are you?" she asked. "I'm hoping that we can get some time to debrief you about your experience. A Sitter traveling to the Negative is always unfortunate, and we have protocols in place to support your recovery. It's just, well . . ." She clasped her hands in front of her and looked back and forth between us. "As I'm sure you can imagine, the events of Halloween were quite a surprise.

We had no idea that Erebus was capable of such a feat."
Her eyes settled on Cassandra, and she looked like she was
waiting for an answer.

Cass hesitated, and for a moment, I thought maybe she
was going to answer Wanda honestly. Instead, she just smiled.
"I'm fine," she said. "I don't think I've ever felt better."

"Oh, that's so good," Wanda said. "One less thing we
have to worry about this weekend." Wanda was dressed
in head-to-toe linen, and she reached into one of the million folds of her cinnamon-colored skirt and pulled out an
iPhone. "I'm going to have my assistant find us some one-on-
one time so that we can really get to know each other," she
said. She looked down at her phone, and what she saw made
her scowl. She cursed under her breath. "That's insane,"
she muttered. "It's not worth that much. At least not yet . . .
Maybe in a few years." She seemed to think about something
for a minute, then tapped her phone a few times, shoved it in
her pocket, and plastered her smile back on.

"In the meantime, the truck should be pulling up outside
any minute now," she said. "So if you could just help with
the library unloading, that would be great. I'll have someone
take care of moving everything that was brought in here, and
you can take all the books to the Cottonwood Room. We'll
be using that as the Mary Anne Spier Library."

A ding sounded from deep inside her linen. She fished
her phone back out. "Woo-hoo!" she said, doing a little fist
pump when she saw the screen. "Now, that's more like it."
Then she turned and scurried out of the room.

"She seems nice," I said to Cass, which seemed like a

better thing to say out loud than what I really felt, which was maybe a little disappointed? All four members of the Synod were powerful, but Wanda was the head, the one in charge, the boss witch. That made her the most powerful Sitter on the continent, and it turned out she was a hugger.

"Yeah, I guess so," Cass said.

"Maybe you can find out more about what's going on when they debrief you?" I said.

"Maybe," she said. The door opened again, and in walked a woman who looked like a Pantone swatch. She wore lavender head to toe, from her scrunchie to her Juicy Couture tracksuit to her lavender Air Force Ones. It had to be . . . it could only be . . . ironic, right?

"Hello," she said, brightly. "You must be the Spring River delegation. I'm Clarissa."

Cassandra and I introduced ourselves. "Are you a Sitter?" I asked, and Lavender Clarissa burst into laughter.

"Oh dear no," she said, waving a hand. "You flatter me. I'm about twenty years too old and never had the kinesis anyway. I'm a Counsel in Salt Lake City. I'm just here to help out. But we should hurry. The truck is parked outside, and we don't want the books to get cold!"

I had no idea what she was talking about. I looked at Cassandra, who shrugged, and we followed Clarissa's bouncing ponytail back through the lobby out to the front of the hotel, where, sure enough, a large moving van was idling.

Clarissa went around to the back, flipped the latch, and then rolled the door up like she'd done it a million times.

Inside, the van was packed, floor to ceiling, with purple velvet boxes, all different sizes, but all the same deep, shimmering violet, wedged in like a winning game of Tetris. Everything smelled strongly of garlic.

"Whoa," Cassandra said. "What are these?"

"Sitter books," Clarissa said. She climbed up on the tailgate and took a box off the top, then handed it down to me with both hands. "Or, more specifically, the boxes the books come in."

"How many books are in each box?" I asked, the box in my hands feeling surprisingly light.

"Only one," she said. "They've very protective of their space and don't like to be crammed in while traveling." She turned, picked up another box, and handed it down to Cassandra. "Now, I think Wanda said they all go in the Cottonwood Room? No need to unpack them, just drop them off and Dierdre will arrange them when she arrives."

"I can take more," Cassandra said.

"Oh no you can't," Clarissa said. "One at a time, and hold them with both hands. I'll wait here and guard the truck. Now, snap to it! We don't have all day." I looked past her into the van. Now I could see that the garlic smell was coming from actual garlic, hung in bunches along the van's sides. There were hundreds of boxes in there, and two girls carrying them one at a time, well, that would take all day.

"You know," I started to offer, "some of the employees helped with our party supplies earlier. I bet—"

"No way," Clarissa said, cutting me off. "Only the

Sitterhood touches these books. That's why I drove this van here myself. Now, hurry up. I drove all night, and I would really like to freshen up before the Summit starts."

Cassandra turned and started to walk back toward the building, and I followed. Neither of us said anything until we made it to the Cottonwood Room, where Cassandra put her book box down on a table and immediately opened it. As soon as she did, a gonging chime filled the air, and she quickly shut the box again. "Well, I guess we won't be doing as much snooping as I would like," she said. "But still, this is pretty awesome."

"Is it?" I asked, still feeling incredulous. "It's awesome that we got here early so that we could help unload a truck?"

We started to walk back outside, and I couldn't help but notice that Cassandra was walking quicker than usual, like she was actually obeying Clarissa's order to hurry. "Well, admittedly, this part is less than awesome," she said. "But this library is like twenty times the size of Brian's. And these books must be special, because they're definitely getting the Oprah treatment. So if there's anything, anywhere, in a book that could help us figure out what's going on with me, it's probably in one of these."

I nodded and flashed back to my conversation with Brian. He hadn't been able to find much about curses in his books, but like Cassandra had said, these books had to be bigger and better. Maybe I could even come to see unloading them as a privilege. Maybe.

• • •

I didn't. Cass and I worked for almost two hours, until my arms were sore and I could walk from the truck to the Cottonwood Room with my eyes closed. We stopped only for occasional chugs from the water dispenser. At one point, Cass even stuck her hand into the dispenser and fished out a few orange slices, because unloading books really works up an appetite and there were no snacks to be seen.

"Good job," Clarissa said, when Cassandra and I returned to a finally empty van. She slammed the door shut with a clang. "Now relax for a minute, and I will see you in the Laurie Strode Auditorium right at six. I'm going to go find a place to park this thing."

Back in the hotel, we plopped down on a couch, and Cassandra propped her feet up on a coffee table, knocking her feet into a flocked wicker basket filled with decorative glitter balls. I couldn't help but giggle, and she looked at me, smiled, and then gave the basket an actual kick so that it fell off the table and sent the balls rolling across the floor. I had just started laughing when someone cleared their throat behind us, which sent me sitting straight up.

I turned around, and sure enough, Brian was standing there, a look of total displeasure on his face. I was pretty sure that Brian wore a tracksuit 364 days a year—he had a closet full of them—but now he was dressed up, in a turtleneck sweater, a tweed blazer (not totally unlike the one Janis had been wearing today), dark jeans that looked like they'd been ironed, and brown leather driving loafers. In that outfit, I practically expected him to pat a golden retriever and squirt some Old Spice in his eye.

"What up, Coach D?" Cassandra said.

"Pick them up," he said. "Now." Cassandra didn't argue, but she did pour herself off the couch and started picking up the glitter balls like all of her limbs were made of dough.

"Did you get the library unloaded?" Brian asked.

"Sure did," I said. "Every last book. Do we get a cookie now?"

"No," he said, all business. "Everyone else will arrive shortly. We need to discuss the party. Come with me." We followed him back down the hall, and with every step I got more nervous, imagining Brian's dismay when he saw what we'd bought at the party supply store versus what he'd sent us to get.

Brian walked briskly, and when he entered the ballroom, he didn't hold the door for us. "B-B-Brian," I started to stammer as he walked straight toward the bags piled in the back, "I–I can explain. We thought that . . ." I faltered, wondering what kind of excuse I could come up with for buying purple maracas when we'd been sent for gray napkins. Brian opened the top of one bag, reached in, and then turned around, holding up something I had never seen before: a chunky gray turtleneck sweater with cream-colored snowflakes woven into the front.

"What the . . . ?" Cassandra said, as Brian lovingly laid it on a chair, then pulled out a different sweater—this one red with green trees. "That is not what we bought."

"Of course it's not," Brian said. "You two managed to spend five hundred dollars—almost eight hundred with our discount—on a bunch of plastic grass skirts and joke sunglasses. Not that I expected anything different. You two are nothing if not predictable in your unwillingness to follow instructions." He held up yet another sweater, and I swear to goddess he stroked it like it was a kitten. "Now, these are hand-knit cashmere," he continued. "I figured it could be an ugly-sweater party without the sweaters actually having to be ugly."

"Wait," I said. "Where's all the stuff we bought?"

"Some of it is still here," Brian said. "I haven't gotten a chance to manipulate all of it yet." I walked over to the bags and was happy to see that it was the one with wigs, and that they were still wigs.

"Oh, good," I said, pulling out a bright-blue bob, "I love these. I'm glad we get to keep them."

"Er, not exactly," Brian said, as he came up behind me. Then he held out one hand and enunciated, "Objeckinesis." Before my eyes, the wigs turned into beanies. Hand-knit cashmere beanies, to be precise. "You understand, I'm sure," he said. "Wigs just scream Halloween, and not holiday."

"Oh," I said, figuring it wasn't worth pointing out that Halloween was a holiday. "So why did you even send us to the supply store anyway?"

"I thought it would be a good opportunity for you and Cassandra to feel involved," he said. "It *is* your party. But really, Esme, I would have been willing to compromise, and I am completely open to your ideas, but nothing that you bought is appropriate for this time of year, and you don't even have a cohesive theme."

"I beg to differ," Cassandra said. "We most definitely

have a theme. It is luau-fiesta-sock-hop-bachelorette-party, and all the kids are doing it."

"Whatever," Brian said, in a way that made me think he needed to spend more time around people of his own generation. "Now, for the fondue, I'm thinking a classic pungent with cherry tomatoes, baby carrots, and a good crusty sourdough—"

"What is fondue anyway?" Cassandra asked, interrupting his reverie.

"Melted cheese," Brian said. "Now—"

"So, like nachos," Cassandra said. I sensed a repeat of the dead versus dried flower routine from earlier this week, and tuned them out before they started to argue.

CHAPTER 9

After it seemed Cassandra and Brian had reached a melted-cheese impasse, Cassandra and I made our way to the Laurie Strode Auditorium, which was marked by a printed-out sign that called it such. The doors were unlocked, so we went in. There was no one else there. I let Cassandra pick the seats and she, of course, led us straight to the back, to two chairs closest to the doors, as if we might need to get up and run out at any minute. There were purple folders on each chair. I picked one up and opened it—the Summit schedule, aka, everything the weekend had in store for us. It looked like we'd be in workshops to help us learn new skills and to hone old ones: There was one about demonology, located in the Fran Fine Fitness Center, and one about spells, which was to take place in the Mary Anne Spier Library; honing our kinesis would happen in the Jill Johnson Room, and Sitter history and hierarchy had us back in the Laurie Strode Auditorium. Meals were to be held in the Chris Parker Cafeteria, and the final closing party—the very one that Cassandra and I were supposed to be planning—would be in the Steve Harrington Ballroom.

"Ha," I said to Cassandra. "Where's the Claudia Kishi fashion closet?"

"What?" she said, looking at me like she had no idea what I was talking about.

"Never mind," I said. I'd long ago learned that trying to explain my pop culture references to Cassandra was more trouble than it was worth. I flipped the piece of paper over to look at the back, and there they were. The names of all the other Sitters, listed in groups of six that were, as far as I could tell, named after popular children's books: the Very Hungry Caterpillars, the Wild Things, the Cats in Hats, and so on and so forth. Cassandra and I were in a group called the Runaway Bunnies, along with Ruby Ramirez, Mallory Schnell, Amirah Rahim, and Ji-A Kim.

From deep inside my pocket, my phone started to buzz. I pulled it out to silence it but froze when I saw that the call was coming from Mom's facility. My heart leapt a tiny bit, thinking that maybe she was calling me, though I knew it couldn't really be the case.

"Hello," I said.

"Hi, may I please speak to Dave?"

"Oh," I said, wondering why someone was calling my phone to talk to Dad. "This isn't his phone."

A beat of silence. "This number was listed as an alternate for Dave Pearl."

"This is Esme Pearl," I explained. "Dave's my dad. Is my mom okay?"

Another beat. "I'm calling from the accounting office, ma'am. We've been trying to reach Dave, as he is the guarantor for . . ." The woman paused, like she was reading something. ". . . Theresa Pearl, and the account is overdue."

"What?" The word involuntarily came out as a shout. "I don't understand," I added, making my voice softer.

"That means her bill has not been paid, ma'am," the woman said.

"I know what it means, I just don't know how that happened."

"It means that—" I stopped her before she got any further.

"I'm sorry, but who am I speaking to?"

"My name is Patricia, ma'am." I'd been going to Mom's facility at least once a week for as long as I could remember, but I'd never met anyone named Patricia.

"Hi, Patricia," I said, trying to keep my voice calm. "Thank you for letting me know. Are you new?"

"Yes, I just started last week," she said. "I'm trying to chase down all of our past due accounts." She cleared her throat. "Which is why I'm still at work on a Friday evening."

"I'm sorry," I said, carefully. "I'm sure this must be hard on you. Has anyone spoken to my dad, I mean Dave, about this?"

"I can't tell, ma'am," Patricia said. "The previous accountant did not excel at record keeping." There was a hint of snarky satisfaction in her voice when she said that.

"What does this mean?" I asked. "I'm sure there's a grace period."

"Yes, ma'am, there is. It ended on Wednesday."

"Next Wednesday?" I asked, my heart stuttering.

"No," she said. "Last Wednesday."

"I don't understand," I said, my voice coming out in a squeak because a deadline that was in the past did not sound like a grace period to me.

"At this point, we need this bill to be taken care of immediately, but since today is Friday and I am definitely not spending my weekend at work, we can give you until Monday."

"Okay," I said. "What happens then?"

"As I'm sure you're aware, our facility is one of the top rated in the state and we have quite a waiting list. Theresa will have to find alternate accommodations." She stopped, and then she actually added, "Ma'am."

At that moment, I wished that my power were teleportation instead of telekinesis, because I wanted to jump through the phone line and smack the snot out of Patricia. Instead, I visualized her office and imagined sweeping all her stuff onto the floor. From her still-contented silence on the other end of the line, I could only assume that my powers didn't work remotely. I forced myself to tell her to enjoy her new job and then hung up.

"What was that about?" Cassandra asked. "Is everything okay?" I shook my head as I called Dad. His phone went straight to voice mail. I called again, and then again. I left him a voice mail, and then hung up. My hands were shaking as I flipped my ringer on. If he did call me back, I didn't want to miss it, no matter where I was. I couldn't swallow. This morning, I'd written off the unpaid bills as forgetfulness on my dad's part, or just plain old irresponsibility. But not paying Mom's bills? There was no excuse for that. The only reason he wouldn't pay that was if he didn't have the money. I wiped my palms on my pants and forced myself to breathe. No matter how awesome this Summit might turn out, I did not want to be here right now.

"I have to go," I said to Cassandra, standing up.

"What?" she said. "You're leaving? Why?"

"I can't be here right now," I said. "Something . . . I don't know." I stopped and took a breath to calm myself down. "Someone just called from my mom's . . ." I turned around and scanned the auditorium. "Have you seen Brian?" I was about to walk toward the door and make a break for it when I heard them.

A chatter, a roar, the sound that filled the school hallway between classes. The other Sitters had arrived, all at once, like a mob descending out of the sky, or at least off the same flight. I was standing there, and they were spilling into the auditorium around me—teenage girls, already the most capable slice of humanity, and these girls with capabilities to the nth degree: Sitters, of every shape and skin tone imaginable, but all looking like they were beyond excited to be here. The buzz was palpable, every molecule in the air was incandescent, and as the energy flowed over me and through me, I felt my heart slow and my palms dry. I needed to go, yes, but I also needed to be here. This was where I belonged.

I forced myself to focus. I wasn't going to panic. I'd find Brian as soon as I could, and he would help. I put my phone away and craned my neck, trying to get a good look at everyone. My eyes settled on two girls a few rows up. One had a half-shaved head, her hair cropped close on one side, then hanging long and over one eye on the other; a glinting nose ring brought out the gold in her skin. The other had spaghetti-straight hair that hung down her back like a black curtain and severe, too-short-on-purpose bangs. She was wearing pale-pink heart-shaped glasses. I could swear that I knew them both. Or, if I didn't know them, I'd definitely seen them somewhere before. With a start, I realized it wasn't them I'd seen, but their clothes. The one with the nose ring was wearing a Rick Owens leather jacket. I'd seen that jacket online before—it cost five thousand dollars. And the other one's heart-shaped glasses? They were Saint Laurent.

I strained so I could get a good look at the rest of Heart-Shaped Glasses's outfit. She wore a long Prince of Wales check blazer with a large, toothlike zigzag cutout at the waist. "Comme des Garçons," I gasped, gripping Cassandra's shoulder.

"Who?" she said. I didn't bother to explain myself, and I couldn't take my eyes off the girls as they sat down. The one in the Rick Owens jacket pulled a tube of lip gloss out of a white leather Alexander Wang fanny pack and dabbed some on her lips, and the one in the CDG blazer tucked a strand of hair behind her ear. Her nails were matte black talons with a tiny stud in each ring finger. Dang. They looked like they'd slay at Returns *and* Fashion Week.

The buzzing died down as everyone waited in anticipation, and the room was so quiet you could have heard a sequin fall. Then, out of nowhere, music started. Simple piano notes that sent chills down my spine in a very good way. It was music I knew well—the *Halloween* theme song—and I sat up straighter in my chair. Others did the same, and I could see that girls were looking around the room, trying to find the source of the music and wondering what was coming next. Then, in the newly named Laurie Strode Auditorium, the real-life Laurie Strode walked onstage. I braced myself for the music to swell and for something to happen, something awesome, something mind-blowing, something so sinister you didn't know whether to poop your pants or dissolve into giggles.

Except, the music didn't swell. It didn't get louder, and even Laurie, er, I mean, Wanda, seemed confused about where it was coming from. The theme song kept playing, small and tinny, almost like a ringtone. Wait, it *was* a ringtone—the music was coming from someone's phone.

Then it hit me. "Oh God," I said, right as Cassandra looked at me with a shocked expression. It was coming from *my* phone. My stupid ringtone that I had set as a joke and then forgot about because my ringer was usually off. I scrambled to pull my phone out of my pocket, hoping it was Dad. It was Janis calling me. The laughter in the crowd was growing louder.

"Sorry!" I shouted to no one in particular. At that moment, I wanted to throw my phone on the ground and stomp on it. Stupid, stupid Michael Myers!

As the laughter died down, Clarissa got up from her chair and headed in my direction. Without saying a word, she held out her hand. I knew what that meant, so I passed my phone over, and then Clarissa returned to her seat. Brian had turned around and I caught him giving me a sriracha stare before he turned back around to face the front.

"Well," Wanda said with a little laugh, "that is the perfect intro for me to lay down the house rules before we get started, as some of you apparently did not get the memo. We have few rules here, yet they are strict. First: cell phones in your rooms only." She smiled, and a small laugh snaked through the crowd. "Your time here is brief, and we want you focused on being here while you are here. Also, I do not need to tell you that you are all very powerful, and you are all very trustworthy. If you were not, you would not be one of the chosen few, selected by destiny to protect the world's innocents from evil." She paused and cleared her throat. "That said, this much concentrated power could quickly dissolve into chaos, so we must lay down some ground rules about magic. When you are in common spaces, such as this auditorium, and at mealtimes, no magic. You will comport yourselves as if you were normies. When you are in your rooms, use your kinesis as you normally would, but no spells."

Next to me, Cassandra shifted in her seat. "Great," she muttered, "so I can light as many candles as I want." I pretended I didn't hear her. After the phone incident, I definitely did not want to get caught talking out of turn, but I could see that a few other people seemed displeased by Wanda's statement.

"Don't worry, though," Wanda continued, "spells are a huge part of why we are here, and there will be plenty of opportunities to practice the old and learn the new. I think you will all be quite happy. Now, as I said earlier, we consider you trustworthy and we expect you to honor the rules. For anyone who is caught breaking them, punishment will be swift and severe." She stopped and smiled again. A grin this time, one that stretched wide across her face. "So with that out of the way, on to the fun part! I am so, so pleased to welcome you to the 2020 Sitter Summit.

"I am sure you all know who I am, and who my fellow Synod members are, but on the off chance that you do not, I would like to take a minute to introduce us: I am Wanda Willis, and I am the Synod's Premier and will be overseeing the operations behind this operation." She gave a little smile and gestured behind her, to the three other women in the Synod, the same ones who had been at the mall with her on Halloween night when they flushed Erebus like the wad of toilet paper that he was. "To my right, I have Janine Guillot, our foremost expert in demonology." A tall blond woman stood up and waved. She wore a black-and-white '80s business suit, white stilettos, and her nails were candy-apple-red talons. It was a fierce look and I 100 percent approved. "To my right, I have Deirdre King, our librarian." Deirdre had an equally fierce, though completely different, look. If Janine was a skinny cappuccino, Deirdre was a rooibos chai: she had thick dreads, almost to her waist, and a wax-print scarf tied around her head and giant gold hoop earrings accessorizing a leopard-print maxi dress.

"And finally, off to the side, is Ana Mora, who will be your instructor for all things related to kinesis." Ana was a triple Americano: she wore a black turban, black turtleneck, black jeans, and black high-heeled boots. Out of all of them, she looked like the one you would least want to mess with.

"We also have several Counsels helping out this weekend," Wanda continued, "all of whom were outstanding in their fields both before and since they were recruited." Wanda went down the line and introduced all the Counsel, which included a guy from Oregon with a mullet, a woman who looked like Oprah and was from Chicago, a few others, Brian, and Clarissa, who had changed out of her tracksuit into an equally amethyst dress.

"We are all looking forward to getting to know you this weekend, as I'm sure you are looking forward to getting to know us," Wanda continued. "A Summit is a chance for the Sitterhood to come together in the name of education and connection, and to reassess where we are in a rapidly changing world. Thanks to us, the mortal world is safer than ever before, but new threats will always arise. And one is rising now. That threat is Red Magic." Silence had returned to the room. It didn't seem like anyone was even breathing, and Wanda sighed, a weary, confessional sigh. I bit my lip and looked sideways at Cassandra, who looked totally passive. So, we were right. They were here, all of them, because of what had happened on Halloween. "Red Magic is a perversion of Sitter magic," Wanda said. "It is selfish rather than altruistic. Instead of protecting, it causes harm. It is greedy, not generous, and rather than being genetically innate, it can

be acquired by anyone willing to sacrifice their moral soul."
She cleared her throat and took a sip of water.

"Many of you are unfamiliar with Red Magic, and as
I stand here today, I want to take the blame for that. We
thought we could protect you from it, but we were wrong,
and I am afraid that our hubris has put the Sitterhood in
danger. Right here, just a few weeks ago, the true powers of
Red Magic made themselves known. We were almost bested,
and unimaginable havoc was almost wreaked, so we are here
now to make sure that never happens again." Wanda paused
and looked around the auditorium, and I swear that her eyes
lingered on me for just a second. I quickly looked down at
my knees.

I tried to pay attention to the rest of Wanda's speech, but
I had a hard time. Her words were powerful, and serious,
but somehow I couldn't make sense of them. Halloween had
been the most terrifying night of my life. It was the first time
I'd seen demons, and a Portal, and MacKenzie had been
kidnapped on my watch. It was a hot mess from beginning
to end. But I was a novice Sitter then. I'd never even done
a real Return before that night, and neither had Cassandra.
We were pantsing it all the way, and we hadn't done a terri-
ble job.

And the villains of the night, Erebus and Dion? They
were Tweedledumb and Tweedledumber. Erebus was powerful, no doubt, and scary, but he was also a total scuzz-
bucket. The Synod had come in and swatted him away like
he was nothing more than a fruit fly. Yet, they had also sealed
the Spring River Portal for almost fifteen years because of

him. This whole Summit was here because of him. He was a creep for sure. But a Red Magician mastermind? That seemed like a stretch.

Suddenly, Wanda's speech was over and everyone was up and heading for the doors.

Casandra stood, but instead of charging ahead like she normally did, she actually waited for me, and we fell in behind the crowd. "So, what did you think of that speech?" I asked, wondering if she was on the same wavelength as me.

"It was weird," she said, glancing around. "What did you think?"

I nodded. "It was weird," I agreed. "Why did *you* think it was weird?"

"You tell me first," she said.

"Well, it made Red Magic sound terrifying," I said. "And it is. But Erebus, well . . ." I struggled for the right words, trying to keep in mind that Erebus was Cassandra's dad.

"Was not terrifying?" she offered, and I nodded.

"Exactly!" I said, happy she had said it, not me. "I mean, don't get me wrong, he was scary. And he was certainly powerful, but there was something about him that seemed a little thirsty." Cassandra nodded, and I kept going. "Like, he seemed like the kind of guy who'd keep his pleather jacket on when it was ninety degrees, just because he thought it looked cool." She nodded again. "He seemed like the kind of person who'd be really into creative facial hair, and turn up the radio and say 'This is my jam!' when Nickelback came on." Cassandra kept nodding, which encouraged me to continue. "He seemed like the type of guy who'd drive a PT Cruiser,"

I said, "and call it a sports car. He seemed like—" Cassandra held her hand up.

"I got it," she said. "You can stop there. Basically, he doesn't seem like someone who would warrant all this."

"Exactly," I said, but before we could continue, I spotted Brian. "I'll be right back," I said to Cassandra, and took off in his direction.

I wove through the crowd, making my way toward Brian. When I caught his eye, he did not look happy to see me. I could see the muscles twitching in his jaw.

"Well, that was quite a show you put on," he huffed when I was finally standing in front of him. Oh God, my phone.

"I'm sorry, I really am," I said, realizing that this was perhaps not the best intro to the question I had to ask. "And I swear that it will never happen again. But I need my phone back. Now."

Brian laughed so hard that he slapped his knees. Rather, he pretended to laugh so hard that he slapped his knees. I gave him a minute and acted like I was impressed when he pretended to wipe his eyes. "Oh, that's rich," he said. "That's just rich."

"I'm serious, Brian," I said. "Mom's facility called and Dad hasn't paid her bill and they are going to kick her out. Dad isn't answering his phone and I have to figure this out. The electricity was off at our house this morning, and if I don't get ahold of him soon, I might have to go home."

"That is not an option," Brian said. "You're here for the duration of the weekend, and the Synod has gone to great pains to make sure no one will notice you're gone."

"I'm not worried about anyone noticing I'm gone," I said, feeling very real, not-pretend-at-all tears come to my eyes. "I'm worried about my mom. And my dad." And Pig, and basically everyone else whom I cared about. In short, I was worried about my entire life.

Brian's face softened. "You can't have your phone back, and you certainly cannot leave," he said. "But I will look into it. We don't want anything to take your attention away from being here." He paused. "Don't worry, Esme. Everything will be fine."

I nodded. "Thank you," I said, slightly calmed by Brian's assurances, though, if Dad truly hadn't paid the bill because he couldn't afford it—because *we* couldn't afford it—then that was a problem no amount of magic was going to solve. Suddenly, I felt my cheeks go hot as a thread of anger coursed through me. "Brian," I said, "Mom was a Sitter, and the only reason she is in the place where she is now is because she was trying to do her job. The Synod owe it to her, and they should be helping make sure she's okay." They owe it to me, too, I thought. I braced myself for Brian to give me another one of his lectures about rules and responsibilities and yada yada all that life-is-not-fair BS, but instead he just reached out and squeezed my shoulder.

"I'll see what I can do," he said. "And I promise your mom will be fine." He swallowed. "Room assignments were handed out, so you should go meet your roommate now. And try to enjoy this as much as you can. It's a very special thing." I nodded and started to walk away when a thought hit me, and I turned back to Brian.

"So, hey," I said, "Wanda . . . I thought her name was . . . well, you know?" Brian shook his head. A cup of yogurt knew more about pop culture than Brian did, but he still picked up on my reference.

"No, but it is not a coincidence they look so much alike. The actress you are thinking of was cast in her iconic role because of her resemblance to Wanda. It is one of those bits of the Sitterhood that has made it into mainstream lore." Suddenly, Brian straightened up and brushed something invisible off his turtleneck. He was looking over my shoulder, staring at something across the room. I followed his gaze to see that he was staring at someone, not something. Clarissa. Even in different clothing, tracksuit still recognized tracksuit, and it looked like someone had a crush.

CHAPTER 10

I got my room assignment, then took the elevator up to the fourth floor. I walked down the hall, and when I found room 402, I tried to push the door open, but it would only open about a foot. The door was hitting something behind it. I tried again, but the door wouldn't budge. Finally, I turned sideways and squeezed through the gap. The doorstop was a massive suitcase, wedged between the door and the wall. And from the looks of it, the suitcase had exploded. There were clothes and shoes and jewelry and makeup on every conceivable surface, and, though the room appeared to be empty, it smelled like skunk. Then I heard a toilet flush and someone appeared in the bathroom doorway.

It was the girl with the shaved side and the Rick Owens jacket, and the smell I'd been smelling wasn't skunk, but the lit joint pinched between her fingers. She must have just taken a hit, because she started coughing and the smoke burst out of her nose and mouth like she was an asthmatic dragon.

She walked over to one bed, and as she did, a piece of ash fell off the joint and floated through the air, landing on said jacket, which was now lying in a crumpled pile on the floor.

"I took the closet," she said. "Because there was only one." She took another hit. "Amirah Rahim," she said as she held her breath. I recognized the name from the Runaway Bunnies.

"Oh," I said. "Esme Pearl."

She smiled. "I mean, is this not the smallest hotel room you've ever been in? The showers at the Standard are bigger than this." I just nodded and didn't offer up the fact that (a) this was probably the only hotel-not-motel room I'd ever been in, and (b) I had no idea what the Standard was.

"Where's your stuff?" she asked. The hotel had dropped off my weekend bag, and it was sitting right inside the door, but apparently that didn't count as stuff.

"I didn't bring much," I said. "Since these rooms are so small," I added. I was torn between looking at Amirah and at her jacket, which looked like it was in pain. Finally, I couldn't take it anymore and bent over to pick it up off the floor. I smoothed it out and hung it on the back of a chair. "I like your jacket," I said. "Is that from the spring/summer '19 collection?" As soon as the words were out of my mouth, I hated myself for saying them. Sure, I was asking because part of me wanted to know, but I was also trying to impress Amirah. And she was clearly not impressed.

"Yeah, but I think I'm going to sell it," she said. "I'm pretty sure my godmother is getting me a Saint Laurent for Christmas."

I nodded like I knew what she was talking about, even though I didn't have a godmother and had never been faced with an embarrassment of leather jacket riches. I crossed over to the bed that she wasn't sitting on and sat down on it. "So where are you from?" I asked, though I already knew the answer.

"New York."

Of course. I'd heard of that place. "Did you get to the room early?" I asked. Wanda had dismissed us just a few minutes ago, so surely there was no way Amirah could have made this much of a mess in such a short time.

"No," she said, looking confused. "Why do you ask?"

"No reason," I said quickly. Amirah stubbed out her joint on the lip of an open La Croix can. I heard a hiss as the cherry fell into the Pamplemousse, then she stood up, turned around, and, in one swift motion, pulled all the sheets and blankets off the bed and dumped them in a pile on the floor.

The hell? Maybe the thread count wasn't high enough, and she'd brought her own sheets from home. But then she pulled out a roll of clear packing tape, ripped off a strip with her teeth, and started taping it on the mattress. Then she stood up, held the tape up to the light, and peered at it.

She was apparently satisfied with whatever she saw, because she crumpled the tape into a ball. Then she turned to me and motioned me off the bed I was sitting on. I stood up and got out of her way as she repeated her performance.

"What are you doing?" I asked.

"Checking for bedbugs," she said. "My dad brought them home once from a Four Seasons in Scottsdale. I thought

Mom was going to divorce him. We ended up having to go to Paris for three weeks while the penthouse was fumigated."

Amirah looked at me like I was supposed to feel sorry for her that she had endured such an inconvenience as having to go to Paris for three weeks. And she had said penthouse, not apartment. I bet it was one of those places where there were no hallways and the elevator opened right into the living room. I wondered whether she always traveled with a roll of tape tucked between Balenciaga jeans and Balmain T-shirts, which I knew she had because they were also strewn across the floor.

"Well, I'm going to head downstairs," Amirah announced. "See what sort of old tires and burlap sacks this place cooks up for dinner. You coming? We're at the same table." I followed her to the door and in the process nearly tripped over a Versace sneaker.

"Are you going to put the sheets back on the bed?" I asked.

She waved one hand over her shoulder. "The maid will do it," she said, and shut the door behind us. "So, where are you from? Wait! Lemme guess! Minnesota?" I shook my head. "Iowa?" I shook my head again, and Amirah crinkled her eyebrows. "Well, it's definitely someplace flat. Gosh, you're not from Oklahoma, are you?"

"No, I'm from here."

"From Kansas?" she asked. I nodded and she laughed. "I've never met anyone from Kansas before. It's kinda cool, in a *Children of the Corn* sort of way." I cringed—that was not a compliment. "So, tell me, what do you do for fun here?"

I sucked my breath in through my teeth. I wasn't sure

how to answer that question—watched movies, ate dough-nuts, went thrifting. But would that seem lame to Amirah? I decided to keep it vague. "Oh, you know, just hang out," I said. "What about you?"

The elevator arrived, and I followed Amirah on. She pressed the lobby button with an elbow. "You know, normal stuff," she said. "Go to clubs, openings, things like that." She swiped her hair from one side of her head to the other. "Or rather, I used to. I've been training so much lately that I barely have time to go to brunch."

"Oh," I said. "Training takes up most of your free time?"

Amirah nodded. "My parents are actually letting me homeschool so I can focus on it. Which kind of sucks, 'cause I miss my friends, but protecting the innocent is more im-portant. Obviously."

"Your parents are supportive of you being a Sitter?" As the question came out of my mouth, I realized that this was the first-ever conversation I'd had with a Sitter other than Cassandra, and that I had a million questions for Amirah, and not just about her wardrobe.

"Of course, they're, like, beyond," she said. "My mom slayed back in her day."

"Is your dad in the Sisterhood too?" I was starting to learn the words that everyone else used when they talked about this stuff. The elevator door opened and Amirah and I stepped out into the lobby.

"Nah, he's just a normie. Well, not a total normie—he's like a billionaire—but he's like obsessed with my mom. He has been from day one. He was actually dating Naomi

Campbell when they met, but he dropped her so fast. I mean, why date a supermodel with you can date a woman with actual superpowers?" She rifled through her Issey Miyake tote and pulled out a little box of mints. She popped one in her mouth, then held the box out to me. I took a mint and regretted it the second it touched my tongue: a sinus-clearing blast ripped through my head, but the mint itself tasted like dirt and shrimp. I coughed a little.

"Good, right?" Amirah said, and ate another one. "Our housekeeper special orders them from Japan." I nodded and forced myself to swallow the mint whole, like a pill, just to get rid of it.

We walked across the lobby, and when we got to the Chris Parker Cafeteria, I was relieved to see a buffet table laden with things that looked worlds away from what I had just had in my mouth. Food that looked normal, and predictable: a fajita bar, chicken fingers, pizza, veggie burgers, french fries, iceberg lettuce with bacon bits and ranch dressing. I turned, ready to ask Amirah whether she wanted to get in line, to see that she had already left. She was running toward Heart-Shaped Glasses, and it looked like they were reuniting after thirty years, not thirty minutes.

I grabbed a plate and got in line by myself. Across the room, I could see Cassandra already sitting at a table, chowing down, with several empty chairs between her and a redhead, the only other person at the table. I helped myself to a couple of slices of pizza and extra breadsticks, then added a salad, extra dressing, for good measure. I walked over to our table, which had a little Runaway Bunnies sign, just like the book cover, in the middle of it, and opted for the empty chair next to the redhead as opposed to the empty chair next to Cassandra. The redhead looked up at me and smiled.

"Hi," she said, holding out her hand, "I'm Mallory." Her hair was curly, the top part held back with a scrunchie, and she had big glasses that kept slipping down her freckled nose. I couldn't help but think how she reminded me of the original Mallory, Mallory Pike, but I didn't bring it up, because it seemed like something she had probably heard a million times before.

"Are you Cassandra?" she asked, which made me realize that even though she and Cass were sitting at the table alone, and had been for a minute, they hadn't exchanged a word.

"No, I'm Esme," I said. "That's Cassandra." At the sound of her name, Cass looked up from shoveling spaghetti into her mouth and gave a little wave. I was about to ask Mallory where she was from when Amirah and Heart-Shaped Glasses approached the table, and Amirah set her tray down with a bang. There was only a small bowl of white rice on the tray.

"This food is not going to work for me," she said, looking at me as if I had cooked it. "I'm going to have to order takeout. Please tell me you have uni in this godforsaken town."

"Jeez, Amirah," Heart-Shaped Glasses said. "This is Kansas. If they had uni, would you really want to eat it?" Her tray was similarly laden to my own, and she used the tips of her talon-nails to pick up two chicken fingers and drop them on Amirah's tray. "Eat some chicken. You're not going to die if you go one weekend without Nobu." Then she turned to the rest of us. "I'm Ji-A," she said. "With a hyphen between the *i* and the *a*."

Mallory introduced herself, and I introduced myself and Cassandra, who was still eating like a seagull was going to swoop in and steal her food. "I like your glasses," I said to Ji-A.

"Thanks!" she chirped. "I got them at a sample sale."

"I didn't know YSL had sample sales," I said, then again wanted to kick myself for trying to show off. But Ji-A didn't seem to notice.

"Well, it was more of a friends-and-family thing," she said, ripping the crust off her pizza and dipping it in ranch.

"So I take it you're from New York too?" I asked.

"Upper East Side," she said, nodding. "But I practically live with Amirah, and she's in Tribeca."

"We share everything," Amirah said, nibbling on a chicken finger as if she were trying to illustrate the point.

"Where are you from?" I asked Mallory.

"Miami," she said, which was not what I was expecting, considering she looked like she'd need an SPF of about 182.

"Huh," Ji-A said. She had taken a bite of quesadilla and was chewing carefully. "This isn't bad."

"It's cheese and a tortilla," Amirah said. "Guy Fieri couldn't mess it up."

"That's not true," Ji-A said. "A quesadilla can be burned, or you could get one where the cheese isn't melted in the middle, or it could be made with muenster."

Amirah rolled her eyes in concession. "Is that all you're eating?" Ji-A asked Mallory, who looked down at her tray, which contained only what appeared to be PB&J on white bread. She was cutting the crusts off it like she was preparing it for a preschooler.

"Yeah." Mallory shrugged. "I'm kind of a picky eater." She said it with the same certainty other people reserve for saying their birthday is in March.

"What *do* you eat?" I asked, which was a legit question since the buffet spread had a bit of everything.

Mallory thought for a minute, twisting a napkin in her fingers. "I really like oranges," she said, "and oatmeal, as long as it's not Irish oats."

"Yum," I said, not knowing how else to respond.

There was still an empty chair at the table, and I was starting to wonder who Ruby Ramirez was when she appeared right behind Cass. I knew it was Ruby because her gold nameplate necklace said so, and I assumed she was Mallory's partner, since she looked like someone from Miami. Ruby was gorgeous, and she was dressed like a model at the airport: low-slung green cargo pants, cropped white tank top, oversized hoodie tied around her waist, and black-and-gold Adidas shell toes. Everything about her was golden: her skin was bronzed gold, and her hair, which was shaved to about a quarter inch all the way around her head, was sunshine gold, and her eyes were the color of the beach. I bet she smelled like coconuts and mango. She glowed, except the look on her face was confused and almost PO'd.

"Hey," she said, pulling out the chair and sitting down.

"I thought we'd come down together, but when I came out of the bathroom, you were gone." She was talking to Cass, and it took me two seconds to figure out what she was talking about. Cass was obviously her roommate, and of course had already been rude as hell.

"Sorry," Cass mumbled, barely looking at her. "I was hungry, and it seemed like you had moved into the bathroom. No offense."

Ruby brushed it off. "None taken," she said. "I guess we've got the whole weekend to get to know each other." With that, Cass pushed back her chair, got up, and walked away. Ruby looked after her, and then turned to Mallory. "Oh, good," she said, "I'm glad you found something to eat."

At that moment, my allegiances were split—I wanted to apologize to Ruby and offer some sort of explanation for Cassandra's rudeness: she'd been sick, or she'd had a rough day. But it seemed patronizing, and also a bit like talking about Cassandra behind her back. So I said nothing as Ruby began to squeeze a lemon over her plate of fresh greens and grilled chicken breast. As soon as she was done with that, she pulled out a little pill organizer from one of the pockets on her pants and started to line capsules and tablets up alongside her plate.

We were all watching with curiosity, and Ji-A was the first to speak. "Nice supplement game," she said. "Is that turmeric?" Ruby nodded as she popped two bright-yellow tablets into her mouth and washed them down with a swig of water.

"My colon therapist had me taking that for a while," Amirah said. "So good for inflammation."

Ji-A nodded in agreement, and then the four of them fell into an animated conversation about omega-3s and vitamin C. I plastered a smile on my face and sat there in silence, as I had nothing to contribute. I hadn't taken vitamins since I was seven, and those were shaped like cars. Finally, Ruby changed the subject. "I'm Ruby," she said to the rest of us, then forked some greens into her mouth. "What can you all do?" She was looking at me when she said it, so I went first.

"I'm telekinetic," I said.

"I'm a quantum tunneler," Amirah said, "so I walk through walls."

"I heal stuff," Mallory said, her PB&J still mostly untouched.

"Sweet!" Ji-A squealed. "You didn't tell me that back in the room. Can you fix my nail?" She held one hand out, and sure enough, one of her talons was broken off in a jagged edge.

Mallory peered at it. "Unfortunately, no," she said, "I can only heal organic matter."

"Worth a shot," Ji-A said, unfazed.

Cassandra came back to the table, carrying a tall glass of soda, no ice, and sat down again. Ruby looked at her. "I already know that Cassandra's pyrokinetic," she said. "Judging by the state of our shower curtain." Oh no, I thought, what the heck did she do to their shower curtain? I tried to catch Cassandra's eye, but she was looking down and drinking her soda very intently.

"I do astrology," Ji-A said. I wondered how that counted as kinesis, but Mallory and Ruby seemed totally impressed.

"Can you do my chart?" Mallory gasped.

"Sure," Ji-A said, "back in the room. You know what Wanda said about kinesis in the common spaces." Everyone nodded gravely.

"So, what about you?" Ji-A asked Ruby.

"I'm psychic," she said, then picked up a napkin and held it out to Cassandra. Cassandra looked puzzled, but took it from her, then immediately spilled her soda everywhere. I'd never seen Cass blush before, but now she was the color of a cranberry.

"Sorry," Ruby said, "I know I'm not supposed to use it in here, but old habits die hard."

"That's sick," Ji-A said. "So can you tell me who is going to win on *The Bachelorette*?"

Cassandra hadn't used Ruby's napkin to mop up the spill, so there was a puddle of soda on the table in front of her. I saw Ruby glance at Cassandra out of the corner of her eye before turning to answer Ji-A. "I can't, actually," she said. "I can't see that far ahead. Usually it's just a few seconds, sometimes as much as a few minutes. But it's really helpful with Sitting, and I had to stop boxing because of it. I always knew what punch was coming next. My uncle made me quit because he said I was getting too good and the normies were getting suspicious."

I looked expectantly at Cassandra, thinking she would jump at the chance to get to know someone who liked fighting as much as she did, but she was still just looking down at the table silently when Clarissa chirped over.

"Hello, girls," she said, cheerily. "I've got an icebreaker to help kick things off." She reached into a pocket and pulled out a stack of index cards and a little pencil, which she handed to Ruby. "You're in charge, dear," she said, and patted her on the shoulder before heading off to the next table.

I jumped up quickly and ran after her. "Clarissa," I said, and she turned around, a stack of cards in her hand. "I'm so sorry, but I was wondering if I could get my phone back."

She smiled a placating smile. "I don't have it, honey," she said. "I handed it over to Wanda right after I confiscated it."

My stomach dropped. Wanda? I was going to have to talk to Wanda to get my phone back.

"Okay, thank you," I said.

"Not a problem," she replied. "Let me know if you need anything else." But she was already on to the next table.

I got back to mine to find everyone waiting for me to start.

"Okay," Ruby said when I sat down, looking down at the cards, "I guess we'll get started. Each card has a common babysitting disaster scenario," she read. "With your roommate as your teammate, you will take turns reading the scenarios aloud and then calling on fellow Sitters at random to solve them. The same person cannot solve two scenarios in a row, and your answers will be scored by your peers, on a scale of one to ten. The winning team from each table will be entered into a drawing for a grand prize."

"What's that?" asked Mallory. Ruby flipped the card over and read off the back, "Free admission to all the indoor playgrounds in your city for an entire year. Complete with free snacks."

Mallory let out a low whistle, and Amirah turned to me. "Don't mess this up, Esme," she said. "I want that prize." She didn't need to tell me twice: I wanted it too, and we both sat up a little straighter and leaned forward.

I looked over at Cassandra, who was staring at her knees. I could also swear that she was slowly moving her chair away from Ruby's, and that the distance between them was growing inch by inch. This kind of grand prize meant nothing to Cassandra, but Ruby was looking at her intently. "That would be great on days when it's too hot to go to the beach," she said, which elicited zero response from Cassandra. Ruby's smile disappeared and she turned back to the cards.

"Okay, first scenario," she read: "You're at a playground with no fence, and you're watching four-year-old twins. They suddenly take off running in opposite directions. Which one do you chase first?" She looked straight at Mallory and nodded.

Mallory shifted a little in her seat, looked at Ruby, and then cleared her throat. "I would chase whichever child was running toward the street, or an area where he or she was most likely to come in contact with some mode of transportation."

Ruby looked around the rest of the table. "Seven," Amirah said. "Solid plan, but you should also yell to alert any other responsible adults at the playground, as one of them could maybe grab one of the twins." Everyone murmured, and Ruby wrote down "7" on her scorecard, then passed everything to Mallory.

"Disaster scenario number two," Mallory read. "You are

babysitting a six-month-old who rolls off the changing table."
Everyone at the table gasped. "What do you do, Ji-A?"

Ji-A put her palms flat on the table. "That has never happened to me," she said. "I take my role as protector of the
innocent very seriously, in all kinds of sitting. But if it did,
I would one hundred percent remain calm, no matter how
much I was freaking out inside." She then went on to list her
steps, which included seeing whether the baby would stop
crying if distracted, checking for bumps and bruises, and
giving the parents a full report as soon as they got home.
Everyone was nodding.

"I give it a nine," Ruby said. "One point deducted for
letting it happen in the first place." Ji-A groaned, but good-
naturedly. Mallory passed the cards to her.

"The next disaster," Ji-A started. This was going to be
our scenario. I was ready, and I also had to admit that I was
kind of having fun. "You are babysitting three children,
and they are playing in the backyard. As you go to get some
snacks and water, you realize that one of them has locked
the door and you are all locked out of the house. None of
the children have shoes, and you do not have your phone." I
smiled. Something almost exactly like this had happened to
me before, so I totally had this one.

Except that Ji-A called on Cassandra. Cass looked up
from where she'd been staring at the floor. "Um, find a brick
and break a window," she said. "And then climb in and open
the door." From the corner of my eye, I saw Ruby's mouth
drop open.

"No," said Mallory. "The kids have bare feet, remember? You don't want broken glass all over the place!"

"Oh," Cassandra said.

"I give it a three," Amirah offered. "I mean, at least she did something."

And so went the rest of the game. At one point, Mallory got called on again, and Cassandra actually interrupted. "You're babysitting for a woman who is really into clowns," Amirah had started, and the table let out a collective "ew." "In the living room, there's a rocking chair with a life-sized clown doll that is really freaking you out. What do you do?"

"I know this one," Cassandra said, slapping the table as if she were hitting a buzzer. "I'd set it on fire."

Mallory grimaced. "I would have said: confirm with the parents that such a clown doll exists in their home, but I guess incineration is another option." She looked around the table.

"Five?" Ji-A offered. Cassandra beamed. It was the highest score she'd gotten all night.

CHAPTER 11

When the game ended, Ruby took our scorecard to the front of the room, Amirah's eyes on her the whole time. "We didn't do too bad, roomie," Amirah said, and at that moment, I wondered if maybe we'd actually end up being friends. Then, all of a sudden, Cassandra stood up so quickly that her chair toppled over. She was looking at me, eyes wide, and I knew what was coming. I jumped up just as quickly, was around the table in two seconds, and took her elbow.

"Hey, didn't you say you wanted to talk to Brian?" I said, turning Cassandra away from the table. "Let's go see if we can find him."

"He's right over there," Mallory said, but I pretended I didn't hear her and steered us in the opposite direction. Cass kept walking slower and slower, and by the time we got to the door, I was practically dragging her. Thankfully, we made it all the way into the hall before she twisted free of my grip to do a pretty good roundoff, throwing her arms in the air when she executed a perfect landing.

I ran over and managed to steer her into a nearby bathroom, which, thankfully, was empty. I figured this was a private space, so I used my kinesis to hold the door shut. If anyone tried it from the outside, they would think it was locked, which was very necessary since Cassandra had pulled her shirt off and was swinging it like a lasso. "Yeehaw!" she yelped, and then flung it at the mirror.

"Cass," I said as firmly as I could, "put your shirt back on." She didn't, of course. Instead, she took off her pants. I watched as she picked up her shirt and stepped into it, pulling it up to her waist. Then she took her pants and tied them around her head. She was starting to look like Little Edie in her best outfit for the day.

"I just don't think it is right that society dictates how we wear our clothes," she said, turning on the hand dryer by headbutting it with a leg of her pants. I would not argue with her on that, but as her shirt fell down to her ankles, I had to think that this wasn't exactly the best argument for it. Then, to my horror, a toilet flushed, revealing that we were not as alone as I had thought.

Whoever had been in the stall had been quiet as a ghost, and I was at Cassandra's side in two seconds, trying to tug her pants off her head. Cassandra, of course, resisted. "Don't cave to mainstream pressures, Esme," she sang, twisting away from me. "When life gives you lined paper, write the other way."

I turned, and in a panic, used my kinesis to hold the stall door shut. "What the heck?" said the person inside, as she gave the stall door a violent shove. "Why won't this open?" I could only keep someone locked in a bathroom stall for so long, so I resumed frantically trying to get Cassandra dressed in a seminormal fashion. Then I heard a grunt from behind me, and I turned to see a woman crawling through the space between the stall door and the floor. I wanted to slap myself in the forehead. I hadn't even thought of that.

I loosened my grip on Cass, and she spun away from me, humming loudly. As the woman pushed herself up off the floor, I saw who it was: Cybill, the woman at the front desk with the caked makeup and the watery eyes. I sighed, then almost laughed: a hotel employee, already bespelled so that she couldn't see anything unusual, like a half-naked girl pressing her nose hard against a mirror and staring intently into her own eyes.

Cybill made her way to a sink, where she washed her hands and then used a paper towel to dab at her still-streaming eyes. I figured she wouldn't even notice us and walk right out of the bathroom. But then, she tossed her paper towel in the trash can and, to my surprise, turned to look right at me, her face twitching. "Is she okay?" she asked. Behind me, Cassandra had closed her eyes and looked calm and peaceful, two qualities that I would never normally ascribe to her. She had turned on the faucet and had one hand pressed against it, so water was spraying out and onto the floor.

"She's fine," I said to Cybill, surprised that anything odd had registered with her. But as soon as I said that, Cassandra pushed herself away from the wall, screamed at her own re-flection, then raised a fist and smashed it into the mirror. The mirror spider-webbed, and as Cass reared back to smash it again, I could see the glass was smeared with blood. Instinctively, I held up my hand and used my kinesis to hold her back, but she struggled against me, blood dripping from her knuckles as I pulled her farther and farther from the spot where she wanted to be.

My kinesis was like a grip. A grip about one hundred times stronger than my actual physical grip, but Cassandra kept flailing around, and whatever had taken hold of her had made her even stronger than she normally was. In two seconds, she'd twisted free. As she ran toward the mirror, her sock-clad foot hit some of the water she'd sprayed on the floor. She slid, and then tripped on her shirt, which was now twisted around her ankles, and fell like someone in a cartoon who'd just stepped on a banana peel.

The woman and I were at Cass's side in two seconds. As she looked up at us and blinked, I was relieved to see that her pupils were back to normal. If the woman was under the Synod's spell, I would have expected this whole scenario to barely register with her, but her breath was rapid and her hands were shaking as she leaned over Cassandra.

"I have something that will help," she said to Cass. "But I need time." She looked at me. "Come find me Sunday," she said. "I'm working the continental breakfast. Not the buf-fet, the bagels and cups of yogurt in the lobby. I don't know if I'll be able to get everything, but I'll try." She looked up sharply as voices wafted into the bathroom from the hall.

"I have to go," she said, standing up quickly. "But Sunday, continental breakfast. Don't forget." Then she turned and ran to the bathroom door. She tugged at it with a grunt, and then looked back at me. I lifted my kenesis, and she pulled the door open with a swing, then ran out into the hallway.

"What, and who, was that?" Cassandra said, struggling to sit up. Then she looked down at herself. "Esme, why am I wearing my shirt as pants?"

That seemed to be the least of her—of our—concerns right now. "Cass," I said, "your hand." It was bleeding, a lot. I helped her up and over to the sink, where she turned on the water and held her hand under it, the water running pink over her fingers. She pulled her hand out from the water, and the blood started to run bright red again. She grabbed a wad of paper towels and wrapped them around her hand. Within seconds, I could see red spots start to appear. "Is your hand going to be okay?" I asked.

"I think so," she said. "The cuts aren't deep enough for me to need stitches, but still. I can't go back in there like this. Esme, this is bad." I could tell Cassandra wasn't just talking about her hand. Her earlier episodes had been inconvenient, and almost funny. She'd seemed happy. But this one was different. She'd been angry, and she had hurt herself. Maybe even pretty bad. I'd become a pretty good liar over the past month, and Cass was no slouch herself in the fib department, but it would be hard for us to come up with a story to write off why her hand looked like she had just punched a mirror. She held her wounded hand above her head, but within seconds, a drop of blood seeped out from the paper towels and started to run in a red river down her arm. "And who was that woman?" she asked. "What'd she mean, she had something for us?"

"I don't think she meant a croissant," I said, the back of my neck starting to tingle.

"Do you think she's a spy?" Cassandra said, her words turning my tingle to a chill.

I swallowed. "Cass, we have to tell someone," I said. "So you stay here and I'm going to go get someone to help us." She started to shake her head, but I stopped her. "It's not Brian, and it's not a member of the Synod," I said. "We don't know if we can trust her, but we have to take that chance." And then, before she could stop me, I turned and ran out of the bathroom.

The dining room had about half cleared out, but to my relief, Mallory was still sitting at our table. Unfortunately, she wasn't alone. Amirah and Ji-A had taken off, but Ruby was still there, and they appeared deep in conversation. I forced myself to walk, and not run, over to the table, but I didn't do a very good job. Sure enough, Ruby's head snapped up when I was still halfway across the room, about five seconds before I would have arrived at the table. And I was out of breath.

"Esme!" she said, half rising from her chair. "Is everything okay?"

"Yes," I said, too fast, "everything's fine. I just need to talk to Mallory." Mallory's eyes widened.

"Okay," she said. "What's up?"

"Not here," I said. "And alone, please." Ruby wasn't buying it, though, and she stood up before Mallory did.

"Where's Cassandra?" she asked, looking behind me at the door.

"She's fine," I said.

"I didn't ask *how* she was," Ruby said.

I shifted from one foot to the other, wasting valuable seconds that I needed before a bleeding Cassandra decided she was done waiting and took the matter of her hand into her other hand. I shuddered to think what that would look like.

"She's in the bathroom," I said.

"Doing what?" Ruby asked. She was looking down at me like she was the babysitter and I was about to get in trouble. I didn't know how it worked to lie to someone who was five-seconds psychic.

"She's not feeling well," I said.

"Is that why you need Mallory?" Ruby asked.

"Ugh," I said, my voice pitching into a whine. "It's none of your business."

"Cass is my roommate," Ruby said. "So if she's sick, it is my business."

"She's not sick," I said. "At least, she's not contagious." Mallory still hadn't said anything and just looked back and forth between me and Ruby.

Then she pushed her glasses back up on her nose. "I can't cure," she said. "Only heal. So if Cass is sick, it won't be instantaneous."

"I said she's not sick," I snapped, then caught myself. I

needed their help, or at least I needed Mallory's help, and I didn't want to piss them off.

"Esme," Ruby said, "I'm going to end up going with you anyway, so let's just go now and save some time."

"Okay," I said, deciding right then that I wasn't picking this battle. "Come on. And hurry." I turned and walked out of the dining hall, and even though I knew that Cassandra wasn't going to be happy about it, there was a part of me that was glad Ruby was coming. I could already tell she was a great Sitter. She could take charge, and her kinesis must have given her a strong sense of intuition. She seemed like a good person to have on our side, and if the events of the past half hour were any indication of the weekend to come, it was going to take more than me to keep Cassandra safe.

People were milling around the lobby and hallway. Mallory, Ruby, and I didn't talk as we walked. When we got to the bathroom, we slipped inside, and then I held the door shut behind us. Cassandra was still sitting on the floor, in her underwear, her bloody hand wrapped in paper towels as she held it above her head. The mirror above her looked like it had been shot, and shards of glass littered the floor and sink.

Ruby gasped and said "Oh my God!" at the same time Cassandra looked at me and hissed my name. As I suspected, she was not happy that we were not alone, which Ruby picked up on immediately. "Esme wanted just Mallory," she said, squatting down by Cassandra, "but I forced myself in. What happened? Who did this to you?"

Cassandra kept looking at me, and I could see some of the

fire in her eyes drain out. She wasn't choosing this battle either. "Nothing happened," she said. "And I did this to myself."

Mallory walked over and motioned at Cassandra's hand. Cass lowered it and then unwrapped the paper towels. "I think it's pretty surface," Cassandra said. Mallory didn't move to touch her, just bent at the waist, like she was searching for a four-leaf clover, to get a better look.

"That one on your index finger is pretty deep," she said. "We should really get a first-aid kit and clean everything thoroughly, but I'm assuming there's a reason you haven't already done that." She looked at me, and Cass's gaze followed.

"Yeah," I said, "we don't want anyone to know."

Mallory nodded and stepped back. "Okay, at least wash it with hand soap," she said. "A wound that isn't clean can still get infected, even if I heal it."

Cassandra washed her hand, the rushing water turning bright salmon. "What'd you do?" Ruby asked. "Punch the mirror?" Cassandra nodded as she dabbed at the cuts to dry them. Ruby let out a low whistle. "Dang, girl," she said. "That's some punch." Cassandra walked back to Mallory and held out her hand. Ruby and I took a few steps closer to them. Mallory held out her own hand, hovering her palm about six inches above Cassandra's still-bleeding cuts. A look of focus swam onto Mallory's face, Cass winced a little, and then the cuts started to zip themselves up. They closed one at a time, like someone was erasing them with Photoshop. After a few more seconds, Mallory stepped back. "Wash the blood off," she said, "and I'll check and make sure I didn't miss any cuts." Cassandra did as instructed, and when she patted her hands dry, this time the paper towels stayed white. She held her hand out and flexed her fingers a couple of times. There wasn't even a scar.

Holy crap. It was one of the most impressive things I'd ever witnessed, and I could see my wonder reflected in Cassandra's face as well, but she shook it off. "Good as new," she announced. "Thanks a lot. I owe you big-time." Then she sidestepped Mallory and started to grab her clothes.

"Wait a sec," Mallory said. "You have to tell us what's going on."

Cass hopped on one foot as she pulled on her jeans. "I told you," she said. "I punched the mirror and hurt my hand, but you fixed it, so now it's fine. Thanks so much. Like I said, I owe you big-time."

Ruby was standing behind Mallory like she was her bodyguard. "Maybe you can start to pay her back by telling her why you punched the mirror," she said. "That seems like a just thing to do, considering both of you are acting real sketchy and Mallory just put her own butt on the line to save yours."

I could feel Cassandra looking at me, but I deliberately avoided meeting her eyes. She had asked me not to tell anyone, and I wasn't normally the type of person who spilled someone else's secret, but I was pretty sure this secret was going to be too big for me to keep all by myself.

"She doesn't know," I said. Ruby and Mallory looked at Cassandra, who had her shirt over her head as she pulled it back on the right way. Her head popped out of the collar, and then she took her time getting her arms through the sleeves.

"Well?" Ruby asked.

"Esme's right," Cassandra said. "I don't know why I punched the mirror. I don't know why I took off all my clothes. I don't know a lot of things these days."

"Are you on drugs?" Ruby asked.

"Heck no," Cassandra snapped. Ruby didn't look like she believed her.

"She doesn't even drink coffee," I said, backing her up with the same argument she'd given me.

Cassandra sighed. "I don't know what it is," she said. "I've been having these episodes. It's like I black out, and when I come to, I don't remember what I was doing. Esme tells me, or else I piece it together. Mostly, it's been harmless. But today I hurt myself. I'm lucky Esme saw it coming and got me out of the dining room in time. Otherwise, I could have really made a scene." She paused. "Or hurt somebody else."

Ruby crossed over to the counter and hoisted herself up so that she was sitting on it, her black-and-gold sneakers dangling. "Huh," she said. "That's it?"

Cassandra huffed. "You lose control of yourself and see how you like it," she said. "It's a big deal, even if it doesn't sound like—"

Ruby waved a hand, interrupting Cass. "I'm not trying to trivialize it," she said. "That's not what I meant. I meant, are you having any other symptoms?"

"You mean aside from occasionally blacking out and

doing things like trying to wear my pants as a hat while I assault a mirror?" Cassandra said. "No, that's about it."

"Wait, Cass," I said. "Before all this started, you said there was something that you couldn't remember."

"Your memory is bad?" Ruby asked, and Cass shook her head.

"No, it's not like that," she said. "It's more like there's one specific thing I can't remember." She sighed and slouched against the hand dryer. "To be honest, it's driving me nuts, almost more than these episodes, or whatever they are. It's what I think about first thing in the morning, and the last thing before I fall asleep, and I don't even know what it is." Suddenly, she straightened up, her face brightening. "Hey!" she said, looking at Mallory. "Do you think—"

Mallory shook her head and cut Cass off. "I can't do diagnostics," she said.

"It wouldn't matter even if she could," Ruby said, "because you're not sick, and you don't have a brain injury. You're just cursed."

"What?" Cassandra and I said at the same time. Just hearing that word out loud threw all my senses into overdrive.

"Everything you're talking about, it's classic cursed behavior," Ruby said.

"But I went to the Negative on Halloween," Cassandra said. "Couldn't it just be from that?"

"You would hope it's that," Ruby said. "Because then there would be a cure. But Sitters go to the Negative all the time. Well, not *all* the time. But it does happen. And sometimes, they're a little effed up after it, but nothing like this."

"That's true," Mallory said. "One of my mom's best friends ended up there for almost a week. When she came back, all she did for like a month was watch reruns of *Three's Company*. But she eventually got her spirit back, and she's been fine ever since."

My heart was starting to race. I had a million questions for Ruby—about Cass, about my mom, about curses in general—and I felt like once again I was staring into the chasm that existed between me and Cassandra and the rest of the Sitters, or at least all the other Sitters whom we'd met so far. They'd all grown up in the Sitterhood, and their powers were expected and accepted. But Dad knew nothing about Sitting, and the various relatives and foster parents who'd raised Cassandra knew even less. It wasn't Brian's fault that Cassandra and I were behind. Even if he was the best Counsel to ever Counsel, there was no way he could ever make up for the fact that Cassandra and I had not been raised by our mothers, and we were behind by a lifetime for it.

"How do you know about curses?" I asked Ruby. "I thought Sitters didn't know about curses since we can't do them."

"We can't," she said. "And you're right—a curse wouldn't come from Sitter magic. It's Red Magic. I know all about curses because my grandma was a Sitter." At the mention of her grandma, Ruby's face lit up. "She was a real badass," she continued, "because she was also a Santeria priestess. People were always coming to her for Santeria curses, which Nana wouldn't do, of course, but seeing how many people wanted to curse someone got her interested in the whole idea. She was very academic, and wrote about it a lot, and actually got special dispensation from her Synod to study the history of Red Magic curses as well. She was looking for ways to remove them without using Red Magic." Suddenly, Ruby started coughing. For me, at least, I had never been so impatient in my entire life for someone to keep talking.

"Excuse me," she said finally, pounding her chest. "I just swallowed wrong." But then she just sat there, and it didn't seem like she was planning to continue.

"And?" I said. "What did she find out?"

"Oh, it's not possible," Ruby said. "Red Magic curses can only be removed by Red Magic."

Cassandra was hanging on every word, just like I was. "But you said there were other kinds of curses," she said.

"True," Ruby said. "But no one would use one on a Sitter. I mean, they might try, but it would be like a drop of rain, whereas a Red Magic curse is a hurricane."

I was starting to feel like I'd been hit by a hurricane. "So, basically, you're saying that a Red Magic curse can only be removed through Red Magic."

Ruby nodded. "That is literally exactly what I just said."

From across the room, I could feel Cassandra's eyes boring into me, and I didn't want to meet them because I didn't want to acknowledge the horror of what we were hearing. Sure, we'd heard it before from Brian, but I knew better than to trust an adult. Yet hearing Ruby say there was only one way out . . . well, that made me pretty sure there was only one way out. "You're absolutely sure there's no other way to break it?" I asked.

Ruby shrugged. "There might be," she said. "Not everyone who's cursed stays that way for their entire life. Sometimes it wears off after a few years. Other times, it can just be gone, and no one knows what broke it."

"Your grandma told you all of this?" I asked.

Ruby nodded, and a faraway look crossed her face. "She and I were close, and I helped her get her papers and stuff in order before she died, so I spent a lot of time with her research."

"I think we have to tell someone," I said, looking at Cass, but speaking to the room.

"No way," Cass said. "What are they going to do about it?"

I looked at Ruby, but she raised her eyebrows. "I mean, I can tell you what they'll do about it: nothing," she said. "That's the only thing they can do." Cassandra gave Ruby a look I couldn't quite interpret, then looked back at me.

"They'll make me leave the Summit," Cassandra said. "And I won't be able to Patrol, or even be a Sitter anymore." She turned to me. "Esme, they're letting your mom rot and they'll do the same to me. If I get packed up and shipped off to some locked room, then we'll never find out who did this." Ruby had barely taken her eyes off Cassandra, but now she looked at me.

"My mom is . . . ," I started, but then I saw Ruby was nodding, and I realized she already knew.

"I recognized your last name," she said. "From my grandmother's files."

I felt like I'd stepped on a swarm of fire ants, and my skin prickled at her mention of Mom. "What did your grandmother's files say?" I asked, my heart pounding in my throat.

"I don't remember," Ruby said. "But that means it probably wasn't much. Nana had records of every Sitter who was cursed." I think she caught the look on my face. "Sorry I don't know more," she said.

I bit my tongue and nodded.

"The same person cursed them both," I said. "Cassandra's dad. He was a Red Magician, and the Synod banished him to the Negative a long time ago. He actually cursed my mom for ransom, but the Synod won't pay, and she's been this way for almost fifteen years."

"It wasn't my father," Cassandra said, her words almost giving me whiplash because I spun my head so fast to look at her.

"We *are* talking about the same person here, right?" I asked. "Erebus, your father, wearer of a pleather jacket?"

"Yes, of course, him," she said. "And you need to get over his jacket."

"So if he didn't curse you," I asked, "then who did? He's the only Red Magician either of us has ever heard of."

"Not necessarily," Ruby said. "Someone could be practicing Red Magic, and you just don't know."

"I thought using Red Magic made someone's Sitter magic go away," I said, somewhat shocked, but Ruby shook her head.

"Only if they get caught," she said. "Then that's their punishment. But it doesn't have to be a Sitter. There could be others like Cassandra's dad."

"So, what if someone's just dabbling?" Cassandra said. "Like, not going full-on, just testing it out."

"The whole thing with Red Magic is that it's addictive," Ruby said. "That's why the punishment is the same whether you're just doing a little spell or trying to bring on a full-blown apocalypse. Once someone starts, they're probably not going to stop."

"So, basically, anyone with access to Red Magic could be using it?" I asked, and Ruby nodded. "Well," I said to Cassandra, "then we've got to start with motive. Who would want to curse you?"

"Who knows?" she said. "Anyone who ever spent more than five minutes with me on a day when I was in a bad mood?"

"You said it, not me," I said.

"I bet it has to do with whatever you're not supposed to remember," Ruby said. "Red Magic curses aren't like regular curses, if there is such a thing as a regular curse. A regular curse just means bad things will happen to you. Like you get lots of parking tickets, you drop your phone, or step in dog crap on the way to a date. But a Red Magic curse, it's like a living death. It makes it so you can't participate in the world, and it slowly cuts you off from everything you love." She glanced over at Cass. "Sorry," she said, "you just don't seem like the type who wants things sugarcoated."

Cassandra nodded. "Thanks," she said. "I appreciate it."

I nodded too. It seemed like we'd learned more from five minutes in this bathroom than we had in all of our studies with Brian. "So, what do we do now?" I asked.

"We stick with the original plan," Cassandra said. "I'm staying here, and we're keeping this a secret." She looked back and forth between Ruby and Mallory, almost daring them to contradict her, but neither one did. They just nodded.

Mallory cleared her throat. "I'm not going to tell anyone," she said. "And I'll help cover for you, if I have to, but if you hurt someone else, I'll have to go to the Synod. I'm sorry," she added, and she looked like she meant it. "But we have to protect ourselves first so that we can protect everyone else."

Cassandra nodded. "Fair enough," she said.

In the silence, Mallory stepped up to the broken mirror and held her palm out to it. "Vitreokenesis," she said, and the cracks in the mirror fused together, healing the same way she'd healed the cuts on Cassandra's hand.

"Wow," I said, and she shrugged.

"Glass manipulation," she said. "I had to learn because one of the kids I babysit for kept hitting a ball through his neighbor's greenhouse."

"So, what do you want to do now?" I asked Cassandra.

"Go back to my room," she said, and again she glanced at Ruby. "And go to sleep."

"I'll walk back with you," Ruby said. "I'm going to hit the gym because I missed my third workout today, so I need to change." Cassandra walked out of the bathroom first, and in the hallway, I could swear she put another six inches between herself and Ruby as soon as Ruby fell in beside her. I had no idea what had happened between them before dinner, but apparently Ruby coming to Cassandra's rescue still wasn't enough to melt that ice block.

"Hey, Esme," Mallory said, "can I talk to you a second?"

"Sure," I said, falling back. "What's up?"

"How well do you know Cassandra?" she asked.

"Pretty well," I said. "I mean, I haven't known her for that long, but we've been through a lot together. She's a good Sitter, and she cares a lot."

Mallory nodded, but stayed silent in that noncommittal, if-you-can't-say-anything-nice kind of way.

"Why?" I asked.

She looked up and down the hall. "When I heal people, I pick up on a lot of their vibes, and Cassandra's are dark." She paused. "That could be the curse, or it could just be her."

I chose my words carefully. "Thanks," I said finally. "For helping her, and for telling me. I didn't mean to, I mean, we didn't mean to, get anyone else involved. I'll look out for her." I swallowed. "And keep an eye on her," I added.

Before Mallory could say anything else, we both heard a loud grumble, and she got a sheepish look. "My stomach," she said. "I'm starving."

"You didn't eat much," I said, thinking of her nibbled sandwich.

"It's cool," she said. "I have a stash of protein bars in my room. I'm going to head up there. See you tomorrow?"

"For sure," I said. "And thanks again for everything."

CHAPTER 12

Mallory took the elevator to her room, but I opted for the stairs. I didn't want to do that thing where you make small talk with someone after you've already said goodbye, and I wanted a few minutes alone to think.

Mallory hadn't needed to explain further about what she'd said, because I knew. Everything I had said about Cassandra was true, and I trusted her, but I also knew that Cassandra had two approaches to rules, and if she wasn't breaking them, she was bending them. I'd seen her steal, get in fights, and turn her brother into her slave. Erebus was her dad, so of course Red Magic was in her blood, but there was more to it than that. From everything we'd learned, Red Magic seemed like a way to exercise great power to get exactly what you wanted and take revenge on anyone who had ever made you mad. And from what I knew about Cass, that all sounded right up her alley.

But still, I couldn't believe it. I'd seen her on Halloween.

She'd jumped into the Portal with no idea what was on the other side, willing to sacrifice herself to save MacKenzie, and that had to count for something. In fact, I was sure it counted for a lot.

I opened the door to the fourth floor and smiled at a few people as I walked down the hall to my room. Smoke hit me in the face as soon as I walked in. Amirah and Ji-A had a joint going that was about the size of a carrot, and the fumes coming from it smelled like a skunk raised on cabbage. The window would only open about four inches, and they were trying to blow the smoke out of the crack, oblivious to the fact that most of it was coming right back in. Amirah held the joint in my direction, and when I shook my head, she turned back to the window. She and Ji-A were deep in conversation, and Amirah seemed heated. I sat down on her bed for a minute, next to an issue of *Vogue Brasil*. I picked it up, then realized that the cover model's face had been scratched out with ballpoint pen.

Amirah saw me looking at it and coughed. "Ugh, my stupid ex-girlfriend!" she said, stomping over and grabbing the magazine from me. Then she ripped the cover off, crumpled it into a ball, and threw it in a corner. "We broke up like two weeks ago, and she's already in another relationship!"

Behind her, Ji-A caught my eye and mouthed, "It's a dude."

"I mean, did the two months we spent together mean nothing to her?" Amirah wailed, before taking another hit.

We still had forty-five minutes before curfew, which meant forty-five minutes of me being the third wheel before

Ji-A went back to her room, and I didn't have the energy right now to try to interject myself into a conversation where I wasn't wanted or needed. "I think I'm going to head down and see what's going on in the lobby," I said to no one in particular, and Amirah waved to me through her tears.

I tried to find Brian, to see if he'd talked to Dad or heard anything about Mom, but he was nowhere to be seen. I thought about asking the front desk for his room number, but after our interaction with Cybill in the bathroom, I wanted to steer clear of the hotel employees. So that left me with nothing, and I didn't know what to do with myself.

The lobby was empty save for a few girls already in their pajamas. I flopped down on a couch that was cozily parked in front of a gas fireplace, and wished I'd brought something to read.

Soft music was playing through the speakers, but instead of being relaxing, it was vaguely disconcerting. Every song was a watered-down version of a watered-down version, and it made my brain itch trying to place the original. I put my feet up on the coffee table and then it hit me what song was currently playing. It was heavy on the jazz flute and drum machine and . . . oh God, of course. Why had I even listened? It was "Jingle Bell Rock."

I groaned out loud and threw my head back, and that was when I realized I wasn't alone. Someone else had had the same idea as me and was sitting in an armchair, feet up on a footstool. But it wasn't another Sitter, or a member of the Synod, or even a hotel employee who at least knew who to talk to about getting my phone back. It was a guy. A very specific guy: the guy I'd seen at the library, and at ice cream after hip-hop class. The hot guy, and now he was here, in this hotel, and he was reading a book. An actual, gosh-dang book, with a spine and paper pages, and it was *Lord of the Rings*.

My heart started to pound. I had no idea who he was or why he was here, but I was sure that I was not prepped to have a conversation with him right now. He had earbuds in, but he took one out and smiled at me, almost expectantly.

"I'm sorry," I said. "I didn't notice that anyone else was here. I promise I won't talk to you." He nodded and put the earbud back in, but not before I could hear what he was listening to. The Clash. "London Calling."

Dang. That was from my gateway-drug album, the one that opened the door to punk, then domino-effected everything so that I discovered half of my favorite bands. I could spend an afternoon just talking about Joe Strummer's hair.

But yeah, I'd promised I wouldn't talk to this guy.

And, ugh, the god of social anxiety himself couldn't have orchestrated a more awkward situation. I didn't have anything to do, or even to look at. I missed my phone violently. I didn't want to leave immediately, because I didn't want him to think I was leaving because of him, so I settled back into the cushions and stared at the fire like the flames were a secret code I was trying to decipher.

Then he said, "Hey." I looked up and I must have looked startled. "Sorry," he said, "but I didn't promise I wouldn't talk to you. You're Esme, right? You live here in Spring River."

"Yeah." I was momentarily shocked that he knew my

name. Since there was literally no way for me to play it cool, I decided to not even try. "I've seen you around town," I said. "Before the Summit. Are you from around here too?" I knew he wasn't, as guys who were from around here didn't look like him. He was a piece of fancy licorice, whereas Spring River boys were stale circus peanuts.

"No, I work for the Synod," he said, taking out his other earbud and winding up the cord. "I had to come early and scope out the town as a Summit location."

"Oh God," I said, laughing. "What on earth did you possibly see that made you tell them this was a good spot?"

He shrugged. "I didn't." It took me a second to realize he wasn't joking.

"Oh," I said, not sure how to respond. "Then why did they choose to come here anyway?"

"I think it was like Wanda said in her remarks earlier," he said. "A lot of stuff has happened here, and they're pretty worried about it. I guess you had something to do with all that?" I nodded, and he smiled. "Sorry, I don't mean to freak you out and talk like I know your life story, but I figure it's less weird to cop to what I do know than to pretend I've never even heard of you."

It still kind of freaked me out to think that he knew about me because someone—i.e., Wanda and the Synod—had been talking about me, and because there was no way they were saying anything good. But I had to admit there was some logic to the rest of what he said. We were both members of Generation Lurk, so why not own it?

"So when you say you work for the Synod, what does

that mean?" I asked. He was too young to be a Counsel, and Sitters were only girls. Something about him piqued my interest, and it wasn't just that he was cute. It was that he was in a hotel full of girls and he had chosen to sit by himself and read a book about elves, listening to punk rock. He picked at a string on his jeans. "It's kind of complicated," he said. "I do odd jobs, and kind of whatever they need me to do."

"Oh, that's cool. How'd you get that job? Are you from a Sitter family?" I asked.

"Eh, not exactly. Wanda's my legal guardian. She kind of adopted me after my family was killed."

"Oh," I said, swallowing. "I'm sorry."

"Don't be," he said. "I was too young to remember when it happened, and even then, it wasn't your fault. That's kind of one of my pet peeves, when people apologize for stuff that's not their fault."

"Oh, I'm sorry," I said again, automatically, then blushed. "Wait, did I do it again?"

"No, you apologized, but it was your fault you apologized for something that wasn't your fault, so that one was warranted."

We sat in silence for a second, just looking at each other. The gas fireplace gave off no heat, but it did give off a glow that reflected off his cheekbones. The corners of his lips turned up, and I couldn't help but smile too. "Okay, I'm confused now," I said. "Which one of us should be apologizing?"

"Neither," he said. "I think we're even." He looked down at his feet, then looked back up at me. "I'm Adrian."

"Esme," I said, while his name pinballed around in my skull. "But you knew that."

A beat passed, and then, because he'd opened the door, I decided to walk through it. "So, Wanda's your mom?"

He shook his head. "Not exactly. She raised me, the whole Synod did, but I wouldn't say that it was very familial. As I said, my family was killed when I was little. Our babysitter, who was also a Sitter, really dropped the ball, and demons got in and murdered everyone while she was busy calling a radio station trying to win tickets to a Justin Timberlake concert."

I had no idea what to say, so I went with the obvious. "But you survived?"

"I hid in the dryer," he said. "And now I really hate 'Sexy Back,' so . . ." He smiled at me, but the smile quickly faded. "Sorry, I shouldn't joke about my family being murdered. It's just, it is what it is, and humor is my way of dealing with it."

I shook my head quickly. "Oh no, I totally get it. I'm the same way. With my mom, I mean . . ." The statement was halfway out of my mouth when I realized it wasn't true anymore. I used to joke about Mom. When I thought things were out of my control and that there was nothing I could do about it, dark humor saved me. But now I knew that Mom didn't have to be the way she was, I knew there was a way out, and there was something I could do, I just didn't know what it was, and I didn't feel like joking anymore. . . .

"Hey," Adrian said, "you okay? Your face just got, like, really weird. You looked like you saw a ghost or something."

"Sorry," I said. "Wait, should I apologize for that sorry? I don't know. I've got a lot on my mind right now. It's nothing you said." I took a quick breath and tried to change the subject. "So, what all did you scope out while you've been here? It's so funny that I saw you twice." As soon as the words were out of my mouth, I regretted saying them. I'd noticed him twice, and maybe he hadn't noticed me at all.

Adrian smiled. "At the library, and when you were baby-sitting, right?" I nodded. "God, I sound like a creepy stalker," he said. "I just had to find a Sitter to get my bearings, see what you do and where you go." He paused. "Which, I am just now realizing, is exactly what a creepy stalker does. So if you want to call the police and file a restraining order, I will not stop you and I will move a hundred yards away."

I couldn't help but think that I wanted him to do a lot of things, but moving away was not one of them. "So, what'd you find out?" I asked him, leaning into it.

"Well, you like thrifting," he said. "And you drink a lot of coffee."

I laughed. "My deepest secrets," I said. "I mean, about Spring River."

He moved over so that he was sitting on the couch, next to me, and quickly glanced behind him to make sure we were still alone. "Honestly, it's kind of odd," he said. "Like, it seems like a normal town to me, with slightly below-average levels of demon activity. It's not easy to get to, public transportation isn't great, though I admire you for your continued patronage of the bus, and there's not a whole lot to do here.

Yet there's a history here, and it scares the Synod to death, Wanda especially—and trust me, nothing scares that woman. I've seen her make the manager of a T-Mobile store cry."

"Oh my gosh," I gasped in awe.

Adrian nodded. "The guy ended up apologizing to her for the fact that she used up all her data," he said. "And he paid her overage charges himself."

"Dang," I said. "That's nuts." I met Adrian's eyes, and all it took was him smiling at me to make me feel like there was no way I could sustain eye contact for anything longer than half a millisecond. So I looked down, at his shoes, and saw that the toes were covered with ballpoint pen scribbles, including Clash lyrics that I recognized. Writing lyrics on the toes of your shoes. It was cheesy as hell but also kinda sweet.

I looked back up at him. "You like the Clash?" I said.

"Yeah, they're my favorite band," he said. "Why? Are you surprised?"

"No," I said, quickly. Then, "Well, yes."

"What, you take me for more of an Ableton and Auto-Tune kinda guy?"

"No way," I answered. "It's nothing personal. It's just that most people seem to like stuff made in this century. Not me, though. I haven't liked anything that came out since I was born."

"Ha," Adrian said. "I get it. What about you? What's your favorite band?"

"That depends on the day," I answered. "And I tend to go more by favorite albums instead of favorite bands, but off the top of my head, I can't think of a single favorite album of mine that came out after 1998." I was well aware that this was the kind of answer that sounded like a cop-out, but I meant it, and Adrian smiled like he knew it.

"Nineteen ninety-eight was an incredible year for music," he said.

"*The Miseducation of Lauryn Hill,*" I replied.

"*Hard Knock Life.*"

"*Celebrity Skin.*"

"*Moon Pix,*" he said, and the mention of Cat Power would have knocked me on my butt if I weren't already sitting down. Was he for real? Was any of this for real? Was it all just a dream, and if I looked down I'd discover I had paws for hands?

But instead, for some reason, I decided to test him. "*Wide Open Spaces,*" I said.

He raised his eyebrows. "I have no idea what that is," he said.

I smiled. "Dixie Chicks. It's, like, a Kansas-girl thing," I said. "But no discussion of the best albums of 1998 can be had without mention of . . ." Then we said "*Aquemini*" at the same time. I blushed, and Adrian laughed.

"Wow," he said. "I guess we're just a couple of music snobs, then."

"I don't think it's our fault that we have good taste," I said. He was doing that thing again, where he was looking at me, and I didn't know what to do back. I had no idea what to say to him, and at the same time I felt fear gripping my stomach, panic that if I didn't somehow keep the conversation going, he was going to get up and leave. "So," I said, casting around for something else to talk about, "what was it like growing up with the Synod?" As soon as it was out of my mouth, though, I wanted to bite my tongue off. That was a superpersonal question, and I'd known Adrian for all of five minutes. But, he didn't seem to care.

"Sometimes it was cool," he said. "Especially for me, you know? I wasn't born with powers, and when I was younger they made the whole losing-my-family thing more tolerable. I'd pretend I was a character in a book or a movie, like a chosen one who was rewarded with powers and magic for enduring all of this mortal suffering. But that wears off as you get older. You realize that life with magic is still life."

His words felt like someone had taken a spoon and dug right into my guts. I didn't know how to convey just how much I knew what he was talking about, that I could have said those exact words myself. It felt like a whole ravine of conversation had been opened up, and we'd both fall in. I looked down on the couch, where somehow our knees had moved so that they were touching. Not much, just barely kneecap to kneecap, but still, it was enough to make me feel warm. Only, there was a curfew, and it almost certainly had to be time for us to go.

I looked back up, and I could tell that Adrian knew it too, because his eyes were scanning the elevator and everything behind me. "Okay, lightning round," I said. "You're a total normie human. What's your dream job?"

"Taco taste tester," he said, without missing a beat. "You?"

"Nail polish namer," I said. "Who trains otters in her spare time."

"No fair," Adrian said. "You didn't tell me we also got to pick a side hustle!"

"Hey," I said, "it's not my fault you're lazy." A beat of silence followed.

Then another, and I couldn't help but hear the music again. "Oh, listen," I heard myself saying, "it's that date-rapey Christmas song."

Adrian laughed, and listened for a moment. "At least it's just the instrumental version," he said.

"I really hate Christmas music," I said, and he laughed again.

"All of it?" he asked. "Or just the old standards that paint coercion tactics as romance?"

"All of it," I said. "If there is a cool Christmas song out there, my ears have never heard it."

"Not even the Waitresses?" he asked.

Huh? I was stumped. "I've never heard of them."

"Oh man," Adrian said, a grin spreading across his face. "Look up 'Christmas Wrapping.' It's catchy as hell. Sometimes I even listen to it in July."

I smiled. "Okay, I will."

"It's almost curfew," he said, standing up. "We should probably get back to our rooms." I nodded and stood up too.

"Yeah," I said. "See you around."

"Good night, Esme Pearl," he said. "See you around." And with that, he turned and walked away.

I felt like I was buzzing the whole way back up to my room. Half my brain was a halftime-worthy happy dance; the other half was going, "Huh, weird." I flashed back to the hollow-heart nervous feeling I'd had the first time I saw Adrian, at the library. It felt like more than just lust at first sight. It had felt, if I was being totally honest with myself, a little like a warning. A warning of what, who knew? That a shiny black crow would break into Janis's car? That Cassandra would start slipping away? That the Sitters were coming? That the Sitters were coming and that Brian planned to force me to host a party while wearing a reindeer beanie? It could be any of these things. Or all of them.

I slipped into my room just a few minutes before curfew. The room was still in a haze. The TV was on, all the lights were on, the bathroom floor was covered in puddles, and there was a wet towel on my pillow. But Ji-A had gone back to her room, and Amirah was out, a satin eye mask on as she snored away.

I got ready for bed, turned all the lights and the TV off, and then climbed in bed, adjusting the pillows so that I wasn't sleeping on the damp one. For my first night at the Summit, it could have gone worse. And as for tomorrow, I had no idea what to expect, but I knew it wasn't going to be boring.

CHAPTER 13

For once, I didn't sleep late, but still, by the time I woke up, Amirah was already gone. I was kind of impressed she'd managed to get ready without making any noise, especially since, judging by the detritus spread across the room, and the makeup-dusted sink, and the still-on straightening iron in the bathroom, she wasn't exactly low-maintenance.

I managed to find my own weekend bag amid all of Amirah's stuff. It was the first time I'd looked in it since I'd packed, and I was not impressed. I was good at getting dressed, but horrible at packing, even with infinite time, and yesterday morning, with only five minutes to gather stuff for forty-eight hours' worth of outfits, had left my options limited, to say the least.

I had one skirt, but it was one I'd found thrifting and had never gotten around to shortening, so it remained a scratchy plaid wool that hit right below my knees. I had an oversized bomber jacket, a pair of chartreuse jeans with zippers at the ankles, three T-shirts—all black, one that said "Eat More Figs" on the back in white lettering—a pair of silver tights with a hole in the toe, a blue slip dress (which was really just a slip), my leggings, a striped short-sleeved sweater (not practical), my sweatshirt, a denim button-up, my Docs, a beret (really, what was I thinking?), a bleach-dyed denim shirt, jean shorts, a pair of leopard-print ballet slippers, and green rubber snake earrings that Janis had given me last Valentine's Day. I was the polar opposite of those fashion articles that are always encouraging you to invest in the basics.

I still didn't know what today was going to entail, so I decided to keep things pretty comfortable. The last thing I wanted to do was end up having to climb a rope in a slip dress. I put on the fig T-shirt, my black jeans from yesterday, my Docs, the denim overshirt, and the snake earrings. At the last second, I said frick it and added the beret. When Cass knocked on my door to go down to breakfast, I answered it as a snake-charming, fig-eating beatnik. She was, of course, wearing the same clothes she'd worn yesterday, though she did look well rested.

"How are you?" I asked, as I closed the door. "Anything—"

Cassandra shook her head before I could finish my question. "I've been fine," she said. "But have you seen her? The bathroom woman from last night?"

I shook my head, and Cassandra looked up and down the hall.

"I keep thinking about what she said, that she had something for me. I know she said Sunday, but if we could find her today, maybe . . ."

I was silent for a minute, then just said, "Maybe we can."
I recognized something in Cassandra right now: hope. Hope
and I were well acquainted, and I knew how dangerous it
could be.

"Where's Ruby?" I asked, trying to change the subject as
we headed down the hall. Cass shrugged. "Did you ask her
more about what she had learned from her grandma?"

"No," Cassandra said, offering no further information.
She pressed the down button for the elevator, then pressed it
again and again and again.

"Did you talk to her at all?" I asked, frustrated by her lack
of communication. I was *trying* to help. And so was Ruby.

The elevator doors opened and Cass answered, "Not
really," then walked on.

I rolled my eyes behind her back. "You should talk to
Ruby. She seems really nice, and it seems like you two would
get along. You know, she's a boxer." Cass responded with a
grunt.

"I just hope we can trust her," she said, jamming the Close
Door button over and over. "That little redheaded girl too."

"Mallory," I said. "And I don't think that either she or
Ruby are going to tell anyone." Something in my gut told me
they wouldn't go blabbing unless, as Mallory had said yesterday, Cass started to put other people at risk.

"They'd better not," Cassandra said, "because I don't
care if I am cursed, if they blow up my spot, there's gonna
be hell to pay."

"No one's going to blow you up, Cassandra," I said. "This
isn't us against them. We're all an us. That's why we're here.

This isn't a reality show. We are here to make friends." At the mention of friends, I thought of Janis, my best friend, who I'd lied to and then ignored, and it made me feel like crap. Janis was the person who made my non-Sitter life bearable, and I wasn't doing a very good job of paying her back for that. If I could get ahold of her, I could at least offer her some excuse and also check in to make sure she was okay. "Hey, can I borrow your phone for a second? Do you have Janis's number?" I asked Cassandra.

"Sure," she said, and whipped her phone out of her back pocket. "I think it's in there somewhere." As soon as she passed the phone to me, I was sorry I asked. The screen was shattered, and the battery was at 2 percent. I opened her contacts to find it entirely empty. She had not saved a single number. "Do you mind if I look at your texts?" Cassandra shook her head, so I opened her texts. I recognized my own number, which she hadn't saved, and there were two others. I gleaned that one was Brian's, and the other—from the string of straightforward directives she'd issued, like "get pizza"— was Dion's.

So, no go on that, but maybe I could at least look up the song Adrian had mentioned. Cass did have a streaming service, but she had apparently never logged in, because it asked for a password as soon as I opened it. The Waitresses would have to wait. I passed Cassandra's phone back to her. "Thanks," I said.

The elevator stopped and the doors slid open. "You get what you needed?" Cassandra asked, pocketing her phone as she led the way down the hall.

"Yep, sure did," I said, stifling a sigh. I'd have to figure out the Janis situation later, and it wasn't Cassandra's fault. Right now, I needed coffee, because there was no way this day was not going to require caffeine, and a lot of it.

We walked into the dining room for breakfast, and Cassandra headed directly to the buffet and started filling her plate. I followed suit, then hit the coffee station. I made my own iced coffee, which was really just coffee-flavored room-temp water, and then sat down with the rest of the Runaway Bunnies. I wondered whether Cassandra would relax at all, because neither Mallory nor Ruby dropped any hint about what had happened yesterday after dinner, but she just grunted into her plate like a goblin and made no attempt at conversation. Ruby seemed to have given up on befriending Cassandra and barely even looked her way. I guess I didn't blame her. Cass would never be an easy roommate, and I would have imagined that now, when she was feeling extra vulnerable and even more on guard, she would be especially hard to handle.

Amirah was still wailing about her ex-girlfriend, Mallory was gorging on oatmeal and orange juice, and Ji-A was doing a crossword. She also appeared to be listening to Amirah with one ear, because every once in a while she'd nod and say something like, "She clearly needs help, but you knew that when you started dating her."

On the other side of the room, Brian and Clarissa sat with some of the other Counsel and a few members of the Synod. I saw Wanda, still looking at her phone, come into the dining room, grab a piece of bacon from the buffet, and then go right back out. I thought I was being sneaky about trying to find Adrian, but apparently I wasn't.

"Who are you looking for?" Mallory asked. The question caught me off guard, and I choked on my coffee.

"I bet it's Adrian," Ji-A said, still not looking up from her puzzle. "I saw you two chatting last night."

"You did?" I asked, surprised. I didn't think anyone had seen us, but then, when I was talking to Adrian, I was focused on Adrian. And his eyes, and his hands, and his taste in music, and . . .

Ji-A finally looked up. "Yep," she said. "But you two seemed pretty into each other, so I didn't want to interrupt."

"You know him?" I asked, and she nodded. I noticed that Ruby and Mallory were nodding too.

"He's been around forever," Mallory said. "Wanda used to bring him to Sitter family weekends."

Jeez! I almost kicked Cassandra under the table. Sitter family weekends? What the eff else had Cassandra and I been missing out on our whole lives?

"He used to be the cutest little nerd boy," Ruby said.

"And now he's a hot nerd boy," Ji-A said, giving me a wink. I tried not to blush.

"He hasn't been around that much since he got his powers," Mallory said. "I guess he was kind of embarrassed by the controversy."

"Powers?" I said. "And what controversy?" The questions tumbled out of my mouth faster than I would have liked, but . . .

"Oh yeah," Ruby said, peeling off a piece of grapefruit.

"Wanda issued a special dispensation to grant Adrian powers, and a lot of the Sitterhood wasn't happy about it."

"What kind of powers? Why weren't they happy?" I asked. Adrian had mentioned his powers last night, but he hadn't gone into detail.

Ruby looked at Mallory to confirm. "This was a couple of years ago, right? Like when we were like thirteen or something?" Mallory nodded, and Ruby continued. "So, you know how Sitters have spells and kinesis. The spells are what we acquire, and the kinesis is what we're born with, right?" I nodded, because I did know this much. "And Counsels can use spells, of course, but they don't have a kinetic power, because that only belongs to Sitters. Except that Wanda gave Adrian a kinesis, and a lot of people weren't happy about it. My grandma was one of them. She said it was a perversion of magic, and she didn't like it at all. But Wanda really pushed it through."

"What can Adrian do?" I asked. "I mean, what's his kinesis?" Now I was kicking myself that I hadn't asked him more last night. Mallory and Ruby looked at each other, and both kind of screwed up their faces.

"Something to do with air, I think?" Mallory said, and Ruby nodded. "That, or he might be able to fly? You'll have to ask him."

I kind of felt like I'd been struck dumb. What could I say to two people who had been raised in a world that was so fantastic that a boy who could maybe fly barely even caused their radar to blip? I had a million other questions, about Adrian and about what went on at Sitter family weekends (like, what did they do? White-water rafting and three-legged races?), but I wasn't going to lob them out there now, and anyway, Ji-A had finished her puzzle, pushed back her chair, and announced it was time for us to get to class.

Our demonology session was being held in the hotel gym, which, for Summit purposes, had been renamed the Fran Fine Fitness Center. When we walked in, Janine Guillot was wearing one of her tweed suits and sitting on a weight bench, her legs crossed as she drummed her red fingernails on the vinyl seat. On the floor next to her was a giant crate with a heavy padlock. When she saw us, she smiled, then raised her palm at the door and muttered something.

"Hello, girls," she said, in an accent I couldn't quite place—she could have been French, or from Louisiana. "I'm so happy that you are all here. Please find a seat." I wasn't the only one looking around wondering where to park their butt. Amirah took another weight bench, Mallory perched on something that looked gynecological, Cassandra sat on what appeared to be a torture rack, and Ruby, Ji-A, and I leaned up against the StairMasters. We were sharing the session with the Very Hungry Caterpillars, who sat in a row on the floor, and their easy small talk with everyone in our group but me and Cassandra further confirmed my fears that the rest of the Sitters were basically besties from way back.

"I'm not going to waste time talking," Janine continued, "as we are here to study demons. Demons are as unique as humans, and each has their own strengths and weaknesses.

The sooner you are able to identify each strain, the sooner you will be able to capture them and ensure your own safety and the safety of those around you." I was listening to Janine, but my eyes were on the box at her feet. I'd seen one of those before, when Brian was first teaching Cassandra and me about demons. This one was bigger, and as I stared, it moved a couple of inches on its own.

"Now," Janine continued, "your goal here is to identify a demon before it can do too much damage. The collection we are working with today has been carefully curated, so I expect there will be quite a few that you do not know." Here, she smiled. "This will make it much more exciting." She nudged the box with one foot, and it let out a howl. Then she took a key from her pocket, bent down, and inserted it in the lock. "Oh," she said, "I almost forgot. Spells and kinesis won't work in this room, and the door is locked. Now, have fun!" With that, she hit the lights and popped the lock off the box. Two seconds later, there was a demon in the room.

He was green. He had a snaggletooth, and feet that looked like they were made from taffy. He oozed out of the box and plopped onto the floor. His eyes stared in two different directions because they were on two different sides of his head. He burped, which was met with universal groans.

"Seriously?" said a Caterpillar with a short blond bob. "We're not in kindergarten. That's Kevin." Everyone except Janine laughed, but I found Kevin's presence strangely comforting. He was the first demon Cassandra and I had ever met, and the one we had trained with, and if everyone else knew him too, then maybe we weren't that far behind. But no sooner had I thought about how easy it was going to be to capture Kevin than he disappeared. A pop, a sizzle, and then he was gone.

The next demon was about the size and shape of a dachshund, but black with amorphous edges that blurred into the air. And it could fly, or float. It rose up out of the box, and hovered, then took off like a fighter jet, straight for Ruby. It collided hard with her shoulder, knocking her back against a mirror and sending a row of dumbbells clanging to the floor. "Think on your feet, Miss Ramirez!" Janine shouted as Ruby struggled to stand. "If you don't know what's going to happen next, you'd better react to what is happening now."

The demon, whatever it was, was back up in the air, ricocheting around the room and sending everyone diving out of its way. It came for me, and I barely had time to flatten myself on the floor behind a treadmill. "I've seen it before!" Mallory shouted. "I just can't remember what it's called." The demon almost took itself out when it collided with an elliptical machine, but it quickly recovered and was going after Amirah when Cassandra picked up a ten-pound weight and hurled it at the demon like she was tossing a tennis ball. It took the demon out with a thud, and dented the wall in the process, but it also gave Amirah time to compose herself. "It's an Asperitas!" she shouted, and the demon vanished.

Save for some light streaming through the window on the door, the room was dark, and I could see Janine lounging in the corner, her arms crossed over her chest. She looked totally relaxed, but everyone else was getting amped up now that we knew what to expect. The next demon didn't crawl or float out of the box, it unfolded, like a sheet of paper unfurling in the wind. It looked like a creased bedsheet, and it headed straight for Amirah, and quickly. "Oh God," she said, turning and running straight into the wall, apparently forgetting that her kinesis wouldn't work and she was stuck in here, just like the rest of us. "Amirah," a brunette Caterpillar screamed, "duck!" Then she swung a barbell at the demon, and it crumpled as it wrapped around the bar.

"Wait, wait!" Mallory shouted, and in the dim light I could see she was pinching the bridge of her nose in concentration, like the name she was looking for was just on the tip of her tongue. "It's a Syncline!" she finally yelled, and the demon dissipated, leaving the brunette holding a bare barbell.

The next one to arrive was a glowing, globby orb, with limbs growing out of its sides. I watched it carefully and jumped when its limbs retracted, with a slurp, into its sides. It moved slowly and deliberately through the air, and as it moved closer to me I could feel it emanating a fierce static electricity several feet in every direction. As the demon moved through the gym, Sitters stepped away to avoid its force. By now, I was starting to feel the hallmarks of the Negative demons. With each new one, I cared less and less, and I steeled myself to fight that feeling. But then the demon did something interesting. It stopped, hovering in front of Cassandra, not like it was about to attack her, but like it was looking at her. And she was looking right back. "Hey," she said. "I know you."

"Then say its name and get it out of here," Blond Bob snapped.

Cassandra shook her head, still looking like she and the demon were locked in a staring contest. "No, I don't know what kind of demon it is," she said, "I know this particular one. We met before. On Halloween." I swear to goddess, the demon gave a little nod. "Do you know what—" she started, and then just like that, the lights were back on and the demon was gone. Janine was striding back toward the box, and then she clamped the lock onto it.

"Well, that's enough for that part of the lesson," she announced. "You did okay, some better than others. Now we'll work on memorization."

We were all blinking in the sudden light, somewhat stunned. "We were just getting started," Ji-A said.

"You've caused enough damage to the gym," Janine said.

"You can fix everything in two seconds," Amirah countered. "And you know that, or you wouldn't have had us fighting demons surrounded by exercise equipment in the first place."

"Take a seat," Janine said, ignoring her. I didn't see where she had gotten them from, but she was holding a stack of thick plastic binders, which she began to pass around. "These are your demonology dictionaries," she said. "Memorize as much as you can. You will be quizzed at the end of the session."

I could hear grumbling, especially from Amirah and two of the Caterpillars, but everyone spread out around the room and started to do as Janine had told them. I tried hard to catch Cassandra's eye, but it felt like she was avoiding me. I sat down between the dumbbell rack and the wall and Mallory sat a few feet from me. Across the room, Ji-A raised her hand, then just started talking. "There are literally thousands of demons in here," she said. "How are we supposed to memorize this in the next two hours?"

"I'm not here to tell you how to do your job," Janine said.

"Actually, I'm pretty sure that's exactly why you're here," Ji-A countered.

"If you have a problem, you can always leave and I will let Wanda know how you felt about the session," Janine said.

Ji-A mumbled something that sounded like "can't wait for the teacher evaluations," but opened her binder and started reading. I did the same, then felt a nudge on my foot. I looked up and met Mallory's eyes. She raised her eyebrows and jerked her head at Cassandra, who was sitting with her binder unopened in her lap, staring straight ahead like her brain was off orbiting the moons of Pluto.

"Do you think she's okay?" Mallory mouthed. I wasn't sure, but after watching Cassandra for a few more seconds, I turned back to Mallory and nodded. Cassandra wasn't having an episode right now. She was just being herself.

We sat in silence, no bathroom or water breaks, until the session was almost over and Janine presented us with a pop quiz—ten demon identification questions. Sure enough, it was an impossible quiz, and Mallory, who got six right, was the only one who passed. I got two, and Cassandra got zero, because she didn't even try. When Janine dismissed us, we flowed into the hallway. "That was a colossal waste of time," Ji-A said. "Why have us come all the way here just to study worksheets?" The Caterpillars stuck close together, and I could swear I saw a couple of them shoot dirty looks our way.

"This is the most budget Summit I have ever heard of," Amirah said. "When my mom went to a Summit, they chased demons through the pyramids! And all we get is frickin' Kevin." She spun so that she was facing Cassandra. "What was that all about anyway? You acted like that demon was someone you were trying to hit on at a club. 'Excuse me, don't I know you?'"

Everyone was looking at Cassandra, myself included, waiting for her to answer and enlighten us, but before she could, or would, say anything, someone called my name from the end of the hallway. We all turned to see Brian striding toward us, his arms wrapped around a miniature Christmas tree.

"The rest of you should head to lunch," he said, when he got closer. "Esme and Cassandra, please come with me. We've got some work to do." He shifted the Christmas tree to his other arm and kept walking down the hall. When he reached the other end, he realized we weren't following. He stopped and turned. "Now," he said.

"I need to go look for someone," Cassandra said.

"Who?" Brian asked. Cassandra glanced at me for a split second, and I knew she was talking about Cybill.

"Can't tell you," she said, and he laughed.

"Yeah, that's not going to happen," he said.

"What about our lunch?" I asked.

"I picked up some salads," he said. "Come on." Reluctantly, we followed him, while the rest of the group headed toward the cafeteria. I looked back once to see that Ruby was still watching us. Cassandra reached over and squeezed my arm, and when I looked at her, her face was a warning, cautioning me not to say anything. Brian turned left into a large room labeled with a sign that said THE STEVE HARRINGTON BALLROOM. All of our now-transformed party decorations were inside, and a table was filled with bags, tissue paper, piles of candles, silver ornaments with "#springriversummit" spelled out in red glitter, and bags of individually wrapped cookies.

"Ooh, cookies!" Cassandra said, grabbing a bag, but Brian smacked it out of her hand before she could open it.

"Those are for the gift bags," he said, "and that's why you're here. I've been trying not to bother you all weekend so that you can do what you're supposed to do here, which is focus and immerse yourselves in your community. But you need to be involved in this party somewhat." He held up a tote. "Which brings me to these bags. We need to stuff them. And I thought it would be nice if the two of you wrote each Summit attendee a personal note to thank them for coming."

"But we didn't invite them," I said. "The Synod did."

Brian fixed me with a look. "I think it would be a nice touch," he said.

"Fine," Cassandra said. "There's probably a spell we can use to get them all done at once."

Brian gasped. "That negates the whole point of it being personal," he said. "And besides, spells aren't allowed."

"Didn't you use spells to conjure all of this stuff?" Cassandra said, gesturing at the pile of ornaments.

"That's different," he said, but didn't explain why. True to his word, there were three salads stacked on the table. Brian cracked the plastic lid off one of them, a smile on his face. "Boy, I just love a good Cobb." I had to bite my tongue to keep from laughing. Sometimes I envied Brian—there must be times when it's very cozy being that basic. "Esme, I also have some news about your mother. We can speak privately if you'd prefer." I looked at Cassandra, who'd taken the lid off her salad and was picking out the bits of bacon.

"No, it's fine," I said. "I'd tell Cassandra anyway."

"Well," Brian continued, dabbing at the corner of his mouth, "I wasn't able to get ahold of your father, unfortunately. His phone must be dead—it goes straight to voice mail when I call." I nodded. Or it could just be that, like with everything else, Dad hadn't paid the bill. "But I was able to speak with someone at your mother's facility, and her outstanding balance has been taken care of."

Everything since the Summit started had been such a blur that I hadn't had much time to think about Mom, but as soon as he said that, my eyes filled with tears. "Oh my God," I said. "Brian, thank you so much. Did you use a spell to erase it from their books?" Brian shook his head and finished chewing a bite of hard-boiled egg before he spoke.

"Of course not," he said. "You know full well that Sitter magic, in any form, is not to be used for material gain." I nodded. Of course I knew that.

"What'd you do, then?" I asked.

"I put it on my credit card."

"A Sitter card?" I asked, and Brian shook his head.

"No, my personal one."

"B-B-Brian," I stuttered, "it was several thousand dollars."

"I have good credit," he said. "And a high limit." My chin trembled, and Brian looked away. He didn't need to explain further, because I just knew: This wasn't something he'd done as my Counsel; this was something he'd done as a friend. As Dad's friend. Maybe their friendship wasn't totally fake after all.

"I'm sure your father will pay me back once everything is sorted," he said, looking down at his salad and trying to gather blue cheese on his fork.

"He will, I'm sure," I said, even though I was less than sure. "Thank you." Those were two paltry words to express how I was feeling right now, but they would have to do. I would have gone over and given Brian a hug, but he didn't seem the hugging type, so I decided to show my gratitude by doing what he had asked me to do: I picked up a pen and started to write some thank-you notes.

CHAPTER 14

Brian kept us busy through lunch, and by the time we were finished, my fingers were cramping from writing "We hope you enjoyed your time in Spring River," over and over again. Our afternoon session was with Dierdre in the Mary Anne Spier Library, and I was excited to get a look at the books that Cassandra and I had spent hours unloading the day before. As we walked down the hall, I grabbed her sleeve and held her back a little.

"Hey," I said, "in demonology, what did you mean, you knew that demon?"

Cassandra looked up and down the hall, then stepped to the side so that we were standing close to the wall. "Just that," she said. "Like, we'd met before. He looked familiar."

"We've never Returned anything like that," I said. "I'd remember if we had."

"I know," she said, nodding. "Which means there's only one place where I could have met him."

I nodded. "The Negative," we both said at the same time.

"That's good, right?" I asked. "Because it means you're remembering something?"

Cassandra's normally calm face wrinkled up like a sharpei's. "Maybe," she said. "But it's just a ghost of a memory. If I could talk to the demon, I could ask him about that night, what I don't remember. It's my best option. I can't ask MacKenzie, and if I can find out what I don't remember, then maybe I can find out why I'm not supposed to remember, and then find out why I'm . . ."

Her voice trailed off. "Cursed?" I said, and she nodded, biting her lower lip. "We'll look for Cybill at dinner. If she's working the continental breakfast tomorrow, maybe she'll also be in the cafeteria tonight." Cass nodded. Just then, Deirdre came walking down the hall, a smile on her face.

"Come now, girls, you're with me this afternoon," she said. "And you don't want to be late."

When it came to clothes, Deirdre and Wanda went for the same silhouettes, but with a totally different vibe. While Wanda favored shades of oatmeal, Deirdre was all about the power clash: hot, feverish wax prints that burst with tropical hues, orange and blue on her skirt, pink and yellow on her top, and red and green on the scarf tied around her nearly waist-length dreads. She smelled like palo santo, and unlike Wanda, who seemed distracted, and Janine, who was as icy as a frozen shrimp, Deirdre actually seemed like she wanted to be here.

And unlike demonology in the Fran Fine Fitness Center, which had remained basically just a hotel gym, the Mary Anne Spier Library had been transformed. There were flickering candles, the tables were draped with brocade fabric woven with thick gold thread, and a pyre of frankincense burned in a goblet. All the books had been removed from their boxes, and some sat in short stacks, while others stood individually. Their pages rustled softly, even though there was no wind, and with all the books' energy, the room felt very crowded.

That was one half of the room. The other half looked like the discount aisle at a dollar store, with spice rack dregs and a recycling bin thrown in for good measure. From where I was sitting, I could see yellow caution tape, a Mr. Potato Head, rolls of recycled toilet paper, giant tins of Folgers coffee, tinsel, candy canes, a California Raisins nativity scene, a dog collar, and on, and on, and on. . . .

At the front of the room, Deirdre sat down at a table and held her hand over a thick volume with black-stained edges and a cover of iridescent scales. She smiled at it, and as she did, the book gave an audible sigh. "They love Reiki," she said, and looked at the book like it was a goldendoodle puppy. "So, as you all know by now, our books are perhaps the Sitterhood's most precious commodity. Like us, they are ever-evolving beings and it is us who are here to serve them, not the other way around. I am assuming that most of you, in your training, have been able to spend some time with your Counsel's books and familiarize yourselves with more than a few spells." She paused and looked around the room at everyone's nodding heads. "Does anyone have a favorite spell they'd like to share?"

This session was just the Runaway Bunnies, and everyone but Cassandra and me raised their hands. Deirdre called on Mallory. "I use spells in most of my Returns," she said, "as my kinesis isn't that great at, you know, getting rid of demons. And I've found architectonikinesis to be really helpful in that regard."

"Ah yes," Deirdre said, smiling. "The ability to manipulate architecture. Three Legos, some double-sided tape, a brown palm oil candle, and one graham cracker, if I'm correct?"

"Exactly," Mallory said. "So if I'm trying to do a Return indoors, I'll use architectonikinesis to manipulate the walls until I get the demon right under the Portal."

"Fantastic," Deirdre said. "Such ingenuity. Anyone else?" She nodded at Amirah.

"So, this one time, we were at Mr. Chow in Beverly Hills and my mom started to panic because she realized she'd lost her wedding ring," Amirah said. "And we had the entire staff looking for it, and my mom was freaking out. Because that ring is, like, serious wattage, and no one could find it, but I used diamantikinesis and realized it was actually at home, by the bathroom sink." As soon as Amirah was finished with her story, she sat back triumphantly and crossed her arms over her chest. In her eyes, this was another time when she had saved the day. Also, did that really mean her favorite spell was a spell for finding diamonds?

"Okay, wonderful," Deirdre said, in a way that I couldn't

tell whether she was serious or not. "Now, the goal of this session is to have each of you create a spell that will be accepted by the books." I sat up a little straighter. Now this, this was interesting. Tentatively, I raised my hand, not sure whether I was about to ask a question that everyone else already knew the answer to. Deirdre nodded at me.

"So all the spells in this book have been written by other Sitters?" I asked.

"Yes," Deirdre said. "Our grimoire is truly a communal effort. Some of our spells have their origins centuries ago, and that's why the books must be able to update themselves, as a Sitter who created a spell in the seventeenth century would have no way of knowing what sort of ingredients would be available to her lineage hundreds of years later." I nodded. That made sense, and my mind immediately jumped to Mom: Were any of these spells ones she had written?

"How do you know who wrote what spell?" I asked.

"We don't," Deirdre said. "There have been some Sitters who were notably prolific, but on the whole, we try to keep things anonymous. As always, our magic is about altruism, selflessness, and protecting the innocent, not gaining personal recognition." Beside me, Cassandra shifted in her seat and I couldn't help but wonder whether that was in response to what Deidre had just said. Cassandra liked power, and while she certainly didn't need the confidence boost that came from people telling her she was great, I was sure she wouldn't have minded it one bit.

"Now," Deirdre continued, "do any of you know the criteria for getting a spell in the books? There are three."

Ji-A raised her hand. "It has to be as near universal as possible."

"Correct," Deirdre said. "Can you explain what that means?"

"Sure," Ji-A said. "It means that a spell has to solve a common problem, not a problem that just you face or that will occur just one time."

"Very well put," Deirdre said. "Now, the second?"

"The ingredients have to be specific, yet widely available," Ruby said, and when Deirdre nodded, she continued. "Like, if you are designing a spell that uses mushrooms, you have to specify what mushroom, since there are so many kinds. But at the same time, you don't want it to be super rare. So it's best to pick something right in the middle, like shiitake or cremini."

"Very good," Deirdre said. "Now, the third rule of spells?"

Mallory spoke up. "Like with everything we do," she said, "it has to be altruistic. You can't create a spell just so you can use it for personal gain."

I was sitting rapt in my chair. "Did you know this?" I whispered to Cassandra, and she responded with a quick shake of her head. I hadn't either. Brian had never told us that Sitters wrote the spells or that new ones were constantly being added, and we'd never asked. It had never crossed my mind to ask where the spells came from. I just assumed they came from the books, and that wasn't a lazy assumption. The books revised themselves, after all, so why wouldn't they write themselves too?

I had missed what Deirdre was saying, but everyone else was scribbling on pieces of paper, so I grabbed a pen and slid a pad of paper closer to me, but then I just sat there with the pen poised in my hand, not writing a dang thing. I had a million ideas—a spell to drive a car; a spell to make food appear in an empty refrigerator (both so handy for babysitting); a spell to keep socks from separating; a spell to walk into a store and immediately find the perfect shade of lipstick. . . . So many spells, but only one I really cared about.

The room was silent except for the sound of pens scratching on paper, and the sound of Cassandra's left knee, which was bouncing and made a soft thud every time it hit the table leg. "Remember," Deirdre said, "wording is everything. That is why we so often use the word 'manipulate,' because it can be interpreted so many ways. If you are too specific, your spell might not have enough impact. Not specific enough, and it could be hard to control."

Ruby was the first to put down her pen and get up, then walk to the back of the room. Amirah followed, then Mallory. Suddenly, Cassandra jumped up to go join them, no doubt worried someone else might take all the good stuff.

I still sat there, going over it in my mind. Like Deirdre said, it had to be just right. A spell could not remove a curse—if it were that easy, then that spell would have been in the books a long time ago. But what if I wasn't trying to remove the curse, or even lessen it? What if I just wanted to pierce it? My spell wouldn't make a curse go away, it would just cleave the cloud for a while. If I had a spell like that, I could talk to Mom, and we could build a relationship. Then, when her curse was finally removed, we wouldn't be starting from scratch—we would have known each other all along.

I was sure this spell was universal. Talking to Ruby had been enough to convince me that Mom and Cassandra weren't alone. There were plenty of cursed Sitters out there, and wherever there was a cursed Sitter, I was sure there were people who loved her and wanted to talk to her. A spell like this could help people. Not just Mom—or, goddess forbid, Cassandra—but a lot of people.

I finally scrawled some words on my paper, then stood up and walked to the back of the room. Ji-A was standing back there and methodically picking up items and then setting them down. It looked like she was going through them one by one.

She looked up and smiled at me. "I want to make sure they feel right," she said, before setting down a pink flamingo swizzle stick.

The thing with Sitter spells was that the ingredients seemed random at first glance, but they were actually very carefully chosen, and everything related back to the ultimate goal. My goal was communication. It was to clear a path so that the essence of the person could emerge through the curse. I didn't want the books to reject this spell, and I wanted it to work, so I had to make sure the ingredients were just right. I spied a blue pillar candle and picked it up. Blue was the color of truth and communication, and in a way, this spell would be lighting a path for the cursed person to follow. Then there was a broom—it was petite and handmade, for cleaning up only the cutest messes. I'd take that too, to sweep away the curse.

I saw something that made me smile: wind-up plastic teeth, with googly eyes on top and flat pink feet on the bottom. Most spells had four ingredients, so now I just needed one more. I made my way down the table, looking at everything. Silver wolf's head charms, tiny pots of eye cream, golden paper crowns, fabric flowers, dried stems of eucalyptus, a pink and purple beer koozie that said "Same Penis Forever," a few different types of dog treats, a cat toy, a yellow bandanna, tubs of neon-hued slime, barrettes, bubbles, anything and everything imaginable. Then I saw it: a package of smoke bombs, the different-colored orbs Dad and I used to light off on the Fourth of July. I picked them up and headed back to my table.

Now that I had my ingredients, I had to think of a name and a description. I'd start with the description first. The power for a cursed person to speak clearly? Eh, no. That could just mean they weren't supposed to mumble, or even that their words would be invisible. The power for a cursed person to speak the truth? That wasn't quite it either, because it might only work on someone who was cursed to lie. I thought for a minute, gripping the pen over the blank paper. Then I wrote it down: the power to manipulate curses so that a cursed person can experience themselves again.

Mom was smart and funny, but under her curse, none of that could come through now. I could see how frustrated she was, like she was looking at the world through a scummy shower curtain, and I could imagine how freeing it would be for her to have a conversation again, even if it was just for a minute, where she could be herself again.

Now I needed a name: identikinesis. Quickly, I raised my hand, which brought Deirdre over to our table. Cassandra was scrawling all over her paper, and she put her forearm over it, as if she were trying to make sure the teacher didn't copy off her paper. I wasn't sure if Deirdre noticed. "Yes, Esme?" she said.

"When it comes to a name, how do you know if it's already been taken?" I said. "If there's already a spell with that name in the books?"

Deirdre smiled as she flipped half her dreads over one shoulder, a move that sent a hint of palo santo wafting through the air. "You ask them." With that, she gestured toward Mallory, who was bent over at the waist and whispering to a book. Suddenly, she bolted back upright as it flew open, its pages rustling like a flock of pigeons. I heard her mutter, "Crap," and then she sat back down.

"All of them?" I asked, and Deirdre shook her head.

"They're very cooperative," she said. "So one will speak for all."

I nodded at Deirdre, then stood up and walked over to where Mallory had just been. I was glad I could whisper and not have to announce it in front of everyone else. I bent and whispered, "Identikinesis," but the book didn't emit so much as a purr. I straightened up and turned around. Deirdre was looking at me, and she gave a little smile and nod. "Looks like you picked well," she said.

I sat down feeling more hopeful than I had in weeks.

• • •

My anticipation grew as we waited for everyone to finish their spells, and soon my knee was bouncing as much as Cassandra's, turning our table into the epicenter of the room's nervous energy.

Which definitely didn't help the wariness aimed at Cassandra, from Mallory and Ruby especially. Ruby kept glancing over at Cassandra in a way that made me anxious wondering whether there was something Cass was about to do that Ruby knew and I didn't. But even Amirah and Ji-A seemed a little distant after the incident with the demon this morning. Or maybe I was just imagining it all, and they weren't distant, just absorbed in what they were doing. I hoped that was the case.

Finally, everyone had finished writing and concocting, and it was time. Deirdre gave us a little speech about how we shouldn't get discouraged if the books didn't accept our spells. "They're not saying *no*," she explained. "They're saying *not yet*. If it's something you really want, you can tweak it and try again later." She did not say when later would be.

Mallory went first. She carried her four ingredients to the front of the room, then held them up one by one—soy sauce packets, raisins, a tongue depressor, and a packet of gold leaf—so that we could all see. Then she carefully arranged them in a line, evenly spaced. Mallory picked a book out of the ones lining the room and carried it back to the table. She set it down and then took a step back. "Umamikinesis," she said. "The power to make gross food taste good." The room was silent as we waited, but nothing happened. She said it again, waited a beat, and then turned to Deirdre.

"I'm sorry, Mallory," Deirdre said, "but it looks as though they are not going to accept it. My guess is that it is too subjective, in that everyone has a different idea of what 'gross' and 'good' mean."

Mallory shrugged; she didn't seem too bummed. "That makes sense," she said. "I was thinking it would be useful to do something like turn sushi into oatmeal, but—"

"Why would anyone want to do that?" Amirah interjected. "Sushi is far superior! I've had sushi that cost hundreds of dollars, but what's the most you're gonna pay for a bowl of oatmeal? $19.99?" I watched Deirdre's face, but her smile didn't slip. Instead, she turned back to Mallory.

"Case in point," she said. Mallory nodded, then carried the book back to where she had picked it up, before taking her seat.

"I'll go next," Ruby said, gathering her items and standing up. She had a tube of arnica, a bottle of foundation, a packet of paper plates illustrated with Elsa from *Frozen*, and red cedar shavings. She set out the first three in a triangle, then sprinkled the cedar in the middle. She picked out a book from the library and placed it a few inches away. "Contusikinesis," she said. "The power to manipulate bruises." Everything was silent for a few seconds, then the book burst open, sucking the ingredients toward it like a powerful vacuum cleaner. As the ingredients hit the pages, they disappeared as if sinking into a bubble bath. The book snapped shut, made a sound like someone swallowing soup, and then popped open again. Ruby leaned forward to look at it. "Holy crap," she said. "It's in there! My spell! It's in the books." She was beaming and bounced up and down on her toes. "It's going to help so many Sitters! You won't have to wear makeup or make up stories the day after a tough Return."

"Well done, dear," Deirdre said. "Well done." She started clapping, and the rest of the class joined in a little round of applause. Ruby still had a look of disbelief on her face as she sat down and leaned over to fist-bump Mallory. I couldn't take the waiting anymore, so I shot my hand into the air before anyone else decided to go next.

"Esme, sure, go ahead," Deirdre said, and I pushed my chair out and stood. I carried my ingredients to the front of the room and carefully placed them on the table, just as Ruby and Mallory had. Then I took my time choosing which book I wanted to represent all the books. I finally settled on a rather slim gold volume with pages tipped in a deep jelly bean purple. I carried it to the table and placed it next to my ingredients, then cleared my mind and said my spell. "Identikinesis," I said, making sure to enunciate every syllable. "The power to manipulate curses so that a cursed person can experience themselves again." Then I waited, my heart falling as it looked like the book wasn't going to do anything. That meant they were rejecting my— But then, the book burst open. Every book burst open, not just the one I had chosen, and the room was filled with a piercing, shrieking sound. Instinctively, I clapped my hands over my ears. That barely did anything; the sound was boring into my body, like my innards were being shredded from the inside out.

It was the books. They were screaming.

Panicked, I spun around to look for Deirdre. She was up and moving toward me, already coming for the book. Her hands were clasped over her ears, and everyone else had done the same. Everyone, that is, except Cassandra, who just sat there, staring straight ahead as if she didn't hear a thing. Then, all of a sudden, she jumped up, so fast that she knocked her chair to the floor, and started screaming too, her mouth open like that Munch painting. She grabbed the table in front of her, and in a flash, I realized two things: First, this wasn't Cassandra; this was Cassandra in the middle of an episode. And second, she was about to flip that table like a Real Housewife.

In the space of a split second, I glanced at Deirdre, who, fortunately, had her back to us as she tended to the scream-ing books. I raised my hand at Cassandra. To hell with not using our kinesis outside of our rooms, this was an emer-gency, and I clamped the table to the floor. That seemed to make Cassandra mad. As she kept trying to flip the table with one hand, she made a fist with the other and raised it, ready to punch through the poor table, which hadn't done anything but just try to do its job and give us a place to take notes. Not wanting to let go of the table, I braced myself for the sound of Cassandra's fist pounding the wood, but just like that, Ruby was behind her, wrapping Cass in a bear hug and literally lifting her off her feet and dragging her out of the room. Mallory was right behind them, and in two steps, I was right behind her.

Ruby must have been strong as heck, and her adrenaline

must have been pumping as well, because Cassandra was fighting her every step of the way. As soon as we were out of the library, Ruby threw Cassandra, who tumbled to the carpet right as the cartilage-cutting sound coming from inside the room died down.

As soon as Cass looked up, I could see she was back, even with her hair in her face. "What the . . . ?" she said, looking at me. I didn't have answers, so I turned to Ruby, who was bent over, one hand on her heart.

My head was spinning, and I had the feeling I'd just done something wrong. Really wrong. "The books were screaming. Why would they scream?" I asked. "Why didn't they reject me quietly?"

Ruby gave a long exhale. "I have no idea," she said, "but man, that sound. It was tearing into my bones."

We both looked at Cassandra, who was still sitting on the floor. Mallory knelt beside her. "Are you okay?" she said. "Ruby stopped you right before you were about to put your fist through a table."

Cassandra didn't say anything, just pushed herself up off the floor. "I'm fine," she said, when she was on her feet. She seemed to shake something off, then looked at Ruby. "Thank you," she said. Ruby's breathing had returned to normal, and she stood quietly, looking at Cassandra, then at me. Cassandra thanking her, and in front of other people, was a huge deal. I knew this, but Ruby didn't, and her expression didn't soften.

"This is the last time," she said, addressing me and Cassandra. "You two have dragged me and Mallory into this far enough, and now we're out. You need to tell someone, and soon, or I will. It's against our code to just stand by when it looks like someone could get hurt." She took a step closer to Cass. "You're a ticking time bomb. It's only a matter of time before something really bad happens. And, Esme, you might think you're helping, but you're not doing her any favors by keeping this a secret."

I wondered how Cass would respond, but then the door opened and Deirdre stuck her head out. "It's safe to come back in," she said. "I calmed them down." The four of us streamed back into the room. Amirah and Ji-A were still sitting at their table, albeit looking a little rattled. Amirah leaned over and I heard her whisper something about "running away."

"What happened?" Mallory asked. "That was awful." Deirdre smiled again, but she looked less certain this time.

"A misunderstanding, I'm afraid," she said. "Esme, I'd like to speak to you for a minute after class, but it's nothing the rest of you need to worry about right now."

No one appeared satisfied with this explanation, but the steely tone of Deirdre's voice dispelled any arguments before they even happened, and the mood was less buoyant for the rest of the class. Amirah had submitted a spell that was—get this—to manipulate scarves and—get this—it was accepted. Cassandra's spell was also accepted, which was a big shock to me. It was about the power to manipulate muscles, and I wondered whether it was about Sitting or just about her getting better results at the gym. Ji-A's spell, surprisingly, was not accepted. She had written a spell to manipulate celestial bodies, and Deirdre pointed out that it was too similar to the kinesis she already had, and that there was already a spell to manipulate stars.

"Yeah, but what about comets?" Ji-A asked.

"Well, maybe that's your answer right there, as to why your spell didn't work," Deirdre said. "Be more specific next time."

"Yeah, but when will there be a next time?" Ji-A asked. "We're only here through tomorrow night."

"Spells are added at Summits," Deirdre said. "And through special, Synod-granted permission. If, going forward with your Sitting, you find the books are lacking a spell you really need, you can always petition the Synod for an attempt to add it. Thank you again, girls. You all did a great job today in spite of the unusual occurrence."

Everyone was getting up to leave, but I hung back, remembering what Deidre had said earlier. "I'm sorry," I told her, when the room had cleared. "I don't know what happened. I didn't mean to do anything wrong, I swear."

"Do you?" she asked, and I couldn't quite read the look on her face. I waited for her to say more, but when she didn't, I just nodded. "It was Red Magic, Esme," she said. "Any spell created to work with Red Magic is, in and of itself, Red Magic. A long time ago, when I first started as a librarian, I would review spells before they were taken to the books to prevent just such an incident as what we saw today, but I haven't had to do that in years."

"How could that be Red Magic, though?" I asked. "I wasn't trying to hurt anyone. I was trying to create a spell to help people."

Deirdre's face softened and she leaned forward a little. "Of course you were," she said. "I know it hasn't been that long since you learned the truth about your mother, and I do not blame you if it's hard to accept."

I felt anger bubbling up inside me. Since I'd found out Mom was cursed, I'd heard that word, "accept," so much and it was total BS. Acceptance was what kept power imbalanced, and it was what kept you simmering, never boiling over, when you were faced with something that wasn't right. "So, I'm just supposed to accept the fact that my mother will be cursed until the day she dies?"

"That is not what I am telling you to do, Esme," Deirdre said, a sharp note creeping into her voice. "You don't know that your mother's curse will last forever. Some curses do evaporate on their own, so you must not lose hope."

"Basically, what you're saying is that I can sit around and hope my mom's curse goes away, but that actually doing anything to make it go away, or even to make it a little more tolerable for her, and for me, is Red Magic?"

Deirdre sighed again, and leaned a little bit away from me. "We're on the same side, Esme," she said. "Everyone in the Sitterhood loves and supports your mother."

I stood up. My mouth tasted like vinegar, and it was all I could do to keep myself from spitting at Deirdre, or at least blowing her a very offensive raspberry. Hoping Mom's curse would go away was just the same as letting her rot. "You're right," I finally said. "I won't ever try to help my mother again." My words were dripping with sarcasm, which was apparently lost on Deirdre.

"Now, you don't need to go that far," she said. "Non-magical help is always allowed. Paint her nails, take her flowers, bake her cookies. Please don't ever despair. There are so many things you can do to help your mother." I was about to reply when something caught my eye—a book just over Deirdre's left shoulder, in the corner of the room. It was directly behind where I'd been sitting, and Ruby and Mallory had been between me and it, so I hadn't noticed it during the session. But I could see it now—small and black, with pages edged in bright bloodred, totally standing out from the purple and gold books. I didn't need anyone to tell me what it was. I just knew: it was a book about Red Magic. And Deirdre was sitting there pretending that Sitters didn't touch Red Magic with a thirty-nine-and-a-half-foot pole when, in reality, information was just an arm's length away.

But I couldn't ask about the book now. There was no way she was going to tell me anything, so I nodded and bit my lip. Covering my shock, I pretended to still be mad but also seeing her point. "You're right," I said. "Thank you for the suggestions. They're all good and I will try them." Deirdre smiled, and she put a hand on my shoulder as she walked me out of the room. She might be powerful, and she might be smart, but she was still just another adult easily placated by a lie. I shook my head as I walked away from her. As if I'd never thought to paint Mom's nails before. How dumb did she think I was?

• • •

Cassandra was waiting for me down the hall, leaning against a wall, behind a door. I jumped a mile when she said my name. I took a deep breath, then ran my hands through my hair, trying to shake it off. "Do you remember what happened in there?" I said.

"Mostly," she said. "But you can fill me in on the details."

So I did. I told her everything, and then told her what Deirdre had just said. I kept my language focused on my mom. I didn't want to think, and I'm sure Cassandra didn't either, that someday she might need the same kind of spell I'd just tried to get in the books. She didn't say anything and her face was impassive.

"Come on," she said finally, with a wan smile. "Let's go get dinner. I'm sure it won't be awkward at all."

CHAPTER 15

Dinner was awkward, and there was no sign of Cybill. At first, I was relieved that no one asked why Deidre had asked me to stay after class. Then it became apparent that everyone was avoiding the topic, and I started to get paranoid that they had all talked about it, sans me and Cassandra, and agreed not to ask. Amirah, as always, dominated the conversation by talking about people and topics no one but Ji-A knew or understood, and I could swear that Ruby and Mallory were inching away from Cassandra and me. Again, maybe that was mostly in my head, but it sure as heck seemed like Cassandra and I were on one side of the table and everyone else was on the other. And it was a round table.

We'd finished eating, and everyone but Ruby was eating brownies (Ruby had opted for a mango) when I excused myself. I was on the way to the bathroom when I heard someone call my name. Specifically, I heard Adrian call my name. I started toward him, then stopped when I realized he was practically jogging my way. Something about the look on his face—amused, with a sprinkle of concern—set the back of my neck on fire.

"Is everything okay?" I asked as soon as he was close enough that I didn't have to shout.

"Yeah, but there's a girl outside asking for you." He paused. "Actually, more than asking. I would say demanding. The girl you were with at the library. That's how I ended up talking to her. I was heading back inside, and she started yelling at me. She called me 'library boy.'"

"Oh my God, Janis," I said, realizing she'd heard zilch from me in more than twenty-four hours, a first in our years of friendship. Why was she here? *How* was she here? "Where is she?" I asked. Adrian looked down, and I saw a smile flicker across his lips. I followed his eyes to see that I had grabbed his arm and was gripping it like it was the only thing keeping me from falling off a building. I quickly let go.

"I told her to wait for you out back, by the dumpsters," he said. "I didn't want anyone to see her hanging around out front."

"What?" I said. "Why?" That was a direction Janis would not exactly love.

Adrian took a step toward me in a way that made my heart flutter, but his expression was serious. "I don't think you're supposed to have visitors," he said. "So I'd tell her to leave before anyone besides me sees her."

I nodded and managed to mumble "thanks" before I turned and walked down the hall as fast as I could. Finding the back door to the hotel wasn't easy. The first two doors

I tried were locked and the third led to a weird computer room. The fourth pushed open into the night. Following the whiff of rancid lettuce, I found the dumpsters, with Janis's car parked between them.

I started toward her car, when a sharp whine from the backseat sent me running. Janis wasn't alone: she had Pig! By the time I reached the car, the rear window was frosted with a thick layer of slobber, and Pig's tail beat like a windshield wiper in a downpour. I yanked the door open, and Pig tumbled out, a squiggling sack of love. I bent down, and she covered my face with dog-smelling kisses. I stood up and turned to Janis, who was still sitting in the driver's seat, window rolled all the way up, looking significantly less thrilled to see me.

"What are you doing here?" I asked. "How'd you find me?"

She cracked the window an inch. "What am *I* doing here? What are *you* doing here? You don't have your phone, and you're staying at a hotel in town when you're supposed to be in Saint Louis visiting an aunt who I'm pretty sure you made up!" I could see she was seriously pissed off but also worried. Her eyes were wide, and she was chewing on one of her braids, an end-of-her-rope habit that she rarely did.

"I'm sorry," I said. "But it's a long story. Really, really long. How did you know I was here?"

"Well, since you bailed on our weekend slumber party, I'm trying to catch up on my orders, and I need that purple burnout-velvet mock turtleneck I let you borrow."

"Okay," I said, not sure yet how this tracked.

"I sold it," Janis said, "and when you didn't answer, I fig-ured you wouldn't care if I went by and grabbed it. I know where your key is hidden. You and your dad never change it up, even though every criminal in the world knows to look under the mat. But when I got there, something was up." Pig had sat down on my foot and was leaning heavily into my leg. "Your dad was gone," Janis continued. "All the lights were still out, and Pig didn't have any food. Esme, I know she always pretends like she's hungry, but this time she really was hungry. I looked everywhere and I couldn't find any dog food. I got worried, because I know you guys wouldn't go out of town and just leave Pig, so I did Find My Friends and saw your phone was here."

"Wait, what do you mean my dad's gone?"

"Exactly what I said," Janis snapped. "His car wasn't there and neither was he. The whole house was pitch black. I had to use the flashlight on my phone, and I'm surprised no one called the cops thinking I was trying to steal your toaster oven or something."

Janis was right, something was wrong. Pig was already looking skinnier. I needed to talk to Dad ASAP, but Adrian's words kept echoing in my head: Janis shouldn't be here, and I didn't want anyone to see her. Or Pig. I couldn't send them away, especially since something told me that I still wasn't getting the whole story from Janis. Which meant I had only one option.

"Janis," I said, "I think you should park your car and come in for a little while. Pig too."

"No way," she said, remaining in the driver's seat. "Not

until you tell me why you're here and what's going on. You keep glancing over your shoulder like you're worried you're going to get caught by the paparazzi or something."

"I can explain everything," I said. "Or most of it at least, but I think you should come inside. It's not safe out here." I wasn't sure why I said that last part. It was like the words just came out of my mouth before I'd thought about them, but then Janis slapped the steering wheel.

"Yeah, no crap," she said. "It's freaking me out, but I'm also freaked out as to why my best friend lied to me and is now holed up in a hotel."

"Wait, what?" I said, caught off guard. "What do you mean you know it's not safe out here?" Then something decided to show me what Janis was talking about. I felt the cold drip on the back of my neck. My senses turned on high, and the sweat glands in my armpits went into overdrive. "Janis," I said, taking a step toward Pig and putting a hand on her, "lock the doors, cover your head, and shut your eyes tight." She started to ask what I was talking about, but then seemed to think better of it and did exactly what I had told her.

It was moving faster than anything from this dimension ever should or could. It was a flicker, and then a blinding burst of light, like a camera flash two inches from your face. I couldn't see anything, just rainbow-tinged black. Pig started to howl, the pitiful sound cutting through the night air, and I could hear the sound of her jaws snapping as she tried to bite something she couldn't see.

"Down, Pig! Get down!" I shouted, keeping my eyes squeezed as tight as I could. I couldn't tell a dog to close her eyes, but I could at least try to keep the rest of her safe. I stumbled forward and my hands connected with Pig's fur. I could tell she was still standing, so I gave her a shove and pushed her to the ground. "Stay!" I hissed. "Stay!"

Keeping my eyes shut tight, I stood back up and positioned myself in front of Janis, my back pressed against the car. Then I raised my hands and tried to shut everything out but the sensations coming through my palms. It felt like a handful of slobbered-on Pop Rocks, crackling and sharp. It was coming closer, and closer, and diving for Janis's car. Pig howled again, but didn't move, and with a sharp twang, the diving demon collided with the car antenna as I managed to grab it at the last second before it hit the roof of the car. Yanking hard, I gave it a spin, and then tossed it, as hard as I could, right into the dumpster.

The sound of metal scraping on concrete tore at my ears, but I didn't dare open my eyes for fear of being blinded again. Janis was screaming, and Pig was howling—no doubt her eyes were burning—but I forced both sounds out of my mind and kept all my other senses focused on the demon. A Flash, so named for the obvious reasons. It was barely fazed by its literal dumpster dive and was already taking to the sky again.

I could feel it diving again, only this time, I barely caught it, and the force of its plummeting mass colliding with my powers nearly knocked me over. I didn't want to think what it could do to Janis's car. I spun it again, flinging it as far as I could. I blinked my eyes open, just for a second, long enough to see that the demon had landed across the street and was tangled in the branches of an oak tree. Crap. How long was this going to take? The Portal was supposed to be sealed for the Summit, but that was clearly not the case. If this thing got out, then surely the Portal would open enough to flush it back in.

I grabbed hold of the demon again and started to whip it around in a circle to build momentum for my toss, waiting for the familiar magnetic tug of the open Portal. But I kept whipping, and whipping, and never felt the tug. Finally, I risked opening my eyes. There was the demon, thrashing above me as it moved through the air in a loop, but there was no swirling Portal in the sky. What the eff? Where was it? Why was it taking so long? The longer I held on to the demon, the more I could feel my strength draining. A drop of sweat formed at my temple, and then trickled down the side of my face. The demon kept thrashing, and I could feel it pry strands off my kinesis, one by one, like they were fingers, and I'd have to clamp them back down. Confusion and anxiety were wearing away my concentration too. I couldn't keep this up forever.

I pulled my senses back into my body enough so that I could speak. "Janis," I screamed, "unlock the door and open it! Then when I say run, grab my hand and follow me!" Using everything I had, I let go of the demon at the same time as I yanked the dumpster into the air, turned it on its side so its lid fell open, then smashed it into the Flash and brought it down on the ground, like I had just captured a gigantic bug in an even bigger glass.

With one hand, I grabbed Janis's, and with the other, I

grabbed Pig's collar, as she was still too dazed and blinded to follow on her own. "Run!" I screamed. The hotel door I came out of had locked behind me. When we reached it, I let go of Janis and Pig, then used the last of my kinesis to pry it open and shove us in. The kinetic shove was so hard that Janis rose a foot off the ground, and when she landed, she stumbled and fell, catching herself with her hands as the door slammed shut.

"What the—?" she panted, pushing herself up and scrambling across the carpet, away from me. She stopped with her back pressed against the wall. Her lip was trembling and she was looking at me like I was the second-scariest thing she'd ever seen. It was déjà vu all over again, and I flashed back to the first time Janis had seen me use my powers. A time that had been carefully scrubbed from her memory. Pig lay on the floor, pawing at her eyes like she was trying to remove a pair of sunglasses. I put my palms over her eyes and bent down so that my forehead was touching hers. "I'm sorry, girlie, it'll go away. And we'll find you some food."

I looked back up at Janis, wondering where to go and what to do next, when I saw someone turn the corner and head toward us, down the hall. Drapey clothing. Silver hair. Wanda, just the person I did and did not want to see. She had a phone in her hand, and her eyes were trained on it, so I had just enough time to shove Janis and Pig into a nearby broom closet. "I'll explain later," I said. "Stay here and stay quiet." Janis stumbled over a mop bucket but nodded, then knelt and wrapped her arms around Pig. As soon as I shut the door, I turned and shouted Wanda's name.

She looked up sharply and pocketed the phone, causing it to disappear into the folds of her winter culottes. "Esme," she said, "is everything okay?"

"No, it's not. There's a demon outside. Trapped in a dumpster. I trapped it in a dumpster. I tried to Return it, but the Portal wouldn't open."

A dark look crossed Wanda's face, and I could hear her phone buzzing. "Why were you outside?" This was a question that seemed totally beside the point.

"To get some air," I said. "But we need to do something about the demon. It's not going to stay there for very long."

"You're sure it's a demon?" she asked, almost smiling. "And not just a big raccoon? The Portals were sealed, remember?"

"I'm sure it was a demon," I said.

"If it was in the dumpster, it could easily be a raccoon." Were we really having this conversation? Why was this woman obsessed with raccoons?

"It wasn't *in* the dumpster," I said. "I *put* it in the dumpster because the Portal wouldn't open."

"Of course the Portal won't open, dear," Wanda said, her eyes flashing toward her pocket, which was buzzing, and her fingers playing with the folds of her skirt. "It was sealed for the Summit."

"But if it's sealed, how is there a demon outside?"

Wanda's face got stony. "The Portal has only been sealed from the time the Summit started yesterday," she said. "If there is a demon outside, then it likely slipped through before that, and you and Cassandra did not notice."

I felt like I'd been slapped, and my mouth fell open a little. I had no idea what to say. "That's imposs—I-I mean . . . ," I stammered, trying to wrap my head around her words. It wasn't impossible, totally, but Cassandra and I had been on top of our game lately. Unless whatever was going on with Cass meant we weren't as connected as we had been. But even then, I would have known something came through, right? Even if Cass didn't?

"Now, don't worry," Wanda said. "You're new, and some Sitters make mistakes. I'll send someone to investigate, and we'll get it taken care of. Now, please, do not go outside again."

She was done with our conversation and turning back to whatever was happening on her phone, and before I could respond she was walking quickly away. Considering I was currently hiding my best friend and my dog in the broom closet, it was probably a good thing Wanda didn't seem to give a flying finger about me at the moment, but still, the whole thing was unsettling. There was a demon, right outside, and not tackling it immediately went against every line of the Sitter code. But I had to choose, and first things first, so I headed to the closet.

I had my fingers on the handle when I groaned. Ugh. I'd forgotten to ask Wanda about my phone. Certainly she, who seemed totally addicted to her own, would understand why I needed my phone back, and ASAP. But I guess that would have to wait even longer.

• • •

I opened the door as calmly as possible, to find Janis standing as still as one of the brooms. There was no way I was sending her back outside, which meant she was staying here. Which meant, I guess, that I was telling her everything.

"You can come out now," I said.

"Oh, so you're giving us permission to stop standing here, pretending to be mops?"

"Yes," I said, "I am."

"That's very kind of you," she said, and theatrically stepped around a push broom that wasn't in her way. She had one hand looped through Pig's collar, and Pig stayed close by her side, radiating dog vibes that let me know she and Janis were a team right now, and I was the odd girl out. "You better give us an explanation in the next two minutes, or we're going to cross from mildly-annoyed-but-mostly-worried-about-you into pissed-as-hell-and-thinking-you're-shady territory. Because something out there thought Pig and I looked like snacks, and not in a good way."

"It's a demon," I said, "from an alternate dimension. From a negative dimension, called the Negative. It wanted to suck all the positivity and good out of you until you were just a sad husk of bleak emotions."

"Well, great. That's fantastic," Janis said. "Glad that didn't happen." Just as I was thinking that Janis was taking this exceptionally well, she took two steps, her knees buckled, her head lolled to one side, and she passed the frick out. I caught her before she hit the ground, and back into the broom closet we went. Pig immediately started licking Janis's face, and I was starting to panic. I couldn't leave Janis in here—she'd start screaming as soon as she woke up, and get discovered. Plus, I was pretty sure "leaving-your-passed-out-best-friend-in-a-closet-full-of-cleaning-supplies" was in violation of every best-friend accord ever written. I had no idea how to revive someone who had just fainted. In old movies, people were always waving smelling salts under their noses, but who knew what smelling salts were. Then, as if she had been reading my mind, Pig let one rip.

"Oh God," I said, quickly blocking my nostrils, and then Janis twitched and sat up.

"What is that smell?" she said. "Did something die?"

"Not yet," I said. "And you know what that smell is, but no more questions right now. Just please trust me. We have to get you to my room or they won't let you stay."

"We're at a hotel," Janis said, swaying a little as she stood up. "I remember now. But you haven't told me why you're here. Are you in a cult? Is it a mime cult? Is that why you're wearing a beret?" She swallowed. "Are they force-feeding you applesauce?"

"Oh my God," I said, grabbing her hand. "I'm not in a cult, and not all cults eat applesauce. Just please, come with me now, and hurry."

Pig, pleased with herself for reviving Janis, licked Janis's face as she bent down to take off her shoes, which were Lady Miss Kier–era Fluevogs. Goddess love Janis—who else channeled Deee-Lite for a day of going to the post office? She even had on a wide elastic headband, a Pucci-esque button-up shirt, and dangly earrings with red plastic hearts.

"Here," I said, "I'll hold your shoes." I took the Fluevogs

in one hand and grabbed ahold of her arm with the other, then led us down the hallway and into the stairwell. Pig's vision seemed to have returned, and she stuck close to our heels. We crept up the stairs, and we were lucky that everyone seemed to still be down at dinner, because when I opened the door to the fourth-floor hallway, it was empty.

"When I say run, we run," I said. Janis nodded, and Pig seemed to understand too, because seconds later, the three of us were sprinting toward room 402. I got the door open quickly, and when we tumbled inside, I breathed a sigh of relief that we were alone.

Not too deep a sigh, though, as the air still reeked like crazy. Beside me, Janis wasn't saying anything, and I turned around to see that she was taking in the state of the room. The sheets were in tangles on the beds, and every flat surface was covered—with clothes, with makeup, with magazine pages that had been ripped out and crumpled into balls. Pig apparently needed no time to adjust. She instantly pawed across the room and made a nest out of Amirah's Moncler puffer jacket, which was lying half in, half out of the bathroom.

I expected Janis to say something about the smell, but instead, she crossed the room, got down on her hands and knees, and partially crawled under Amirah's bed. "Esme," she said, crawling back out and holding up a hot pink satin Louboutin. "Seriously, what the eff?"

"I'm sure the other one is around here somewhere," I said.

"Beside the point!" Janis snapped, pushing herself up to her feet. Then she held the shoe out and waggled it in my face. "Why are you here? Why don't you have your phone?

Why did you lie and say you were going to visit a made-up aunt and then come stay in a hotel in downtown Spring River? And who the heck owns this shoe?"

I decided to be honest, to start with the easiest of those questions. "My phone got confiscated because I forgot to turn the ringer off," I said, "and I haven't been able to get it back. And I'm here for a thing. I didn't want to tell you, because it's kind of weird. But it was a thing my mom did. Cassandra's mom was in it too, back when they were friends, and now we're doing it. Kind of in their honor, I guess. I didn't really have a choice, and I'm not supposed to talk about it. But I'm here to learn about stuff, and meet other people . . ." I wasn't sure where I was going with this, because contrary to everything I was saying, it sounded like I'd joined a . . .

"Esme," Janis gasped, "you *did* join a cult!"

"No, it's not like that at all," I started, "or wait, it's only kind of like that. And that shoe belongs to my roommate. She's from New York. And she's rich."

"Why are you keeping her, and her wardrobe, from me?" Janis said, pointing at a shirt flung over the back of a chair. "That's Versace!"

"I just met her yesterday," I said. "She's in the cult too. Wait, I mean, there is no cult, but her mom knew my mom. I think. Or they were coworkers."

"And what is this shadowy organization and its dream wardrobe?" Janis asked.

"It's like Girl Scouts," I settled on finally. "Where you learn skills, and how to be a good citizen. It's not a cult, but there are rules, and secrets."

"No one puts LSD in the applesauce?"

"No," I said. "There's no applesauce, at all. I mean, there is, but you don't have to eat it." I was having trouble keeping my own story straight, and Janis's focus on applesauce wasn't helping. When someone knocked on the door, I jumped so high I practically levitated.

"Bathroom, bathroom," I hissed at Janis and Pig, yet neither of them moved an inch.

"I'm not hiding from anyone until you tell me what's going on here," Janis said. Pig seemed to be taking her side, since all that moved was her ears as she perked them toward me.

"Fine," I said, walking to the door, but I relaxed when I looked through the peephole and saw that it was Cassandra. I opened the door and yanked her in. Cassandra surveyed the scene, and a smile crept onto her lips.

"Wow," she said. "You've been busy. Are you bringing your dad here next?"

"I wish," I said. "And you have no idea. Cass, there was a demon outside. I trapped it in a dumpster and told Wanda, but she tried to blame it on us and—" I stopped when the Louboutin went whizzing by my head, so close I could feel it. Cassandra ducked, and I spun around to face Janis, who crossed her arms over her chest.

"So, she's in the cult too? Who's her roommate? Someone from Beverly Hills?"

"There's no cult, and I don't know the people from Beverly Hills—" I started, but Janis cut me off.

"Esme," she said, "I'm not playing, and neither is Pig. An explanation now, or I start screaming and Pig starts barking and we don't stop until we've brought the whole cult running."

"Cult?" Cassandra said.

"She's obsessed with applesauce," I said, by way of explanation. I could feel three sets of eyes on me, everyone waiting to see what I was going to do or say next. Really, there was only one option. "Cassandra, I think we should tell Janis," I said.

Cassandra looked at me. "Tell Janis what?"

"Yeah, Esme," Janis said. "Tell Janis what?"

"Everything," I answered, and Cassandra raised an eyebrow.

"Your call," Cassandra said. "If Esme Pearl wants to break a rule, I'm certainly not going to stop her. Besides, Janis is *your* friend, not mine."

"Thanks for clarifying that," Janis said. "Because I was just sitting here thinking that I came to visit you."

"Okay," I said to Janis. "You have to promise you won't get mad."

"What? You want me to pinkie swear or something? This isn't middle school, Esme, and I will promise no such thing."

"The Synod will just microwave her brain again," Cassandra said.

"No, they won't," I said, somehow sure of myself. "I won't let that happen."

"Oh yeah?" Cassandra said. "And how will you manage that?"

"I don't know. I'll figure it out."

"There's a spell that will make her immune," Cassandra said.

My head swiveled so fast, I thought my neck might snap. "What?"

"I don't remember what was in it, but I saw it. In one of Brian's spell books," Cassandra said.

"And you're just mentioning this now?"

"It wasn't relevant before now," Cassandra said.

As usual, I was filled with competing urges. One, to hug Cassandra; the other, to throw an alarm clock at her or strangle her with the bedsheets.

"Excuse me," Janis said. "You're talking about microwaving a brain like that brain isn't sitting right in front of you still trying to decide whether it should make its mouth start screaming." She gave me the Janis look. The don't-mess-with-me babysitting look I'd seen doled out before, but never been on the receiving end of.

I held out my pinkie. "I know we're not in middle school anymore, and you can get mad. I just want you to swear you believe me, that I never meant to hurt you and I will never mean to hurt you."

A beat passed, and then Janis held out her pinkie and I looped mine through it. "You're my best friend," I said.

"Freaking heck," she said. "I know that. Just tell me."

So I did. About my powers, and the Sitter spells, and meeting Cassandra, and Brian. Dion dressing as Voldemort and trying to kidnap Andrew Reynolds when Janis was babysitting. I told her about Halloween, and about Erebus and MacKenzie and the Portal and Mom.

She held up her hand. "Wait a second," she said. "Cassandra's brother, the hot, dumb one—I hit him with a chair?"

"Yeah, but you didn't know it was him," I told her. "And he's not really that dumb. Or wait, he is dumb, but he's not as dumb as he seems."

Janis nodded. "And the football coach, the one who's always in a tracksuit, he's in on it too? And he's an interior designer?"

I nodded. "And he actually has really good taste," I said. "If you like things that match."

Pig had moved over to sit next to Janis, who stroked Pig's ear as she thought. "So how long does this thing last?" she asked finally.

"Just until tomorrow night," I said. "Then we all go home."

"No, not this Summit," Janis said. "I mean you being a Sitter."

"Forever, I guess," I said. "I mean, at some point, my powers will fade and I'll stop having to chase demons, but I'll always be a Sitter."

"Do you like it?"

"I don't think it matters whether I like it. It's what I do, and it's what I am."

Janis took a deep breath and crinkled her nose. The room still smelled like pot if you sniffed hard enough. "So what does this mean for me?" she asked. "Now that I know about you, does this mean I get to hit someone with a chair again?" She coughed. "I mean, have to hit someone with a chair."

I laughed. "I hope not," I said. "But it does put you in

danger. We were specifically told not to tell you. Every time a non-Sitter finds out about Sitter stuff, the Synod knocks that knowledge right out of their brains. I don't want that to keep happening to you if you don't want it to. Like Cass said, there's supposedly a spell that will prevent the memory eraser from working. I don't know what it is, but I can try to find out. On the other hand, if you don't want to know any of this stuff, that's cool too."

Janis had a faraway look. "That thing in the dumpster," she said. "It was awful. You have to deal with those a lot?"

"Not that one specifically, but yeah, things like it. They're all awful." I looked at Janis sitting there, her Fluevog shoes lying on the floor amid all of Amirah's stuff, her headband slightly askew, but still with more groove in her heart than ten thousand non-Janis people. She was the bravest person I knew. I would have hidden under the bed by now. "Honestly, Janis, I don't blame you at all if you don't want to know any of this. It's a lot, and it's not . . . pleasant."

Janis rolled her eyes. "Of course I want to know. It's the truth, right? I'm not trying to sit here in a bubble." It sounded like the wind was picking up again outside, and Janis's eyes flickered back to the window. "So, you're in this hotel until tomorrow night?"

I nodded. "There's like a party thing that Cassandra and I are supposed to be planning, and when that's done, we get to go home."

"A party?" Janis said. Even though we were best friends, in a lot of ways Janis and I couldn't have been more different. For one, she loved parties.

"It won't be any fun," I said. "It has this après-ski theme and—"

"Ooh," Janis said, "I like it. Are there going to be drinks with cinnamon sticks in them?"

"Probably," I said. "But really, I'll call as soon as it's—"

"No way," Janis said. "I'm staying."

"The party really won't be that cool," I said.

"Not for the party," she said. "Though it sounds very festive. But I'm not going back out there, and Pig isn't either. Not by ourselves at least."

Cassandra had been quietly sitting on my bed this whole time, but now she cocked her head and looked at Janis. "What do you mean?" she asked.

"Well, for one, that thing Esme trapped in a dumpster is probably still out there," she said. "And for two, my family's out of town, and for three, I bet it's not the only one. I swear there was something outside my house last night."

The skin along my spine prickled. "Wait," I said, "some*thing*, not some*one*?"

Janis nodded. "But it wasn't that dumpster thing. It was different. It sounded like a dog, but bigger, and more gooey. That was when I started to call you. And then when I saw my feed this morning, I knew I wasn't the only one. People have been seeing stuff all over town."

My mouth went dry. "What people?" I asked. "And what are they seeing?"

Janis pulled out her phone and handed it to me. It was open to Natalie Bedecker's account, and a dark, shaky story that had been posted thirteen hours ago. Natalie's voice was a whisper as she pointed the phone at a tree barely visible on the edge of her backyard. "It's right there," she said, her voice trembling. "I've never seen a bear run so fast. It was like its feet didn't even touch the ground." I felt the back of my neck prickle, and my fingers started to go numb. That sounded like a demon, all right, and not a Flash. How many were out there? I handed the phone to Cassandra, who watched the video, her eyebrows twitching. When she was done, she looked up at Janis.

"Go to Pete Anderson's page," Janis said. "He's got one too." Pete Anderson was a guy who had graduated last year and who Janis still followed because he posted sneaky shots of the customers who came into the gas station where he worked. He was pretty funny and was well known for breaking a car windshield with his forehead, from outside of the car. But in this video, he was hiding in a closet, crying, because he was scared to go outside.

Cassandra handed the phone back to Janis. "Have you seen stuff anywhere else?" she asked.

"There was something on the news this morning," Janis said. "But I guess the city's trying to say it's a bobcat? But that's a lie. It's not a bobcat."

"What do your parents say?" I asked.

"I haven't told them," she said. "Because they don't know I'm home alone. They still think you're staying with me, remember?"

Guilt washed over me. "Okay," I said. "You're definitely

staying here, but you have to stay in this room and hide. No one else can know about you, because you're not supposed to know about them."

And with that, I heard a click as the door unlocked. Fortunately, I'd bolted it after I let Cassandra in. "Just a second!" I called to Amirah as I hurried Janis and Pig into the bathroom. I'd just shut them in when Cassandra unlocked the door and stepped aside. Amirah came in and started tossing pillows and pieces of clothing in the air. Ji-A, close on her heels, perched on a table. They both seemed high.

"We're going down to watch the movie," Amirah said. "And I need my mints. Have you seen them?"

"I haven't," I said. Amirah looked back and forth between me and Cassandra.

"Are you sure?" she continued. "If you ate them, that's cool. Just tell me."

"We most certainly did not eat them," I said, and Cassandra raised an eyebrow. I'd never licked the bottom of a rowboat, but I was pretty sure the taste of Amirah's mints was comparable.

Suddenly, she stopped her search, and her nose wrinkled. "Why does it smell like dog in here?" The question caught me off guard, as I was surprised she could smell anything other than leftover smoke. Instinctively, I glanced at the bathroom door and wondered how intensive Amirah's mint search was going to be.

"You're being paranoid," Ji-A told her, then turned to me. "Amirah hates dogs." Great, I thought, that's awesome. Also, how could anyone hate dogs?

"I don't hate dogs," Amirah said, crawling out from under her bed, still without mints. "I just think they're gross, and I don't understand what the big deal is. Like, if you want to carry around poop in a plastic bag, just start babysitting." Amirah kicked a Kenzo pouch out of the way, and I saw her eyes drift toward the bathroom door. Then, I spotted them, on the bedside table, half obscured by an Hermès scarf.

"Your mints!" I screamed, lunging toward the bedside table. Everyone looked at me, probably wondering why I was so gosh-darn excited about finding Amirah's mints. I turned and handed them to her.

"Thanks," she said, opening the tin and popping one in her mouth. "You want?" I shook my head. Ji-A did the same, but Cassandra, who didn't know any better, took one.

"Thanks," she said, tossing it into her mouth.

"See you down at the movie?" Amirah said.

"Yeah." I nodded. "We'll be down in a sec."

I waited as long as it took Amirah to pull the door closed behind her, then ran to the bathroom to let Pig and Janis out.

"Sorry," I said to Cassandra. "I didn't have time to warn you about the mints."

"What about them?" she said. I could hear the mint clacking around in her mouth.

"You like them?" I asked, incredulous.

"Sure," she said, "I mean, they're not orange Tic Tacs, but then what is?"

CHAPTER 16

Tonight's post-dinner activity was a showing of *Better Watch Out* in the Laurie Strode Auditorium. The room was dark, and the movie was already a few minutes in when Cassandra and I arrived. I'd seen the film before, and liked it a lot: creepy, misogynistic twelve-year-old decides Christmas is the best time to confess his crush to his babysitter, with murder and torture served as steaming side dishes. I clearly wasn't the only one who'd seen it, as the crowd booed every time the kid came on-screen, and cheered for the babysitter. It was my kind of movie, and my kind of crowd, but I couldn't concentrate. There was so much going on in my head that I felt like I should make a list. The world's most impossible to-do list:

- Solve Dad's money problems
- Remove curse from Mom
- Remove curse from Cass. Who did it?!?
- Demons outside. Why? Make sure no one hurt.

- Host holiday party
- Hide BFF
- Hide dog
- Get dog food

"I'm going to the bathroom," I said to Cassandra, before realizing she'd fallen asleep. Maybe a walk, even if it was just around the hotel lobby, would help me think. I'd barely left the auditorium, though, when I ran right into Adrian. My heart started to pound, and I could feel that gonna-smile-real-big feeling build, but I wasn't totally sure I was happy to see him. I made a mental note to add "Cute boy—what's his deal??" to my list.

Adrian was confusing, and more confusion was not what I needed. But we were the only two people in the hall, and he was walking right toward me. Plus, he was holding something that I could not ignore: a venti iced coffee.

"You drink iced coffee in December?" I gasped. By now he was standing just a few feet from me, and he looked me straight in the eyes and took a long drink, almost like it was a dare.

"Aw," he said, when he was finally finished. "So refreshing. And I don't care what you say: it's always iced coffee weather."

"N-n-no, no, I would never!" I stammered. "I mean, I never want to go to Antarctica because I'm pretty sure they don't have Starbucks there, but if I did, and if they did, I would definitely order iced. In fact, I'm kind of jealous right now. Like, really jealous."

He smiled and then, to my shock, he reached out and took my hand. "Come on, then," he said, pulling me down the hallway. "Let's go find you a glass. I'm happy to share."

"So, you got to leave the hotel to go to Starbucks?" I said, making small talk to distract myself from the feel of his fingers intertwined in mine.

"Well, technically, I was working," he said. "But you know, if I'm working and there happens to be a Starbucks, and I just happen to need a coffee, then yes, I can go." We reached the dining room, and Adrian pushed the door open, but didn't flick on the lights. In a corner, a still-on Christmas tree cast little pools of white light on the floor and on a nearby table and chairs. By now everything had pretty much been cleaned up, and dishes were already out for tomorrow's breakfast. Adrian took a water glass off the stack, then cracked the lid on his iced coffee.

"So, when you were outside, was everything okay?" He was concentrating on pouring half the coffee into the glass and trying not to spill, so I couldn't see his face.

"Yeah," he said, as he handed the glass to me. "Why do you ask?"

"Much obliged," I said, raising my glass in a cheers before I took a sip of the cold, bitter, burned, watery deliciousness. "When I went out to meet my friend earlier, there was a demon. It tried to attack us, and when I tried to Return it, the Portal wouldn't open."

"Well, the Portal is sealed," he said, though I could almost swear I heard a note of hesitation in his voice when he said it.

"I know. But then how did the demon come through?"

"Maybe it came through a while ago." Even though the fact that Adrian hadn't seen anything made me think that Wanda had handled it, my shoulders sank at this statement. It was the same thing Wanda had said, though it hurt a lot more coming from Adrian. The implication was, of course, that Cassandra and I sucked at our jobs. I started to say I was heading back to the movie, when Adrian pulled a chair out from the table nearest the Christmas tree and sat down.

"Was everything okay with your friend?" he asked.

"Oh, yeah," I said, sitting down in the chair next to him. "She just, uh, wanted back a shirt I'd borrowed. It was no big deal." It struck me that this was twice now Adrian had been outside tonight, and my curiosity was piqued, especially after what everyone else had been saying about him earlier. It felt like asking him, straight out, what his powers were was maybe a little too blunt.

"So, when you're working, what do you do?" I asked instead.

"It could be anything," he said. "I'm kind of like an assistant, so I help out with what's needed. But really, it's a lot of errands. Really boring stuff."

"Like returning library books?"

"Boringer," he said.

"Picking up dry cleaning?"

"Boringer than that, even," he said. "For example, I went to the post office twice today."

I laughed. "That is the boringest. Why on earth?"

He took a sip of his iced coffee and then traced the

stick-on label with his finger. "Can I tell you something? And you promise you won't tell?"

"Of course," I said, instantly, then hoped I didn't sound too eager, like, "Oh, Adrian, tell me all your secrets."

"So, Wanda's kind of an addict. That's why I've been working so much."

"What?" I gasped. The statement shocked me. There was nothing about her that seemed like she was on drugs, but then, you could never tell. But wait . . . "What kind of addict needs someone to go to the post office all the time?"

"She's addicted to eBay," Adrian said, his voice low as he leaned forward. "And it's gotten really bad."

I started to laugh. "What the heck? Is she collecting baseball cards?"

"Worse," he said. "Beanie Babies." I waited for the punch line. Wait, Beanie Babies *was* the punch line. But Adrian wasn't laughing; actually, he looked very serious.

"I thought it was harmless at first," he continued, "but now she's buying two or three a day. She's spending thousands of dollars, and she's selling her own stuff to pay for it. Last night, she had me take her mother's wedding ring to a pawnshop so that she could get money to bid on a tie-dyed crab."

I still couldn't believe it. Beanie Babies? Tiny stuffed toys? Granted, I knew tons of people who were obsessed with Beanie Babies and would do anything to get a new one, but all of those people were . . . in preschool. The whole thing was preposterous, but staring at Adrian's face, I could see there wasn't a hint of humor in it.

"That's insane," I said finally.

"His name is Claude."

"Who?"

"The crab. Claude the Crab. That's the one Wanda wants. She said it's really rare, and this one has a misprint on the tag, so that makes it even more special." Adrian sighed and took another sip of coffee. "When I accepted her offer, I thought I'd be doing important stuff. You know, like what you do—trying to save the world and all that. I don't know if I would have said yes if I'd known this was what it was going to be. It's gotten to the point where managing Wanda's watch list and all her bids is almost a full-time job. Like, she's bidding on stuff that I know she doesn't have the money to pay for. Those purple Princess Diana bears are not cheap, if you know what I mean."

"We are talking about the same Wanda here, right?" I said. "Because I'm talking about the one who looks like she thinks heaven is an Eileen Fisher store? Who looks like she gets really excited about tea?" He nodded, and then my mind caught on something else. "Wait, what do you mean, her offer?" I asked.

Adrian just smiled and poured some more coffee into my glass. "Never mind," he said. "I don't want to talk about it anymore. I mean, we don't get many chances to hang out one-on-one, so I don't want to waste this one complaining about my job."

"I like hearing you complain about your job," I said, which was the truth, but I was also hoping he would answer my question.

"Well, I don't," he said. "Tell me about you. Are you having fun this weekend?"

I traced triangles in the condensation on the side of my glass. "I guess," I said, "but it's also stressful. I'm learning a lot, but not all of it is good."

"What do you mean?" he asked.

"Like, I didn't know that there were Sitter family weekends," I said. "And that most of these people have known each other almost all of their lives. It makes me feel like an outsider, you know?"

"Trust me," Adrian said, "you should be glad you missed all those family weekends. I've attended enough talentless talent shows to last me my entire life. Juggling can get ugly. Besides, I think it's cool you weren't raised in the Sitterhood. It can get pretty insular. But you've got a different perspective, and you know about all kinds of things the other Sitters don't."

"Like what?"

"Like music," he said. "Most of these girls don't even know who André 3000 is. And you know about fashion."

"Amirah knows about fashion."

"Amirah has money and she buys designer stuff," he said. "That's different from knowing about fashion."

I smiled at him. "Okay," I said. "If you insist. But I'm still a little jealous of her wardrobe, and I would take a single shoe if she ever offered it to me." Adrian laughed, and I was glad we were in a dim glow, so he couldn't see me blush. "So, post office runs aside, there have to be some perks to working with the Synod."

"Sure," he said. "We travel a lot, so I've already been to forty-three states."

"Wow," I said, "that's a lot. Which was your favorite?"

"Montana," he said. "It's like the sky is a living thing there. What about you? What's your favorite place you've been?"

"I haven't been to that many places," I said. "Just Colorado, Missouri, Oklahoma. And Illinois once, but that was by accident."

"Accident?"

"Long story," I said, "but my dad missed an exit."

"I like Colorado," Adrian said. "The mountains are cool."

I nodded. "Dad and I used to go camping, before we realized neither one of us likes camping. On one trip, we stayed right by a lake, and there were all these small, round rocks at the edges of the lake in the morning, and I thought they were fallen stars. I collected dozens of them in a ziplock and took them home. The next night was cloudy, and I got totally freaked out that there weren't any stars in the sky because I'd stolen them all. I started crying, so Dad and I went into the backyard, and we threw all the rocks I'd collected up into the air. Dad told me we had to wait for them to resettle, and then the next night, it wasn't cloudy and I could see all the stars, and I thought I could pick out the ones that had been mine because they glowed a little brighter."

"The girl who gave the stars back," Adrian said. There was something different in his voice when he said it, and the way he was looking at me made me want to look down at my feet, but I forced myself to hold his gaze. The lights from the Christmas tree reflected off his cheekbones, and his eyebrows had an arch that would make a beauty blogger salivate with envy. He could tell I was looking.

"What?" he said, a smile creeping onto his face.

"Nothing," I said. "I should get back to the movie before anyone notices I'm gone."

"Of course," Adrian said. "You don't want to miss it."

"I've seen it before. Have you?"

"No way," he said. "Too scary for me. But not you, you're fearless."

"Oh God, no way," I said. "I'm afraid of everything."

"Like what?"

"Heights," I said. "I don't even like standing on a stepladder." I couldn't help but notice I'd said I needed to go, but neither of us was moving.

"So," he said, leaning toward me and resting one arm on the table, "you love scary movies, but you're afraid of heights?"

I nodded. "Two totally different things."

"How so?"

"Heights are real," I said. "You could slip and fall, or you could be so focused on not going off the edge that your brain gets the wires crossed and makes you jump."

"Does that actually happen?" he asked.

"I don't know," I said. "But there's no reason why it couldn't."

"So how is that different from scary movies?"

"Horror movies flip the scary paradigm," I said. "Like, your whole life, everybody is telling you not to be scared.

Don't be scared of the dark, don't be scared of the roller coaster, don't be scared of having to sing a solo in front of your entire seventh-grade class. But in horror movies, the message is 'be scared.' It's like terror in a safe space. You can scream your head off, and know that Candyman is staying right there, on the screen."

Adrian shook his head and smiled. "Oh man, not for me," he said. Now I leaned forward. I couldn't help it. My body did it on its own.

"You don't like horror movies?"

"No way," he said. "I'm never convinced anything is going to stay on the screen. Like, I still don't go in the basement, and it's been years since I saw *The Conjuring*."

I raised my hands. "Want to play hide-and-clap?"

He pointed a finger in my face. "Esme Pearl, do not, or I will spend the rest of the weekend drinking all the caffeine in this building so that you get none."

I held my hands up in surrender. "Okay, okay," I said. "No clapping. But you should know that the call is coming from inside the house."

Adrian shrugged. "Isn't it always?" he said. "Hey, did you like the song?" he asked, suddenly changing the subject.

"The song?"

"The Waitresses? Their Christmas song."

"I couldn't listen to it," I groaned. "My phone was confiscated last night and I still haven't gotten it back. I tried to listen to it on Cassandra's phone, but, well, long story."

"That sucks," Adrian said, then thought for a minute. "Want to hear it now?"

"Sure," I said. He pulled his phone out, tapped it a few times, and then placed it on the table. He started to press Play, but then paused, his finger hovering above the screen.

"Wait," he said. "Is it weird to just sit here and listen to a song? What if you don't like it? That would be like standing there while someone watches your favorite video and thinks it isn't funny. . . ."

"Just play it," I said. He hit Play, and the music started. The first few bars were good—a little Christmasy, sure, but kind of post-punk. The beat was strong, and I could imagine dancing to it in my room, bouncing up and down and bobbing my head. Then the lyrics kicked in, and the first words were "bah humbug." Oh my God, this song was awesome!

"This is rad!" I said. "Who's it by, again?"

"The Waitresses," he said. "I can't believe you've never heard of them. They're totally your kind of band. They broke up in 1984." I looked down at the table and smiled, wondering whether he could see how hard I was blushing right now. From what I'd heard so far, this *was* 100 percent, totally, my kind of band. I looked back up and Adrian was smiling at me and bobbing his head along with the song. Then he raised his hands and started shrugging his shoulders, moving in a little dad dance equal parts cool, hilarious, and to-die-for adorable. The song was catchy as heck, and before I knew it, I'd kicked in with air drums and was tapping my toes, my smile matching his in width. Then all of a sudden, the music cut out, replaced with a shrill sound that made us both jump.

"Wanda," Adrian said, shaking his head when he saw the

screen. "And I am not going to answer right now, because we were in the middle of a song." He hit Silent, and a split second later, before the music could even start back up, his phone dinged with a text. He read it and groaned. "Ugh," he said. "She got Claude."

"What?" I said.

"That stupid crab. The Beanie Baby," he said. "She won it, and she needs me to come help her figure out how she's going to pay for it."

Jeez. I almost shook my head in disbelief—Wanda had given us this entire speech about staying focused and had confiscated my phone in front of everyone to prove the point, all the while she was using hers to obsessively collect tiny stuffed animals. Whatever Christmas magic the Waitresses had conjured was gone. Adrian stood up, and I followed.

"I'm sorry you have to deal with this," I said, as we walked toward the door. Adrian tossed his cup in the recycling bin, and I put my glass in an empty bus bin. "But who knows? Maybe this crab is really cool?"

"Ha," he said. "Trust me, it's not." Then, right before we reached the door, Adrian turned and looked at me again. "This was cool, though," he said, "hanging out with you and talking. Maybe we could do it again some time."

I nodded. "Over coffee," I said. "And more songs."

"Yeah," he said. "Over *iced* coffee."

Then, in the hall, we went our separate ways.

CHAPTER 17

When I got back to the auditorium, the movie was still playing and Cassandra had woken up. "Where were you?" she hissed as I slid back into my seat. "I can't follow this plot at all."

"I went to the bathroom," I said.

"So what is happening here?" she asked.

"I have no idea," I answered, thinking she was talking about Better Watch Out.

"I thought you'd seen it before."

"I have," I said. "But I'm not talking about the movie!" My leaving the auditorium had done the opposite of what I had hoped—I hadn't cleared my brain. Instead, everything Adrian had said just made things even muddier. "Listen, we have to keep Amirah out of our room," I said. "We have to get her to switch and stay in someone else's."

"Easy," Cassandra said.

"Easy?" I asked. "How is that easy? You've met Amirah!"

"Don't worry about it," she said. "You go upstairs, hide Janis and Pig, and I'll take care of Amirah." I had about a million questions, but the credits were starting to roll, which meant Amirah was going to head upstairs any minute. Also, there was a part of me that was relieved to delegate one task on my mental to-do list to Cassandra, especially if she considered it NBD.

I made it to the elevator before Amirah did, and the fourth-floor hallway was still empty when I ran down it to our room. When I got there, Janis and Pig were curled up on my bed, watching *Vanderpump Rules*.

"We're hungry," Janis said.

"Get in the closet," I said. "Now."

"Is there food in the closet?" Janis asked, but still, she got up and started moving, and Pig followed. I ran over to the closet and threw the door open. Fortunately, Amirah kept her clothes on the floor instead of on hangers, so I wasn't worried about her looking in there if she wanted to gather up some of her stuff. Janis and Pig were taking their sweet time, and I just managed to get the door shut behind them when there was a knock on the room door.

I looked through the peephole and exhaled, relieved. It was just Cassandra.

"Get in bed," she said, as soon as I opened the door, "and act like you're in pain." I did as she said, pulling the covers up to my chin, and she sat on Amirah's bed. Two seconds later, Amirah's key beeped the lock and she walked in.

"I'm just going to grab some stuff," she said. "I won't be long. Thanks again for switching with me," she said to

Cassandra. "I appreciate it." Then, turning to me, she put a look on her face that appeared to be her version of resting pity face. "How are you feeling, Esme?" she asked, keeping her distance. "It sounds really . . . gross."

I groaned and Cassandra nodded. "WebMD says it's only contagious for the first three hours," she told Amirah. "So I'm screwed, but there's still hope for you." Amirah grimaced as she grabbed clothes off the floor and stuffed them in a Gucci tote, then she gave a little wave as she headed back out the door.

As soon as the door clicked shut, I sat up and looked at Cassandra. "What did you tell them?"

"I told everyone we thought you were coming down with a case of aspartamevirus."

"What's that?" I asked.

"I made it up," she said. "But trust me, be glad you don't really have it. It's awful."

"Excuse me," came a voice from the closet. "How long are we supposed to stay in here?"

"You can come out now," I said, opening the door to let Janis and Pig out. "So, you're hungry?"

Janis shifted from foot to foot. "Well, Pig definitely is," she said. "I don't think I've ever heard a dog's stomach growl like that before."

"And you?"

Janis shrugged. "I wouldn't mind a nibble."

"But you'll survive without one?"

"Yes."

"Well, good, because we don't have any nibbles." I looked

at Cassandra. "But Pig needs to eat. What are we going to do about dog food?"

"Don't look at me," Cassandra said. "I just exposed myself to a very serious fake illness for you."

Pig whined and licked my hand, then looked at me with those Hershey's Kiss eyes. I leaned down to nuzzle her face. Where was I going to find dog food in a hotel where you weren't even supposed to have a dog? I wished there were a spell to conjure kibble.

Then it hit me. Meat. When Cassandra and I had first discovered her mother's spell book, we'd tried all of the spells, even the ones that didn't seem like they would ever be useful. Like kreaskinesis—the power to manipulate meat. Cassandra had tried to make herself a hamburger, but she basically just succeeded in destroying the kitchen so badly that I had to use a different spell to clean it up.

Purina wasn't in my repertoire, but a raw chicken might be, and Pig could definitely eat that. Dad and I had tried to put her on a raw-food diet at one point to see if it did anything about the farts, but we'd given up when it only seemed to make them worse. And sure, we weren't supposed to be casting any spells, even in our rooms, but I also wasn't supposed to have my dog here, or my best friend, so if you're already breaking two rules, why not break them all?

Amirah might be a total slob, but I felt like she would have a reasonable objection to me splattering the room with raw meat. Plus, that might actually give me whatever illness Cassandra had just made up. So I figured the bathtub was the safest place for a relatively untested spell. "Give me a minute," I told Janis and Cassandra, then I motioned to Pig to follow me into the bathroom.

"Don't do anything I wouldn't do," Cassandra called.

In the bathroom, I told Pig to sit, and then closed the door to make a little more room. I closed my eyes so that I could concentrate and held out one hand as I thought, "Raw chicken." Almost immediately I felt a current run through my body, which told me the spell had worked. Then I heard something that made my eyes snap open.

There was a chicken in the bathtub all right, and it was most definitely raw. So raw it was still covered in feathers, and alive. It scratched and pecked at the bottom of the tub and Pig started to whimper. Not because she wanted to eat it, of course, but because she was scared of it. She backed up until she had wedged herself between the sink and the toilet.

"It's okay, girlie," I said, calmly. "Don't be scared." Sure, I was calm-talking to my dog, but inside I was freaking out. Then the chicken started to flap its wings, and with a squawk, took off, flying up to sit on the sink, sending Pig scrambling to get away from it. Crap! I thought these things weren't supposed to be able to fly!

I was looking at the chicken, and it was looking at me, and as though it had read my mind and wanted to prove me wrong, it took off again, this time forcing me to duck as it launched itself off the sink to fly up to the shower curtain rod.

From outside the door, I heard Cassandra's voice ring out loud and clear. "Oh, hi, Amirah!" Crap. Crap, crap, crap. Two seconds later, there was a knock on the bathroom door.

"Who's in the bathroom?" It was Amirah's voice. Who the frick did she think was in the bathroom? And why was she back?

I coughed as the chicken flew over to perch on the sink again. I shouted, "It's me, just a minute!"

"I forgot my toothbrush," she said.

I flushed the toilet. "It might have germs on it!" I yelled.

"That toothbrush was three hundred dollars. I need it," she called back. "And it has a disinfect mode, so it will be fine."

A three-hundred-dollar toothbrush? What? How? Was it solid gold? I looked around, thinking I could crack the door and hand it to her, but I didn't see a toothbrush.

"I don't see a toothbrush!" I yelled, and flushed the toilet again.

"Esme, are you okay?" Amirah asked, a note of concern creeping into her voice. "Do we need to call someone? It sounds like you're about to break the toilet!"

"I'm feeling better," I said. "I'm just using the bathroom!" It wasn't a total lie. "Are you sure your three-hundred-dollar toothbrush is in here?"

"I'm sure," she snapped. And then I saw it. It was right under the mirror, obscured because the chicken was sitting on it. I coughed again and shooed the chicken away. The toothbrush was solid white and looked pretty regular to me. I ran it under the faucet, and then cracked the door an inch and held it out.

"Thank you," Amirah said, and I shut the door. I heard nothing as I counted to five, and when I opened the door again, she was gone. Cassandra was sitting on one bed, flipping through the remnants of the *Vogue Brasil*, and Janis was crouched on the floor, between the bed and the wall, under a comforter, her eyes wide as bagels.

"I hid . . . but still . . . did she just . . . ?" Janis asked, pointing at the wall where Amirah must have disappeared. "I mean . . . I saw . . . no door?"

"Yes," I said. "And she has a three-hundred-dollar toothbrush that disinfects itself." Then the chicken launched itself at the bathroom door, which I managed to shut just in time to keep it in the bathroom.

"What's going on in there?" Cassandra asked. I really didn't feel like dealing with her right now.

"Like I said," I snapped, "nothing. I'm just getting ready for bed!" But my heart was pounding as I opened the bathroom door and ducked back in before the chicken could come out. I had somehow managed to double our hotel room's illicit animal count and broken one of the Summit's biggest rules in the process. I tried to think. Another one of the first spells Cassandra and I had tried and never really mastered was for bird manipulation, but I wasn't sure how that was applicable in the current situation. What did I want to manipulate this chicken into doing? I didn't think I could manipulate it into not existing.

What I knew about chickens amounted to nuggets. Except birds needed nests, right? I grabbed one end of the toilet paper and pulled until I'd gotten almost all of it off the roll. Then I opened up the cabinet under the sink and threw the toilet paper in there in a pile. I looked back at the chicken.

I'd figure out a long-term plan later, but right now I wanted it to go into the cabinet and be quiet. I held out one hand. "Avekinesis," I said. The chicken's onyx eyes were shifty, and I knew it was a formidable opponent. It stared at me and I stared at it and I held my breath. Then, finally, like it knew it was doing me a favor, it took off from behind the sink, and with a couple of wing flaps, landed on the floor. Then, taking its sweet time, it waddled over, jumped up into the cabinet, and started pecking at the toilet paper. I closed the cabinet door and exhaled. One problem postponed.

With the chicken out of sight, Pig seemed to relax a little and started to inch away from the toilet. "Okay, Piggy," I said. "I'm going to try this again." I held my hand out and closed my eyes. This time, I imagined a steak, fully cooked, because the last thing I wanted to do was to conjure a cow. Suddenly, the smell of charred meat singed my nostrils. I opened my eyes and breathed a sigh of relief. It was burned as hell, but it was a steak all right and it was definitely not moving.

"Bon appétit," I said to Pig, who wasted no time in devouring the steak. As soon as she had scarfed down the last bite, I pulled open the cabinet door to check on the chicken. It was still shredding the toilet paper, but it was doing so quietly and it didn't seem to mind being in a dark box. Then I opened the bathroom door and Pig and I went back into the room.

"Whatever you do," I said, "stay out from under the sink, okay?"

Cassandra didn't even look up. "Sure," she said.

"I'm done with questions for tonight," Janis said, pulling the covers up over her. "But won't Pig also have to pee?"

"Maybe," I said. "But she can hold it for a long time. She probably hasn't had much water today."

"I gave her a La Croix," Janis said.

"You did what?"

"I found a case under the bed," she said. "I was drinking one, and she was giving me those eyes. You know those eyes?" I did know those eyes. They made you think that Pig had never eaten in her entire life. Still, what did a dog care about La Croix?

"So you gave her one?"

Janis nodded. "Tangerine," she said for clarification. "I just dumped it in the ice bucket." I glanced over. So that was why the ice bucket was on the floor by the bathroom door.

I sighed. "Okay, girl, come on," I said, opening the bathroom door and motioning Pig in, and then I shut the door behind us. A minute later, we were back out, and Cassandra and Janis were both staring at us.

"Um, what just happened?" Cassandra said.

"Desperate times call for desperate measures," I said. "But if either of you were thinking about taking a bath, I would suggest you reconsider."

Pig took the other half of Janis's bed, and Cassandra took the other half of mine, and we watched reality TV for a while. Cassandra, of course, had no idea what any of the shows were. "I just don't understand why any of these people are important," she kept saying.

"That's the whole point," Janis would always reply. "They're not."

Pig fell asleep first, of course, and then Janis. They both

snored, and together they made an off-kilter cadence that sounded like a bagpipe with postnasal drip. So what if I was breaking every rule? I was very happy they were here.

The thing about blackout curtains is that they really black things out, and I wasn't sure how long my eyes had been open before I looked at the clock: 1:32 a.m. glowed red in the darkness. By 1:34, I was out of bed and sliding into my shoes.

I crept to the door and opened it slowly. Pig grunted and shifted in her sleep and I froze for a second, then slipped out and eased the door shut with a small click. The hallway was quiet, the only sound the air blowing through the vents. The carpet muffled my footsteps, and I wondered if this was what it felt like to be a jewel thief.

I opted for the stairs, sure the ding of the elevator would ring out like a gong at this time of night. I walked down the four flights, and when I stepped out onto the ground floor, it was as quiet as the fourth. My feet were moving of their own accord, and I couldn't remember making an actual decision to do what I was about to do, and I had no internal debate about what I was about to do.

I had fully expected the Mary Anne Spier Library to be locked, which my kinesis could have taken care of immediately. But when I got there and grabbed the door handle, the door swung wide open. I guess physical locks weren't that important in a hotel where everyone was either under a mind control spell or in possession of superpowers.

I stepped into the room and could feel it, just like I had

this afternoon: the sense that I wasn't alone, and that it was crowded in here. I stood very still, not even breathing, and listened. The books had not been packed back into their boxes for the night, and there was the faintest pulse in the room, not audible to my ears, but to my Sitter sense—that spot on the back of my neck—that told me the books were alive and watching me. I didn't want to turn on any lights, because I didn't want to draw attention to the fact I was here, on the off chance someone was walking by outside. It also seemed rude. I wouldn't like it if someone came into my room in the middle of the night and turned on all the lights.

Carefully, I made my way to the corner where I had seen the Red Magic book earlier. I figured I could take the book up to my room, read it, and then have it back before anyone noticed it was gone.

Except, it was already gone.

Well, crap.

I strained to make out the titles of the books, hoping it wasn't actually gone, just moved. But as I crept up and down the rows of books, I grew more and more uncomfortable. I'd made them scream earlier today, and I wasn't sure they liked me. They might not just be watching me, they might know exactly why I was here. . . .

I walked quickly back to the door and let myself out. My heart was pounding and I felt super jumpy. I took the stairs back up to the fourth floor and couldn't help but note how weird it was—the very book that I had gone to the library planning to steal wasn't there anymore. Maybe Deirdre packed the more valuable ones up at night? I'd check again in the morning.

I let myself back into the room and crawled into bed. I was readjusting my pillows when Cassandra shifted next to me.

"Where'd you just go?" she asked, making me almost leap out of my skin.

I let out a breath. "To see if I could find something," I said.

"Did you?"

"No."

"Well," she said, "good night."

CHAPTER 18

The next time I woke up it was morning. Everyone else was still sleeping as I dug through my luggage and made an attempt at an outfit: my chartreuse ankle-zip jeans under my blue slip dress, which was over a black T-shirt and under my bleach-dyed denim shirt and my bomber jacket. Thinking about Outkast, I dubbed it "Layers Ball," which was essentially a sad attempt to spin the fact that I'd packed poorly and was now wearing two outfits at once to try to stay warm.

Cassandra and I decided to go down to breakfast, get whatever we could, and then bring it back up to share with Janis and Pig. Rather than taking the elevator, we walked, a path that took us back by the Mary Anne Spier Library. As we passed the room, I slowed down to try to see in, and Cassandra seemed to pick up on my slowed steps.

"So, where'd you go last night?" she asked, casually.

I had to hand it to her, she knew me pretty well. "I came here, to the library," I said. "There was a book that I was pretty sure was about Red Magic. I mean, it was red, so I just assumed . . ."

"And you snuck out to steal it?" she said.

"No, of course not," I said quickly. "I didn't want to steal it. I just wanted to see what was in it."

"So, what was in it?" she asked.

"I have no idea," I said. "It was gone."

"So you went to steal a book someone had already stolen?"

I sighed. "I wasn't going to steal anything, Cassandra," I said.

As we walked through the lobby, Cassandra slowed. She chewed her nails as she scanned the room. "It's Sunday," she said. "But where's the continental breakfast?"

I nodded. True, this was when, and that was where, Cybill had told us to meet her, but there wasn't a bagel or a box of cornflakes in sight. With Cassandra following, I walked up to the desk.

"Excuse me," I said, speaking to the man behind the counter. "I'm looking for the continental breakfast."

"I'm sorry, ma'am," said George, whose eyes were as black as his hair. "But there is no continental breakfast this morning, as the hotel is entirely booked for a private event."

"We're supposed to meet someone there," I said. "One of your employees."

George looked at me blankly, like he had no idea who I was talking about. "I'm sorry," he said, "but there is no continental breakfast this weekend. However, I do think you will find our buffet more than satisfactory, and with many more options."

"But someone who works here told me there was," I said. "A blond woman. Her name is Cybill."

George shook his head. "I apologize, ma'am, but we do not have any employees by that name," he said.

"Her hair is kind of shaped like a helmet, and she's wearing a lot of makeup and her clothes don't totally fit." I realized that everything I was saying to describe the woman was awful.

"Is there anyone else who can help you?" George asked.

"We were supposed to meet Cybill at the continental breakfast," Cassandra said, stepping up to the counter from behind me.

"She checked us in," I said. "And then I ran into her in the bathroom Friday. I know she's here."

George beckoned someone over, a short, wide man named Julio who also had onyx orbs for eyes. "This young woman is looking for someone named . . ." George stopped and turned back to me.

"Cybill," I said.

"Right," he said. "She is looking for someone named Cybill, who she says checked her in and who told her to meet her at the continental breakfast."

"We don't have a continental breakfast," Julio said.

"That's what I just told her," George said.

"When did you arrive?" Julio asked.

"Friday evening," I said, and Julio smiled.

"You must be thinking of Suzanne," he said. "She was on duty Friday night."

I shook my head. "Not Suzanne," I said, firmly. "I'm looking for Cybill." Even with their black eyes, I could tell

George and Julio were exchanging a look, like I was one of *those* customers.

"I'm sorry, ma'am," Julio said. He must have been the manager, because something in his voice said this conversation was finished. "But we have no Cybill, and we have no continental breakfast."

"Try the hash browns from the buffet," George said.

I gave up. "I will," I said. "Thank you for your time." Cassandra and I turned and started walking toward the fabled hash browns. "What do you think all that was about?" I asked Cassandra.

"They weren't lying," she said. "They clearly had no idea who Cybill was."

"I know," I said. "But then, who was she?"

"Who knows?" Cassandra said. "But now I'd really like to find her. I don't like that . . ."

Cassandra trailed off as we walked into the cafeteria and the smell of scrambled eggs hit my nose in a way that made my nostrils flare. Instead of sitting down and eating with our group, Cass and I each took a plate and piled it high from the buffet with the plan to ferry the food directly back upstairs.

"Janis hates beans," I whispered to Cassandra, as we worked our way down the line, "so that breakfast burrito better be for you." I put as much meat on my plate as I could, plus a couple of waffles, because Pig really liked those. I wondered whether it was against the rules for us to not eat with our group, but I figured that between Cassandra's odd behavior and my supposedly contagious virus, no one was going to miss us.

As we headed out the door, I glanced back at our table. Amirah was talking, and everyone else was doubled over in laughter, Ruby collapsed on Mallory's shoulder and Ji-A sitting there with a huge smile and a look like she'd heard it all before. I liked them, even Amirah with her name-dropping and her hatred of dogs. They were probably the people in this world whom I had the most in common with, the people who might understand me better than anyone except Cassandra and Janis. And yet somehow, even in this innermost inner circle, I still felt like I didn't belong. They wore their Sisterhood status like bejeweled crowns. I schlepped mine around like an overstuffed backpack, or a plate of smelly sausage, like the one I was currently holding.

Cassandra and I rode the elevator up to the fourth floor in silence and let ourselves into room 402. Janis was in the bathroom, so I put the meaty half into the ice bucket for Pig and the other half—the half with the melon and waffles and scrambled eggs—way up high, out of her reach. Then we headed to our first session of the day. Cassandra ate her breakfast burrito on the way, and since I rarely got up early enough for breakfast, I was fine with my DIY iced coffee and half a bagel.

"I can't believe you're not taking advantage of this buffet," Cassandra said when she'd finished off the burrito. She burped, and then pulled a cinnamon roll out of her pocket. "Want?" she said, holding it out to me and gesturing toward her other pocket. "I snagged two."

"Thanks," I said. "I'm good." As we were about to walk into the session, I stopped and whispered her name. She turned around, her mouth full of cinnamon roll. "I don't think we can do this much longer," I said. "No one's going to cover for us if anything happens again." Cassandra wiped a fleck of icing off her lip and nodded. "There's no way we can get through the next three hours without something happening," I said. Not finding Cybill had left me feeling deflated. What I didn't say was that I wasn't sure I could get through the next three hours just waiting and watching for something to happen, and by the looks of her gnawed-on fingernails, Cassandra probably couldn't either.

She shook her head, and then I saw an idea move across her face like a shadow. Her eyes lit up. "For the next three hours, no," she said. "But I bet I can make it fifteen minutes."

I looked at her. Through the open door to the Jill Johnson Room I could see that, as per usual, we were the last to arrive. "What does that mean?"

She followed my gaze, then turned back and spoke hurriedly. "If she asks for volunteers, you go first," she said. "Insist. Don't let anyone else go, and then as soon as you can, pick up the heaviest thing in the room and throw it right at me." She stopped and clapped me on the arm. "I'll take care of the rest."

The Cats in Hats were also in this session, and everyone had already partnered off, leaving one empty table with two open chairs in the back for Cassandra and me. Mallory caught my eye and gave a little wave as we sat down, but nobody else seemed to even notice us. This session was taught by

Ana, who wore all black and looked like the kind of person who could intimidate someone into buying a really expensive piece of art they didn't understand. She made her entrance by suddenly appearing at the front of the room without even a pop, sizzle, or wisp of smoke, and her entrance made several people, including Amirah, jump.

Ana's voice made everyone sit up straighter in their chairs. "Kinesis," she said. "It is something you are born with, but it will take a lifetime to hone. Kinesis is diverse, and in this room alone, we have telekinesis, pyrokinesis, psychic propinquity, intangibility, astrological prowess, and curakinesis, among others. Now, would any of you like to demonstrate and explain how yours works?"

It was like we had laid a trap and Ana had walked right into it. It was so clear and obvious that there was no way I could have missed my opportunity, even if Cassandra hadn't kicked me, way harder than she needed to, under the table. Still, I hadn't expected it to happen so soon, and I'd barely had time to think about what Cassandra had told me to do. "I'm Esme, and I'm tele—" As I spoke, I picked up the nearest large object—which happened to be an empty chair—let my body be racked by a string of sneezes so that I looked like someone who had momentarily lost control as opposed to someone who never had control in the first place, and flung the chair at Cassandra.

She had told me to throw the heaviest thing I could at her, and the chair couldn't have weighed more than a few pounds, but when it hit her, it looked like they were wrestling. Somehow she got one of her arms wrapped in its legs, and then the chair was clattering to the floor, and Cassandra was standing up, cursing at me while covering one of her eyes with her hand. I heard a snicker that I was pretty sure came from Amirah. Ana was saying something about how that was a perfect demonstration of how not to use kinesis, but I couldn't hear her over Cassandra, who was still cursing as she dragged me to my feet. "I think you tore my contact," she snarled. "Walk me back to the room so I can get my glasses." I didn't look back as we left, and she kept up the act until we got to the end of the hall and turned the corner.

"Wow," Cassandra said, happily. "That was easy."

"Too easy," I said. "So easy it makes me nervous."

"Don't be," she said. "You messing up like that was totally believable."

"Wait, is that supposed to be a compliment?" I said. "Because it sure doesn't sound like one."

"Chill," she said. "I just mean you played your part well."

"Come on," I told her, "let's go kill time in our room so that getting hit in the eye with a chair is the worst thing that happens to you this session."

"Yeah," she said. "Lots of time to kill, because my glasses are going to be really hard to find."

Back in our room, I found myself pacing with nothing to distract myself. I had planned for a weekend of educational, community-building mind expansion, and instead I was trapped in a hotel room, spinning my wheels and trying to keep myself from spiraling out.

"Shouldn't we go back?" I asked. "I think I should go back, at least."

"Sure," Cassandra said, "if you want to, go." But as soon as she said it, I realized I didn't want to go back. It felt like a dream I'd had a million times before, where it's the end of the semester and I have a test in a class I haven't been to once. It was disorienting.

Janis kept peering out the window, trying to catch a glimpse of her car and freaking out about her Depop orders, which were sitting in the back of the Honda, unsent. "People want this stuff by Christmas!" she whined. "My rating is going to drop to subzero."

"Tell them you're Jewish," Cassandra said. She was sitting on our bed and flipping through the room service menu for the twenty billionth time. At this, Janis turned and gave her a look like Cass had ramen for brains, but Cassandra didn't even notice. Finally, it was time for lunch.

"Let's go get something to eat," Cassandra said, tossing the menu on the bed. "I'm starving."

"Me too," Janis said, "and Pig definitely wants her lunch."

"Dogs don't get lunch," I said.

"You're kidding," Janis said.

"Nope," I said. "Only breakfast and dinner."

"How unfair is that?" Janis said, scratching Pig's ears and mushing her face. "Well, bring some extra meat stuff, then."

I promised to grab meat stuff and other food and come right back. It seemed safest, and by now, we'd missed breakfast and most of our morning session, so Cassandra and I figured we might as well miss lunch too. The Runaway Bunnies would have been shocked if we had shown up. We did our usual cruise through the buffet, where I opted for spinach ravioli for Janis and a burger, no bun. To count as "extra meat stuff." I'd eat the fries. Cassandra, having recovered from her eye injury, piled her plate twice as high as she had at breakfast.

We could hear the screams as soon as the elevator doors opened on the fourth floor. And they sounded like they were coming from . . . our room. I started sprinting—or walking as fast as I could carrying a plate of marinara—and fumbled with the lock and then threw open the door to 402. The screams were coming from Amirah, who had a pillow in one hand and was swinging it wildly at the chicken, who was either trying to attack her or trying to escape. Pig was sitting on a bed, watching the whole thing like it was lucha libre. When the chicken finally landed on a desk chair and sat down in a puff, ruffling its feathers, Amirah spun around to face us.

"You're not sick!" she said. "You just wanted me out of this room so that you could fill it with animals!"

"Amirah," I started, setting the plate of food down on the table near the bathroom. "I can explain. It's my dog, and she couldn't stay at my house, and I had no place else for her to go." As I spoke, I covertly scanned the room. Janis had to be in here somewhere.

The chicken squawked, which made Amirah jump. It stood up and started to turn in a circle. "Oh my G-G-God," she stuttered. "It's not going to lay an egg, is it?"

"Of course not," I said, with much more surety than I felt. "It's not a real chicken."

Amirah glared at me and plucked a feather out of her hair. "It looks pretty freaking real to me." We all watched the chicken as it flew to the floor and walked into the bathroom. I had to agree: it looked pretty freaking real to me, too.

"It was a mistake," I said. "I conjured it when I was trying to get something for Pig to eat."

"There's a pig in there too?" Amirah's voice was a helium squeak.

"No, there's no pig!" I said. "It's the dog. Her name is Pig."

Amirah was looking at me like I was something she'd accidentally sat in. "If you get caught I'm not going to cover for you," she said. "I don't even like dogs."

I couldn't help myself. "How can you not like dogs?" I asked. But Amirah didn't answer me and instead started screaming as she ran toward the bathroom. "Shoo! Shoo! You filthy fowl! That's prescription!" She had spilled her weed on the bathroom floor, and the chicken was pecking away at it. At least now I knew what chickens ate.

Amirah scooped the weed that remained un-fouled by the fowl back into its canister and then left the room in a huff. I waited a bit to make sure she wasn't coming back, then called to Janis, "You can come out now." She didn't answer, and when I opened the closet door, it was empty. I was starting to worry when I heard a grunt and looked over to see Janis pulling herself out from underneath a bed.

"She's a trip," she said, pushing herself up to her feet. "How can she babysit when she smokes so much weed?"

"Well, apparently it's medicinal," Cassandra said, smiling.

Then she turned to me. "So, now we know what you were doing in the bathroom last night. But what do you plan to do about it?" She gestured toward the bathroom, where the chicken was sprawled on the floor.

"It looks dead," Janis said.

"I doubt it can die," I said. "Since it was never born." As if it had been listening to me, the chicken clucked itself back up to its wiry bird feet and then sprinted directly toward Pig. Pig scrambled to get away from it and backed herself into a corner with the chicken pecking at her paws.

"Okay," I said, walking over to the chicken. "Back in the cabinet you go." I meant to pick it up, but when I was standing next to it, I realized I had no idea how. It started flapping its wings as soon as I bent down, and I managed to just grab a handful of tail feathers, which seemed to really make it mad. Pig whimpered.

"Oh God," Cassandra said. In two strides, she was standing next to me. "I can't believe you're from Kansas and don't know how to pick up a chicken."

"Excuse me," Janis said, "Esme and I hang out at the mall, not the barnyard."

Cassandra shot her a look. "Spring River doesn't have a mall, remember?"

Janis sat down on the bed. "I know," she said, totally unoffended. "It just sounded good. Where *do* we hang out? The thrift store? The coffee shop?"

Cassandra ignored her. "When you pick up a chicken," she said, "you want to pin its wings to its sides."

"Okay," I said. "But how the heck do you know that?"

Cassandra didn't answer. Instead she bent down, but right as she was about to grab the chicken, it screeched and took off, flapping its wings like its life depended on it until it landed on the bed that Janis wasn't sitting on.

"That easy?" Janis said with a smirk.

"I thought these things aren't supposed to be able to fly," I said. Cassandra was creeping up behind the chicken for round two, and again, it managed to avoid her, making a hop just out of reach and landing on my pillow.

"This one seems to be an exceptionally tricky chicken," Cassandra said.

"That's probably because it's made from magic," I said. The bird was now trying to tear a hole in the pillow with its beak. "Stop that," I pleaded, swiping at it. "Please don't do that. If you ruin that pillow, we'll have to pay." Cassandra swooped in again, and this time she grabbed the chicken, but no sooner had she lifted it off the pillow, than it started hard-core pecking at her hand.

"Ow!" she said, dropping it again. "It bit me." She held out her hand, and sure enough, it was bleeding. "I will turn you into soup," she snarled at the chicken.

"No offense," Janis said, "but you two have superpowers and you are literally getting owned by a bird right now."

At the same time, Cassandra and I both raised our hands at the chicken and said, "Avikinesis." I was about to say "jinx" when I realized what had happened. I said, "Oh no," instead. Getting hit with double bird manipulation had indeed manipulated the chicken. There were now two of them.

"Frick," Cassandra said, then looked at me. "How did you conjure this thing in the first place?"

"Meat manipulation gone wrong," I said.

"Maybe no more magic?" Cassandra said. "We'll just keep them in the bathroom and go in there only when necessary."

"Well, let me use it first," Janis said, walking in and turning on the shower.

"You're going to shower now?" I called to her in disbelief.

She stepped into the doorway to answer me. "Yes, I'm going to shower. What are you, the hygiene police? I smell like dog."

Then, before she could shut the door, one of the chickens—either the real fake thing or the replica of the real fake thing—launched itself at her. It made a sound like a broken kazoo and its wings flapped furiously. The other chicken started to run in circles, and Pig began to bark. "No," I hissed. "No barking. Bad dog! Bad dog!"

Faced with a flying chicken coming right at her nose, Janis screamed and grabbed the handheld showerhead, squirting a stream of hot water at the bird. Then she dropped the showerhead and ran out of the bathroom. Through the door, I could see water shooting at the walls and the toilet and puddling on the floor.

"Janis! You're flooding the bathroom!" I yelled. "It's just a bird." Then one of the chickens came at me, and I dove out of its way. Pig barked again and the other chicken took off. I think it was aiming for the TV, but it flew close to Cassandra, who reached out and managed to catch it by one of its feet. It flapped like crazy as Cassandra tried to keep ahold of it.

She and the chicken were locked in a vicious battle, and the bird became a blur as it flapped its wings trying to get away. Cassandra closed her eyes as one of its wings hit her in the face. As she carried it toward the bathroom, she stepped in the ice bucket right outside the bathroom door. Cassandra knocked into the table, upsetting the lunch plates and sending ravioli hailing down on the floor.

Cassandra crashed into the bathroom door, which sent the chicken slamming into the side of the bathtub. Cassandra then fell through the spraying water, hitting the floor with a splash followed a millisecond later by the sickening crack of her head making contact with the base of the toilet before it joined the rest of her body on the floor. Thinking it had won, the chicken twisted away and then jumped onto Cassandra. It squawked triumphantly.

"Cass?" I said, but she didn't move. In an instant, I was in the bathroom. With one hand, I swept the chicken off her and then turned off the spraying showerhead before kneeling next to Cassandra. The water that had pooled on the floor soaked through my jeans.

She was out.

"Cassandra?" I said. "Cassandra? Can you hear me?" I was just about to panic and run screaming for Mallory when Cass's eyelids fluttered. She groaned as she started to shake her head from side to side.

"Ugh," she said, wincing as she pushed herself up. "What happened? Were we doing a Return?"

"Um, not exactly," I said. "You fell and hit your head on the toilet trying to catch a chicken."

"Oh God," she said. "Why am I all wet?"

"Janis tried to spray the chicken with the shower and things got a little out of hand." I helped Cassandra up and, with water dripping off her, we walked to the bed, where she sat down. The chickens and Pig, seeming to sense that things had gotten serious, had called a truce and were sitting together, silently watching us. Janis came over and squatted down in front of Cassandra, then leaned forward and pried one of her eyelids even farther open. Cassandra jerked away.

"Your pupils are fine," Janis said, standing back up. "And considering you were only out for a few seconds, it's probably nothing serious. Does your head hurt?" Cassandra put one hand up and started to feel around on her skull.

"A little tender," she said, "but nothing too bad." She pointed at the chickens and gave them the evil eye. "So, you've won for now," she said. "But later, you are going in that fricking cabinet. Come on," she said, standing up and turning to me, "we'd better get to this session."

"You're soaked," I said. "Do you want to change?"

"I don't have any other clothes," she said, and shrugged. "I'll dry."

Janis settled back onto the bed as we got ready to leave. "You know, I don't think I need to shower after all," she said.

"That's probably a good idea," I said. "And don't let Pig eat all the lunch."

"Too late," Janis said. She was right—Pig was already scarfing ravioli off the floor.

CHAPTER 19

The party was looming in the near future, though it seemed like something we'd hardly thought about as we took the elevator downstairs for our final session of the day: Sitter history, with all groups in the Laurie Strode Auditorium and Wanda herself doing the lecturing. Cass was being her usual self, walking about ninety mph and at least five feet in front of me, and I practically had to run to keep up as I followed her into the auditorium. Suddenly she stopped, and I stumbled out of the way so I didn't smack into her. My heart stuttered in panic. Not another episode, I thought, not right now, but then I saw she was staring at something in her hands.

It was an old photo, one she had shown me before, one of our moms, and me and Cassandra when we were babies, proof that our moms had been present once and that Cassandra and I went in-the-womb way back. Now the photo was soaking wet, and the image was starting to peel away from the paper in some places.

"It was in my pocket. It's soaked," Cassandra said, sounding as distraught as I'd ever heard her. "It's my only copy."

Gently, I took the photo from her. "It's okay," I said. "It's not ruined, we can blow-dry it once we get back . . ." My words dried up in my throat as I looked at it, squinting. "Oh my God," I said, then I turned and ran.

Cassandra chased after me. "Esme, where are you going? Give it back!" she yelled, catching up to me just as I practically slammed into the front desk.

Unfortunately, our good friend George was working. "Excuse me," I said. "A woman who was working here on Friday night, her name was Cybill. I need to find her immediately."

"I'm sorry, ma'am," he said, his lips tight around the words, "as I've told you before, we have no employees by that name." Then, clearly done with me, George turned and busied himself with the printer.

"The woman who helped us in the bathroom," I said, turning to Cassandra. "Did you notice anything unusual about her?"

Cass shook her head. "I was bleeding and wearing a shirt for pants at the time, so no."

"Something seemed off," I said. "Her eyes were black like everyone else's, but they were watery. She was the only one who looked like she was physically bothered by the spell. I remember it, because it made me feel bad for her because it looked like she was uncomfortable. But it's because she wasn't under a spell. She was wearing contacts, and they were uncomfortable!"

"I don't get it," Cassandra said.

"It was a disguise," I said. "She wanted to look like she was under a spell without actually being under a spell."

"Why would a hotel employee wear a disguise to look like she was under a spell?"

"Because she wasn't a hotel employee," I said. "That's why she told us to meet her. She wanted to help us. She wanted to help you, because she's your mom."

Cassandra's face twisted and she took a step away from me. "Esme, don't joke about this. It's not funny."

"I'm not joking," I said. "She was there when you had an episode in the bathroom, and she didn't act like someone under a spell, and I thought she looked familiar, but I didn't place her until I looked at the photo."

Cass turned and stared at the desk.

"They have to tell us where she is, then," she said, but before she could walk away I grabbed her arm.

"They don't know," I said. "They're under a spell that makes them not notice anything unusual. Your mom was unusual, so they wouldn't have blinked a black eye at her presence."

Cassandra looked shocked. Her eyes were wide, and her hair was still wet and plastered to her neck. "If she's here, this close, then where is she? Why would she leave before she talked to me?"

"There must be some reason why she's hiding," I said. "It must not be safe for her or . . ."

The look on Cassandra's face changed, like some switch

had just been flipped. Her eyes and mouth turned into ovals of surprise. "Oh my God," she said. "I remember."

"Your mom?" I asked, and she shook her head.

"No, not that," she said. "But everything else. Everything I learned in the Negative. Everything I wasn't supposed to."

"Holy crap," I said. We both just stood there, silent, and I could tell from the glint in Cassandra's eyes that her brain was working at light speed.

"Esme," she said, "I think this means the curse is gone."

"W-w-wait, what?" I stuttered. "What do you mean? How?"

Cassandra's eyes darted around the room and settled on the hotel entrance. "I have no idea," she said. "What happened back in our room?"

"You hit your head and lost consciousness for a second," I said. "But that couldn't be all it takes to remove a curse. That'd be too easy."

She bit her lip and nodded. "What else was going on?"

"Well," I started, "there were two fake chickens flying around, and Pig was barking, and Janis was spraying water everywhere, and then you put your foot in an ice bucket and spilled the tomato sauce and—"

Cassandra held her hand up to stop me. "We'll have to figure it out later," she said. "We don't have time now, because we have to go talk to my dad." She started toward the elevator, then paused. "Do you think Janis will let us borrow her car?"

But her question barely registered with me, because I was

standing there, rooted to the floor, my mouth open in disbelief. "W-w-wait," I stammered. "We have to go talk to *who*?"

Yes, I had heard her right. Her dad. I chased Cassandra into
the elevator, and we rode in silence up to our room, where
we interrupted Janis, who appeared to be in the middle of a
photo shoot, trying to get the chickens to balance on top of
Pig's head.

"Look," she said, "they're friends now!"

"Janis, Cassandra remembers!" I gasped as the chickens
tumbled off Pig.

"Remembers what?" Janis asked, momentarily giving up.

"Everything!" Cassandra said. "Look, I'll explain later.
Janis, we need to use your car."

"Oh, heck no," she said. "Isn't this the same crap you
pulled on Halloween?"

"Not exactly," Cassandra said. "That time, we were chasing down a kidnapped kid. This time, the stakes are much
higher."

Janis nodded slowly. "And what am I supposed to do while
you two go crashing around in my Honda?"

"Stay here, and stay out of sight," Cassandra said.

"No way," Janis said. "I've had enough of that. You can
borrow my car, but I'm coming with."

Cassandra and I exchanged a look. "Fine," she said. "But
we have to go now."

"Do you think we can just leave?" I asked.

"Of course not," Cassandra said. "But right now is our

best chance to sneak out. Everyone's in the auditorium, so there's a greater chance no one will notice we're gone."

Janis sighed. "Okay," she said. "Let me get my keys." Pig was keeping a close eye on us, sensing she might be about to get left behind.

"We should take her," Janis said, noticing Pig's jumpiness also. "She doesn't like being cooped up in here any more than I do. I tried to get her to pee in the tub again, but she's freaked out by the bathroom now that it's all wet. She won't even go inside it."

"Oh, Piggy," I sighed. I bent down and stroked her head. "Such a sensitive blockhead you are. Okay, come on." As I was grabbing Pig's leash, Cassandra opened the door and shut it again immediately.

"How are we going to get Janis and Pig out of here?" she asked.

"The way I got them in," I said. "We take the stairs and we run." Cassandra shook her head.

"No way," she said. "It's too risky. It's one thing to get caught sneaking them in; it's so much more to get caught sneaking them out. The Synod will zap their brains for sure."

At this, Janis froze and started to shake her head. "No, no, no," she said. "I don't want that to happen." She looked at the door. "I guess I'm staying here, then. But before I give you my keys, you at least have to tell me what's going on."

Cassandra still had one hand on the door. "When I came back from the Negative, I remembered everything at first," she said. "But I was tired, and we had to get that kid home, and I'd basically just had my world rocked by the revelation that my brother, who I'd always thought was an idiot, was even dumber than I had imagined and that he was also a backstabber. And it was confusing. I wanted to sleep and needed time to process everything. To write stuff down. So when we got home that night, I locked Dion in a closet and then passed out. But when I woke up in the morning, my head was empty. I couldn't remember the very thing I had wanted to spend time thinking about. I don't know if you've ever come back to your room, and you can just tell someone has been there, even though they tried not to leave a trace?"

I shook my head, but Janis nodded. "Jason, my little brother. He's always going through my stuff, looking for quarters. He thinks he's being sneaky, but I can tell, because everything's just a little neater than it was before."

Cassandra nodded. "Exactly," she said. "But it was like someone had done that to my brain. And when I tried to think of the Negative, I knew it was bad, but I couldn't remember any specifics, even though I knew I'd known them at some point. But now I do remember specifics," she said. "A lot of them, which is how I know the curse is gone. You can't use mnenokinesis on a Sitter, but you can curse them so they won't remember stuff and so no one will take them seriously if they do. That's what all the demons said had happened to your mom."

"Wait, you talked to them?" I gasped. "And they talked about my mom?"

Cassandra nodded. "They know about her because my dad talks about her. That has to be why I was cursed too. It wasn't to get us back for anything, or for ransom. It was so that we wouldn't be able to remember or to talk. But now I remember everything I learned on Halloween." She stopped, and paused for so long that I wasn't sure she was going to start again.

"And?" Janis said. "Don't leave us hanging."

"The demons talked to me," Cassandra continued. "They knew I was Erebus's daughter, and so they talked to me about him."

"What did they say?"

"Some of them wanted to complain about him. Apparently, half my genes come from a person even demons find annoying. But others wanted to find out what I thought about everything he's saying."

"What is he saying?" I asked, trying to follow.

"He claims he was falsely imprisoned and that he's innocent of the charges brought against him," Cassandra said.

"Ha, isn't that what all guilty people say?"

"Sure, but they seem to believe him. And they're demons, so wouldn't they be able to spot a lie?"

I huffed. It was a flimsy argument, but also the only argument we had at the moment. "Sure," I said, "why not?"

"Apparently, he told everyone down there that there was one person who could corroborate his story and that he was going to find her as soon as he got out."

"Your mom?" I asked.

Cassandra shook her head. "No," she said. "*Your* mom."

"No way," I said, shocked. "*He's* the whole reason my mom is the way she is. She can't even string together a sentence because of him, and he thinks she would stand up for him?"

"I don't know!" Cassandra protested. "I'm just telling you what they told me."

"Erebus thinks my mom would help him?" I asked. I wanted to laugh at how ridiculous that sounded, but there was a part of me that was starting to take it seriously. "The first thing she said when she came back was, 'Don't let him leave.' She hates him." I sat there and let what Cass was saying wash over me. "What do we do? We can't ask her. And if he didn't curse her, then who did?"

"I have an idea," Cassandra said, "but it's a long shot, and I need some proof. So we're going to ask him."

"You're not thinking of opening up that hole again?" Janis said, and to my relief, Cassandra shook her head.

"No way," she said. "We'll use the 8 Ball. We just have to go and get it. So . . ." She plastered a smile on her face and batted her eyelashes as she held out one hand to Janis. "Your keys, please."

For what felt like the millionth time already that morning, Cassandra and I took the elevator back downstairs. She was right—everyone else was in the Laurie Strode Auditorium, waiting for Wanda's Sitter history lecture, and when we turned the opposite way and headed down the hall to the back entrance, we didn't pass a single person. I was starting to get used to this feeling. Everyone else was learning, or dining, or hanging out—and Cassandra and I were in the hall.

We pushed the back door open. Janis's car was still parked in the same spot where she'd left it that night. Its doors weren't locked, and the backseat was filled with packed and ready-to-go Depop boxes. Cassandra climbed into the driver's seat, and I got in and buckled my seat belt. When she turned the key to start the car, I braced myself for the sounds of "Jingle Bell Rock." Instead, there was just static.

I took a closer look at the radio as Cassandra pulled out of the parking lot. That was weird. It was tuned to a station that I knew for a fact existed. I hit Scan and it stopped on the next frequency up. There were a few notes of "White Christmas" before the DJ cut in.

"Folks, sorry to interrupt that classic," he said, "'cause I know how much ya love it, but I've got an emergency update here from animal control. As of now, they have still not been able to capture that bobcat everyone's been seeing around town."

"I'll tell you what, Bob," a female voice broke in, "it sure doesn't sound like a bobcat to me."

"Well, that's what they're saying it is, hahaha," Bob said, laughing nervously. "And they're suggesting that everyone stay inside, with the shades drawn and the doors locked, until they get a handle on the situation."

"Sure, sure," said the female voice, "We will let you know updates as we hear them, but in the meantime, here's some 'Jingle Bell Rock' for you, and our condolences go out to our fellow station, KMWA over at 102.5." She cleared her throat. "Apparently this bobcat took out their tower last night." Then the music came back on, and Cassandra switched the radio off.

"Bobcat, my butt," she said, as she ran a red light to make

a left turn. It didn't seem to matter—there were no cars on the street.

"That sounds like a demon to me," I said. "Exactly what those people were talking about in Janis's feed. The one I saw yesterday was a Flash, and even the city government couldn't pretend that was a bobcat, so there has to be more than one. What's going on? The Portal is supposed to be sealed."

"It's clearly not, though," Cassandra said, slowing down as she swerved around a large tree branch that had fallen in the middle of the street, looking like it had been ripped right off the rest of the tree.

"When I told Wanda about the demon outside the hotel, she said it was probably one that we let slip through before the Portal was sealed."

"She's lying," Cassandra said. "Because we don't make mistakes like that."

"But it is sealed in a way," I said, "because I couldn't get it open for a Return. So maybe it's like a one-way seal? But why would the Synod do that? Why would they want all the demons to come out of the Negative, but not go back in?" Just saying it out loud sent a chill down my spine.

"I don't know," Cassandra said, "but there's no way it's good."

When we pulled up at her house, I could tell she was worried about Dion by the way she jumped out of the car and practically ran up the sidewalk. I was on her heels as she went straight to Dion's bedroom and threw the door open without knocking. Even though it was the middle of the afternoon, he was asleep, a pizza box with a half-eaten pizza taking up the other side of his bed.

Cassandra went down the hall to her room and came out holding a block of ice. She turned on the hot water in the bathroom sink and put the ice block under it. As the ice melted, she kept stepping out into the hallway and looking toward Dion's room. He must be a really heavy sleeper.

"Do you want to bring him back to the hotel with us?" I asked.

"No," she said. "But I am going to order him to stay in the house and hide, until this thing is over. If I tell him to do it, he will."

The ice was melting, and Cassandra banged it against the side of the sink, breaking off a chunk, and then she set the 8 Ball in the sink. She went back to Dion's room and kicked his mattress. He grunted and rolled over, but didn't wake up. Cassandra grabbed the edge of his comforter and yanked it off the bed. Sudden exposure to the cold air shocked Dion into sitting up, and he looked around, confused as hell. Even in my pretty-much-hating-Dion state, I had to admit that just-waking-up-Dion was a good look.

"What the . . . ?" he choked out. The panic on his face was replaced with annoyance as he realized the *what* was his sister. He took the edge of the comforter and yanked it back. "What time is it and why are you even home?" he asked, pulling the comforter up to his chin.

"It's after noon," Cassandra said. "Most people are up by now."

"There was an *Are You Afraid of the Dark?* marathon on last night," he said, pushing himself up to sitting, "and when it was done, I realized I *am* afraid of the dark, and couldn't fall alseep until the sun came up."

Cassandra sighed. "Listen to me for a second," she said, and Dion's face got serious. "I'm not staying here, and you can sleep all day if you want, but you have to do it in the basement, and you cannot leave the house. Under no circumstances do you leave here," she repeated. "Esme and I are leaving, and you dead bolt the door behind us, and go to the basement, okay?" She paused. "You can leave the light on."

Dion didn't argue, but just stood up and grabbed his comforter like it was a blankie. "Hi, Esme," he said, looking out into the hall at me.

"Hi, Dion," I said.

Cassandra went back in the bathroom, where the ice had melted and the 8 Ball sat in the bathroom sink under a stream of running water. She turned off the faucet, dried the 8 Ball off, and then wrapped it in a towel. She headed toward the door. I followed her, and Dion followed me. When Cassandra and I were on the porch, she turned to him. "Go to the basement, remember?" she said. "And don't come out until I come back and tell you it's okay."

Dion nodded. "Got it," he said, then gave us a cheery wave. "Have fun!" He shut the door, and I heard the dead bolt slide into place with a click.

Cassandra and I walked to the car, and when we were both in, she tossed the 8 Ball into my lap before she started the car. "Come on, you a-hole," I said, shaking the 8 Ball, "talk to us." I flipped it over. Blue bubbles and then an icosahedron floated to the surface.

Reply hazy, try again.

So I did. "Come on, you a-hole. Talk to us."

My sources say no.

I turned to Cass. "Cass, when you were in the Negative, you used it to talk to me. How?"

"It was easy," she said. "I just thought about it, and then you answered."

"So we can't talk to Erebus," I said, "unless he wants to talk to us."

Cassandra nodded, as she suddenly spun the wheel into a right turn. "Which is why we're taking him to the person he most wants to talk to."

"My mom," I said, and swallowed nervously. Cassandra floored it.

We pulled up to Mom's facility and Cassandra parked in a loading zone. She took the 8 Ball from me, and we got out and ran up the steps two at a time. The entrance was locked, but I was able to use my kinesis to open it easily. The front desk was usually staffed with at least three people, but only Marie was sitting there. "Girls," she said, gasping, and jumped up from her seat. "How did you get in here? Wasn't the door locked?"

Crap. I liked Marie and didn't want to worry her. "It wasn't," I lied. "But we made sure it is now."

Marie frowned as she sat back down. "I don't like that at all," she said. "We're trying to make sure no one, or no thing, gets in or out." Her voice dropped as she looked around quickly to make sure no residents might have heard her. "You two shouldn't be out by yourselves," she said.

"It's okay," Cassandra said. "We can handle it. We've got a gun." I almost kicked Cassandra in the shin, but Marie actually seemed to find it comforting.

"You've seen the news, then?" she said. "What do you think it is? They're saying it's a bobcat or something, but I don't know. . . . My husband says I'm being silly and that I've got too much imagination."

I didn't want to say anything that would make Marie distrust her own correct intuition, but I also didn't want to worry her. "It's probably a bobcat," I said, slowly. "Or something."

She swallowed and nodded. I noticed a holiday tin sitting next to her, filled with tiny brown balls that, truth be told, did not look appetizing at all. "Ooh," I forced myself to squeal, "are those your rum balls?"

Sufficiently distracted, Marie clapped her hands, then reached for the tin. "Oh, you know it," she said, holding it out to us. "One per person, please."

Cassandra and I each took one and popped them into our mouths. "Wow," I said, as my tongue was coated with chocolate and spices. I had been totally wrong. "These are delicious."

Marie beamed, and Cassandra nodded. "This is the best Christmas cookie I've ever had," she said.

"There's rum in them," Marie said, with a wink, "so

don't tell your mom. Come on, I'll let you in the ward." We waited for Marie to walk out from behind the desk, and as soon as her back was to us, Cassandra reached over the desk and grabbed two more rum balls.

Mom's ward was half-empty, and she was sitting outside of her room wearing a Fort Lauderdale sweatshirt and a pair of acid-washed jeans. Her hair was pulled back with an Arizona Razorbacks scrunchie, and she was gripping the arms of her chair.

"Hi, Mom," I said, talking to her the way I had ever since I'd learned she could hear and understand everything I was saying. "Some bobcat, huh?" I held out the 8 Ball. "We brought someone who wants to talk to you." I took her by the elbow and she stood up, and then we walked back into her room. Cassandra shut the door behind us, and I helped Mom sit down on the bed. "We need to ask Erebus some questions," I said. "We can talk to him through this toy, because it's somehow enchanted to make one-way calls from the Negative." Suddenly, I had a thought, and I looked up at Cassandra as I held the 8 Ball. "This is Red Magic, isn't it?" I said. "Whatever it is that makes this a communication device."

"Oh, most definitely," she said.

I turned back to Mom. "We don't know how to get ahold of him, but we know he wants to talk to you," I explained. "We were hoping that if you held it, he would show up." I put the 8 Ball in Mom's hands and then wrapped my hands around hers. Then I shook our hands and turned the ball over.

You may rely on it, it said. Then, before my eyes, the icosahedron started to spin, and when it surfaced again, it said, *Ah, Theresa,* and I could practically hear Erebus's slimy voice saying the words. *It's been too long.*

We had him.

I took the ball from Mom and shook it again.

"Sorry, loser," I said. "It's us. We need to talk." I passed the 8 Ball to Cassandra, who shook it.

"Hello, Father," she said. "Remember me?"

She held it out so I could see the answer. *Haha.* Then, *How could I forget?* It spun again. *How are you?*

"Doing pretty good," she said. "Except I was cursed for a while. I'm not anymore, but the town is being ravaged by demons and we're supposed to be shut up in a hotel for a Summit."

The icosahedron started to spin furiously, and when it came up, it just said *Moan.* Then it spun again. *Summits are the worst,* it said. *A bunch of Sitters getting together to pat themselves on the back.* It was amazing how sneering insults seemed to lose their vitriol when delivered just a few words at a time.

"Do you know who would want to curse me?" Cassandra asked.

No one down here, it said. *I wouldn't let anyone curse my daughter.* Cassandra looked at me and rolled her eyes.

"But you did curse my mom, right?" I said, deciding to see whether I could provoke him.

Did not.

"Did too."

Did not, it still said, and I stopped myself when I could see where this was going.

"You hate my mom," I said.

I do.

"And she hates you."

She does.

"But . . . ," I started, not sure where I was going with this, and then it hit me. "But you have common enemies."

The icosahedron flipped again. *True.*

Cassandra took the 8 Ball from me and shook it. "When I was in the Negative, the demons down there said you swear you're innocent."

False, it said, just like Dwight Schrute.

"So you're guilty?" she asked.

As charged, it said. Cassandra and I looked at each other. Mom was sitting on her bed, and I could tell from her stiff, straight spine and clenched fists that she was paying close attention. *But I'm not the only one.* Flip. *They want the power.* Flip. *But I take the blame.*

Cassandra looked at me. "Who do you think he's talking about?"

I knew exactly who he was talking about. I just knew. And when I looked at Mom, her face still and blank, with all of her thoughts and emotions Saran-wrapped inside so tightly that they'd never reach the surface, I didn't have any doubt.

"It has to be the Synod," I said, looking at Cassandra. "I mean, I always thought that maybe he just discovered Red Magic on his own." I placed my hand over the 8 Ball's window, just in case Erebus could hear me. "But I think that's giving him too much credit. It makes a lot more sense if someone gave it to him." I uncovered the window and then shook the 8 Ball so that he would hear me. "So the Synod had you training in Red Magic, and when they got found out, they cursed my mom and banished you, sealing the Portal so you wouldn't come back and talk." I shook the 8 Ball again. "Is that what happened?" I asked.

You are smarter than you look, it said. I rolled my eyes and resisted the urge to smash the 8 Ball. I wonder whether this was how my mom felt—needing the help of someone she despised.

"Why would they do that, though?" I asked.

The answer was one word. *Power.* For a moment I was dumbfounded. That made no sense. Who could be more powerful than the Synod? They could erase an entire town's memory. They could appear out of thin air. They had everything. Except . . . Beanie Babies. My mind flashed to Adrian telling me about Wanda, and how she was selling off her possessions so that she could buy more Beanie Babies off the internet. That didn't sound powerful. That sounded pathetic.

I looked at Cassandra, who walked over and slowly took the 8 Ball back. "I think we need to get back there. Now," I said, then stood up and went over and threw my arms around Mom in a big hug. As I squeezed her, I didn't want to let go. "I love you, Mom," I said, pulling away. "I'll see you soon." She remained totally still.

When we were in the hallway, I pulled the door to her

room shut. There was no way to lock it, but I glanced up and down the hall to make sure no one was looking, then raised my hand and used my kinesis to slide her heavy dresser in front of the door on the other side. For now, that would have to do.

Back at the front desk, we said goodbye to Marie. "You girls be safe," she said.

"We will," I said. "You too."

"Rum ball for the road?" Cassandra asked.

Marie smiled and held up the tin. "Oh, sure," she said. "Go ahead and take two."

CHAPTER 20

When we got back in the car, the street was just as quiet as when we left it. It was like all of Spring River had become a ghost town, not a single person or living thing to be seen. I could tell the demons were out there, though, by the emotional pull and the weird skittering feeling I'd get occasionally, like something was just on the other side of a wall or behind a bush. Then Cassandra turned a corner, about half a mile from the hotel, and in the distance I saw something that made me do a double take. A person walking alone.

"Turn here," I said. "There's someone ahead." Cassandra turned, and as we got closer to the walker, I could see it was a woman, her hair pulled back under a baseball cap. Closer still, and I could see she was about our age. At the sound of the car, she turned around, and that was when I could see her face. And it wasn't just any girl. It was a girl I knew well: turtle-smashing, dodgeball-dominating Stacey Wasser, Spring River's biggest bully, my own personal demon before I ever knew that real demons existed. She'd destroyed my projects in freshman-year art class, pelted me with sporting goods in junior-year gym and delighted in every sadistic second of it.

Cassandra rolled down her window. "Hey!" she called to Stacey. "What are you doing out here?" Cassandra was not known for her grace, and I could almost see a ridge of fur rise up on Stacey's back as she took the concerned question as an accusation.

"What are *you* doing out here?" she shot back. And then I gasped. Not at Stacey, but at what had just appeared behind her. It must have been hiding behind a car, crouching, but now it stood and drew itself up to its full height, its claws like Argentine steak knives, its vicious face dripping goo, and the hole in its neck gaping. I recognized it from the demonology books—it had no eyes, so it went by smell. If Stacey moved a few feet downwind, she'd be fine, but right now, she was exactly in its line of sniff.

I leaned over. "Stacey," I said, keeping my voice steady, "move slowly and quietly and start walking backward. Do it, *now.*"

The logo on Stacey's baseball cap was a hand, made from a weed leaf, giving the middle finger. "Yeah, right, loser," she said. "Since when do you tell me what to do?" Then, of course, she did the exact opposite of what I'd just told her to do. She took two steps in the wrong direction, turned, and that was when she saw the demon.

I could see its face twitch as it took in her scent, and then it lifted a paw, claws flexed and glinting. Its swing cut through the air the same time as Stacey's scream. She dropped to the ground and it just missed her, one of its claws catching on her hat. Cassandra and I were out of the car in an instant. Cassandra's fire engulfed the demon, but it was so wet and sticky that it hissed and crackled like damp wood and didn't catch. It was about to strike again, so I held out my hands and managed to grab one of its limbs with my kinesis. It was strong, and I grunted with effort as I pulled its arm and twisted it behind its back. The demon roared in pain, and Cassandra took advantage of its open mouth to shoot a ball of fire straight down its throat. Stacey was screaming a stream of expletives more creative than a comedy special, and this time when I told her to run, she didn't argue.

The demon was slippery, and Cassandra hit it with another fireball just as it wriggled out of my grasp. I managed to get ahold of its head and tried to push it to the ground. Stacey was running, but not fast enough. I could see a ripple of recognition move across the demon's face as it got its bearings and figured out where she was and then started striding after her. Stacey was running at full speed. Faster, even, than I'd ever seen her move in gym class when she wanted to slam someone into a pole or elbow them out of the way. The demon threw one of its arms back, ready to strike. I tried to grab it, but missed. Fortunately, Stacey was kind of zigzagging, which caused the demon to miss. This also pissed it off. It raised its other arm to strike, and I knew it wouldn't miss again.

In that second, I didn't even think, I just did. I raised both hands, mustered everything I had, and grabbed the demon's head with the pure concentration of all my power. This time, I didn't pull, or push. I twisted, and twisted, until I heard a snap, like chopsticks breaking in two. It took a second. The demon stood there, wavering, and then gravity took over. It fell to the ground in a pile like a dropped ice cream sundae.

Stacey was on her butt, looking back and forth rapidly between the pile of demon, me, and Cassandra. I walked over to her and held out my hand to help her up. She looked dazed, and it was hard to tell what she was thinking. She took my hand, and when I pulled her to her feet, she still didn't say anything.

"Are you okay?" I asked.

She nodded, but she wasn't looking at me. Her eyes were over my shoulder and moving, and I turned, wondering whether there was something else coming our way. Cassandra was standing stock-still, staring at me. I met her eyes for a second, and then we both looked away. We both knew what I had just done, and we both knew I had no other choice. Stacey gave a little grunt of joy. She'd spotted her hat. She walked over, picked it up, and slapped it against her legs a couple of times to knock off any dust, then she put it back on, even though the top had been sliced to shreds.

"What was that thing?" she asked, and I decided to level with her.

"It's a demon from the underworld," I said. "They're running rampant around these parts." I sounded like a B-movie cowboy talking about coyotes. "Haven't you seen the news?" She nodded. "Spring River's kind of under siege right now. You shouldn't be out and about."

"You're out and about," she said.

"True," I said. "But we're equipped. We have special powers. Remember that time I threw a dodgeball at your nose without even touching it?" But of course, she didn't, because her memory was wiped just like everyone else's in our town. The Synod had done that for practically anything before—a few weird incidents that could have been explained away, and demons that didn't even leave the mall. Now our whole town was being destroyed. What kind of heavy-duty spell would it take to erase all memory of that? Stacey was still looking at me blankly. "Never mind," I said. "We're kind of in a hurry. Where were you going anyway?"

"I was going to the Kros N' Go," she said. "I want chips."

I grimaced, because I empathized. "You should probably just go home. Where do you live?" She pointed back down the street. "We can take you."

"Yeah," she said. "But I'm really hungry. And we don't have any food at my house. I was going to get lots of chips so that I don't have to go out again later." She took a step toward me, and I instinctively flinched. But she was smiling, and she didn't stop until she was standing really close. "Have you seen the Kros N' Go?" she almost whispered.

I looked at Cassandra, and then we both shook our heads. "Someone ran a car into it or something," she said. "The front window is all smashed in, and the people who work there left. The Icee machine ran out, but other than that, you can just take whatever you want."

I felt my eyebrows furrow. "So this isn't the first time

you've come out of the house?" I asked, incredulous, and Stacey shook her head.

"How many times have you gone to the Kros N' Go?"

She shrugged. "I don't know," she said. "Whenever I want a snack."

"Stacey," I said, "you've been risking your life for Cheetos?"

"Of course not," she huffed. "Cheetos are gross. I take the Funyuns." Then she frowned. "Though I took the last bag of Flamin' Hot yesterday, and I don't like the original as much, but if that's all they have left, that's fine."

I sighed. "So you're not going to go home?" I asked.

"Not without a tasty treat," she said. I looked over at Cassandra, and I couldn't believe I was about to do this, but it seemed like the only option if we didn't want Stacey Wasser to become the nibble.

"Come on," I said, "we'll take you there. But like I said, we're in a hurry, so you have to be fast."

"Oh, I'm fast," she said, proudly, "'cause I don't want to be there when the workers come back from their break."

Fortunately, the Kros N' Go was only a block away, so we piled in Janis's car and were there in two seconds. Cassandra parked on the sidewalk, and we entered the store by climbing through the broken window, which had been completely smashed out, and then Stacey walked behind the counter and grabbed a couple of plastic bags. She handed one to me, and one to Cassandra, and then she started walking up and down the aisles, filling her bag.

At one point, she turned to me and smiled. "See, isn't this great?" she asked. "It's like shopping, but you don't have to pay for anything."

I was about to tell her there was a name for this, and it was looting, when I looked over to see Cassandra, who was filling up her own bag. Then I spotted a bag of Gold-Bears, and my mouth started to water. Oh, what the heck? I'd already killed a demon, so today was not the day to stand on principle. I grabbed the bag, ripped it open, and shoved two greens and a white straight into my mouth.

Stacey took all the Funyuns the Kros N' Go had to offer, and also got several jugs of milk, a few packs of gum, and whatever else she could stuff into her pockets and bags, and then we all climbed back in the car to take her home.

"This is me," Stacey said, pointing to a house midway down an empty street.

"Okay," I said, as she got out of the car. "Be careful. And stay inside!"

She stopped and turned around. "I'm gonna," she said. "And I'd thank you for saving my life back there, but I guess we're even now."

"Wait, what?" I asked. I had no idea what she was talking about.

One of the bags of chips was starting to slip from under her arm, and she shifted a bit so that she could get a better hold on it. "I told you about the Kros N' Go," she said. "You probably got at least forty bucks of stuff there." She shifted the chips again. "So, I don't owe you nothing."

I was sitting there, looking at Stacey Wasser, who was wearing a shredded baseball cap that was stupid even when it had been in one piece, her arms full of stolen snack foods, and I had a hard time remembering why I'd spent almost every day of my freshman year scared to death of this person.

"Yeah," I said. "You're right. We're totally even. So, see you around."

I tried not to think about how much time Cassandra and I had lost to this insane interlude, but Stacey Wasser's life was worth it. Anybody's life would have been worth it.

We zoomed back toward the hotel, and Cassandra was having fun with the fact that the streets were empty. How could I tell? Because she drove on the left side of the street and went the wrong way down one-ways whenever the opportunity presented itself. When we reached the hotel, she drove through the parking lot and slammed on the brakes, parking Janis's car where we had first found it.

Cassandra grabbed the 8 Ball and we got out of the car. As we ran toward the hotel, she started laughing. "I have to give you credit, Pearl," she said. "I can't believe you snuck an eighty-pound dog and a full-sized human in here."

"Seventy-two-pound dog," I corrected her. "Pig is very svelte these days."

We ran for the hotel's back entrance, which was, of course, locked, but I was able to use my kinesis to open it and Cassandra and I slipped back inside. As soon as we did, she turned and smiled at me. Our timing was perfect. The Sitter history lecture had just been dismissed, so everyone was milling in the hallways getting ready for the party.

Ugh. A party that was supposed to be our responsibility. A party that I hadn't even thought about all day. I wondered how much Brian hated me, hated both of us right now. Then again, maybe us shirking our soiree duties was the best thing that could have happened to Brian because it let him do what he loved.

We ran up the stairs, exiting on the fourth floor like I was Bill Murray and it was Groundhog Day. The hallway was pretty empty save for a couple of girls at the other end, so Cassandra and I walked down it as calmly as possible and let ourselves back into our room.

As soon as we stepped inside, I could tell something was wrong. It was too quiet, and there was no sign of Janis, Pig, or our feathered friends.

"Janis?" I called softly, and then the closet door burst open and all four tumbled out. Janis looked terrified and she came running over to me.

"There was someone in the room," she said, half whispering and looking around like maybe they weren't gone. "Someone came into the room."

"Maybe Amirah?" I asked. "Coming to get something she forgot?"

Janis shook her head. "No, I've met Amirah, and she's not quiet," she said. "Whoever this was, they were sneaking. I couldn't even hear their feet. But they moved stuff around, and then left again."

"Housekeeping?" Though from the looks of the room, it had not been housekeeping.

Janis shook her head, grabbing the corner of a pillow and twisting it with her hands. "At first I thought so," she said. "So I locked the big lock. But then they kept trying, and I could see that the big lock was starting to move on its own, so I grabbed everyone and hid in the closet."

Cassandra and I stared at her, not quite believing what she was saying. "You grabbed the chickens?" Cassandra asked, and Janis nodded. "Both of them?" Janis rolled her eyes.

"That's beside the point," she said. She was starting to get frustrated. "I just pinned their wings, like you said."

"And they were quiet when you were in the closet?"

"Yes!" she snapped. "They're intuitive creatures! They knew I was scared, so they shut up. But can we stop talking about the chickens? I'm trying to tell you that someone broke into your room."

"Do you think they took anything?" Cassandra asked. Janis looked at her, and then straight-up chucked the pillow at her face.

"Neither one of you is getting it, at all," she said. "Someone unlocked the big lock to come into this room. Which means they had to know someone, or something, was in here. Because you can only lock that lock from inside the room."

"I could lock it from outside," I pointed out. "With my kinesis."

"Of course you could, Jean Grey," Janis snapped. "But why would you, unless you had something to hide? And as you just pointed out, the big lock doesn't do a darn thing in a hotel full of people with superpowers." She swallowed. "Someone knows you're hiding something," she said. "What if they know it's me?" Pig let out a low growl, as if she was backing up Janis's story.

I nodded slowly as I let her words sink in. What if I'd put Janis and Pig in more danger than I'd saved them from? Still, it was too late now. "I don't think you want to leave the hotel right now. It's bad out there," I said.

"If it's so bad out there, then why are you two in here?" Janis said. "Isn't it your job to make it not so bad out there?"

Cassandra and I looked at each other. "That's what we're trying to figure out," I said, standing up. "It's bad out there, but I think it's bad in here too, and we're not sure which to tackle first." Janis grabbed another pillow, and I flinched, expecting to get it in the face again, but instead she shoved it into her lap. "Come on," I said to Cassandra, "let's go." Then I turned to Janis. "We're going to figure out how to get you out of this hotel room, and we'll be back ASAP."

"What am I supposed to do if someone comes back?" she asked. I didn't have a good answer. I wished there were something magical I could tell her, a spell she could cast or a tool she could use that would keep her safe. But there wasn't.

"Scream," I said. "All four of you."

With a weak smile, Cassandra held up the Kros N' Go bag. "At least we brought snacks," she said. Janis swiped it from her with a scowl.

• • •

Cassandra and I headed back down the hall and joined several other girls getting on the elevator. When we reached the lobby, we let them walk ahead of us, and when they were out of earshot, Cassandra whispered to me, "How are you going to get them out of that room? And where else are they going to go?"

"I have no idea," I whispered back. "I was hoping something would come to me." As we walked toward the dining room, I noticed Cassandra was moving way slower than usual, still looking for Cybill—her mom—behind every potted plant and around every corner. But of course she was—her mom. Then, just as we were about to walk into the dining room, I felt a hand clamp down on my shoulder.

"So, how did you enjoy that lecture on Sitter history?" It was Brian, and he had Cass and me each by a shoulder.

"I personally found it to be very informative and I learned a lot," Cassandra said, easily. Brian's grip was like a vise, and instead of letting us turn in to the dining room, he propelled us forward, right past the entrance.

"What was your favorite part?" he asked.

"I liked all of it," I said. Brian stopped outside the Steve Harrington Ballroom, and then opened the doors and pushed us in.

"Cut the crap," he said when the doors had closed behind us. "I know you weren't there, and so does everyone else. I had to cover for you and say I sent you on a last-minute run for party supplies. I had to pretend like I didn't know that was against the rules, and now I look foolish, and inexperienced, in front of the Synod and the other Counsel."

Oh no. "Brian," I started, "we can explain." He turned from us and stomped over and hit the light switch. As soon as the lights came on, I gasped.

"What?" I asked, slowly turning in a circle.

Cassandra was as shocked as I was. "Whoa, B, this looks awesome." Brian had been busy, and the whole room was transformed. When we'd entered, I'd thought the room smelled like Brian's car, and now I could see why. The Steve Harrington Ballroom had been turned into a snowy alpine village: one whole corner was a tiny forest of real trees piled high with fake snow. The other corner was filled with tiny houses, the size of gnome homes, with sloped roofs and candles flickering in their windows. The tables had centerpieces of holly and greenery, and huge glittery ornaments, fit for a giant's tree, hung from the ceiling. There were snowdrifts in the corners and up against the wall, and a sleigh, complete with what looked like really cozy blankets, set up for a photo booth. There was even a campfire for roasting s'mores, and all of Brian's carefully chosen pale-gray plates and napkins were the color of snowdrifts in moonlight.

"Brian, this looks amazing!" I gasped. "You did all of this?"

"Of course I did!" he said. "You two bought blow-up dolls and wigs. You can't be least of all with party planning." All of a sudden, I noticed Brian looked tired. "We have approximately ten minutes before our guests start to arrive," he said, as he looked over at the door. "Whatever. My guests. I'm done with covering for you, and I'm just going to tell it how it is from here on out. And you both," he said, stone-faced, "are going to sit down right now and tell me what's going on."

"Can I bring a marshmallow with me?" Cassandra asked.

"Absolutely not," Brian said. He walked over to a table and pulled out three chairs, then sat down in the middle one. Cassandra and I joined him on either side.

"Start at the beginning," Brian said.

Cassandra took a deep breath and looked at me. I could tell by her face that she felt like I did: this was not the time for joking. I nodded, and she started, at the beginning, just like Brian had said. She told him about waking up the night after Halloween, and the feeling that she couldn't remember something, and about her curse episodes and how this morning she'd accidentally removed it by knocking herself out with a toilet base and a chicken.

I told him about the demon in the dumpster, and what was going on outside, and how we figured it was true that the Synod brought the Summit to Spring River because Erebus had scared the hell out of them on Halloween, but not for the reasons everyone thought.

"But why would they be so scared of him?" Brian asked. "Didn't they dispatch him pretty quickly the night of Halloween? From everything you've told me of your encounter with Erebus, he sounds like a gumwad." I couldn't help but smile at Brian's choice of words.

"They're scared of him because he's their protégé," I said.

"Who told you that?" Brian asked.

"He did, basically," Cassandra said, and told him about

the 8 Ball. This was the first time Brian had heard we'd—or rather, she'd—kept it, and his lips went white with anger, but he seemed to swallow it.

"And you believe him?" he asked, looking back and forth between us.

"We do," I said. "It makes sense. Where did Erebus get Red Magic in the first place? Someone had to give it to him, or at least point him in the right direction. And if the Synod was interested in experimenting with it, it makes a lot more sense for them to use someone else as a guinea pig rather than themselves. My guess is that Cassandra's mom, Circe, and my mom started to freak out, so the Synod came in, cursed my mom, banished Erebus, and then Circe got the heck out of town before the same thing happened to her."

"I can't imagine that's the case," Brian said. "Red Magic goes against everything the Synod stands for. Why would they want anything to do with it?"

"Beanie Babies," I said, causing Cassandra and Brian to both stare at me with open mouths. "I heard a rumor," I started, evasively. I didn't want to bring Adrian into this if I could help it. "And I saw Wanda's phone. It's why she's texting all the time. But that's just Wanda. I don't know what the rest of the Synod want."

"Wealth and power," Cassandra said.

"Ha, that's not Beanie Babies," Brian scoffed.

"No, I'm serious," she said. "It looks different for everyone, right? For Wanda, it's stuffed crabs full of beans."

"They're not actual beans—" I started, then shut up when Cassandra put her hand up.

"You can't tell me that you two have never thought about it," she continued, looking back and forth between Brian and me. "Being in the Sitterhood brings you all kinds of power, right? But you can't ever use it for yourself. You can be a Sitter your whole life, and still never get yours. I mean, take the three of us, and then look me in the eye and tell me that we're all living the life we want." She leaned over and ran a finger down a branch of the centerpiece. "I mean, come on, B, you should be having full-page spreads in *Martha Stewart* or some crap like that, not coaching football."

Brian sat silent for a minute, then swallowed. "Don't tell me that you're condoning the use of Red Magic to get what you want," he said.

"I'm not condoning anything," Cassandra said. "I'm just saying I understand. Being a Sitter is about having power, but you can never use that power for yourself. It's only for protecting the innocent, and no matter what you do, no matter how much you sacrifice, you get nothing in return."

"You get the satisfaction of a job well done," Brian said.

"Oh, come on, B," she said. "Stop talking like a high school teacher."

"The Synod wanted to get theirs," I said. "And Red Magic was, and is, a way to do that. With Red Magic, Wanda could write a spell so that every time someone went to list a Beanie Baby on eBay, they shipped it directly to her instead. She could build herself a house with a wing just for BBs." It was an atrocious, silly example, but Brian looked like he got it. He had a tiny twig reindeer in his hand, and he was making it trot along the table. "And that's just the beginning," I added, "because with Red Magic, she could basically have anything she'd ever wanted. They all could."

"I never bought it," he said suddenly, bringing the reindeer to a stop.

"What?" I asked.

"The whole story about your mom," he said, and sighed. "No offense, but Spring River wasn't exactly top on my list of where I wanted to be posted. There were plenty of places where I could have been a Counsel and been more or less myself. But when I was assigned here, I knew it was important, not just for me but for the whole Sitterhood. Then, Esme, the more I got to know you and your dad, and see the pain you were in, it just didn't make sense to me. If I'm being totally honest, that was probably why I waited so long to start your training. I knew the more you learned, the more questions you were going to have. Legitimate questions that had no satisfactory answers." He swallowed again. "I apologize," he said. "To both of you." We all sat in silence for a second, seemingly hypnotized by our own thoughts and the glowing lights of the gnome village.

"We're sorry too," I said, speaking for Cassandra and myself. "For not helping with the party, and for buying a whole bunch of wigs, and for just generally being jerks all the time."

Cassandra rolled her eyes. "Oh God," she said. "We're not all going to hug now, are we? We can heart-to-heart later. There's a demon apocalypse brewing outside right now, remember?"

Brian grimaced. "That, I don't get."

"Me either," I said. "Why would you get all the Sitters in

one place, lie about the Portal being sealed, but really close it just enough so that nothing can be Returned, and then let the demons build up outside? It's almost like . . ." All of a sudden, the blood in my veins turned to slush and the realization hit me in the face. "Oh my God," I said. "It's a trap."

The words were just out of my mouth when the doors burst open. Our first party guests had arrived.

CHAPTER 21

Quickly, Brian reached into a bag and pulled something out. Next thing I knew, he was jamming it on my head: it was one of his knit hats. He put one on too, and then pulled one down over Cassandra's ears. His was red with white snowflakes, hers was gray with brown reindeer, and I could only imagine what mine was. "Brian," I whispered, "you know that spell you used to turn the wigs into these?" He was looking over my shoulder, a fake smile plastered on his face, waving at someone.

"Yes, why?" he whispered back, still grinning and waving.

"I need a women's elf costume, size medium, and a pair of reindeer antlers for a dog, size XL," I said. "And I need them quick."

"Why on earth?" he asked, scanning the room.

"Janis and Pig are up in my room," I said, "and it's not safe for them there." Now I had his attention, and he looked at me without saying a word.

"Fine," Brian said, finally. "It will give me something to do with this." He slid a box out from under the table, and I got a glimpse of the pea-green Grinch adult onesie I'd picked out before Brian waved his hand over it and it changed before my eyes. "Now, hurry," he said. "People are going to be looking for you, especially since you've been MIA all day. And remember, if anyone asks, or even *suggests*, you've both been working really hard on this party." With that, he turned and gave a big wave at Janine, who was at one of the snack stations. "You have to try the fondue," he called out, plastering a smile on his face as he walked toward her.

I grabbed the elf costume and the reindeer horns, then looked up just as Mallory and Ruby came walking in. "I'll be right back," I told Cass. "But you should go talk to the rest of our group. Do what Brian said—pretend we've been working hard on the party, and also pump them for info about the demons. Find out if anyone knows anything."

She smiled. "Will do," she said. "And just to double-check, we *are* allowed to eat the snacks now, right?"

I nodded, and she spun around to head Mallory and Ruby's way.

"Cass," I called, "be subtle." But she was already walking away. I gave a quick glance around the room. It looked spectacular—people were already huddling around the sleigh to take pictures. The snacks were over the top, and the decor was on point, but something seemed off. I was almost out the door when it hit me: there was no music. It almost made me smile, because Brian *would* plan a picture-perfect party that was totally silent. I couldn't have asked for a better

setup: Janis could be the elf DJ. She would fit right in, and no one would bat an eye. And Pig was always festive, but throw a pair of antlers on her and she'd be the star of selfie squads all night. Brian was by the door, geometrically plating snowman cookies, so I ran up to him on my way out.

"Brian!" I said. "There's no music!" He looked up at me, expressionless, but I could tell my words had stressed him out because he squeezed a frosted Frosty so hard that it crumbled in his hand.

"Stupid, stupid Brian," he said, "I knew I was forgetting something."

"You have your phone, right?" I asked, and he nodded, brushing cookie crumbs off his pants. "Just turn a few boxes into speakers. I'll be right back."

As I ran back up the stairs to our room, I couldn't believe that I actually cared about this party. But as I passed the third floor, it hit me that wasn't quite true. Brian cared about the party, and I cared about Brian. There was no doubt everything about this Summit was weird as heck, but if we could just get through the next couple of hours without incident, then maybe we could figure out why.

On the fourth floor, I ran down the hall to our room and knocked on the door. "Janis, it's me," I called as I pushed it open.

Inside the room, Janis stepped out from behind a curtain. "Here," I said, tossing the elf outfit at her. "Put this on."

"What the . . . ?" she started, as she caught it and held it out. "Wait, this is kinda cute." I crossed over to Pig and put the antlers on her. They had a tiny bell that jingled every

time she shook her head. "Oh my God," Janis squealed, pulling on the elf skirt. "She looks adorable."

I turned to face her. "I can't explain everything now," I said, "because I don't have time. But we're having a party downstairs, and you're going to DJ."

"Okay," she said, nodding. "What do I play?"

"Stuff people will like," I said. "Stuff normal people will like and want to dance to, and some Christmas music." Janis clapped her hands with glee. "Pig will be your sidekick, and that way I'll be able to keep an eye on you guys the whole time, because you'll be out in the open. But here's the thing: you can't talk to anybody, and don't let anyone catch you looking at them. You basically have to act like a DJing robot. Don't dance, don't bob your head, just act like a robot and press buttons on the phone. You have to pretend to be under a spell where all you know is how to do your job."

"Got it," she said, nodding. "And that job is DJ."

"It's for your own safety," I said. "And there's one more thing." She had pulled on the elf top and was adjusting the hat. I had to admit, she was right—it was a really cute outfit. "You don't get any snacks," I added, "because if you were really under a spell, you wouldn't even be aware of the snacks. Same goes for you," I said, addressing Pig.

"Are there good snacks?" Janis asked, raising an eyebrow.

"I'm sorry, yes," I said. "There are lots of good snacks. Now come on."

"Wait!" she said, running back to the bathroom and throwing open the cabinet. "What about them?"

I grimaced at the chickens. "They have to stay here," I

said. "An après-ski pit bull is already pushing it—I think two chickens might really blow our cover."

Janis looked torn. "But they're being so good," she said. I walked over, grabbed her arm, and started to pull her toward the door.

"Janis, come on," I said. "I don't have anything for them to wear. They'll be fine, I promise, they're not even real. Okay, ready? The spell starts now."

Janis made her face blank, and out we went, Pig trotting obediently between us. We went downstairs, and I led them toward the party. It was hard to walk with Janis and not talk to her, but she played the part well, though I could see her eyes go wide when we walked into the Steve Harrington Ballroom. We'd barely stepped foot in the door when the squeals began. "Squee, a dog!" It was like Pig was Taylor Swift, and she was mobbed within seconds. "This isn't a dog!" I said, loudly and full of cheer. "It's a reindeer!"

I figured Pig could fend for herself in a gaggle of admirers, so I put my hands on Janis's shoulders and marched her toward the DJ booth that Brian had impressively set up in our few minutes' absence. He'd even set out his phone, or at least a replica of it, open to his music. I turned so that my back was toward the crowd and I was standing between Janis and everyone else.

"This is amazing," she said, under her breath and without moving her lips. "What is all this?"

"Brian did it," I whispered back. A beat passed.

"Of all the crazy things I've heard," she whispered, as she picked up the phone and began scrolling through it. "Esme,

there's nothing on here but Michael Bublé and John Legend," she hissed.

"Use the internet, Janis," I said. "Figure it out, I have to go." Two seconds later, I wasn't surprised one bit when the first few notes of Mariah Carey started to fill the air. Over in a corner, I could see Cassandra talking to Mallory and Ruby, and I wondered whether she was telling them about her fortunate accident today. Brian and Clarissa were by the hot chocolate bar, and he was filling a mug with marshmallows just for her. I had to hand it to Brian—the place looked amazing. It was the classiest Spring River party I'd ever been to.

But it felt weird. Off. It felt like the Summit had barely even started, and now we were supposed to celebrate the fact that it was over? I still couldn't wrap my head around that, and the more I thought about it, the more anxious it made me. I decided to get myself a gingerbread-person cookie and a whipped-cream-topped mocha to calm my nerves, and then I was going to force myself to do something that terrified me. I was going to mingle and find out whether anyone else in this crowd of Sitters knew anything about why we were here, wearing cashmere hats and nibbling on peppermint bark when there were demons terrorizing a town. Not just any town—Spring River. My town.

Halfway across the room, a group of girls had gathered around Pig. Just as I predicted, she was a hit in her reindeer ears, and she gave me the perfect excuse to introduce myself. I had just slugged down half my mocha when the music suddenly cut out. Panicked, I looked at Janis to make sure nothing had happened. She was still behind the DJ station, eyes and face blank, braids tumbling out of her elf hat, standing a few feet back from the DJ booth because Wanda had stepped up and taken the mic.

The sudden silence had gotten everyone's attention, and now we were all looking at Wanda. Crap, crap, crap. Whatever was happening, it could not be good. I didn't want to tear my eyes away from Wanda, because I didn't like the fact that she was so close to Janis, but I didn't have to, because Cassandra was at my side before I could even look for her. Wordlessly, we started to weave through the crowd. On the way, Brian caught my eye. He was still smiling, holding a mug, but I could tell by the set of his eyebrows that he was worried too. "Pig," I mouthed, and he gave a minuscule nod, then started to look for her. I tried to slow my breathing and tell myself that Wanda could be up there for any reason, and maybe she was just going to give a nice little goodbye speech. Deep down, though, I knew that wasn't true, and I knew that Cassandra and Brian knew it too.

"It brings me great pain to interrupt what should be a joyous and festive occasion," Wanda said into the mic. "But something very unfortunate has been brought to my attention." She cleared her throat. The room was dead silent and my heart was racing. "There has been a theft, and a very precious book has been stolen from the library."

The announcement almost made me laugh out loud in relief, and I relaxed to the point that my bones might as well have been made of marshmallows. This wasn't about me or Cassandra. It had nothing to do with us.

"Fortunately," Wanda continued, "we know who took it, and we know where it is. However, until we fully understand their motives, we are taking some precautions." Each of her words fell through the air and landed on the floor with a thud like beanbags. "I hate to do this, but it is for everyone's safety." Then she raised her hands, palms out, a gesture that was both familiar and terrifying, and I felt like I was standing on a sled that was about to shoot out from under me. Wanda moved in a circle until she'd done a complete 360 and was facing us again. I suddenly felt very tired. "As of now, this building is sealed, and all use of kinesis and spells has been suspended," she said. At this, a collective yelp escaped from the crowd, half, I'm sure, at what Wanda had said, and half because she had just erased the magic of Brian's party.

The beauty of a few seconds ago was now replaced by reality. We were no longer standing in an alpine village, but a bleh hotel ballroom studded here and there with a few cheap party decorations, and those of us, like Cassandra and myself, who had donned hand-knit cashmere beanies, were now wearing wigs. I put my hands to my head and felt the synthetic strands of an Orangesicle ombré bob. My heart ached for Brian, as his picturesque sleigh photo op was now a kiddie pool with a couple of inflatable palm trees. Across the room, I could hear someone start to cry and I hoped it wasn't him.

"Silence, please!" Wanda yelled. "We are doing this not because it is an issue of magic, but one of inexperience. We want to give you the benefit of the doubt and attribute this theft to youth and curiosity, not to malice. That is why we are giving you the chance to come forward and resolve this with a conversation." She paused and smiled, then clapped her hands in front of her chest like someone had just presented her with a cake. "Now, if you are innocent, you have nothing to fear, and I want everyone to enjoy what is left of this party. It looks like our ever-competent hosts have provided you with"—she peered over at the snack table—"some corn chips and a tub of hummus! Now, those of you who are guilty, we can work this out, so I beseech you to find me and confess." She smiled again. "Otherwise, I will find you. Now, the rest of you have fun."

I kept my eyes on Janis, who was now clothed in a Grinch onesie several sizes too big, lime-green fabric pooling at her feet. She was still holding the phone, but all of the rest of the DJ setup had vanished. Certainly, this was going to take every ounce of acting skill Janis had to not register something strange was going on at this already strange party, but she just moved slowly and deliberately, and soon started to play Wham!, as loud as she could get it, out of the phone's wimpy speaker. "What was that all about?" Cassandra held out her hand. "Crap," she said when nothing happened. "Our kinesis really is gone."

Wanda's words had dropped a downer bomb in the middle of a good time. I was about to ask Cassandra who she thought had stolen the book when it hit me: no one had stolen any book. This was all just an excuse, and now Wanda had us all together, in one room, and no one had any powers. "Cass," I said, "we have to get out of here. All of us."

"If that's what you're thinking, then I'm sure you won't protest when I tell you to come with me." Cassandra and I spun around with the synchronicity of backup dancers. Wanda was standing behind us, with Deirdre a few feet away. They both wore the inscrutable expressions of potatoes. It was impossible to tell what they were thinking or feeling.

"Okay," I said, at the same time as Cassandra said, "No way." But then we were walking with Wanda and Deirdre toward the door, and Cassandra was keeping pace with me. Our eyes met and hers were wide, but her mouth was shut tight in a line, and that was when I realized it.

Stop walking, I told myself, but I couldn't. Something other than my brain or my body was moving my feet and clamping my mouth shut. I could still breathe deeply, though, and with every exhale, I told myself we had done nothing wrong, but I couldn't say that to the dozens of pairs of eyes watching us as we moved toward the door. Wanda stopped, and I saw Brian look up from where he was panickily dumping Fritos into a plastic bowl, and when he met my eyes, he threw the bag on the table and started to stride toward us. His hat had become an orange mess of a wig, and he looked like Drop Dead Fred.

"Now, I hope you feel bad that you are going to make your Counsel miss the very party he put so much work into," Wanda said, "but we need him as a witness to your misdeeds."

"We didn't do anything!" my brain was screaming at Brian, but nothing came out of my mouth. I could tell by the set of Brian's jaw that he was worried, but it was probably a good thing he wouldn't meet my eyes. "What's going on?" he asked, looking at Wanda.

"Something very unfortunate, I'm afraid," she said. "Now if you'll please come with me." Wordlessly, Brian nodded, then held the door for everyone as we walked out of the ballroom. Wanda did most of the talking as we made our way down the hall and toward the elevators. I tried to protest, but whatever spell Wanda was using to make my feet march made my mouth useless as a mouth. My lips couldn't form words, and my tongue kept hitting the back of my teeth like I was trying to swallow a spoonful of peanut butter—the organic, no-sugar-added kind that I hated.

"Now, Brian, please understand that we only hold you marginally responsible for their actions," Wanda was saying, and I strained to hear everything. "You've served the Sitterhood well for years, and these girls, well, we would not expect a few months of guidance to make up for a lifetime lacking in it." Rage zinged around inside me, creating a headache and heartburn, but nothing came out. I wondered if this was how Mom felt, like a mute mannequin in a sea of the loud living.

At the bank of elevators, Deirdre pushed the Up button. "I see, I see," Brian murmured, not meeting my eyes and looking confused. "What did they do this time?"

"They stole a book from my library," Deirdre said, and my neck snapped around. Every atom in my body wanted to defend itself. I most certainly had not stolen a book from her library. I wanted to ask where we were going but I couldn't. My tongue was tied with a million other questions. The elevator opened and we stepped on. Deirdre pressed the button for the fourth floor, and I figured we were heading to our room. From the corner of my eye, I could see Cassandra was in the same state as me, silent and staring.

Brian cleared his throat as the doors closed. "A spell book?" he asked. Deirdre pursed her lips and shook her head.

"Not just that. It's Red Magic, I'm afraid," she said.

"Part of why we suspected these two from the beginning," Wanda said, "is, of all the current Sitters, they are the two most closely connected to Red Magic. It's in their blood, after all. Cassandra, obviously, is Erebus's progeny. I have no doubt that Circe's attempts to conceal Cassandra's destiny were to protect the child from her own father." I couldn't speak, but I could bite my tongue, and I tasted the blood seeping between my teeth. I wanted to scream. What if Circe was trying to hide her daughter from you, you Beanie Baby–hoarding hound?

"And we always had problems with Theresa," Wanda continued. I wanted to kick her in the shins. Problems with my mom? Who had given everything to being a Sitter? I was sure if Wanda had looked into my eyes, she would have seen the hate pouring out of them.

Ding. The doors opened onto the fourth floor, and the five of us moved down the hall toward our room.

"What are we doing up here?" Brian asked.

"We need to search their room and see if our suspicions prove correct," Deirdre said.

"And what if they do?" Brian asked. At this, I saw Deirdre swallow and look at Wanda.

"Cases of treason are always handled by the Premier alone," she said, as Wanda nodded.

Brian stopped. "Treason?" he asked, surprised. "That's a serious charge for a missing book."

"It is," Wanda agreed. "And it is one that would not be levied for any other kind of book. But with Red Magic, we cannot take chances, especially with two Sitters who already have such close ties to the practice." I could practically hear the blood careening through my veins, and I could feel Cassandra's anger radiating like fire.

"I'm sorry," Brian said. "You know I would never undermine your authority, but they are hardly *close ties*. The events of Halloween happened when Esme and Cassandra were relatively inexperienced and unprepared, both of which I take responsibility for. They acted on instinct and were able to save the girl, which should be commended, not punished. If they did steal a book, which I highly doubt, I am sure it was only to satisfy a curiosity that could not be sated anywhere else. This is their family history, after all, and we have given them no information."

Wanda reached out and put a hand on Brian's sweatered arm. "Don't worry," she said. "You will be reassigned, and we will make sure you get a position in a much more desirable location. You've always loved Minneapolis, right?" She stroked his arm. "And really, we will all be better off." She glanced at Deirdre and smiled. "We have been working on something that will take care of Spring River for good. Then we can be free of this hellhole once and for all. I have always hated coming here."

Take care of Spring River? What the heck did she mean? She was talking like this whole town—full of people—was a decrepit dog she couldn't wait to put to sleep. I wanted to kick her shins, gouge her eyes out, and spit in her face. Spring River was my home, and I was the only one who got to call it a hellhole.

We stopped at room 402.

"You think the book is here?" Brian asked, his voice low and slow.

"Yes," Wanda said, shaking her head slowly. "Esme and Cassandra haven't socialized with their peers much since they've been here; they've been skipping meals and hanging out just with each other. It's obvious they were up to something. Erebus and Circe were the same, always thinking they were better than the rest of us, even when I was promoted to Synod. I don't know why, but I had hoped better for their progeny." She looked at Cassandra and me with mock pity in her eyes and let out a sigh. "It's such a shame when people disappoint you, even when you expect them to." She raised one hand toward the door, and the lock flipped. I hated her.

Wanda pushed the door open and stepped inside first. Immediately, she shrieked and jumped back. I could hear the sound of flapping wings. Deirdre pushed forward. "Oh dear," she said, "it's worse than we thought." Wanda recovered herself, and the rest of us followed her into the room. Cassandra and I entered last to see one chicken perched on the TV and the other nestled on top of a pillow.

"Chickens?" Brian asked, looking at me and Cassandra.

"They were clearly preparing for a sacrifice," Wanda

said. "And the presence of two chickens suggests they were planning two different rituals, or one large one." I wanted to scream that I was just trying to feed my dog.

"Wanda," Brian said, turning to her, his voice pleading, "surely you don't think . . . I don't mean to disrespect, but they're just girls. This has to be a misunderstanding."

"Aha!" Deirdre yelped from behind us. Cassandra and I couldn't turn to see her, but soon she was standing in front of us, brandishing the very book that I'd tried, and failed, to steal. Yet here it was, in our room, no doubt planted there just an hour or so ago by whomever Janis had heard snooping around. "It also appears they were smoking marijuana," Deirdre added, "as there's some spilled on the bathroom floor."

Brian was shaking his head and twisting his fingers together. "Wanda, surely there has to be some sort of explanation for this," he said. "They're children, and we have to take some of the blame. . . ."

Wanda shook her head. "If we listened to your arguments—they are just girls, they are just children—we would discount the entire Sitterhood," she said. "And we cannot take chances anymore. You know as well as I do that we have a zero tolerance policy when it comes to Red Magic. It must be eliminated swiftly and without indecision. I live every day with the regret that I showed sympathy toward Erebus and Circe all those years ago. It was my leniency then that puts us in this situation now."

I could tell that Brian was growing angry. "Charge them if you must," he said. "But give them a trial, at least. This is a fascist action, and I can't let you do it." He turned, about to stride out the door, when Wanda raised her hand at him.

"Oh, that's unfortunate," she said, as Brian's body went rigid, his arms clamping down at his sides and his mouth sealing shut. "Because I'm afraid you don't have a choice."

Brian looked like a statue. He was standing as straight and rigid as a broomstick. Wanda walked over to him, and when she poked him on the shoulder with a finger, he fell to the floor, landing with a thud.

"Deirdre, dear," Wanda said, turning toward her cohort, "please go back downstairs and let everyone know that everything has been taken care of. I imagine there will be some gossip, so do your best to reassure them and keep them calm. I will be down as soon as I am finished with these two."

Deirdre turned, stepped over Brian, and headed out the door. One of the chickens made a piercing squawk as she passed.

As soon as Deirdre had left, Wanda turned to us and sighed. "You know, it really is a shame your mothers aren't around to see you now. They were such a pain in my butt, it's no surprise you two grew up to be the same. Still, I'd like to show them, once again, that rebellion within the Sitterhood does not bode well for anyone." She shook her head. "Cassandra, I still can't believe that I took Circe at her word when she said her daughter did not inherit the gene, but she cloaked you well. She was one of our most powerful, I give her that." She was silent for a few seconds, then opened the door and marched Cassandra and me down the hall, toward the elevator. Then, instead of Down, she pressed the Up button. The doors opened a few moments later, to emptiness.

Wanda pressed the button for the top floor, and when the doors opened again, I wondered whether she was taking us to her room. Instead, she directed us down the hall, to the stairwell, and then up a short flight of stairs to the roof. She gestured for us to follow her, so right foot, left foot, right foot, left foot, we climbed like a couple of marionettes.

I wondered why Wanda was taking us to the roof, but I didn't have to ask. She answered my silent question almost immediately when she marched us out onto the tarred surface and over to the edge, then forced Cassandra and me to bend so that we had no choice but to look down and see the one inch that separated us from a six-story fall.

"Long way down, isn't it?" she said. "But the perfect height for a couple of girls who might get tossed off in the middle of a battle." I was most definitely afraid of heights, but now when my body gasped a gasp that it couldn't physically express, it wasn't because of the ground smirking at us from all the way down there. It was the demons, dozens of them, that were milling around the parking lot like they were tailgating before a Judas Priest concert. The air was thick with them, creating a heavy blanket of despair that I could feel settling over me.

"Oh, goodie," Wanda squealed, like a kid who has just been told she's going to get a cupcake. "Our party crashers have arrived. But don't worry, they're for your friends, not for you. You guys are going out with a good old-fashioned splat." Wanda's spell still had us bound with a gazillion invisible ropes, but my mind was crystal clear. This had nothing to do with the book. She'd probably planted it herself and painted us as Red Magic dabblers so that the rest of the Synod, who certainly didn't seem to be in the habit of asking Wanda the hard questions, would take her at her word that Cassandra and I deserved the harshest punishment around.

Now we were up here and everyone else was downstairs, trapped with corn chips and a bunch of cheesy party decorations, their powers suspended while Wanda's party crashers—a frothing demon horde—gathered on the other side of the wall. Wanda hated our parents, and still held a grudge, so it made sense, even if it was hella immature, for her to hate us. But what did she have against everyone else? Why take out all the other Sitters too?

Then it hit me. She had to take out all the other Sitters because they would never stand for this. Me and Cassandra first, then all of Spring River, and whoever else she needed to sweep out of the way on her path to world Beanie Baby domination. The Synod was clearly full of yes-women, but the Sitters? Girls like Ji-A and Ruby? They'd see right through this, and they'd never let Wanda get away with having anything she wanted if it meant sacrificing the innocent instead of protecting them.

Wanda turned Cassandra and me away from the edge and marched us over to two folding chairs that had been placed in the middle of the roof and sat us down. "I know what you're thinking," she said. "And no, this is not going to be like one of those evil gloating scenes in a movie where the villain confesses everything so that the hero gets all the answers they've been seeking. For one, I am not the villain and you are most definitely not the heroes, and for two, I don't have any need to explain myself."

She pulled a piece of chalk out of one of her pockets and held it up in front of her. The chalk rose, hovering just above her fingers, and then dropped to the ground and started drawing a complicated crosshatch of symbols. They began at my and Cassandra's feet and then spiraled out, the design growing quickly until it encompassed almost the entire roof. My eyes nearly popped out of my head as I noticed the objects that Wanda had carefully placed on the roof: a teddy bear, torn in two, and a deflated balloon. I knew this ritual well: it was the same one Dion had used on Halloween to call Erebus out, and the fact that Wanda was about to use it now meant she must be getting ready to do the same.

But then, she reached into her skirt and, as if it were Mary Poppins's bag, she pulled out a metal cup etched with tiny symbols, and a dagger. The dagger was short, with a sharp, glinting blade and a handle of polished onyx with a faceted garnet affixed to the front. Clutching these in each hand, Wanda edged closer to us.

Next to me, Cassandra's arm jerked straight out in front of her. "Trust me, this is going to hurt you a lot more than it's going to hurt me," Wanda said, and laughed. "I've always wanted to try this immortality ritual, and I figure why not get all I can out of you while you're still here? You'll be in such bad shape by the time this is over, it's not like anyone will notice." Then she took the dagger and dug it into Cassandra's arm, and twisted it. I couldn't imagine how much it must hurt, but, through no will of her own, Cassandra remained a statue. Blood bubbled up in the wound instantly, and then it started to drip down her arm. Wanda leaned in to catch some of Cassandra's blood in the cup. My brain was whirring a mile a minute as I tried to connect the dots between everything that was happening. Immortality ritual, sure—how boring. The oldest trick in the evil-witch book. But the ritual to call Erebus out? What did Wanda want with him? Erebus certainly wasn't a friend, or even a frenemy, but I had no doubt he'd take our side over Wanda's, and certainly she didn't want to create yet another adversary.

Rooted to the chair by Wanda's kinesis, I kept my eyes fixed firmly behind her, on the rooftop door, and despite the horror of what was happening next to me, I realized that something weird was happening to the door. In the quarter inch between the bottom of the door and the ground, something was appearing. It looked as if it was being pushed beneath the door. Something long and black, that looked like . . . hair? A second later, something black and roundish appeared in the middle of the door. It poked a few inches out, wriggled a bit, and then both things disappeared.

At that moment, Wanda stepped in front of me, and my own arm jerked out against my will. Wanda plunged the dagger in and my arm lit up in agony. Then she twisted the blade and my whole body flooded with pain. "See?" Wanda said. "Didn't hurt me a bit." As my blood started to flow over my arm, she waited until a few drops fell to the ground, then leaned forward to catch some of it in the chalice. I'd never liked getting shots or giving blood, and always turned my head away. Wanda must have known that, because she had positioned my arm in front of me in a way that I had no choice but to stare right at it as my blood, bright as red nail polish, pooled and rolled down my arm.

Movement behind Wanda caught my eye. The door—it was happening again. First, the thing under the door. Now I was sure it was a tendril of hair. Long, curly, dark hair. And then, just like before, the circle in the middle, even bigger than before. In fact, it almost looked like . . .

Wanda moved, blocking my view. She positioned herself facing Cassandra and me, right in front of and between us. She swirled the cup, mixing our blood, and then she began to chant, raising the chalice in every direction as she did quarter turns. By the time she was facing the door, the apparitions had disappeared again. When she was facing us again, Wanda gave the cup one more swirl, then, to my gag-if-I-could horror, she took an enormous swig. Our blood was clearly hard for her to swallow, and after she did, she made a horrible face and stuck out her tongue.

"Ugh," she said. "I never have developed a taste for blood, especially someone else's." Then she chucked the cup over her shoulder. It clattered to the ground, blood splattering as it rolled to a stop in front of the door. Wanda had released our arms, but she was coming for Cassandra again, dagger still in hand. This time, she reached out, grabbed a fistful of Cassandra's hair, and pulled it taut, then hacked it off in one big chunk.

Wanda came for me next, yanking off the wig I was still

wearing and tossing it away, before she went for my real hair. She had a harder time with mine, since it was so short. She gouged my scalp with the dagger at one point, and finally settled for pulling some of it out by the roots, a few strands at a time. My individual cells were screaming in agony, though my body made no sound. I was a black hole, or a building on fire, ready cave in on itself any second. When she had some of Cassandra's and my hair in her fist, she resumed her position, chanting as she held the hair up in each direction. As soon as she was facing us again, I braced myself. She wasn't going to, she wasn't going to, she wasn't going to, and then, yes, she did. She opened her mouth and shoved the hair right in it. Watching her, I went from wanting to scream to wanting to barf.

But I barely had time to comprehend what was happening, much less what it meant for me and Cassandra, because at that moment Amirah came tumbling butt-first through the door, feet in the air, head and hands on the ground. Ruby was with her, her arms wrapped around Amirah's waist. They crashed to the ground in a pile of limbs, but both of them were on their feet in a second. Amirah dove right back through the door, while Ruby reached down the front of her sweatshirt, pulled out a large bottle of water, and started to unscrew the top.

Wanda was just standing there, dumbfounded, strands of Cassandra's and my hair poking out of her mouth, when Ruby threw the water in her face. Wanda started to laugh, and then choked on a strand of hair. "What, you think I'm going to melt?"

Amirah tumbled butt-first back through the door, and this time she had Ji-A with her. "Not *her!*" Ji-A yelled at Ruby. "Throw it on *them!*"

"Oh, crap!" Ruby shouted, then turned and splashed the water in my face. Some of it went up my nose, and I started to sputter, then realized that I *could* sputter. The water had broken the spell. Cassandra realized it before I did, but Wanda realized it before both of us. She spat our hair onto the ground and let out an ear-boggling scream. It was a word and a language that I didn't understand, not something we'd been taught in any seminar or book. It was a word Sitters weren't supposed to know, a word no one was supposed to know.

In our haste, I hadn't had time to wonder what the demons were waiting for, but now I knew. They were waiting for Wanda to say the word, the very word she had just said. Within a half second, the sky above us was filled with flying creatures and I could feel the building begin to shake as the wingless ones started their climb. We were beyond outnumbered. Five Sitters on the roof, with dozens of demons coming our way. Amirah was still bringing Sitters through the door one by one, as Wanda's spell must have kept it impermeable to anyone who couldn't walk through walls, and it was slow and messy, and the demons were fast and messy. And then there was Wanda, who was shoving our hair back in her mouth as she chanted fast and furious. Cassandra took a page from Janis's book and picked up her chair and swung it at Wanda's head. Wanda took a page from Erebus's book and disappeared. Amirah's ass appeared in the door again and I ran over, about to use my kinesis to pry it open from the outside, when all of a sudden it was flung wide open. Not by magic, but by Janis, one hand holding up her giant green Grinch suit, the other planted on the door handle.

"Esme, what the . . . ?"

"Watch out!" Ruby screamed from behind me, and I dove at Janis, knocking her away from the door and then covering her as we rolled on the ground. I felt a demon dive-bomb us like a flying stingray and swoop just inches from our feet. A split second later, it went up in flames in midair. The burning demon shrieked until it stopped, dropped, and rolled to put the fire out. Ruby picked up the remaining chair and whacked it. I couldn't imagine her strength, because the demon had to weigh at least three hundred pounds, but Ruby batted it off the building like it was a Wiffle Ball. I used my kinesis to blast away a demon that was coming up behind Ruby as she went hand to hand with another one.

Suddenly, Wanda appeared right in front of my face and I jumped back. I raised my hand to use my kinesis to push her away, but I felt the now familiar, slamming-into-glass feeling of it being thrown right back at me. She forced my arms to my sides and approached. She still had strands of hair stick-ing out of her mouth. In one of her hands she held a tiny vial, and in the other something I couldn't identify. A white crescent-shaped thing that she swiped at my face. I couldn't move my arms, but I could still jump, which is exactly what I did every time Wanda swung my way. She snarled at me and it felt like something invisible wrapped around my knees and yanked me off my feet. I hit the ground, and I couldn't move as she shoved the white thing in my face, right under my nose. Then I knew what it was. It was a freaking onion. A raw onion. She pressed the glass vial to my cheek and its edge scraped my skin.

"Just cry, you little brat, and make this easier for both of us," Wanda stammered, still waving the onion at me and gouging me with the vial. Cry? Then I realized—whatever it was she was trying to do took more than just blood and hair. It took tears.

I started to breathe through my mouth, but Wanda used magic to clamp it shut. Now I had no choice but to inhale deeply, and my eyes started to water. But it still wasn't working fast enough, because she called the onion a string of bad words and tossed it off the roof. I felt a tear start to slip from my eye, and Wanda used one hand to shove the little vial into my cheek again as she tried to catch the tear. With her other hand, she pinched a piece of skin on my arm between her thumb and forefinger and gave it a sharp, strong twist.

Suddenly, she let me go, and a telekinetic blast sent me shooting backward several feet. Wanda walked to the center of the roof, and I saw her tip the contents of the vial into her mouth, and then raise her arms to the sky in a big V.

Janis's opening the door had brought a torrent of Sitters onto the roof. Except for Ruby, Ji-A, and Amirah, they didn't know what was going on with Wanda, but they all knew demons when they saw them, and there were plenty to see. All around me, Sitters and demons were locked in battle and the air crackled with magic. I startled when a demon launched itself at me, but then, *zap*, all of a sudden it was one-eighth its size, like a Pokémon, and almost cute. In the center of the roof, I could see Wanda chanting as she turned slowly in a circle, her arms still raised in a V. But over the commotion, I couldn't hear what she was saying.

"Stop her!" I screamed, to no one in particular, and so no one heeded me. I had no idea what Wanda was doing, so I started to run toward her, when a demon broke loose from Ruby's grasp and made a zooming beeline toward me. I managed to get my palms up to deflect it just before it launched itself on me.

"Where is the Portal?" Ruby screamed. "We can't Return anything!" I was just about to scream at her that the Portal wasn't coming when I felt it, that magnetic pull, and sure enough, I looked up and there it was, huge and swirling. I gave a little yelp as I grabbed the nearest demon and tossed it. Except it didn't get sucked up and flushed like I expected. Instead, it was as though I had thrown the demon straight into the wind. It flew back and thudded against the roof in a collision that made the whole building shake. The Portal was swirling right above Wanda, her hands still held up toward it, the wind it emitted blowing violently and sending her open-placket cardigan flapping and whipping in the air.

All around me, Sitters were flinging demons at the Portal and the Portal was flinging them right back. Wanda stood in the middle of it all, undisturbed. After all, everyone who knew why she was really here was locked in battle with the demon horde. I raised my hand and started to shoot my ki-nesis at her when a flash of flames licked up the back of her skirt. From across the roof, Cassandra was focused on Wanda as well, but no sooner had the flames flared than they were out again. I focused my kinesis on Wanda's arms and tried to pry them out of the V shape. Gripping her felt like trying to grab an eel, slippery and gross and impossible to get ahold of, and then, with nothing but a flick of her head, she knocked me off my feet, so hard that I did a backward somersault and landed facedown on the ground. I was seeing stars, and I didn't know whether that was because there was a Flash nearby or because I'd just hit my head. I started to push myself up, but I couldn't. I could see Cassandra was also on the ground and struggling to do the same on the other side of the roof, but something was holding us down, like we were rubber-cemented to the roof.

Wanda continued to spin, and the center of the Portal grew darker and darker, and then something moving toward her caught my eye. Not a Sitter, not a demon, but a white pit bull, barreling toward her at full speed. A seventy-two-pound cannonball with teeth was a formidable opponent for almost anyone and anything. But as Pig launched herself into the air, Wanda saw her. With nothing more than a quick nod of her head, her powers grabbed Pig and threw her right over the side of the six-story building.

I screamed like Freddy Krueger was clawing out my insides. I couldn't tell who else had seen what just happened. I had no idea where Cassandra was, or Amirah, or anyone else, because all I could see was Wanda. She was more powerful than me. She had more magic and more experience and she was mean, but right now, in that moment, every atom of my being had been flooded with hatred. My mouth was still open, and I think I was still screaming, but my ears were immune to any sound coming out of me as I instinctively held out my hands and used my kinesis to pull Wanda off her feet and into the air. I was going to do to her exactly what she had done to Pig. I was going to throw her off the roof.

With everything I had, I yanked and threw. But somehow, instead of flying off the roof, Wanda flew *up*. Straight into the Portal, into the dark heart of it that she had been working so hard to open. Now the flushing sound was deafening. It felt like the air itself was vibrating and it forced me into a ball, my hands clamped over my ears as tears streamed down my face. When the sound and the vibration finally died down, I could hear the screams as everyone around me tried to figure out what had just happened, why Wanda had disappeared but the demons were still here.

But I didn't care. I started to run toward the stairs, and that's when I saw him. Adrian was standing there, with a look on his face that was a mix of horror and disgust. He was right in front of the door, and I was ready to push him out of the way if I had to. But I didn't, because he vanished.

Or, more specifically, he transformed into a giant crow. Shiny black wings flapped wildly as the bird cawed out of my way. For a split second, I stopped, the reality of what I'd just seen slapping me in the face, but time to think about Adrian was time I didn't have. I'd never moved so fast yet felt so slow in my life as I practically fell down the stairs. I was dimly aware of someone shouting my name and running after me, but I didn't turn to see who it was. On the ground floor, I pushed through the door to the parking lot, my sharp breath turning my lungs to shredded paper, and braced myself for what I might find.

Pig was tough. At times it seemed like she was cast from concrete as I tried to pry her from my seat on the couch. But this was different. She wasn't indestructible. She was a dog, and no dog, no matter how much of a good girl she was, could survive a six-story fall.

I spun in circles, trying to find her. "Esme, I can help, I can help." I turned toward the voice, and through the haze of tears, I saw Mallory running toward me. Behind her, I could see a demon, and without thinking twice, I held up my palms, grabbed it with my kinesis, and then smashed it into the ground, over and over, until it was dead. I felt numb as Mallory caught up to me, out of breath, and grabbed my hand. We started to run around the side of the hotel.

"She has to be here," I babbled. "Somewhere, and she's hurt . . ." My eyes moved over every inch, looking for white fur. A crumpled, broken pile of white fur, the body of the gentlest creature that had ever lived, better than 99.999 percent of these trash humans.

"We'll find her, we'll find her," Mallory said, stumbling as I pulled her along. But we didn't. We went all the way around the building, and we didn't find Pig.

I screamed her name. Maybe there was a chance she was just injured, and she'd managed to drag herself to a hiding place, but again, I didn't see any sign of her. I was starting to sob, and I ran faster, letting go of Mallory. I stopped at a patch of bushes and pawed through them. Nothing but old Taco Bell wrappers and a dirty sock. I started running again, and suddenly Cassandra was next to me and wrapping her arms around me.

"You have to help me find her!" I screamed into her shoulder. If Wanda wanted my tears, well, here they were. It felt like my eyes were melting and pouring down my cheeks. I couldn't see clearly. I was starting to hyperventilate, and I felt like I couldn't stand up anymore.

Janis was here now too, and Amirah behind her, and they were talking, but I couldn't understand what they were saying. Then Cassandra was in front of me, holding out her hand, and the world went black.

CHAPTER 22

I was lying in a bed in a hotel room. Not my room, but it was still a disaster and it smelled like skunk. The TV was on, and someone was sitting in bed next to me. I felt like I'd OD'd on Benadryl, and my head felt fuzzy. I groaned and pushed myself up on my elbows. The person in bed next to me jumped and then started screaming, "She's up! She's up!" The bathroom door banged open, and Amirah came out. Ji-A was the one in bed next to me, and now she was on her knees, leaning over me on one side while Amirah leaned over me on the other.

"Hey," Amirah said. "How are you feeling?"

I moaned. "Like I've been run over by a whole train of shopping carts," I said, wincing with every word. "What happened?"

Amirah grimaced. "You were really upset," she said. "Cassandra cast ypnos on you, but it barely put you under, so Ji-A and I had to do it as well. Triple-layer spell, basically."

My mouth felt dry, and my head was throbbing, and I was wondering why they were all piling on me when it came flooding back. Pig. Flying over the side of the roof. Me, running down six flights of stairs to find her. The memory felt like a knife in my belly, and my tongue was a swollen sea cucumber. "Did you find her?" I croaked.

Amirah shook her head, and I swear it looked like even she was trying to blink back tears. "No, not yet," she said. "Cassandra and Mallory are looking, but it's kind of chaos out there. We're hoping she's just scared and that she'll come back when things have calmed down."

I pushed myself up to sit, and it felt like the hardest thing I'd ever done. "Jeez," I said, "what did you guys do to me?"

"You're not injured," Ji-A said. "It's like you're waking up with a really bad hangover. It will wear off soon. Drink this," she said, wrapping my hand around something cold. "It'll make you feel better." I looked down, expecting to see some sort of healing potion, but instead it was a can of La Croix. Still, I took a grateful chug.

Amirah's phone rang and she answered it quickly. "Whew, okay, good," she said after a bit. "See you soon. Love you." She hung up and turned to us. "My mom's chartering a jet and picking a few people up along the way. She'll be here tonight." She laughed. "And man, is she pissed. Everyone's pissed. She's lucky you flushed her, Esme. Mom wants to flay her alive."

I started to ask who Amirah was talking about, but my mouth refused to form the name. "Wanda," Amirah said, saying it for me. "As soon as she was gone, the other members of the Synod ratted her out. Apparently, she'd been planning this for years, and then I guess when Cassandra's dad got out on Halloween, it bumped up her timeline."

Everything on the roof was coming back in nonlinear chunks, but I remembered the Portal. Wanda standing under it, nothing going in as she tried to call something out. Still, I had flushed her. How? "What was she trying to do?" I asked. "It looked like a Red Magic ritual to . . ." I trailed off. Amirah was still on her phone, furiously texting, but Ji-A was nodding.

"Only Wanda knows for sure, but what we think is that she was trying to call Erebus out so that you could all, um, take care of each other." Ji-A grimaced. "You know . . . ," she said, drawing one finger across her throat.

"Why all the demons, though?" I asked.

"We don't think you guys were the only ones she was trying to get rid of," Ji-A said. "I think she thought that if we were all trapped in the hotel with no powers, then she could wipe most of us out. The weaker the Sitterhood, the easier it would be to bring her Red Magic use out into the open."

I nodded as I sipped the La Croix. "What happens now?" I asked. "The Synod can't stay the Synod. They suck." Amirah tossed her phone onto the bed, where it made a dent in the pillow it landed on.

"No one knows what's going to happen, because it's not like we've ever had to replace a whole Synod before," Amirah said. "But my mom's coming, and several other former Sitters too, to help figure things out and make sure everyone's okay. Maybe we won't have a Synod for a while?"

I was holding the La Croix can in both hands, and I didn't want to look away from it, afraid I might start crying again if I met anyone's eyes. "How did you know?" I asked.

"Know what?" Ji-A asked.

"That something was up when Wanda took us away," I said. "That Cassandra and I didn't steal the book."

Amirah came over and gave me a side hug. "Oh, come on, Esme," she said, "no one who's spent five minutes with you would ever actually believe you were a Red Magic mastermind. I mean, you can't even conjure dog food."

Was that a compliment? It sure as heck didn't sound like one, but Amirah's arms were still around me, and I could smell her mints on her breath. I reached up and wrapped my arms around her. "Thanks," I said. "For everything."

"No problem," she said, shrugging. "Sitters stick to-gether." She plopped down on the bed, then looked over at Ji-A. "Do you think it's too late to ask my mom to bring me some uni?"

I tuned them out and went back to staring at my hands. I wanted to ask about Adrian, but there was a part of me that didn't want to know. If he was a part of this, then he was a part of Pig . . . I squeezed my eyes shut to trap the tears, then blinked them open again.

"Where's Janis?" I asked.

"She went to get you coffee," Ji-A said. "Which is prob-ably a good thing, because it looks like you're going to need it. But don't worry, Ruby and a couple of the other girls are with her. We think we got all the demons, but we're not tak-ing any chances."

"Where's the rest of the Synod?" I asked.

"The Counsels are debriefing them right now," Amirah said. "Brian told me that they're probably going to have to blast the whole town again first thing in the morning, and then as soon as that is done, all the Synod will be stripped of their memories and their powers." I winced at hearing that Spring River's brain would be blasted yet again, but I assumed it had to be done. There were probably already local forums devoted to investigating mysterious bobcat sightings.

Then the door to the room opened, and it was Janis, holding a tray of coffee cups. She was no longer dressed like Lady Miss Kier—instead, she was clad head to toe in Amirah's clothes, including the Louboutins. I leaned forward a little so that I could see what shoes Amirah was wearing. Sure enough, they were Janis's Fluevogs. I couldn't help it—I felt a little pang of jealousy, as lots of bonding had clearly happened while I was passed out.

Janis squealed when she saw me awake, turned and set the coffees down on a table, and then ran over, throwing herself on me in a hug. Ruby came in and closed the door behind her.

"Oh my God, Esme! You're awake!" Janis ran back and got one of the cups of coffee, then brought it over to me. I wrapped my hands around it, the condensation cold and welcome on my palms.

"Janis," I started, then found that I couldn't get the words out. "Pig," I said finally. Each time I thought about her, I felt like I'd been ripped in two again.

Janis's eyes started to water, but she smiled and nodded. "I know," she said. "Everyone's looking for her. She had a lot of fans. I would have gone too, but I wanted to stay here until you woke up."

"Thanks," I said, taking a sip of coffee and then a sip of La Croix. I was starting to feel better. Maybe it was the beverages. Or maybe it was just . . . friends.

I must have fallen asleep again, because the next time I opened my eyes, Cassandra and Mallory had joined us. Cass and Ruby were actually sitting in the same chair, deep in conversation, but Cass jumped up and came over to me when she saw me stirring.

"That was some move you pulled on the roof," she said, sitting down on the bed.

"What do you mean?" I asked.

"You totally overpowered Wanda's ritual," she said. "That was supposed to be a one-way Portal, but you powered right through and pushed her in."

"I don't understand," I said. "I just did what I always do and . . ."

Ruby stood up and walked over to us, though she hung back a little. "You were really mad, though," she said. "And anger is its own kind of Red Magic. You're really powerful, Esme."

I didn't know what to say. All I could do was nod. "You didn't find Pig, did you?" I asked finally.

Cassandra shook her head. "The whole town is a mess," she said. "But we asked everyone we ran into, and no one has seen a white pit bull."

Ruby leaned forward. "But I think that's a good thing. If Pig was that injured, she wouldn't have been able to get far. So hopefully she was just scared and is hiding somewhere."

"Yeah," I said, even though I knew that wasn't true. All Pig ever wanted was to be with her family, so if she was scared, she wouldn't be hiding, she'd be trying to find us. "I want to go home," I said, and Cassandra nodded. I was still woozy from the spells that Wanda had cast on me, so she and Janis gathered up my stuff, and then she and Ruby walked Janis and me out to Janis's car.

"Do you want us to go with you?" Ruby asked, but I shook my head. I wanted to be alone right now, and being with Janis was the next best thing to being by myself. We got in the car, and Cassandra tapped on the passenger window, then waved goodbye. Janis turned the key, and as soon as the car started, "Jingle Bell Rock" started playing on the radio. I groaned and leaned back, turning my head so that I was looking out the window.

"Janis, please," I said.

"I'm changing it, I'm changing it," she said, hitting something on her phone. Missy Elliott started to play. We had just pulled out of the parking lot when I remembered.

"Oh my God, Janis!" I said. "The chickens!" She tossed me her phone so I could text Cassandra, which, considering the state of Cassandra's phone, was only slightly better than

come, how would you have known? Why did Pig need a dog sitter anyway? Where were you?"

He pulled out the chair opposite me and sat down. In the candlelight, I could see how weary he looked, and that the lines around his eyes seemed deeper, like they'd been gouged with a butter knife. "I'm afraid I haven't been honest with you," he said.

"No crap," I said. He leaned forward and picked at some wax that had melted onto the table.

"Es, I lost my job," he said. "I didn't want to tell you, because it seems like you've been pretty stressed out lately, and I was hoping I would get another one soon and just tell you then. But that hasn't been working out."

"And we're running out of money," I said.

He nodded. "I've been trying to pay whatever bills seemed the most important," he said. "But the electricity bill got away from me. I went out to Sunflower City this weekend to see about selling your grandma's old farm, but that won't happen for a while. In the meantime, we'll have to really cut back and try to save."

"Dad," I said, "Mom's facility called this weekend. Her bill's way past due, and Brian paid it to make sure she could stay."

"Brian?" he asked, looking confused. "Brian Davis?"

I nodded.

"How did he know?"

"I told him," I said, "because I didn't know what else to do. I couldn't get ahold of you and I was freaking out." He slowly nodded, let out a long sigh, then gave a fake laugh.

"Man, Brian's a good friend," he said. "And I've messed things up big-time. I'm sorry, Esme. And I'll apologize to Pig too." At this, he gave a sharp whistle, then waited. But instead of the jingle of a collar, there was silence. His face grew confused.

"Esme," he asked, "where's Pig?"

"Dad," I said, my voice cracking, "I haven't exactly been honest with you either." He nodded again, and then I told him everything.

CHAPTER 23

It's been almost two weeks since Spring River's collective brain was wiped, and everything seemed back to normal, or at least as normal as it was ever going to be: "Jingle Bell Rock" every five minutes, children subsisting on powdered sugar and sprinkles, the resident jokers turning the inflatable snowmen displays into a page from the Kama Sutra. You know, the normal holiday stuff.

Cassandra and I weren't able to figure out the spell that would protect Janis's and Dad's brains before the new Synod zapped the town to erase all memories of what had happened the weekend of the Summit, but we got it eventually, and now I was pretty sure they were safe from all future mind melts. Or, at least we could hope.

Of course, we had to tell them everything, again, but Brian let me borrow his PowerPoint, and I could see why he'd made it. It did make things easier to explain. In a certain way, it was funny to see Janis and Dad on the same team. They were each other's one-person support system for navigating how to be a normie in a world of Sitters, and I told them I'd better never catch them ganging up on me. It brought Dad and Brian closer too, and I think Brian was enjoying not having to talk about football all the time. Dad landed an interview at a countertop place next week, and I'd been helping him with his résumé and coaching him for his interview.

In the meantime, we were slowly draining my college fund to pay for our life. I wasn't super happy about that, but it was what it was, and we'd started talking about bringing Mom home again. To save money, obviously, but also because that was something we wanted.

Cassandra and I were back on Returns, and I daresay we were kind of nailing it. We could now scout, battle, and Return a demon in less time than it took most people to floss their teeth. I'd been babysitting every chance I got, and Cassandra got a job too. But not babysitting—at the fro-yo place. She loved it, mainly because no one wanted fro-yo the week before Christmas, so she didn't have to do anything.

Cassandra and I didn't talk about it, because we didn't talk about that kind of stuff, but I was pretty sure she talked to Ruby every day, and I'd never seen her so happy. In fact, I'd never even seen Cassandra happy, and I was happy for her, but also, I admit, a little sad. It kinda made me wonder when I was going to fall for someone who didn't turn out to be a total loser. Or a bird.

So yeah, things were working out in a lot of ways. And

they weren't working out in some major ways. Mom was still cursed. And Pig was still gone.

"Here ya go, miss." The copy shop guy snapped me out of my head as he slid my stack of flyers across the counter. "You can put one up in the window here if you want. I hope you find your dog. She looks like a real good girl."

"Thanks," I said. "She was. I mean, is." I took the flyers and went outside. This was the third bunch I'd put up around town. We'd gotten a few calls, and last weekend, Dad and I drove out to the county shelter because someone had brought in a white female pittie. She was sweet, but she wasn't Pig. Not even close.

I ripped a piece off my roll of hot pink duct tape and wrapped it around a lamppost to hold up the flyer. It had started to snow last week, so the flyers weren't lasting long. I was ripping off a second piece of tape when I heard someone say hi behind me. I turned around with the tape still in my mouth and jumped when I saw who it was: Stacey Wasser, mouth full of Funyuns, an open bag in hand. I'd spent much of my high school career avoiding Stacey Wasser, except for that time I saved her life, which she of course didn't remember. She looked at me and chewed, and I wondered what was coming next. There was no sporting equipment in sight, so she'd have to get creative if she wanted to throw something at me. But she just stood there and chewed, a John Waters mustache of onion dust on her top lip.

"You lost your dog?" she asked. I nodded. "That sucks," she said, then held out her free hand. "Gimme one." I handed her a flyer, half expecting her to crumple it up into a ball and throw it in the gutter. Instead, she read it. "Her name's Pig?" she asked.

"Yeah," I said sadly. "She snores a lot."

Stacey laughed, and sprayed Funyuns on the flyer. "A dog named Pig," she said. Then she shoved the flyer in her pocket. "I'll look for her."

"Thanks," I said. "My number is there, if you do see her."

She nodded, then held the bag out to me. "Want one?"

I hated Funyuns, but Stacey clearly loved them, and I took it that this was her making some sort of peace offering, even if she didn't really understand why, so I nodded and reached into the bag.

"Thanks again," I said.

"I love dogs," Stacey said. "I hope you find her. See you at school." Then she turned and walked away. I put the Funyun in my mouth, and I was surprised. It wasn't as bad as I remembered.

I was putting up another flyer at the library when my phone rang with a FaceTime call. It was Amirah, who had called me every day since she'd gone back home. Even though she never asked me a single question, I knew this was her way of seeing how I was doing. I clicked Accept and was greeted by a ceiling. Then Amirah's face popped into the screen on one side, and Ji-A was leaning over from the other. It was early evening in New York, and they were getting ready to go out.

Amirah modeled her outfit, which included crystal-studded stiletto boots, while Ji-A was wearing a draped, one-shoulder velvet minidress that was probably Balenciaga. She'd paired it with a dirty pair of black Converse All Star high-tops. "I wish you were here," she said, and the image shook as she flopped onto the bed.

"Me too," I said. The sentiment was true, though I had a hard time mustering much emotion for it. "What are you guys doing tonight?"

"There's a party at the McDonald's in the East Village," Amirah called from offscreen.

"A party at the McDonald's?" I asked, not sure I'd heard right.

"Yeah, it'll last like ten mins max before everyone gets kicked out."

"I'm getting a McFlurry," Ji-A said wistfully. "With extra Oreos."

Ugh. I had to admit that a party at McDonald's sounded like more fun than anything I had ever done in my entire life.

Amirah took the phone from Ji-A. "So, we're booking tickets back to Spring River for Presidents' Day weekend!"

"Ha, really?" I asked, totally confused. This was the first time I'd heard about such a plan. "I don't think I even know when Presidents' Day weekend is."

"It's basically Valentine's Day," Amirah said.

"Excuse me," Ji-A said. "Galentine's Day!"

"Of course, of course," I said.

"Anyway, we get a day off school," Amirah continued,

"and our Counsel said New York will be a dead zone that weekend because all the demons will be lying low 'cause they hate romance."

"I get that," I said, since I was pretty sure I hated romance too. "But what do you guys want to do in Kansas?"

"We want to go thrifting!" Amirah squealed. "I just got off the phone with Janis. She said we can stay with her." Ji-A stuck her head in front of the camera and nodded emphatically.

"I want to find, like, a hilarious T-shirt," she said. "From a softball team or something."

I laughed. "We have those," I said.

They were both quiet for a minute.

"Are you still looking for Pig?" Ji-A asked, and I nodded.

"I'm sorry, Esme," Amirah said. "But I do have someone here who wants to say hi." She flipped the phone around and focused on a corner of her room. The chickens, who clearly did not want to say hi and couldn't give a flying frig about a FaceTime screen, were sitting comfortably on a pillow.

"How's that whole thing going?" I asked.

"Amazing!" Amirah beamed. "Everyone thinks it's hilarious that I have chickens in my apartment. I started an account for them: at city underscore chicks. You should follow!"

"I will," I said. I wanted to say something else, but I didn't have much in me for conversation.

"Okay," Amirah said. "We just wanted to call and see what you were up to. Excited to hang when we come back."

"Yeah, me too," I said, and I meant it, even though I

wasn't exactly doing backflips to prove it. Then they both waved and hung up.

I finished hanging up the flyers, then bought myself a coffee for the walk home. The barista seemed incredulous, and asked me three times to make sure I wanted an iced black coffee, and not a hot peppermint mocha, but I held my ground, frozen fingers and all. When I got to the house, Brian's Ford Explorer was parked in the driveway. I went inside and my dad and Brian were sitting in the kitchen, drinking beer. I stuck my head in and said hello before heading to my room. A few minutes later, there was a knock on the door. I expected it to be Dad, asking me what I wanted for dinner, but instead it was Brian.

"Oh, hi," I said. "Come on in." I stepped aside, and Brian got a good look at the mess behind me and gave a visible shudder.

"Hey," I said. "It's called punk shui. You should look it up on Pinterest."

He smiled. "I'm glad to see your sense of humor has returned," he said.

"I'm only operating at about fifteen percent," I said.

He nodded. "I'm sorry, Esme. Your dad said you were having a tough time."

I bit my lip and nodded. "Do you want to come in?" I asked.

"That's okay," he said. "I have to get going. But I wanted to tell you something."

"About Mom?"

He shook his head. "About your dog."

"Did someone see her?" I asked, practically jumping down his throat.

"No," he said. "But I've been doing some research, and I got to catch up with Clarissa last night, and she confirmed that she'd never heard of such a thing either."

"Of what such a thing?" I asked.

"I haven't been able to find a single other instance where an animal has successfully taken part in a Coven ritual," he said. "It's unheard of."

"What do you mean?"

"Well, it seems it's not for lack of trying. There are a lot of recorded instances of Sitters attempting to use animals to form Covens, but it's never worked."

"That's weird," I said, my mind flashing back to Halloween, when I'd successfully cobbled together a last-minute Coven of myself, Janis, Mom, and Pig.

Brian shook his head. "I don't think so. The purpose of some rituals requiring a Coven of other Sitters, preferably, but at least of other humans is a safety precaution of sorts. Otherwise, our most important rituals could be conducted with one Sitter and a few pigeons. The ritual you did on Halloween, with Pig, shouldn't have worked."

"Well, it did," I said.

"I know," Brian said. "And I'm trying to find out why, because it seems like that means there's something unusual about you."

"Or Pig," I said.

"Yes," he said. "Or Pig. We will find her."

"I know," I said, nodding, trying to convince myself of that very thing. "How's everything going?" I asked, half because I wanted to know, half because I wanted to change the subject. Brian hadn't flat out said so, but I got the feeling that the events at the Summit had bumped him a few rungs up the Sitterhood ladder.

"It's proceeding," he said. "Janine, Deirdre, and Ana have all been installed in their new lives."

I nodded. From what Brian told me, it had been decided that Wanda's punishment would be to stay where I put her—in the Negative—but the rest of the Synod had been stripped of their powers and most of their Sitter knowledge. Deirdre had apparently been working closest with Wanda, and now she was substitute teaching in a middle school somewhere in Alabama. I hadn't heard, nor did I really care, where Janine and Ana ended up.

"Nominations for the next Synod will likely happen in the next few months and the election later in the spring," Brian continued. "In the meantime, the interim has been doing a very good job, and they are getting lots of things cleaned up."

"That all sounds good," I said.

"I'd better get going," he said, "but see you tomorrow for training?"

I nodded. Then Brian surprised me and did something he'd never done before. He reached out and gave me a hug before he turned and headed back down the hall.

• • •

I heard his car start in the driveway, and then there was another knock on my door. It wasn't Dad this time either; when I opened my door, Cassandra was standing there. She was wearing an old zip-up hoodie over a monogrammed khaki-colored polo shirt, and her hair was pulled back into a ponytail under a matching khaki visor, a few short bits sticking out from where Wanda had hacked off a handful.

"Not fired yet!" she said, and then held up a tub. "I brought you some fro-yo. Mango cappuccino swirl!"

"Oh, wow," I said, not sure what else to say about a flavor profile that sounded so totally disgusting.

"I made up the combo myself," Cassandra added. I took the lid off. It was orange and brown, all right.

"Bestseller?" I asked.

"No way," she said. "But I do think it's helping keep the customers away. The other handle we have right now is wasabi and peanut butter. Someone came in this afternoon asking for eggnog and peppermint, and I told them to put it in the suggestion box."

"What do you do with the suggestion box?"

"I clean it out at the end of every shift and throw the suggestions in the garbage," Cassandra said. "I was flushing them down the toilet, but apparently that isn't very good for the pipes." She came in and sat down on my bed. "I miss her," she said. "I even miss her farts."

"I know, me too," I replied, knowing immediately whose farts she was talking about. Cassandra's phone dinged with a text, and her face lit up when she looked at it. She typed something quickly and then shoved the phone back in her pocket.

"I have something to tell you," she said, looking at me seriously.

"You and Ruby," I said, "I know. I mean, I figured . . ." The glow returned to her face, but she shook her head.

"No, it's not that," she said, then took a deep breath. "I've been talking to my dad. Through the 8 Ball."

I wasn't sure what to say to that. Certainly, the way Cassandra had prefaced the statement meant she totally expected me to disapprove and give her another lecture about doing something dangerous. And maybe, before the Summit, I would have. But now, I wasn't so sure. After all, what did I know? Rules weren't always right, and breaking them wasn't always wrong.

"Wow. I didn't know you had stayed in touch," I said finally. I hadn't forgotten what Cassandra had said about Red Magic—that she didn't condone it, but she did understand why someone would use it—and so I wasn't sure how to feel about her getting cozy with a Red Magician, even if he was her dad.

She shrugged. "He's a sucky dad, but he's the only one I've got, so I figured I might as well."

"What do you guys talk about?" I asked carefully.

"Stuff," Cassandra said. "We're just getting to know each other. Taking it slow. I mean, like really slow. Having a conversation through an 8 Ball takes all night." She laughed, and I smiled, and then she got serious again. "He doesn't have any idea where my mom might be."

"And you think he's telling the truth?" I asked.

"Yeah," she said. "I think if he did know, he'd want me

to find her. For selfish reasons, of course. He still wants out of there. He said he hasn't seen Wanda, so wherever you sent her must be the bowels of the bowels, if you know what I mean." I cringed at Cassandra's metaphor but was happy to hear that wherever Wanda was, she wasn't coming back. Anyway," she continued, signaling she was done with the subject, "Janis and I put this together." She pulled a folded piece of paper out of her pants pocket and handed it to me.

I unfolded the paper. It was covered with frozen yogurt stains, and a massive list: marinara, spinach, cheese, lukewarm water, medicinal marijuana . . . Janis's tiny writing covered the entire piece of paper in columns.

"What is this?" I asked, turning the paper over to see that the yogurt stains and the list continued on the back.

"It's an inventory of everything that was in the room when my curse broke," Cassandra said. "I'm sure we missed some stuff, but this was everything we could remember. Which means that some combination of some of these things will remove a curse. I figure if we don't have any other options, we might as well start trying with your mom."

I looked up from the list and smiled at her. I didn't need to be a statistics major to know the chances were slim, but still, she was right. It was a start.

"Thanks," I said. "This could definitely help."

"Any word on Pig?" she asked. I shook my head but then remembered what Brian had just told me. I was halfway through telling Cassandra when she started grinning from ear to ear. "It means that Pig isn't a dog," she said.

My own lips stretched into a smile, because that was exactly what I was thinking too. "What do you think she is, then?"

"No idea," Cassandra answered. "But we can ask her as soon as she comes back. You know she's going to come back, right?"

"I do," I said, and realized I believed it more every time I said it. "Amirah and Ji-A are coming for Presidents' Day," I said. "Which I guess is also Galentine's Day? You should have Ruby come too. You know, get the old gang back together."

Cassandra nodded. "We've already talked about it," she said, and I swear she blushed. Holy crap—was Cassandra the kind of person who cared about Valentine's Day?

"Mallory's coming too," she quickly added.

Cassandra stood and zipped up her hoodie. "If you're not going to eat your fro-yo, that's okay. I'll take it home to Dion." Relieved to be free of the mango-capp, I handed the carton back to her.

"You bring Dion fro-yo?" I asked, because that did not seem like something Cassandra would do for her brother.

"No way," she said, "I take home the empty containers and put them in the freezer so that he gets all excited when he sees them." I nodded. Of course. That was totally something Cassandra would do.

"I found a Nintendo Switch box in our neighbor's recycling," she said, "so I'm going to wrap it up and give it to him for Christmas."

"What are you going to fill it with?" I asked.

"I dunno," she said with a shrug. "A bottle of callus remover and a bathmat, maybe?"

Oh, she was evil, all right.

I walked her down to the kitchen, where she rinsed out the fro-yo bucket and then left. Dad had been to the store earlier, and now I had my choice of what to feast on: ramen, mac and cheese, spaghetti . . . Okay, so I had my choice of noodles. I had just ripped into a blue box when the doorbell rang. "I'll get it," I called to Dad, figuring Cassandra had forgotten something.

I walked to the door and opened it, then did a double take. No one was there. The back of my neck immediately started to tingle, even though I'd never heard of a demon playing ding dong ditch. I stepped out on the porch and looked up and down the street but couldn't see anything. I was about to step back inside when I looked down and saw it on the mat. A CD, with a homemade cover of a Gremlin in a Santa hat. I picked it up and flipped open the case. "Esme's Merry Xmas Mix" was written on the CD in black marker, then a note, in smaller letters, on the inside of the cover. *I figure a girl who only likes albums that came out before 1998 will have a CD player. —A*

I shut the CD case quickly, then looked back up and down the street, really straining this time. I could feel myself starting to smile as I stepped back inside, and right as I shut the door, I thought I heard a crow caw, but it could have just been the wind.

THE COVEN RETURNS

FALL 2021

ACKNOWLEDGMENTS

Krista Marino, my incredible editor, thank you so much for all your support and guidance. When it comes to books, you complete me, and I'm in awe of your talent, dedication, and sense of humor. Le freak c'est chic, always. Can we toast a Zima the next time I'm in town?

Kerry Sparks, my equally incredible agent. Without you, I'd sell my books for a tub of pasta salad and some scratchers, so thank you for going to bat for me as my agent and my friend. Many thanks to Dominic Yarabe and the whole team at LGR as well.

Beverly Horowitz, publisher extraordinaire, and Lydia Gregovic and everyone at Delacorte Press. You all are the baddest witches in the game, and I'm so honored to be in your house.

Joshua Redlich, publicity master and the best Sanderson sister. Thank you for being so much fun to work with.

Regina Flath and Rik Lee. Thank you for making my books so freaking beautiful!

Copy editors Heather Lockwood Hughes and Colleen

Fellingham, and sensitivy reader Jasmine Walls—your work is invaluable. Thank you for catching me before I fall.

Amy, for laying the groundwork for the Coven to take over the world (eventually), and Papa Joe, for your support, interest, and willingness to travel.

Bridge Club (especially Patty, Stephanie, and Harvey), for throwing me one hell of a book launch party.

Daria, for being the zookeeper to our little otter. Thank you for keeping him safe and entertained.

Rosie, for being a very good girl.

Kansas, because there's no place like home, and California, for being a teenage dream.

Mike Worful, for fifteen years of friendship and Photoshop.

Carolyn, our eyebrows have improved since we were eighteen, and I daresay so have we.

Star, for Negronis, many memorable meals, and a sincere appreciation of Biggie Smalls and Mary J. Blige.

Molly, Poppy, and Zack. If we had to fly thirty hours to come see you guys, it would still be worth it.

Joe and Diane, I know this is no *At Grandma and Grandpa's House* but then, what is? We are all so grateful for your love, support, and a lifetime of books.

The little one who decided not quite yet—we don't blame you. Take your time, and we are ready when you are.

The Arroyo Boys, my adventure partners and number one and two favorite people on the planet. You are my whole world, and I love you more than anything.

And lastly, to my readers. Y'all are a bunch of weirdos, and I adore you for it. I can't thank you enough for reading, posting, sharing, and talking about this book. It still blows my mind that we found each other, so let's break out the Ouija board and have a slumber party.

ABOUT THE AUTHOR

Kate Williams has written for *Seventeen, NYLON, Cosmopolitan, Bustle,* Vans, Calvin Klein, Urban Outfitters, and many other brands and magazines. She lives in California but still calls Kansas home. She is the author of *The Babysitters Coven* and its sequel, *For Better or Cursed.* To learn more about Kate and her books, go to heykatewilliams.com or follow @heykatewilliams on Instagram.